SOLDIER OF MISFORTUNE

CHUCK DRISKELL

Soldier of Misfortune

Copyright © 2015 by Chuck Driskell
Published by Autobahn Books
Cover art by Nat Shane

First Edition: January 2015

autobahn
BOOKS

In loving memory of Charles Hamilton "Chuck" McKeever.
He did so much for me.

Chapter One

ONE YEAR AGO – Lima, Peru

JIMMY DeLAND was nervous about his summons to the roof of the main building of Nuestra. He had no reason to be anxious; it was just a gut feeling. The request came via text – no way for Jimmy to gauge Sonny's face or tone. So, why be concerned? Other than Sonny Calabrese being utterly insane, Jimmy could think of no reason.

Think about it: Sonny sometimes uses the roof for parties. Five minutes from now, I might find myself eating a fine dinner, enjoying the view and receiving a big bonus for the fine work I've done. And I had two confirmed kills on that ambush a few weeks back. Two. Maybe they're finally going to recognize me for my prowess with a rifle.

Right. Keep telling yourself that, Jimmy.

Jimmy was right about one thing: the roof of the main building, known as "the terrace," was occasionally used for meetings or gatherings during times of good weather. Perfectly square, it had been coated in a reddish rubberized material, making it pleasant for standing, though hot during the midday. There were large planters in the four corners, each exploding with colorful vegetation of different varieties. In the left center of the terrace was a wide, shuttered structure that acted as the bar during parties. Surrounding the terrace was a sturdy steel railing, aimed at preventing anyone taking a potentially deadly fall. On this day, however, one section of the railing, directly above the concrete loading pad at the building's rear, had been removed.

As Jimmy exited the stairwell onto the terrace, he saw Sonny Calabrese leaning against the nearby railing, smoking one of his cigars. Sonny exhaled a stream of smoke into the early evening breeze. He turned, smiling at Jimmy.

"You called for me, sir?" Jimmy asked.

"Ah, Jimmy, the good soldier...you're right on time."

That was spoken just before Jimmy was tackled from behind. As Jimmy struggled gamely, his hands and feet were bound together by prison-grade manacles. The two tacklers were part of Jimmy's team.

"Easy, fellas," Sonny crooned to the Alfa soldiers as they lifted Jimmy. "I don't want him injured."

"He be jus' fine," the swarthier of the two said, lightly slapping Jimmy's cheek. Jimmy spat at the man. As the swarthy man pulled his hand back to retaliate, he was halted by a scant sound from Sonny. Sonny then hitched his head at the Alfa Seguridad men. They silently took their leave, stepping into the stairwell and pulling the door shut behind them.

"I should take a picture of your face," Sonny said, beaming as he moved in front of Jimmy. "It's the very definition of horror. And you don't even know what's coming, do you? I find that fascinating."

Following his time in the United States Navy as a SEAL, Jimmy DeLand had come to Peru to work as a contract soldier for Alfa Seguridad, a "specialized security company." While Sonny Calabrese wasn't Jimmy's day-to-day boss, Jimmy had been with Alfa long enough to know that Sonny was the man in charge. Sonny's company, Nuestra, was Alfa Seguridad's largest customer. And, if one believed the rumors, its *only* customer. Sonny had taken Nuestra from a tiny business operating in a tin-roof building to a multi-million dollar concern with varying interests known only to a few.

Sonny stood calmly in front of Jimmy, eyeing him closely. A rather short man, Sonny was the type of gentleman who'd become more handsome with age—and money. Being shorter than average, his genetics had pushed him to the portly side, but Sonny had fought back with a rigorous diet and exercise—along with years of human growth hormone injections. His skin was richly tanned and his cosmetic teeth straight and gleaming. Sonny wore his lightly-graying brown hair short and fashionably styled. His clothing, while understated, was handmade and always top shelf. Despite his small stature, he oozed confidence and rarely raised his voice.

Sonny Calabrese, with all his quirks and peccadilloes, was the picture of a successful businessman.

He was also quite bizarre.

"Why are you doing this?" Jimmy asked. His eyes darted all around as the full realization that he was in genuine trouble came to him.

"I'm not doing anything," Sonny replied. "You did this and...you *will* do this."

"Do what?"

"Come with me." Sonny placed his hand on Jimmy's elbow until he started moving. "There you go," Sonny encouraged. "Just shuffle along with small steps." He led Jimmy over to the railing next to the void at the roof's edge. Beside the void, on the rubberized roof, was a small blue hand towel. It appeared to cover something.

"What are you going to do?" Jimmy whispered just as the evening breeze ominously increased, making the height of the roof somehow seem more daunting.

"Again, I'm not going to do anything, Jimmy. You are." Sonny's command was peremptory. "You're going to make a simple choice...A or B."

Jimmy stared, in abject terror, at Sonny Calabrese. He was obviously aware of Sonny's infamous "chastisements," in which Sonny insisted his subjects choose the method, then perform the punishment on themselves. "Please, sir...whatever I did...whatever I can do..."

"How many years has it been?" Sonny asked.

"Years?"

"That you've been with Alfa...with us?"

"Almost seven, sir."

"Jimmy, you know I despise the word *almost*," Sonny remarked, closing his eyes for a moment. "Such a weak term."

"Six years, sir. I'm sorry."

Sonny opened his hands to the heavens. "There went another one."

"Yes, sir. My mistake."

"Indeed it was. You've made several lately." Sonny sucked on his veneers as he narrowed his eyes. "In six years, I would like to think you, a ranking soldier, would know that bragging about *anything* you do for Nuestra is highly frowned upon."

"But I—"

Sonny silenced him with his raised hand. "And you certainly know the lengths, and great expense, I go to in order to secure Nuestra's respected position here in Peru." Sonny stepped back, his face registering hurt. "Do I prohibit Alfa's soldiers from socializing? From enjoying life? From earning excellent money?" Shook his head. "Some organizations like mine rule over security people with an iron fist. But not mine. I'm quite benevolent."

"You're very kind, sir," Jimmy said, hoping a bit of schmoozing might help his cause. Sonny ignored the compliment.

"And you know my fastidious rules for Alfa's soldiers, Jimmy, don't you?" Sonny asked.

"Yes, sir."

"Name them."

"Know your job. Avoid married women. And, er..."

"Never, ever speak about Nuestra," Sonny finished.

"But I didn't do any of those things. I've never—"

Jimmy was again silenced as Sonny produced a slim camera phone from his pocket. With a few swipes, it glowed brightly in the growing dusk, displaying Jimmy, standing at a crowded bar down at Punta Hermosa, audibly boasting about the Peruvian cocaine boom.

"*...last year was Peru's biggest coke year ever!*" Jimmy exclaimed in English, his hand sliding lower on some partially obscured, well-dressed woman's back. "*I don't mess with that crap but I've been told by connected people that this country is now dealing in the world's finest stuff.*"

Sonny tapped the phone, freezing the frame. He eyed Jimmy.

"Sir, I...I...I'd had some drinks and was just talking about Peru in general. Hell, Sonny," Jimmy said, trying to sound folksy, "everyone knows about the Peruvian coke industry."

"And you think your discussing these things, with such authority, is helpful to our mission?"

"It was just a harmless conversation." Jimmy said with a shrug. "I don't even know what Nuestra does. I just do security work."

Sonny offered a pinched smile. He lifted the phone again, touching the screen. The video resumed.

Jimmy was seen leaning close to the woman. Although it was difficult to discern his voice from the din, his words were clear enough. "*I've personally had my hands on millions of dollars of product, okay? I'm not gonna say more than that, but you can imagine how much dough I make,*" he said with a wink. Jimmy then leaned back, viewing the woman top to bottom. "*Damn, you're a hottie.*"

"Just a harmless conversation?" Sonny asked, pocketing the phone.

Feeling himself sweating, Jimmy said, "That woman, boss...she didn't even know what I was talking about."

"That woman, Jimmy, was here in Peru with an Air Force lieutenant colonel, her father."

"A lieutenant colonel?"

"Indeed, Jimmy. A man who will someday command an entire wing."

"But...we were in a large crowd. Everyone was drunk, sir." A bead of sweat dangled on Jimmy's nose. He shook his head and said, "There was no harm done."

"And that woman you were bragging to...she's engaged to be married to a young man back in California."

"Oh," Jimmy whispered.

"She told you that," Sonny said, arching his eyebrow. "That's on the video, too."

"I must not have heard her."

"You didn't sleep with her, Jimmy?"

"I swear I didn't, sir. I didn't do anything with her."

"But you *did* try. You suggested something very salacious to that young lady, despite the brilliant ring on her tan finger." Sonny wagged his own finger. "Don't try to argue this, Jimmy. A warning."

Jimmy dipped his chin to his chest.

"The lieutenant colonel, Jimmy, is a friend. A dear friend. In fact, I'm the reason he and his family were here on 'vacation.'"

Jimmy breathed a sigh of relief.

"But, Jimmy...the lieutenant colonel had to contain the leak." Sonny took a half step in Jimmy's direction. "His daughter, his niece, their friends—all the ones who heard you running your mouth...the lieutenant colonel had to go to uncomfortable lengths to make sure they weren't suspicious about anything. While I don't believe him for a second, I still had to compensate him for his trouble. All because of you...*Jimmy*."

"I'll pay you back," Jimmy answered, his head snapping up.

"Indeed."

"I've saved, sir. Saved a lot. Let me just pay you the amount you had to pay the colonel. That way everyone gets back to work and my lesson's been learned."

Whatever merriment had remained on Sonny's face evaporated. His head shook slowly back and forth as he said, "Your case has been heard and the jury has found you guilty. And, Jimmy, the judge has *already* levied his decision regarding your punishment."

"Please, Sonny," Jimmy pleaded. Tears welled in his eyes.

"Be a man," Sonny replied coldly, his nose turning upward.

Jimmy sniffed, blinking away the tears.

Sonny bent down, removing the blue towel from the roof, displaying a regular butcher knife. The knife appeared quite old, with a dark brown handle and a blade that was slightly curved due to years of use. He lifted it.

"Choice one," Sonny said academically, twisting the knife, "is the amputation of either of your hands. If memory serves me correctly, you're right-hand-dominant. Hold this," Sonny ordered, slipping the butcher knife into Jimmy's manacled right hand. Then Sonny removed a Sharpie from his own pocket, uncapping it and drawing a line on Jimmy's left wrist, directly over the joint at the hand and just forward of the manacle.

"I've made an assumption," Sonny said, capping the pen and taking the butcher knife. "I've assumed that you'll want to remove your left hand. Please let me know if you choose the right hand and I'll gladly make the line on your right wrist."

Jimmy's mouth hung open as his eyes wildly darted between his wrist and Sonny's face.

"You must amputate the hand *above* that line. Anything to the hand-side of the line won't count and you'll be penalized by having to hack further up your arm." Sonny took a few steps to the right and gestured to the gap in the rail.

"Choice two involves your jumping from this terrace down to the loading dock area." Sonny grasped the railing with his hand and motioned Jimmy over to have a look. "Of course, sitting or squatting before you jump is *not* allowed. The jump must be done from your feet." Sonny pointed downward. "In my estimation, even if you were an Olympic long-jumper, you couldn't reach the grass over there, but you can certainly try. People have displayed super-human abilities in times of duress. But, if it were me, I would probably aim to the right, to the elevated loading dock. My hope would be to hit that with my feet, then fall down and to the left. The theory being that the dock might provide a slight break to your fall and, by hitting the dock, you reduce four feet from the sum of your fall."

Jimmy's breaths were loud and raspy as he eyed the ground with dread.

"Oh...the fall is thirty-seven feet to the lowest point, Jimmy. About thirty-three to the loading dock. I'm sure you were wondering." Sonny cocked his head quizzically. "Say, weren't you Airborne qualified?"

"What?" Jimmy gasped.

"Airborne...don't SEALs go to jump school?"

"Y-y-yeah."

"So you know PLFs, parachute landing falls?"

"I...um..." Jimmy stared over the edge before his eyes came back to Sonny. "I did...I did know how to do them."

"And isn't the tower you jump from during jump school a thirty-four-foot tower?"

"I think so. It's been a...you know...a while since I was there," Jimmy replied, unable to focus. He chanced another look over the edge and hoped this was just some deranged scare tactic.

"I, also, went through the Army's jump school, during my PJ training," Sonny said, referencing his time as Airforce Pararescue. "It was a cakewalk, but I do remember one black hat saying that, long ago, some psychologist determined that thirty-four feet is a human psychological barrier." Sonny held the rail and leaned out over the edge. He pulled himself back, making a hissing sound and fake-shivering. "The psychologist determined that thirty-four feet was the lowest height that man would deem high enough to be fatal." He eyed Jimmy gravely before bursting out laughing. "I agree with that shrink! This height scares the shit out of me."

Aghast, Jimmy shuffled backward and shook his head. "I won't do it. I won't jump and I won't cut off my arm."

Sonny chuckled as if he'd heard a clever joke that wasn't overly humorous. "Oh, I think you will."

"No," Jimmy said resolutely. "This is utterly insane and I can make up for what I did. I'll fix everything." Jimmy's face contorted as he suddenly began to cry. "I promise you, Sonny! I swear…never again."

"I already fixed everything, Jimmy. It's all done. All that's left is the meting out of your punishment." Sonny checked his watch. "Now, I'll give you precisely three minutes to choose. That's a minute to cry like a bitch. A minute to pull yourself together. And a minute to make your choice like a man. If you still refuse, I'll summon Desgreaux."

"No!" Jimmy wailed, shaking his head.

"Oh, yes," Sonny replied, his voice a satisfied whisper.

As the time ticked on, Sonny puffed on his cigar, eyeing his subordinate. The human psyche under stress had always fascinated Sonny.

199 SECONDS LATER, Sonny burst through the doors one level down. Sil and Desgreaux jumped to their feet as Sonny pointed to the radio. "It's done. Get the doc over here as fast as possible and have him take care of Jimmy. Tell the doc to do it quietly."

"Which did he choose?" Sil asked.

"Call first," Sonny said. Once the doctor was summoned along with the on-call company nurse, Sonny told them the full story. Sil chuckled and Desgreaux roared with laughter.

Afterward, as Sonny walked down the spanking-clean office hallway, he turned to the Alfa men, walking backward as he grinned in wonderment. "Never in a million years would I have thought he'd have chosen that. Just goes to show all of us the unpredictability of the human psyche under duress."

Famished, Sonny took the main elevator down before being whisked by private car to one of his favorite waterside restaurants.

Despite the doctor's best efforts, Jimmy DeLand died seven hours later.

7

A YEAR LATER – JANUARY

IT HAD BEEN a very long six months. Gage Hartline was ecstatic to be back in Vancouver, having flown in only an hour before. He'd found his old truck in the long-term lot, right where Justina had emailed him that it would be. Gage was mildly disappointed that she hadn't welcomed him back with one of her short notes on his seat, the ones she always filled with hearts and smiley faces. He was disappointed but not surprised. On the occasions they'd spoken on the phone during this last trip, it was obvious that she'd grown weary of the back-and-forth nature of his current job. But that was all over now, at least until the spring thaw. Starting today, Gage was staring at ninety days off and, boy, did he ever need it.

After passing through the traffic of rainy Surrey, Gage motored to the east. He continued past Hope, watching as the rain turned to wet snow, and puttered on toward their small rental cabin in the shadow of Mt. Outram. Since landing, he'd tried calling Justina three times. She didn't answer.

"She's probably just distracted getting things ready for my arrival," Gage told himself, drumming nervously on the steering wheel. This last trip had been his longest stretch away during this job. Gage's employer was the recently-retired CEO of one of the largest credit card companies in the world. He now owned a sprawling ranch an hour's drive from Whitehorse, up north in the Yukon.

The former CEO, when he'd first hired Gage, had been fanatical about security, positive that some crazed Canadian (he'd said "Eskimo") would infiltrate his ranch and kidnap him for his wealth. However, once the man had met enough of the vibrant and peaceful, privacy-loving Yukoners, he'd stopped worrying about security. Instead, as the daylight-drenched northern summer had turned to fall then winter, Gage was instead paid to essentially be a handyman and companion.

And Gage would be lying if he said he hadn't enjoyed the former CEO's company. The executive was quite pleasant, if a bit disconnected from the real world—probably the reason he'd desired a sequestered ranch in the wilds of the Yukon. Now, with the New Year only days old, the credit card magnate was off to the South Pacific on his yacht and would be protected at sea by two former Navy SEALs.

In his contract with the former CEO, Gage agreed to work nine months straight through, with four days off each month except December, when Gage was required to work the whole month. Thus, Gage had been gone for nearly sixty days on this stretch. Even though the job had taken Gage away for large chunks of time, the pay was transcendent and the work, thus far, completely nonviolent. But his absence had taken a toll on Justina, and something in Gage's gut told him that this would be a difficult return.

He was correct.

As Gage motored into the gravel drive of the hillside lot, he saw a late-model Subaru wagon idling in the turnaround, marked by a trace of white vapor drifting from the tailpipe. The passenger door of the Subaru opened and Justina stepped out. Judging by her puffy eyes and splotchy cheeks, she appeared to have been crying. Gage noticed his dog, Ranger, a Shepherd mix, in the back of the wagon, panting as he stared through the foggy window at Justina. Lowering his head, Gage was able to see someone with long blonde hair in the driver's seat.

He stepped out of the truck, forcing a smile. "Hey babe, what's all this? What's going on?"

"I'm leaving, Gage," she said, her voice breaking.

He digested the news neutrally, steadying himself with a great breath pulled in through his nose. "Hold on. First, who's driving the car?"

"You remember me telling you about my friend, the nurse?" Justina had met her a few months before. The nurse was second-generation Polish, and had become quite close with Justina. Gage had looked at the budding friendship as a positive, but now he wasn't so sure.

"I remember you telling me about your friend. Is this her idea?" Gage asked, making certain he removed any trace of anger from his query.

"No," Justina said, wiping tears. "She doesn't want me to do this, and I don't want to do this. But I have to, Gage. I can't live this way."

"We should talk this through."

"I tried! I've talked to you for months, asking you to quit, but you never did. Well, now everything's fallen on me." Her lips crinkled as it appeared she was fighting back a wave of tears. "My mind is made up. I'm sorry."

"You're taking Ranger, too?"

"I think he'd rather be with me."

Gage walked to the Subaru and opened the backseat door, making a clicking sound with his mouth. Ranger hopped out but ignored Gage. He shot straight to Justina's side and sat next to her, nuzzling her leg.

Lowering his head, Gage massaged his closed eyes with his fingers.

"You don't let anyone get close to you," Justina said, her lip quivering. "Even Ranger."

"If you truly believe that," Gage said, "then I can't tell you how sorry +I am."

"I do believe it. And I also believe you're sorry. That's what makes this so difficult."

"So, this is really *it*?"

"I just can't do this with you anymore. I need someone all the time, not just *some* of the time."

"I understand. Wait just a moment." Gage turned and walked to his truck. He returned with a wad of money. She shook her head.

"I don't want your money, Gage."

He held it out for her. "This'll cover the bills from last month."

"I had plenty of money left over from November."

"Please, just take it."

"No, thank you."

Pausing for a moment, Gage said, "Justina, my career is the only way I know to make a living."

She lifted her index finger to halt him and, for the first time today, he saw genuine anger. Her full Polish accent could be heard as she said, "No!"

"Excuse me?"

"I'm tired of hearing you say things like that…'the only way I know to make a living.' It gives you a permanent excuse."

"I don't understand."

"I'm sorry, Gage, but it's the only way you're *willing* to make a living." The harshness of her expression faded, replaced again by sorrow. "And I can no longer fault you for it. You're doing what you love, so I'll set you free, because I feel you love your career more than me." Justina tussled Ranger's ears. "And now you must set me free, too."

"Look, I understand you're upset. And you're right, Justina, I do love what I do. But things can change."

"No, Gage…you told me that after the Caymans. You stayed home for three weeks and you were going crazy the whole time. You were miserable."

She's right, Gage grudgingly admitted to himself. *There's no juice in dawdling around the house.*

Her face contorted and she began to cry again. "Do me one favor, yes?"

"What is it?"

"Don't call me," she said, beginning to sob. "Don't start missing me and come back for me."

He drank in her words. "Justina, why would you say that?"

"Because I'll come back to you, Gage. You know I will." She took a few steps closer and lowered her voice. "So, please, leave me be. So I can get over you."

Gage was sad—sad with his own life. "Do you really mean what you're saying?"

"Gage, if you truly love me, if you want what's best for me, don't *ever* call me again. Because I'll come back to you, always, and that's bad for me." She wiped her eyes again and took a few steadying breaths. "If you love me, you'll let me go and leave me alone. Someday, I will find a man who will always be there, and be a father to my children, in a home that's stable. That's what I want, Gage, and it took me loving you to learn that. To *yearn* that." She straightened. "Promise me this, Gage."

The car idled quietly as Gage viewed his former girlfriend. His emotions ranged from sadness to bewilderment. But he knew this woman, this strong young lady, very well. And she was quite serious. "I promise, Justina. I won't bother you again. And I...I wish you well." It was a struggle for him to get it out.

Justina walked back to the Subaru and got in. She looked back at him, her face contorting as she began to cry heavily. She stepped in and closed the door.

Her friend wheeled the car to the left, making a circle and heading back out. Ranger went nuts, barking and trying to chase the car. Gage held fast to his collar.

At the top of the gravel drive, the Subaru stopped, the back-up lights blipping as the car was put in park. There was a lengthy delay before the driver's door opened and the nurse stepped out.

"I'm sorry to be in the middle of this," she said, shrugging.

Not knowing what to say, Gage said, "It's my fault, believe me."

"Justina wanted to know what you want to do about the dog."

Gage knelt, getting in Ranger's face as he petted and scratched the dog. "You wanna stay with me, buddy? Huh? You wanna stay?"

Feeling a pang of melancholy, Gage recalled the day he and Justina had adopted Ranger over in Alberta, in the midst of a two-week road trip when they'd first come to British Columbia. They'd taken the pup straight to the vet for shots and he'd immediately become one of the family.

Gage had a feeling about what would happen next.

He stood and took a steadying breath. After murmuring his fondness for his dog, Gage released Ranger's collar. He watched as the dog darted for the Subaru, his paws hardly touching the ground. When Ranger jumped into the car, it nearly caused the nurse to fall.

"Thank you!" the nurse yelled.

Gage felt sick. He turned away, walking to his truck and grabbing his duffel. Using the bed of the truck for support, he watched the Subaru as it wended down the gravel road, the tail lights eventually disappearing westbound on the Crowsnest Highway.

Minutes later, hating himself, Gage trudged into the cabin. He eyed the empty, lonely nothingness before he went to the bathroom and retched for ten minutes.

Then Gage Hartline tore the cabin apart.

SIX DAYS LATER, Gage repaired the cabin as best he could and cleaned it top to bottom. On the dark early morning of the seventh day, as massive flakes of wet snow plopped on the steep tin roof of the cabin, he left a month's rent in an envelope, then called the landlady to inform her he was moving out. Yes, he knew he'd have to forfeit his deposit. He also informed her that he'd left an extra month's rent to cover the remaining damages.

"Nothing too serious," he said. "But one of the cabinets still has a busted door. And I had to patch a hole in one of the walls." Gage listened before shrugging. "I may have punched the wall. Sorry." He thanked the landlady before bursting from the lonesome cabin, happy to be out of its confines. After gassing up the truck, Gage headed east on the winding and scenic Crowsnest Highway, into the colder temperatures of inland British Columbia. As gray light grudgingly materialized in the winter skies, Gage motored along in the light snow. He didn't have a plan. Didn't know where he was headed. He just wanted to get away. Eight hours later, Gage entered the United States at the border crossing just south of Creston.

A short time later, he idled into the snow-covered, rustic town of Sandpoint, Idaho. He'd decided to stop there a few hours earlier, which is why he'd headed to the border crossing. Gage had a few Special Forces friends who'd settled in Sandpoint a number of years ago. While he'd have been wise to call ahead, he was staring at 83 more days of time off. With all that time ahead of him, Gage was grateful for the distraction of a wild-goose chase. If his friends were no longer here, he'd just keep on driving south. He had a number of other friends down in Texas.

Sandpoint was nearly the way Gage remembered it. On the shores of the extremely deep Lake Pend Oreille, the northwestern town had an outpost feel to it. The last time Gage had been there had been, what, a decade ago?

"Damn," he muttered. "A decade. And here you are, all alone…again."

"Don't do it!" he yelled to the empty truck, for the thousandth time on the long ride. He had to quit thinking about the tall, lithe Polish girl who asked him to leave her alone for eternity.

What if I give her a month? Give her enough time to calm down? Surely she'd be happy to hear my—

"Stop!" he roared to the car. "You promised her."

Growling in frustration, Gage decided to turn around. He'd passed through the center of town and had entered a residential area, notable due to the large lots and timber-built homes. He figured he could go back into the town center and try to find a phone book. Or maybe he'd act like someone in the 21st century and actually use the Internet on his phone.

As Gage turned left, a sight off to his right made him hit the brakes. In a large, snow-covered field, a dog cowered below a man. The man was wiry, wearing jeans and a sweater and tall snow boots. He was holding something above his head and also holding something in his left hand.

The dog was medium-sized and obviously terrified. Now that the truck was stopped, Gage could hear the man yelling, even through the glass. Wanting to hear clearly, Gage rolled down his window and leaned out as the man bellowed.

"…dumbest animal on earth! Now, sit, damn you!"

The man was straddling the dog, continuing to hold something over the dog's head as if he might hit him with it. It was a stick—a thick, broken branch about the size of a child's baseball bat. In the man's other hand was a painted tube on a handle, probably a dummy launch to train the dog in the art of retrieving. Gage slid the selector lever into the park position and twisted all the way around to watch.

Don't you dare hit that dog…

Backing away slowly, the man lowered his voice as he spoke to the dog. "Now…for the last damn time, I want you to wait. Wait…wait…wait."

As the man backed away, the dog came off his haunches.

"Sit, damn you!" the man yelled, cocking the stick. Seeming puzzled at the man's lengthy commands, the dog sat with obvious trepidation. Despite the correct action, the man gave the dog no positive reinforcement.

You stupid asshole. That's not how you train an animal.

The man lifted the dummy launcher, aiming it in the distance and firing it with a pop. The "bird" flew, aided by what was probably a .22 shell. It tumbled into the snow about 30 yards away.

The dog, petrified, anxiously watched the bird fly before looking at his master. Judging by the animals' jerky movements, he was scared and confused, probably unsure of what to do and fearful that, no matter what he did, he'd be beaten for it.

"Get the bird!" the man bellowed, pointing. The dog ran a few steps before halting and dropping to his belly in the snow.

Mister, go calm your dog. Soothe him, then get him interested in the dummy trainer, and use simple commands.

Boy, Gage sure missed Ranger.

Unfortunately, the dog's owner did not follow Gage's mental advice. Instead, the man stalked to the dog, the thick branch cocked back at the ready. Gage watched the scene for just a few seconds. He actually felt his own hot blood rushing to the crown of his head.

Squeezing his eyes shut, Gage gripped the steering wheel.

Do you really want to do this?

Hell yes.

The torturous sounds from the man and dog continued.

Are you sure?

Hell yes!

Gage opened his eyes.

While the owner cursed and abused his animal, he was blissfully unaware of the "training" that he would soon endure. Because, sprinting through the snow at a speed that would make a biathlete proud, Gage Hartline was on the move.

As ready to deliver a beating as he'd ever been, Gage launched himself at the animal abuser, catching the unknowing man squarely in his backside. The man had just straightened, pulling back for another vicious blow when Gage tackled him, making the man's voice box squelch uncontrollably. The two men plowed forward in a foot of white powder. Although Gage wanted to make hamburger out of the man's face, he made the quick decision to give the man the same treatment he'd been dishing out.

So, while the man cursed the powerful stranger who'd just leveled him with a form tackle, Gage scrambled in the snow for the man's "training stick." When he found it, he swung it at the snow-dusted man, catching him in the ear and sending him sprawling.

Meanwhile, the bewildered dog was barking at Gage but keeping his distance. The dog's hackles were up and he was baring his teeth, but he didn't seem the type of dog inclined to bite. The poor dog was still confused—and who could blame him?

When the man with the bleeding ear staggered to his knees, Gage stepped forward with the stick cocked back and yelled his query to the dog abuser. "What am I thinking?"

Regaining some of his piss and vinegar, the man struggled to his feet with a hand over his ear. "You're going to jail, you sonofabitch!"

"Wrong answer!" Gage bellowed, walloping the man again. This strike, while swift, was somewhat softened by the man's stocking cap. As the stocking cap flew, the man went down again.

A car stopped on the street, just behind Gage's truck. An older gentleman jumped out, asking in a yell if anything was wrong.

"Nah! Just training this man!" Gage yelled back. "Don't worry…these are *his* own tried-and-true methods." He turned back to the dog abuser, who was trying to get up but still down on all fours. This time Gage yelled at him in German, telling him to stand and clap his hands. When the man didn't do it, Gage repeated the command. When he still didn't do it, Gage smacked him again with the stick, sending him face down in the snow.

"Hey!" the man on the street protested.

Gage shrugged animatedly. "He just doesn't seem to understand my commands."

"But you keep hitting him!" the man on the street yelled back.

"I know! Like I said, these are *his* methods." The dog had ceased barking and was prancing nervously in a perimeter around Gage and his owner. "This is how this man trains his dog, so I'm just following suit."

Gage stepped to the downed dog abuser, lifting him to his feet. Staring face-to-face with him, Gage guessed he was around fifty years old. A trickle of blood ran down the side of the man's face, mingling with the snow. The man's eyes registered fear and shock as he looked back at Gage.

"Why are you doing this?" the man breathed.

"You wanna end it?"

"Y-y-yes."

"Then crawl on all fours and retrieve that bird," Gage said, pointing to the hole in the snow where the dummy had fallen. "And retrieve it with your mouth, you sonofabitch."

"I'm…I'm…I'm not going to do that," the man said, doing his best to muster some defiance to his countenance.

"Don't you know you don't train an animal by beating him, and by using complex demands?"

"Well…fr-fr-from now on I won't."

"Good. But we're not done here."

"What?"

"I told you to go retrieve that bird."

"I won't."

"Then the beatings will continue."

A sudden fire burned in the dog abuser's eyes. "You go to hell!"

Gage stepped back and cocked the stick again, watching with satisfaction as the man cowered. When Gage didn't hit him, the man peeked out from his arms that had shielded his face. Through a maniacal smile, Gage pointed to the dummy bird and yelled one single command.

"Fetch!"

Chapter Two

THE INTERIOR of the Bonner County Detention Center was not at all like Gage would have guessed. It seemed new and was sparkling clean, quite a difference from the rustic town it served. Though Gage didn't realize it until after he'd been placed in a private holding cell, the detention center, while much smaller, hit many of the same notes as the newish Berga Prison—the Spanish prison Gage had "done time" in. Fortunately for Gage, on this day he didn't have to fight for his life upon reaching his cell. Instead, he was given a stack of hunting magazines, a bottle of water and a tasty Payday candy bar.

"Sheriff's coming in," the youngish deputy told Gage before locking the cell. "He'll be here in about an hour."

Gage had trumpeted his cheeks and nodded, pondering what sort of punishment he'd have to deal with. There'd be an assault charge, hopefully of a simple nature. When he'd been brought in, the deputy allowed Gage to check the phone book for his two friends. They weren't listed—no great surprise. So, after washing up in the sink, Gage ate the candy bar and drank the water. All the while, he willed himself not to think about what Justina was doing.

Having dozed off, Gage was awoken by the snap of locks in the steel door. Through the door stepped a bull of a man in a wool sport coat and poorly matching tie. Gage sat up and rubbed his face.

The man nodded. "I'm the sheriff. Mind if I sit?"

Gage shook his head, watching as the sheriff lowered the fold-up bunk on the other side of the small cell. Guessing him to be in his early sixties, Gage also estimated the sheriff weighed north of 250 pounds. His puffy face was affable and intelligent. Judging by the man's taste in clothes, Gage would hazard that the sheriff only dressed in a coat and tie because he had to. He'd probably rather be wearing jeans or a hunting getup—or, perhaps, just a regular patrol uniform. The sheriff sat, his girth making the two hinges groan under the strain. He immediately twirled his ankles, both joints popping like ladyfinger firecrackers.

"Ahh, that feels good," he grunted. "Been walking the floor at a show in Spokane all day." Seeing the look on Gage's face, the sheriff said, "Police and rescue equipment. I'm not big on spending the people's money but we gotta keep our tools sharp."

From the door, the same deputy asked, "You okay, sheriff?"

"Yeah, Chip. This one come peacefully?"

"Was as nice as could be. After he'd beat the shit outta Roberts—er, the victim, Hartline here came over and put his arms behind his back for the cuffs."

"Good. Close us in, will you?"

The deputy shut the door but didn't lock it. The sheriff eyed Gage. "Got a few problems, Mister Hartline."

"Well, I guess that makes two of us."

The sheriff's walrus moustache moved with his slight grin. "The citizen who stopped and called in your *incident* is one of the wealthiest men around these parts. Owns about half the real estate in town. He's a good man and he's been very good to me."

Gage listened.

"And the man you beat the shit out of, he's—"

Lifting his hand, Gage said, "Sorry, Sheriff, but I have to stop you there. I didn't beat the shit of anyone. If I'd beat the shit out of that jerk, Roberts, he'd have known it. I popped him a few times because—"

Mimicking Gage's raised hand, the sheriff said, "May I finish?" When Gage nodded, the sheriff continued. "That jerk, as you called him— Lawrence Roberts—is actually a full-blown asshole of the worst degree. All the year-rounders here know him and, if they knew about the whipping you put on him, they'd probably chip in and award you with a medal."

Gage wasn't expecting to hear that.

"But he's got a little money, too, and that wealth, unfortunately, has netted him some influence. And he wants me to throw the book at you."

"He was beating his dog."

"Yes, I heard. But you've got no witnesses to prove that. The man who called us didn't see anything but you hitting the victim. And believe me, those two men don't care for one another. The witness would love to have seen the victim doing something wrong."

"The *dog* was the victim."

Tugging on his moustache, the sheriff nodded. "I agree, Mister Hartline, and I believe your story." He leaned back, resting against the block wall. "And, before I came in here, I broke the law, too. After I'd read all three statements, I went to see the so-called victim. After allowing him to curse me for about five minutes, I told him that several witnesses had come forward and verified *your* story. I told him they'd seen him beating his dog in a cruel fashion." The sheriff's eyes twinkled. "You might say Lawrence was a bit surprised. I then informed him, if he wanted to continue forward with charges against you, that I was going to press on with animal cruelty charges against him. Unfortunately, that's a misdemeanor in Idaho and his team of lawyers would know that. But I can take a thousand bucks from him and, for a first offense, get up to six months of jail time. If I actually *had* witnesses, if I had a prosecutor who would support me, if I had an animal-loving judge, and if I had a pissed-off jury I might actually get him a little bit of jail time."

"But you don't," Gage said.

"The pissed-off jury part would be easy. This 'victim' has exploited this area. Enough said. But even if I had impeccable witnesses, the DA probably wouldn't go full bore on him. So, it was all a bluff. Thankfully he didn't call his lawyers, or he hasn't yet. I'm guessing he's ashamed, though he'd never admit it."

"So, what's the bottom line, sheriff?"

"The bottom line is this: I'm going to shake your hand and instruct you to please get the hell out of Sandpoint and Bonner County. No charges, for now, so I'd prefer you haul tail. Clear?"

"Yes, sir."

"Once you're long gone I seriously doubt we'll pursue you over a little, very deserved butt-kicking."

"Understood."

The sheriff turned his head a fraction, narrowing his eyes. "Tell me something, Mister Hartline. Why do I get the distinct feeling that there's more to your story than what I saw on the computer?"

"What did you see on the computer?"

"Vanilla. A taxpayer listed as a 'security consultant.'"

"That's me, sir."

"Well, I've been a law enforcement officer for thirty-five years. Before that, I did two late tours of 'Nam. I've been around long enough to know when a man's been through the battles. He's got 'a look' in his eyes… it's indefinable."

Gage said nothing.

"You know what I mean about that 'look,' don't you?" the sheriff asked.

"Yes, sir. I do know the look."

Slapping the bed, the sheriff stood. He led Gage back out into the bay and to the rear of the detention center. They passed through the laundry and stepped outside, into the frigid night air. Gage's old pickup idled in a parking space, the light snow drifting down in the beams of the truck's headlights.

"Deputy got your truck warmed up for you. Your things are on the front seat." The sheriff extended his hand.

When Gage took it, he said, "I've got one request, sir."

"What is it?"

"I want the dog."

His chest hitching, the sheriff shook his head. "I can't do that."

"Sure, you can. You've still got him, don't you?"

"He's over at animal control, but we'll have to give him back."

"No, sir. Don't give that dog back to that asshole. I want him, Sheriff," Gage said, speaking the words slowly. "No animal deserves to be treated that way. In fact, I want two things. I want the dog, and I want you, or someone you choose, to tell that prick Roberts that I said someday I *will* be back here. Even though he won't know it, I'll be here, watching him. And if I ever see him do such a thing again, well…you just tell him what I said. Believe me, he knows what I'll do. This first time will be a pat on his butt compared to the next time."

There was a moment's pause before the sheriff went through the menu on his phone. He called and spoke a few sentences before hanging up.

"Animal Control is two blocks that way. Get the dog and go. And I mean *go*."

"Thank you, sheriff."

When Gage opened the door of his truck, the sheriff said, "If and when you come back, I don't want to know about it."

Ten minutes later, Gage headed south on Route 95, toward Coeur d'Alene. Beside him, the young Golden Retriever mix sat upright, happily panting as he watched the snow swoop over the windshield. Gage petted the dog and, 8 miles into their 2,685 mile journey, he gave the dog a new name.

"We'll call you Sheriff."

FIVE DAYS after leaving Sandpoint, after driving through blinding snows and bitter, whipping January winds, Gage and Sheriff awoke before the sun in the converted shipping container out behind Colonel Hunter's home. It was chilly outside, probably in the upper 30s. Though rare, it occasionally snows in Fayetteville, usually in January or early February. Typical weather in January is lows just above freezing and highs in the upper 50s, and that was exactly what was forecasted for this day. Gage made a small pot of coffee and let Sheriff do his business before eating. As the pup, who Gage estimated to be about a year old, destroyed his breakfast of puppy chow, Gage sipped his coffee and pondered his day.

He'd go for a run and maybe some calisthenics over at Lake Rim Elementary before school got started. After that, he'd take Sheriff to the vet and then call up a few friends to see how they'd been. He also needed to run by a few stores to pick up a few things he needed.

"Got to make home feel like home," he mumbled.

Just as Justina's striking image roared into Gage's mental picture, Colonel Hunter called, asking Gage to come to the house and bring the pup. Gage put on his running clothes and crossed the broad backyard with his new dog. The sun was heading up and the temperature slowly climbing. He glanced back at the converted shipping container hidden at the rear of the Hunter property, camouflaged by a stretch of broad white pines. His simple little home.

His lonely little home.

Wiping the weak thoughts from his mind, he viewed the charming Hunter homestead, grinning as he recalled Colonel Hunter's gripes about money, fussy contractors and pastel colors. That had been years ago when the Hunters had begun restoring the old farmhouse.

The Hunter home belonged to Alice Hunter—no one would argue that. It was nearly a hundred years old and was situated on a large piece of land south of Fayetteville. Appealing yet understated, typical of southern farm style, it was two stories and boxy, with a wide shotgun porch that ran around the sides and the front. Painted in a faint yellow that Colonel Hunter dared not criticize in earshot of his wife, the house was surrounded by lush evergreen landscaping. Window boxes bursting with red winter flowers matched the amaranth red roof. As Gage followed the stone walkway to the back door, he noted the dormant azaleas, trying to recall their April color. Hunter met him and Sheriff, leading them inside, directly to a small corner room. It was the only room in the house that fell under the colonel's command—his den.

The colonel sat forward in his reading chair, slapping his knees. Sheriff jumped up, placing his dewy paws on the colonel's lap and immediately slobbering all over the retired officer's legs.

"Coffee?" the colonel asked, giving Sheriff a vigorous neck and ear massage.

"Had plenty," Gage replied, frowning over the fact the colonel had encouraged the dog to jump up. Then Sheriff, all 75 pounds of him, leapt into the colonel's lap.

"Aw, c'mon, don't encourage him to jump up on you, sir," Gage said. "If we start him off that way, he'll jump up the rest of his life."

"Bah," Hunter admonished, as the dog bathed his face with kisses. "A friendly dog jumping up never hurt anybody." Typical of the colonel, he charged right into his questions.

"So, how are we feelin'?"

"Fine."

"First full day outta that truck felt pretty darn good, didn't it?"

"Yes, sir. My buns were numb."

"I used to hate driving. Hated it," Hunter said, scratching behind Sheriff's ears and making him moan gutturally. "But now that I'm an old fart, I like cruising on long trips, enjoying little things along the way. I like the old diners…scenic little towns…fruit stands…and boiled peanuts."

"Look, I know you're getting long in the tooth, sir, but please tell me you don't drive slow in the left lane with one of your turn signals flashing," Gage remarked.

"People who drive slow in the left lane should be at fault if they get rear-ended. We ought to make our driving laws like the ones in Germany."

After agreeing, even though he knew American drivers were too free-spirited to ever obey laws like the Germans, Gage said, "I was just getting ready to take a little run and do some P.T. over at the school playground. You mind watching him?"

The colonel scratched Sheriff some more. "Nah. Happy to do it." Hunter stood and followed Gage outside as he began to stretch his quads.

"Not a bad day for January," Gage noted.

"Winter in the south." Hunter cocked his eye. "So…you and that Polish gal are finished, are you?"

"Sir, I told you, I don't want to—"

"Talk about it," Hunter finished. "It's amazing to me that a regular old gal can get a decorated warrior all twisted up in himself. Look at you, son, all torn up like some lovelorn seventh grader. How much weight have you lost since she left?"

"About ten pounds."

"Gotta eat, son."

"I would if I could."

"Force yourself. Man up."

Gage was dangerously close to retorting with a few questions about the way Alice Hunter led the colonel around by his nose. But he tamped down his rebuttal, acknowledging with what was supposed to look like an uncaring shrug.

"Will Sheriff run off out here without a leash?" Hunter asked.

"Nah. As long as you don't leave him alone."

The colonel detached the leash. "Come over to the house when you get back. We'll have a sandwich."

"That sounds good."

"Something I want to run by you."

Gage had moved to the back stairs and was stretching his calf muscles. "What's that?"

"Got a line on some jobs down at the coast. They're looking for four people, actually."

"For what?"

"Simple stuff, kinda like what you were doing down on Grand Cayman."

"Personal security?" Gage asked, fighting not to curl his lip.

"They're makin' a movie down in Southport. A-list actors, supposedly. They've made a bunch of movies around there and Wilmington in the last twenty years. Supposedly, due to tax breaks North Carolina gave 'em, they've got to hire a certain percentage of locals, including security. Assuming you still have a North Carolina driver's license, you'd be rubbin' elbows with the jet-set."

Gage couldn't help but grimace. "Sorry, sir, but I'm not interested in that at all."

"Just think about it on your run. You make the right contacts in that biz, you could find yourself out in Hollywood, set for life guardin' those pinkos who've got money to burn."

"Still...no interest."

As Sheriff lifted his leg on one of the azalea bushes, Hunter eyed Gage and opened his hands in frustration. "Don't tell me you're wantin' time off? That's not like you."

"It's not about time off," Gage said. "It's about wanting the right kind of job."

"And what might that be?"

Gage shrugged. "I was thinking maybe I'd head out to Raeford in a day or two...throw out some feelers."

"Throw out some feelers at Raeford, huh?" Hunter said, shaking his head in disgust. "You're gonna toss your line in and reel in a tire or, worse, a friggin' water moccasin."

"Well...maybe I need a little adventure," Gage said. "Clear my head. Start eating again."

"Be real careful what you wish for," Hunter said. "Have a nice run." He attached Sheriff's leash and took him around the front, leaving Gage alone with the thoughts he tried not to have.

Wasting no time, Gage clicked the timer on his watch and set out at a brisk pace. As he jogged north on the winding trail that ran alongside Puppy Creek, he had to admit to himself: He was curious about what sort of leads he might get from some of his Special Forces and Delta contacts out at the Raeford Parachute Center.

It had been years since Gage had blindly thrown a hook in the water.

3,266 MILES TO the south of Gage, Sonny Calabrese awoke with the summer dawn, stretching luxuriously before he ambled onto the cool of the open terrace. The long fronds of a Peruvian pepper tree swayed through the marble balusters, tickling the hairs of his tanned leg. He leaned forward, his hands caressing the smooth marble railing, staring out over the twinkling lights of the Lima morning. Sonny felt magnificent. More than two years ago, he read an article in a health magazine about the body's internal clock. The author claimed that it was healthiest to awake naturally, without the aid of alarms or wake-up methods. Since then, Sonny had arisen on his own, typically before the sun—unless he'd taken part in significant nocturnal activity the night before.

Following his battery of stretches, Sonny performed 82 push-ups in a row. These were done to military regulation without stopping. He then did 91 sit-ups, using a workout pad and placing his feet under a notch in the patio. His last wake-up exercise was 20 wide-arm pull-ups, which he executed slowly, alternating pulling his chest and back to the bar, at which time he took a three-second pause. As he did almost every day, Sonny performed each of these exercises in the nude.

Lowering himself to the ground, he poured lemon-imbued ice water from the pitcher that had been discreetly left for him sometime during the last hour. As he took a great drink of the refreshing water, he admired his charming, understated *casa*. Technically, it was more of a *palacio*, but its grandness was well-hidden. To the discerning eye, Sonny's large home seemed nice but not remotely extravagant. Like many of the homes in Lima's San Isidro District, his home had the normal features such as a high wall, electrified fence and visible security features designed to keep intruders at bay. It was there, however, that all similarities ended.

Sonny had paid more than a million dollars to a Japanese security firm to install their proprietary security system, originally designed for one of the world's wealthiest families. The system was so robust, it had a triple redundancy feature and, because of its massive battery backup, could operate without electricity for a full ten days.

Just down the road from his house was a platoon of security police, paid for by the residents of Sonny's community. If Sonny's alarm tripped, the security police—on call 24 hours a day—would arrive in less than two minutes. The alarm system and the security police's proximity gave Sonny peace of mind—when he was home, he was safe.

He heard a shuffling inside the patio door. That would be Chief Mikkelsen. Sonny knew she wouldn't dare come out while he was nude—though he wished she would. He donned his silken robe from the gold hook and announced that he was now decent.

Chief Mikkelsen promptly marched onto the broad patio. Sonny gave her credit for at least attempting to smile. She halted and formally stood at parade rest before him.

"Sir."

"I wish you'd relax, Abi."

"I'm fine, sir."

Sonny looked her up and down. She wore a different version of the same outfit every day. A trim, short-sleeved button-down shirt, this one light blue. Her pants were utilitarian, with cargo pockets on the side. She wore black tactical boots but didn't blouse the pants. If she had, she'd truly look like a soldier in a plain uniform. Abi's narrow, attractive face displayed no emotion as she awaited his next command. Her short, sandy blonde hair was pulled back so tightly it seemed to tug on the skin around her blue eyes.

Abi Mikkelsen was Danish and carried around a massive chip on her shoulder.

And Sonny was obsessed with her.

"Well?" Sonny crooned.

"How was your sleep, sir?"

"Quite nice. Strange dreams, however, and I need to develop the habit of jotting them down." Sonny leaned against the marble and crossed his arms. "Perhaps there's something to be learned from my subconscious."

"How interesting," Abi observed, her curiosity poorly feigned. "And what do you need from me today?"

"Yesterday, in your email, you mentioned something about Jimmy DeLand?"

"Yes, sir. I was informed that someone's been poking around in Lima, asking questions of the coroner and M.E."

"Informed by whom?"

"A source," she replied, using a tone that told Sonny she would say no more.

"And?"

"I don't have other pertinent intel yet, but I'll let you know if I hear anything."

Sipping the ice water, Sonny narrowed his eyes. "You keep me posted, Abi. And if you find who is asking the questions, you send Desgreaux and Sil. You tell them to interrogate the questioner. When they've got the information, they're to make the inquisitor's death slow and agonizing."

"Sir, as I've told you before, I'm a soldier and I lead a team of soldiers. We are not, nor will we be, a hit team."

At moments like this, Sonny missed the old chief. Unfortunately, he'd caught the man stealing. Then he gave the man one of his infamous choices. Of course, both choices involved death and, in the end, the man predictably chose the less painful of the two conclusions.

But the old chief had been pliable. He would do anything that was asked of him, other than keeping his hands out of the cocaine. Abi Mikkelsen was far more stubborn. But, despite her impudence, she was also far more skilled. Sonny's income had doubled since her arrival, making him a bit more tolerant about what she would and wouldn't do.

"Is your team ready for the next job?"

"Barely. We need another person."

"Prospects?"

"I've got multiple candidates," she replied crisply. "None of which I'm crazy about."

"Get more and keep me informed."

"Yes, sir." She opened her mouth but no words came out.

"What is it?" Sonny asked.

"DeLand, sir. What happened last year?"

"He perished."

"I realize that, sir. But I've been told by a number of people he didn't actually die in the ocean."

Sonny shrugged. "If that's true, I'd like to know more, myself."

For a moment, the only sounds were the numerous squawks and calls of the birds in the trees. Abi asked, "May I be dismissed?"

"You're welcome to stay," Sonny said, smiling.

"Good day, sir. I will send Pedro to you." Chief Mikkelsen exited with great haste.

Sonny's nostrils flared as he watched her go. He focused on her perfectly shaped ass. There was something about her that drove him utterly mad.

Pedro appeared, wearing a handsome brown suit. He was Sonny's butler and one of only four house servants. With an aristocratic air and a shiny bald head, he managed to be obsequious and snobbish all at the same time. The butler was a poor substitute for Mikkelsen, and Sonny noticed a sour taste in his mouth. He was ready to get on with his day.

"Your breakfast, señor?"

Sonny gave off the expression of a man pondering a major choice, such as life-altering surgery. "You know what?" he asked, suddenly inspired. "I'll take a light breakfast down at the courts, on that sunny strip of lawn between the courts and the cabana. I've never eaten there before. And have Raul standing by for a long match, will you?"

"Of course, señor," Pedro said, producing his phone and dispatching several quiet yet terse orders.

When Pedro hung up, Sonny stared at the brightening horizon and said, "My day?"

"Indeed, señor." Pedro removed a crisply folded sheet of linen paper from his suit coat. "Your morning is largely free. You're having lunch with the outgoing Minister of Agriculture in the executive dining room at Nuestra. After that, your afternoon is open."

Sonny pulled in a breath of the velvety Peruvian summer air through his newly thin, surgically-altered nose. "It sounds like a fine day, Pedro. I will greet it with my customary zest."

"Indeed, señor." Pedro motioned inside. "Lupita is preparing your shower. I assume you'll desire another one after tennis?"

"I'd prefer a rubdown from that Japanese woman from Miraflores. Call her up here, will you?"

"It will be done."

"And I'll follow the rubdown with an ice bath, Pedro. Have Lupita prepare that down in the cabana. I'll dress there."

"Very good, señor. I'll see that everything is prepared."

While Pedro hurried away to give orders, Sonny entered his dimly-lit bathroom, dropping his robe to the tile floor. Lupita, the sixteen-year-old daughter of a trusted servant, stood demurely with her eyes down. She held the glass shower door open for her master. Sonny didn't acknowledge her presence but he couldn't help but grin when he saw, as she took her leave, her taking a generous peek at his nakedness.

It was good, *quite* good, to be king.

THREE DAYS LATER

FAR WEST ON the range of Fort Bragg—an area of rolling sand hills, tall pines and angry rattlesnakes—is Holland Drop Zone. Just south of Holland is one of the deepest firing ranges on the famed Army post, set up with 1,000 meter targets for sniper practice. Colonel Hunter had called a few friends and finagled an invite to a fun little shoot-around that was just winding down.

Gage lay prone, completely still. Colonel Hunter crouched behind him, waiting. Finally, as Gage's ribcage deflated ever so slightly, the final shot rang out from the Dragunov 7.62 sniper rifle. Releasing the magazine, Gage came to his knees and rotated his head, stretching his neck. He turned and looked at Hunter, who was viewing the target through the high-powered spotting scope.

"Well?" Gage asked.

"I take it you were going for a center mass shot on that one?"

"No," Gage replied irritably. "I already did that. I was going for a head shot. Jeez, was I that far off?"

"Well...you mighta hit him in his kidney," Hunter replied, taking another look.

Gage stood and nudged his former commander out of the way. Peering through the scope, Gage noted the bright yellow mark on the silhouette of specially treated target paper. He turned and glared at the grinning retired colonel. "I got him right in the mouth."

"Just a little sniper humor to kill some time," Hunter chuckled.

"How'd you guys like it?" an approaching soldier asked, referring to the Dragunov. The soldier wore the towering stripes and chevrons of a sergeant major. He was roughly Gage's age and had looked after them since they'd arrived a few hours before. Gage didn't know him personally, but knew of him. He was one of the senior NCOs at the JFK Special Warfare Center. The sergeant major had let the two former soldiers fire all manner of weapons over the last few hours, and was doing the same for several other groups of people.

"I think the young'un here favored that Russkie rifle the best," Hunter remarked.

"Yeah," Gage agreed. "Well-balanced and just a nice feel. I didn't think I'd like the magazine feed but it seems to work great."

"I like it, too," the sergeant major said, clearing the rifle. "The Russians didn't build too many things all that well, but this is an exception. Unfortunately, those ISIS bastards like it, too."

The three men each appeared to have sucked on a lemon.

After a moment, the sergeant major said, "Hope you gents had fun.

We're about to call Range Control and tell them we're going red so we can head to the house, assuming y'all got enough."

Hunter shook the sergeant major's hand. "Thanks for inviting us and please thank Colonel Norris for us."

"Will do, sir." The sergeant major shook Gage's hand before walking away and storing the Russian sniper rifle with the other weapons.

"Let's grab some water and have a chat," Hunter said. The two men took bottled waters from the cooler and crossed the sandy lot to a grouping of picnic tables. Gage sat on top of one while the colonel leaned his back against another.

"That was fun."

"You were drilling those silhouettes," Hunter remarked.

"Me? I saw you put three, center mass, at six hundred meters with that Colt, sir. That's impressive."

"Old codger got lucky." Hunter pointed west. "Didn't I first come recruit you out here, somewhere?"

"Yes, sir. We were in ROBIN SAGE. Can't remember exactly where…I was a tad sleep-deprived. It was in an ammo shack by some woods. You were wearing your greens."

"Heady days. Hated those damned greens. Always had to wear 'em when meetin' with the brass."

The two men sipped their water.

"Let's talk about this job you're thinkin' about," Hunter said.

Gage crossed his arms. *Here it comes.* He was in no mood to hear one of the colonel's persuasive diatribes that the grizzled soldier disguised as "just tellin' it like it is." That straight-talk mentality is what made the man so damned convincing.

"Just look at you," Hunter said, gesturing to Gage. "I haven't said a word yet and already you're closed off to anything I have to say."

Gage opened his mouth to respond but changed his mind. He uncrossed his arms and nodded, knowing he should approach this chat with equanimity.

"Listen, son, I realize you really liked that Polish gal. And the little bit I was around her, I liked her, too. How could a man not?"

Gage nodded again.

"And I know how tough things can be in your line of work. Don't forget, I used to be like you, always on the go, having to put myself into my job one hundred percent. It's either that or lose focus and get dead, and that leaves the loved ones empty-handed. A damned life of catch twenty-two."

Hunter sipped his water and settled back on the picnic table, resting on his elbows. "I remember one time when I came home after a long stretch...Beirut and Tripoli...Alice greeted me out in the garage of that little Hope Mills crackerbox we were livin' in. Without sayin' a word to me, she went into the glove box of my old pickup and got her extra pair of sunglasses she kept in there. Then she walked straight to me, handed me a stack of divorce papers and told me her Raleigh lawyer'd be in touch." He shook his head. "She even took the light bulbs—all of 'em. Helluva way to come home. I just sat there in the dark that night, paralyzed."

"I didn't know about that," Gage replied, genuinely surprised. "She threatened to divorce you?"

"Threatened, hell. She *did* divorce me. Eighty-three to eighty-six. Took the girls and went back to her parents' in Kansas. I'd just made light colonel." He twisted his mouth into the vinegary semblance of a smile. "When we got remarried, she told me she'd dated a few men and learned that I wasn't the world's only asshole."

"I honestly didn't know about that," Gage mused again, watching as the three HUMVEEs pulled away. The occupants waved and Hunter and Gage waved back.

"Nice of those boys to let us come out and fart around with 'em." Hunter leaned forward. "Back to this job of yours."

Here comes the hard line.

"The thing is, son, unless you choose another vocation, these things'll continue to happen. But look how well you're doing. Your head's clear again. You're not limpin' anymore and havin' bad dreams and flashbacks. You even got a great gig up there in Canada with that wacko gazillionaire payin' you just to bait his damn hooks."

"I can't stand it. I'm not a professional sidekick."

"You think every man and woman in this country loves their job?"

Gage didn't respond.

"The thing is, Gage, you're well. You'll get over the woman. There'll be more, believe me."

"Yeah, yeah..."

"All right...tell me about this gig."

Gage shook his head. "You won't like it. You'll try to talk me out of it. So, there's no point getting into it."

"You didn't take it already, did you?"

"Told the man I might be interested."

"The man...let's start with him."

"Why?"

"'Cause I'd like to know, okay? I've earned that much," Hunter said, his brow lowered. "I won't try to talk you out of it. Not yet."

Gage told Hunter about his meeting with the attorney out at Raeford.

"How'd you connect with this lawyer?"

"When I first went out to Raeford, I saw Mal Odom and Dobie Waxman. You remember them?"

"Only enough to nod hello. Third Group, right?"

"They were. They're now working executive security, going back and forth to Afghanistan for some defense contractor that's paying obscene fees."

"Didn't those two know you before you became 'Gage'?"

"Good memory," Gage said. "They went through Selection with me. Anyway, I told them I was looking for some work and they put me onto a guy who'd been sniffing around for weeks, interviewing a number of operators for some clandestine job."

"Did they know anything about this job?"

"Not really. They said the lawyer seemed pretty selective and had quickly turned down a few people. Good people." Gage shrugged. "That got me curious so I called the number they had for him. He was there within the hour and we danced around my background and the job he was interviewing for."

"I'm assuming the lawyer is an intermediary."

"He is. I sure as hell wouldn't work for him. He annoyed the crap out of me within a minute of meeting him."

Hunter adjusted himself on the bench seat. "So, what did he tell you?"

"If I tell you…"

"I just want to understand. I won't even comment."

Gage eyed Hunter knowingly. "There's a security and assault team of some sort, working outside the U.S. They're made up of spec-ops types, working for an American concern that's thought to be a cover for a major narcotics operation."

Screwing up his face, Hunter said, "Simplify that—I'm already confused."

"There is an American company doing business in another country. With me?"

"Yeah."

"The company is allegedly a cover for an illegal narcotics operation."

"Okay."

"And working for them is a team of operators who are all former special ops."

"Doing what?"

"Stealing drugs from drug cartels. Assassinating rivals. Things like that."

Hunter was quiet for a moment. "Okay, assuming that's all true, how do you fit in?"

"He wants me to get hired by the team of operators."

"Why?"

"He described me as a Trojan horse."

"I get that. But what is your mission?"

Gage paused. "That hasn't been divulged, yet."

Using his index finger, the colonel scratched his short stubble all around his face, as if checking to see if he missed a spot while shaving. It was a long delay tactic so he could think things through. "Son…"

"You want to know who the lawyer who's hiring me works for and, more importantly, what do they want me to do?"

Hunter showed his palms. "I said I wouldn't comment."

"Please do."

"You're right, Gage, those two questions I'd want to know. And I could come up with a helluva lot more questions in very short order."

"The attorney assured me he and his backers are on the up-and-up. In fact, he hinted that his backers were somehow related to some of the spec-ops individuals who've served in this little unit. That this is a mercy mission, of a sort."

"A mercy mission," Hunter said flatly.

"I knew I couldn't explain it in a way that you'd accept."

Hunter abruptly stood, pacing the sandy area between them. "I'm not gonna lecture you, son, but we're talking about illegal drugs in a foreign country. That leads me to believe it'll be Mexico or Central or South America." He looked up at Gage. "Now, just think for a minute about drug cartels…about the blood they've spilt. Or, better yet, do a little research. Okay? And then consider that you could be escorting starlets back and forth to L.A. who'll brag that they've got a nice lookin' former Green Beret looking after them. Hell, one of 'em might even invite you to come over to their house in Beverly Hills."

"Matthew Schoenfeld was a former Green Beret, sir. I'm Gage Hartline and, according to D.O.D. records, I'm just a former grunt."

"Whatever. Everybody around here knows you were on my team.

You've got enough juice to get hired for that security job and I'll vouch for you."

Gage stood. "I just want to look further into this job. Never hurts to listen."

"I have a question," Hunter said.

"Go ahead."

"You said the team down there is comprised of special ops."

"Yeah."

"But like you just said, Gage Hartline wasn't in special ops."

"I told him I was. Told him I was involved in some stuff and the D.O.D. changed my files. Odom and Waxman vouched for me."

"See, I don't like that either. Puts you at a disadvantage."

"How?"

Hunter's face softened. "You damn near got yourself killed in Spain, son. I take the blame for that."

"You didn't know."

"But now you've got yourself a nice gig and three months off. Why the sudden urge to jump into something that could be worse than that mess in Berga?"

Gage paused for a moment, thinking about the question. "I guess I'd kinda like to get my hands dirty."

Hunter's eyes narrowed to gun slits. "Bloody, you mean."

"No, sir. I don't want that."

"You go dickin' around the cartels, somebody's hands are gonna get bloody. And just remember, the blood may be yours."

"I just want to look into it."

Hunter began to walk to the truck. "I'm not gonna try to stop you."

That was the end of the conversation. They didn't speak about it on the drive back to the Hunter homestead. Five hours later, unable to sleep, Gage phoned the number the lawyer, Josephson, had given him. It was nearly 10:30 p.m. and Gage could tell he'd woken him.

"Sorry for calling so late, but I'd like to move to the next step. I want to know the details."

"Ah, good," Josephson said, smacking his mouth a few times. "I'll let you know tomorrow when you can meet the others involved. It'll probably take a few days. Travel arrangements, and what not."

"That's fine."

Gage thought making the call would have allowed him to sleep. But it didn't. Colonel Hunter's words about bloody hands kept ringing in Gage's ears.

As Sheriff snored next to him, Gage stared at the metal ceiling and whispered, "Is that what I truly desire?"

The question bothered Gage until sunrise.

Chapter Three

THE MEETING took place at 11 a.m. at the Renaissance Raleigh North Hills Hotel. Mr. Josephson booked a suite for the meeting and asked Gage to free himself for the remainder of the day. Gage arrived fifteen minutes early and Josephson slid a non-disclosure agreement across the table. Gage slid it right back.

"I didn't come here to sign papers. You either trust me or you don't."

Frowning, Josephson slid the papers back into his briefcase. After briefly considering, he relented, revealing his official identity as R. Thomas Josephson, a lawyer practicing in the Washington D.C. area. That done, he opened a set of adjacent doors and asked an unseen person to join them. Gage watched as an attractive woman of perhaps fifty-five made her way to the sitting area. She wore a burnt orange suit with matching jewelry. Her brilliant teeth, her outfit and her accessories threw off the powerful scent of old money. After politely introducing herself as Linda DeLand, the lady sat across from Gage with Josephson sitting on the sofa adjacent to them.

Clasping his hands, Josephson sounded every bit the verbose lawyer as he said, "You'll pardon us for the unfortunate legalities, Mister Hartline, but it's paramount that we trust you implicitly before revealing the many aspects of what we hope to retain you to assist us with."

Not knowing what to say to such a wordy preamble, Gage nodded.

"Mister Hartline, Missus DeLand was the mother of—"

"Excuse me, Mister Josephson. I'm perfectly capable of explaining," she interrupted.

Dipping his head, Josephson gestured for her to go ahead.

"Mister Hartline, my son, Jimmy, served in the Navy as a SEAL. Like my other children, he grew up with privilege, although we were determined not to spoil them. But, being the youngest and a free spirit from the time he took his first steps, he began to rebel during his teen years, especially after his father passed." She flinched. "Passed far too early."

"I'm sorry to hear that," Gage said.

Linda DeLand returned the condolence with a fleeting smile.

"Following the briefest of stints at a university, Jimmy up and joined the Navy without even telling me." Smoothed her skirt. "Jimmy served for several years as something known as a mineman before applying for the SEALs. He broke his foot during his first attempt. According to what I've learned, due to his tenacity during the selection process, he was invited to come back. He made the SEALs on his second attempt."

"No small feat at all," Josephson added. Gage eyed him until the lawyer broke eye contact and stared at his hands.

"Jimmy was so proud to have made the SEALs," Mrs. DeLand recalled. "Back then, he called often." Gage watched as the woman's face contorted. She produced a tissue and dabbed her eyes.

"Very difficult," Josephson said gravely, as if he were the offstage narrator. Gage didn't look at him this time.

Pulling herself together, Mrs. DeLand tugged at the edges of the tissue. "Anyway, my son served without much distinction for six years. In fact, as is my understanding from considerable inquiry, Jimmy was a bit of an agitator. While the SEALs apparently desire men who can think for themselves, my son isn't remembered as a good team member. And, according to what I've been told, his penchant for mischief grew worse over time."

Clearing his throat, Gage felt compelled to say something. "I understand."

She stiffened and pulled in a breath through her nose, as if steeling herself for the morbid denouement Gage knew was coming. "Jimmy departed the Navy more than seven years ago. He phoned me on his final day, drunk, at a celebration he termed his hail and farewell."

"Where was he stationed?" Gage asked.

"Coronado."

"That's in California," Josephson added. Again, Gage flicked eyes at him.

Mrs. DeLand dabbed her eyes. "And that was the last time I spoke with him. Jimmy had a trust fund at his disposal but, after he joined the Navy, he never touched the account in which his disbursements were deposited. Once he departed the Navy and we couldn't find him, we watched that account with hope but it was never accessed. We hired batteries of investigators to find him. None did. After a few years, we assumed he was dead."

Genuinely interested, Gage leaned forward. "Please, go on."

"But Jimmy wasn't dead." Mrs. DeLand pushed a few stray hairs behind her ear. "Unfortunately, there is no joy in this tale, Mister Hartline. My son's body was discovered in the Pacific Ocean about a year ago. He was found just off the shore of Isla San Lorenzo, an island near Lima, Peru." She slumped a bit as her eyes sparkled. "We soon found he'd been in Lima for all those years he'd been missing. Through considerable time and effort, we learned that he'd been employed by Alfa Seguridad."

Gage glanced at Josephson, who unnecessarily said, "The team of former special operations soldiers I told you about."

"Although Jimmy's body had been partially…" She tapped her lips with her index finger, summoning strength. "Although there wasn't much to be learned due to the results of his being in the ocean for some time, the medical examiner said his body had several broken bones not consistent with the injuries his body sustained due to…"

"Aquatic life," Josephson added.

Linda DeLand joined eyes with Gage. On her face was a forced, pained smile. "So, now you know. While I wish I could tell you more, I'd prefer my portion of this meeting come to an end," she said. "I'd hoped my sales pitch might be more convincing but it's not an easy thing to talk about."

"Yes, ma'am," Gage replied, filling the gulf of silence.

She stood, followed by Gage and Josephson, and stepped around the Victorian center table, her blue eyes intent as she stared at Gage. "If you're our man, Mister Hartline, all I'd ask is that you put your heart into this job. And if you don't feel compelled to do that for me or my son, do it for your own mother, wherever she may be." She offered her hand and Gage took it. Then, she departed the suite, holding the tissue under her nose.

Mr. Josephson audibly deflated when she was gone. "So gut-wrenching." He motioned Gage to sit again. "Do you have kids?"

"No."

"Well, for me, as a father, to hear that sort of pain…" He shook his head as if trying to clear the thoughts from his mind. "Missus DeLand is funding this operation, Mister Hartline. She's the backer, but there are four other families who've joined her in this undertaking. All of them lost sons who worked for Alfa Seguridad."

"Go on."

"The group I represent believe their sons were murdered."

"By whom?"

"We'll get to that."

Leaning forward with his elbows on his knees, Gage said, "Will you please explain, succinctly, what it is that you want me to do?"

"I'd like to, but this is as far as I can go. To learn more, you'll need to meet your handler."

"And who is that?"

"He's the man who will run this job."

"I know what a handler does."

"Sorry. Will you meet him?"

"I'm not committing to anything, yet," Gage said firmly. "Got it? But I would like to meet him."

"That is a satisfactory condition. Can you meet today?"

"You told me to clear my schedule."

Josephson reached into his coat pocket and removed an outmoded flip phone with a red stripe around it. "After I prompt him, he will call you on this phone. Follow his instructions, please, and don't use the phone to call anyone else." Josephson handed it to Gage.

"How long?"

"He should call you shortly after I send a message through a third party."

"Then send it soon," Gage said, wagging the phone. "I'm not big on carrying someone's tracking beacon around."

"Of course."

"What can you tell me about this handler?"

Josephson frowned importantly. "He's American and, according to what we know about you, his background is similar to yours. He's older than you. I know he served in the military."

"Served with whom?"

"That I don't know."

"Has he run jobs like this before?"

"Dozens. I'll let him tell you about those."

"What does he look like?"

Josephson gave a brief description.

"How do you know he's capable?" Gage asked.

Seeming to regain his confidence, Josephson's face brightened. "This man is top drawer. He has great knowledge of this operation, and the techniques needed to pull it off. So, you can take my word for it or you can quiz him to your heart's desire."

"Did he approve of me?"

"He did."

"What about the others you interviewed before me?"

"He found fault in them."

"What's his name?"

"Falco."

"Falco?"

"Yes."

"Falco," Gage said again.

Josephson chuckled and shrugged. "That's how he wants you to address him."

Their business done, Gage elected to remain in the suite while Josephson grabbed his briefcase and departed to catch a quick flight back to Reagan National. After he'd departed, Gage searched the suite, finding nothing of interest other than a few empty cans of Diet Coke in the adjacent room. He lifted one with his pinkie, seeing lipstick around the rim. Gage placed the can by his keys and stretched out on the sofa, hoping to catch a catnap.

SEVERAL MILES away, in a second-floor Residence Inn hotel room, the man known as Falco sipped a bottle of water as he awaited the lawyer Josephson's arrival. Falco glanced at his $25,000 Girard-Perregaux pilot's watch, cursing under his breath at the time. Despite his American citizenship, if an experienced traveler spotted him in an airport, they might guess he was from a Mediterranean country. He stood a few inches shorter than average, his body fit and muscular for his age. His skin was deeply tanned, made more stark by his short white-gray hair. Even the hairs of his sinewy forearms were of white-gray color, contrasting sharply against his sun-burnished skin. Falco had chosen his pseudonym from the Italian language, his heritage.

He was an arrogant man who, despite the danger, liked to leave subtle clues to his true identity.

There was the sudden sound of a car door shutting. Then footsteps on the wooden stairs leading up to the room. Falco checked the peephole. He snatched the door open, catching Josephson by surprise as he'd pulled back his hand to knock.

"Get your ass in here," Falco growled.

"I see you're anxiously awaiting my arrival," Josephson remarked. He eyed Falco's hands. "Surgical gloves?"

"Fingerprints. Give me the briefcase," Falco commanded, snapping his fingers. He walked to the small kitchen table, dialing in the correct sequence of numbers to open the briefcase. Inside was a tablet, similar in size to an iPad but more durable. Falco disconnected the USB cable that had connected the tablet to a wide angle camera with microphone deftly mounted through the side of the case. With a few expert swipes, Falco rewound the video to the portion when Gage Hartline entered the room at the Renaissance Raleigh North Hills Hotel.

Josephson pointed to the tablet. "You'll see I adroitly had him sit exactly where—"

"Shut up," Falco snapped. He watched the video in its entirety, all 37 minutes, without saying a word. Behind him, Josephson occasionally dabbed sweat with his mottled handkerchief. When the video was over, Falco shut the tablet and stood.

"You did exactly what I wanted." He offered no reassuring smile and he spoke monotone, as was his habit.

"I said I would."

"How about DeLand? Any calls from her afterward?"

Josephson shook his head. "I told her I would check in once a week. I don't expect to hear from her except when I call. Too painful."

Falco walked into the bedroom and came back with twin bricks of hundred-dollar bills wrapped in cellophane. "Today's compensation." He tossed the money, shaking his head when Josephson fumbled the packets, allowing them to tumble to the floor.

"Wasn't expecting that…usually good at sports," Josephson mumbled as he lifted the money.

"You've done your part, Josephson…*so far.*"

"Thank you."

"As I told you before, you'll likely be needed again."

"I understand."

"Do you remember all my conditions and warnings?"

"Mister Falco, this has been, and *is*, an opportunity of a lifetime. I will do nothing to jeopardize what I hope will continue to be a long-term—"

"Get that out of your mind," Falco said, cutting him off. "After this job, there will be nothing else. But cross me…tell someone else…try to take my picture…go to the cops or the FBI," Falco paused for a full ten seconds, "and I will guaran-damn-tee you that your children, your wife *and* you will die in the worst way imaginable."

Josephson turned pale. "You've threatened that before, sir. Frankly, it's over the top, unnecessary and unnerving."

"You knew those conditions *before* you named your exorbitant fee and accepted the job."

"That doesn't mean you need to repeat them every time we meet."

Falco narrowed his eyes at Josephson.

"Sorry," the lawyer said, lowering his eyes. "But will you please reassure me that, provided I comply with your conditions—which I most certainly will!—that you won't harm me or my family?"

Falco grinned. It was a strange, humorless smile, the type one might see on a wicked boy who tortures cats for fun. "I don't give a shit about you, Josephson. So don't go flattering yourself by thinking I have time to worry about you, assuming all goes well. Just be available when I call and you should definitely expect to get checked up on by Hartline or retired colonel crony, Hunter. Got it?"

Swallowing, Josephson nodded. "I understand."

"That's a lot of cash, buddy boy. Tell me you're not stupid enough to fly with it."

"I'm driving back to the District."

"Good. Now get the fuck outta here."

"Indeed," Josephson said. He extended his hand. "Well...it's been good—"

"Haul ass."

The lawyer sprinted from the hotel room. After he'd roared from the parking lot, Falco sat on the couch and made the call, speaking politely but firmly.

"This is Falco. It's important we meet today. You're at the hotel?" He listened and nodded. "Okay. Pardon the precautions but I think you'll understand. I want you to leave the hotel and drive to Triangle Town Center & Commons. Leave your personal phone in your car. Take the phone the lawyer gave you and go into the Starbucks and use the men's room. Reach under the sink and remove the note that's taped there. Follow the directions on the note. Can you go right now?" Again he listened. "I will see you soon."

Falco leaned back on the sofa and shut his eyes for a moment, going through his mental checklist. He thought about the airplane. Even if Hartline ran the registration number, he wouldn't be able to trace it back to Falco's true identity.

But he'll know I'm a pilot.

Falco smiled. Another clue.

Several minutes later, he grabbed his items and departed the hotel, ripping the surgical gloves from his hands as he descended the wooden stairs. It was time to go flying.

FALCO'S LITTLE scavenger hunt took Gage's mind back to Germany, back to his days of doing low-level espionage work for shadowy people like the rogue DGSE agent, Jean Jenois. Despite all the gadgets that had emerged during the techno-revolution of the new millennium, spooks still loved basic tradecraft. They enjoyed the power of the written word, honeypots, cut-outs and hushed meetings over neat bourbons in dark bars.

The first note from Falco had instructed Gage to flush the SIM card from the burner—the prepaid phone he'd been given—in the toilet at Starbucks and to discard the phone and battery elsewhere. He was then to walk casually through the open-air mall, heading north into the Belk department store. Gage assumed he was being watched. At Belk's, on a specific hanging rack of Lucky Jeans, Gage would find his next set of instructions in the back pocket of a robust pair with a size-42 waist.

Gage followed the bizarre directions, finding flaw in them. Ignoring his pang of concern, he did as the second note instructed and walked out the north exit of Belk's. Parked in the small knot of cars near the exit was an older model Chevrolet pickup truck. Gage entered the truck, found the keys in the ashtray and waited—as he'd been directed. Several minutes later, a phone could be heard ringing. He eventually located it under the passenger seat, identical to the one he'd been given earlier.

"Yeah," Gage answered.

"Did you leave your own phone in your car?"

"Yes."

"Do you have anything else that's transmitting or trackable?"

"Just this phone I'm holding."

"Good. Pardon my caution but it's necessary. Drive the truck up 401 north to the Triangle North Executive Airport. Park in the main lot and walk out onto the tarmac. I'll be in a Piper Archer, white with blue trim. It'll be idling, so get in. We're going to take a ride. That okay?"

"Why all this caution?" Gage asked. "We're just going to have a chat."

"I trust you, or we wouldn't be talking. But I've been off the grid for a while and I'd like to keep it that way."

"By flying?"

"I'm someone else today," Falco said. "Just a relaxing flight to get to know each other."

"Okay," Gage breathed, nonplussed.

Fifteen minutes later, Gage sat in the right seat of the small aircraft. He felt mildly relieved when his contact diligently performed all the basic pre-flight maneuvers Gage had grown so familiar with over the years. Soon they were buzzing off to the northeast, climbing gracefully over the brown winter landscape.

After Falco had completed a few actions following takeoff, Gage spoke through the intercom, asking, "How do I know you're a good pilot?"

"You don't. You'll have to take my word for it when I say, if something were to go wrong that put us in danger, I'm the guy you want at the yoke. Besides, this little baby's a paper airplane compared to what I'm used to."

"And what's that?"

Falco grinned. "I'm rated for all types of aircraft." They were in a slight bank and he pointed to a forest. "If we lost our engine, I could pancake her into the top of those trees so soft you'd think we landed on a big pillow."

"Well...you've certainly got plenty of confidence."

"I wouldn't fly with any pilot who doesn't."

"What's the reason for the flight? Why couldn't we just meet in a crowded place and chat?"

Falco turned his head at Gage. He looked every bit the archetypal pilot with his deep tan and his gold aviator sunglasses. "Sometimes it's nice to just make an excuse to fly. I don't get to do it as much as I used to."

Gage got the distinct feeling that Falco's pleasant nature was forced. While he couldn't put his finger on what the tell was, some tiny marker told Gage that Falco, in reality, was an asshole. And that was okay. Some of the best operators Gage knew were assholes. And since Falco was still recruiting Gage, he was in sales mode.

But there was something else about the man—something he was hiding.

Gage settled into the leather seat of the Piper, watching the altimeter as the plane passed through 2,000 feet AGL. The airspeed during their climb was just under 100 knots as they resumed a northeasterly course. Viewing the landscape below him, seeing all the brown, all the deadness of winter, somehow made Gage think about Justina.

Where is she right this second? What's she doing? Is she thinking about me?

Needing the distraction of the job, Gage said, "Let's get down to it. I've got some stuff to do this evening."

"Roger, that," Falco said. He began explaining the remarkable details of Alfa Seguridad and Nuestra Corporation, going into far more detail than Josephson had. Those details set off a bevy of questions from Gage, followed by more explanation from Falco. They flew to the east, over Elizabeth City, turning south before swooping down and west, flying low, making their way back over the narrowing body of the Albemarle Sound. The flight wound up taking two hours and they spoke the entire time.

After Gage had scrutinized the facts from every angle, he looked at Falco and said, "You've still not told me what it is you want me to do."

Falco stared straight ahead, controlling the yoke with one finger. His nostrils flared as he pulled in a deep breath. "You're to go down there and get hired by Alfa Seguridad. You're to prove yourself, and I mean *really* prove yourself. That means flex all your muscle, use all your skills."

"You told me that already."

"And when Sonny Calabrese finally shows himself, when the time is right, I want you to kill him. Kill him stone dead. That's the job. Get hired. Gain trust. Kill Sonny Calabrese, the murderer."

Gage said nothing.

"Once he's gone, I've been assured by powerful people in the Peruvian government that they'll go in there and bust things up."

After a moment, Gage said, "Why won't they just bust it up now?"

"Sonny's paying off a lot of people. Has been for years. But he's isolated himself. Get him out, and that whole snake pit goes away."

Gage saw the airport off to the north. He didn't respond.

"Well?" Falco asked.

"Tell me about you," Gage said. "What's your story?"

Holding up his hand, Falco spoke with ATC. After complying with their instruction, he switched back to Gage. "Do me a favor while I talk and keep a lookout for other aircraft." While Gage peered all around them, Falco kept speaking. "While you and I are different, especially in age, we have one glaring similarity."

"You got a pretty large jet approaching from the east but he's at least a thousand feet above us," Gage said, pointing.

"Roger." Falco spoke to ATC again.

When he was quiet, Gage asked, "So, how are we similar?"

"While you call me Falco, I do have an actual identity that I live under. I live in a place in the United States where my neighbors and my few acquaintances believe I'm a business consultant. I'm gone often but, being single and type-A, no one thinks a thing about it. I don't mingle and I don't bother anyone, either. About the only time I relax is when I'm flying or out on the water."

Falco pulled off his sunglasses and turned to Gage, revealing green eyes. They had yellow sunbursts around the irises—like the eyes of a crocodile. "But I'm not a business consultant and I'm not the man whose identity I live under." Falco faced ahead again, settling into his seat as he slid his aviators back on. "I run operations, Hartline, like the one I hope you're going to participate in. I run them for governments, for individuals and for corporations. And I'm the best in the business."

Gage stared at the man. Something told Gage that Falco was lying.

"And I know a little about who you were and what you did," Falco said. "I know who Hunter is, also. I don't know him personally but, like you two, I was in the military, before Uncle Sam moved me to something a little more clandestine."

"What did you do in the military?"

"I've said enough about myself. The job is the job." Falco let that hang for a moment. "Nut-cutting time, Hartline. Someone's going down to Lima, Peru to represent the five families whose sons never came home. That person is going to kill Sonny Calabrese."

"I'm no assassin."

"But you've killed bad people plenty of times."

Gage said nothing.

"Do you believe everything I've told you about Sonny Calabrese?"

"I'd like more proof."

"I can provide that. Does that mean you'll take the job if I do?"

"I'm going to be frank, Falco. Something tells me you're misleading me about something."

"Only about who I am. I can't let that out, nor would I compromise your identity. But everything I've told you about Sonny Calabrese, Nuestra and Alfa Seguridad are true." He stared at Gage. "Will you take the job?"

"I'm interested."

Falco grinned. "Let's get in the pattern." He banked steeply to the north. Ten minutes later, after a baby-soft landing, they taxied back to the ramp.

Sitting there on the tarmac, Falco removed a briefcase from behind him. He produced sheaves of paper containing numerous eyewitness testimonies of Sonny Calabrese's atrocities.

"Damn," Gage muttered, reading. "How can this guy keep operating?"

"Hundreds of millions of dollars, Hartline. It's the same the world over. This is not an assassination I'm hiring you for. This is an extermination job. You're smashing a cockroach."

When they were finished, after Falco discussed compensation, Gage said he needed a day or two to think about it. By the time Gage reached his own truck—despite the uneasiness he felt—he'd just about made up his mind.

THAT NIGHT, Gage sat in a lawn chair on the rear edge of Colonel Hunter's property. The fire had died down and a cool wind ushered in scattered clouds with the promise of morning rain. Sheriff lay beside Gage on the winter rye, snoozing peacefully after an hour of *proper* retrieving. As Gage stared into the embers, he pondered the facts he'd learned today, ordering them in his mind. When Gage finally saw Hunter's imposing silhouette heading in his direction, he slid two more split logs into the hot coals, satisfied as the resident heat set the seasoned logs quickly aflame.

"Sorry I took so long," Hunter said, arriving in his bathrobe and slippers. "Alice had me changing a bulb in our bathroom that's a pain to get to. I'd like to whip the ass of the idgit that designed the fixture."

Chuckling at his former commander's domestic uneasiness, Gage said, "Like I mentioned, sir, I want to tell you about the details of the job. I want your honest opinion."

"Let's hear it," Hunter said, plopping into the chair opposite Gage. He immediately grabbed a stick and began making adjustments to the fire.

"The job will take place down in Peru…in Lima. Been there?"

Hunter shook his head.

"Me neither. Anyway, here's the elevator version before I get into details. There's six ex-military down there working at a security company called Alfa Seguridad. As I told you before, this security company works for another company, Nuestra. Nuestra is a manufacturing company that sells all sorts of products. They sell coffee. They deal in rubber. And their biggest division is medical, so they make and sell a lot of ancillary products like pill casings, syringes…that type of thing."

"I remember."

"What I'll tell you now is new information. The CEO of Nuestra is a fellow by the name of Orson Calabrese…goes by the name of Sonny. He was Air Force Pararescue, a PJ. Got himself booted about a decade ago after it was discovered he was running an illegal scheme on base. Test scores were extremely high. Fitness scores good enough to make PJ. His evals were supposedly a mixed bag—seems he was loved or hated by the brass. Got himself busted on a regular basis."

"How old is Calabrese?" Hunter asked.

"About my age."

"Young."

Gage laughed. "All depends on viewpoint."

"Keep going," Hunter said, sitting back as the fire roared, cracking and popping.

"Although Nuestra is run by this Calabrese character, the handler thinks both Alfa and Nuestra fall under Calabrese's command. He just created the security company as a separate entity to distance his company from the bloodshed."

"I'm still with you."

"Anyway, the handler says that when they went deep into Calabrese's past, they were surprised by some of the stories they dug up. The guy is fascinated with the human mind. Used to present people with all sorts of crazy scenarios."

"Like what?"

"According to the handler, one time an airman had gotten his lower leg crushed while out on maneuvers. They were medevacking the guy out and he complained that Calabrese offered him a choice rather than just take care of his leg."

"Yeah?"

"Said they were in the back of the bird and Calabrese offered him morphine or, if the airman could take the pain, five hundred bucks instead. Said Calabrese pulled out the money and waved it all around his face."

"What PJ's got five hundred bucks to give away?"

"Calabrese, based on what eventually got him kicked out of the Air Force. But before I tell you about that, the handler said Calabrese still does that kind of thing, but on a much greater scale. The handler said he got intel that when Calabrese orders people killed, he gives them bizarre choices of death and tries to predict what they'll choose based on their personality type."

"Sounds like a seriously sick sonofabitch to me."

"Agree."

Hunter snatched a weed from the ground, sticking it in his mouth. "What got him booted?"

Gage crossed a leg over his knee. "He got a court martial over drugs he was dealing all over Vandenberg."

"Sounds like a fine, upstanding PJ."

"But, again, showing that he's not your run-of-the-mill scumbag, Calabrese was dealing pharmaceutical grade drugs, none of them narcotic, and was selling to a number of officers as well as enlisted. And, because he'd steered clear of narcotics, and because he cut a deal to name names of some of his ranking customers, he got himself a special court martial and avoided the general."

"And now he's in Peru living it up as a CEO?" Hunter snorted. "What a world we live in."

"After Calabrese got put out of the Air Force, he bounced around for about a year before he headed to Lima. Intel after that is sketchy. Then he popped back up as the head of this company, Nuestra, that's supposedly been growing like this fire with gas thrown on it. I don't know how big the company is, but my guy said they're believed to be extremely profitable."

"So, what's the issue?"

"Five men who worked for the security company, Alfa Seguridad, have gone missing in the last three or four years. A few turned up dead but they're *all* presumed to be dead."

"That's no good."

"Even worse, each of them was American and each of them was a veteran. They had all served in some type of special ops. There was a sixth one, a Brit, who never turned up, either, but his family isn't a part of this consortium."

"What consortium?"

"This job is being put together by the five families of the missing."

"What's the mission?"

Gage licked his lips but didn't say anything.

"Tell me, son."

"They want me to get hired by Alfa Seguridad…"

"Yeah…"

"…and kill Sonny Calabrese."

Hunter didn't respond. He blinked a few times but showed no other emotion.

"Sir? You gonna say something?"

"I have a feeling you don't wanna hear it."

"I do."

Flicking the weed away, Hunter leaned forward and softened his voice. "There is a difference, Gage—a huge frigging difference, and you *know* this—between a trained soldier who sometimes has to kill people to do his job…and an assassin. You are *not* an assassin."

"I know that, sir. But this is not some politician, or some rival businessman to be rubbed out for someone's personal gain. This guy is a killer and a blight on humanity." He raised his finger for emphasis. "And you know I will not go through with it until I confirm for myself that he's the genuine article."

Hunter's voice was flat. "How do they want you to go about all this?"

"I have to gain trust in Alfa Seguridad to get close to him."

"Why can't this handler just hire a sniper and be done with it?"

"They want everything to implode and feel it will collapse if the kill comes from within. Besides, Calabrese is too insulated and too unpredictable."

Hunter sat back and steepled his fingers under his chin. "Question: you go get mixed up with these assholes down in Lima…assuming you don't get dead, who's to say you don't get swept in and prosecuted if the Peruvians decide to bust up the joint in the meantime?"

Gage shook his head. "The lady I met with today, the mother of one of the dead, is named DeLand. They're wealthy and connected and they've already done the back channel work to make sure we're covered if that kind of thing happens."

"Oh, they're wealthy and connected," Hunter said. "Yeah, I'm sure the DeLand family will look after a soldier of fortune named Gage Hartline."

Gage sank back into his chair, saying nothing.

"And when you do kill him? Will you have an alibi? You said if the kill comes from the inside, the operation implodes. Do you think the others are just gonna stand by and watch you walk?" Hunter leaned forward. "I bet this Calabrese character pays a pretty penny to all those mercenaries. They're not gonna take kindly to you killing their golden goose."

"I can figure out a way to manage this once I'm there. And I will bail if I think it's a suicide mission."

"There's an easier way to bail," Hunter said. "Don't take the job."

Gage looked away.

"Tell me about the handler."

Knowing this was going to be a point of contention for Hunter, Gage shook his head. "No, sir. You're just going to crap all over it when I tell you."

"Just tell me," Hunter said, opening his hands in a gesture of goodwill.

"I don't know his real name. He's probably mid-fifties and he's a capable pilot."

Hunter's nostrils flared as he pulled in a deep and loud breath. "Do you have confidence in him?"

"He seemed legit," Gage replied. "But, in the interest of full disclosure, there was something about him I didn't like. He actually had me jump through a bunch of hoops before he took me flying. I felt it was unnecessary, diversionary and…"

"And what?"

"Amateurish."

"That's a pretty big strike," Hunter remarked. "How's the pay?"

"Very good. If I choose to go back to Canada, assuming I can get this done inside the time I've got left, I'll go back with a knot in my pocket."

"What about your identity?"

"They claim they have the juice to give me a new identity, even down to a Special Forces file with the D.O.D."

"You know how much you'd have to pay to bribe someone to do that?"

"A lot, I'd imagine."

"Yeah." Cracking his knuckles, Hunter said, "It's damn near midnight. You ready for my unvarnished opinion?"

"Yes, sir," Gage said, although he felt he could predict, almost verbatim, what Hunter was preparing to say.

"I don't think you should take this job. No way in hell. Your mind's not in a good state after all that mess with your gal Justina. You're running from what's bothering you, and when people do that, even brilliant people like you, they tend to make poor decisions. Plus, you said the handler is amateurish. Even if everything is set up perfectly, the fact is you're wading into a bloody industry." Hunter paused, raising his index finger. "And if one *single* person finds out what you're up to, you're a dead man. Even if your cover holds, you're gonna be pirating coke from cartels while you wait for a chance to kill this psycho? Shit, son…I'm not sure I could dream up a more dangerous mission."

"But, sir—"

"Lemme finish." An expression of pain shown on Hunter's face. "I almost got you killed in Spain and it's bothered me ever since. I'm getting old and, well, son, you mean a great deal to me. I realize you're hurting inside and I know you want some action. You're just like I was, once. The only way to deal with things you can't control is by pressing into things you're used to…things you're trained for." As the light from the fire danced on Hunter's lined face, he closed his eyes as he said, "But I've got twenty more years of experience than you to fall back on, and you'll have to believe me when I tell you that this job they're offering you is a snake pit. Don't take it. You're a soldier, not an assassin."

Gage allowed an appropriate amount of time to pass. "I appreciate everything you've said, sir. I do."

"But," Colonel Hunter added.

"Yes, sir…*but*…I'm going to take the job. I'll be headed out in few days to spend a little more time with my handler. If something during that time doesn't seem right, I'll bail, okay?"

Colonel Hunter stood, staring down at Gage. It wasn't a reproachful stare. Hunter wasn't angry, either. The look he gave Gage seemed a combination of dissatisfaction and affection, the way a parent views an independent child. Without another word, Gage's longtime commander and advisor turned and walked back to the house, leaving Gage alone, awash in a vortex of swirling disapproval.

Chapter Four

THE PETITE LADY completed her computer search. She carefully replaced the paperclip on the top left corner of the paper. Grabbing her pen and notepad, she told her co-workers she'd be back shortly. Then she walked, exiting human resources and passing down the elevated, window-filled hallway known by the locals as *"el tubo."* The floor was rubber-coated and immaculate, dampening the click of her heels as she walked from the administrative side of the Nuestra building to the center, where the CEO maintained his suite of offices.

After swiping her keycard to enter the outer security area, the woman passed by a guard and stepped into Sonny's outer office. There, an older executive assistant—known behind her back as *La Bruja*, the witch—was on the phone and ignored the human resources lady. La Bruja eventually hung up, making several notes and taking her sweet time. She'd still not acknowledged the lady from HR. When she finished with her busywork, she removed her reading glasses, massaged her nose as if mentally preparing herself to speak to this peon, then offered a pained smile as she said, "What do you want?"

Ignoring the obvious contempt, the efficient human resources worker spoke matter-of-factly. "There's an American over at Alfa Seguridad. He's applying for a job."

"Oh, goody," La Bruja said flatly. "Perhaps I should call Viva TV."

The human resources lady maintained her patience. "He claimed to have served in the American Special Forces and everything on his application checks out. They gave him the randomized test of two hundred questions and he scored very highly. Per Señor Calabrese's orders, I'm to notify him when Alfa gets applications like this."

"Where is Chief Mikkelsen?" La Bruja hissed.

"She's *out.*"

La Bruja seemed disappointed that the human resource worker's visit was completely necessary, almost as if she'd looked forward to belittling her. Without another word, *La Bruja* stood and, after knocking on the closed door, disappeared into Sonny's office. After just a moment, she reappeared and gestured the human resources woman in with a hitch of her head.

"Be brief."

Smiling victoriously, the human resources worker stepped into the office, apprising Sonny of the taciturn, yet well-mannered, man who currently waited in the small conference room across town at Alfa Seguridad.

SONNY SIPPED his Perrier as he eyed the man on the high-definition television set. His name was Jeffrey Burrell, originally hailing from Missouri. Slightly larger than average, Burrell sat patiently, hardly moving a muscle. Sonny would describe Burrell as capable-looking, the type of man that, during his own military career, Sonny expected to find piloting F-15s or leading a specialized task force. Burrell's clothes seemed quite understated and utilitarian—and certainly not what most people would choose to wear for a job interview. His shirt was vented, slightly wrinkled and rolled up at the sleeves. It was gray but had probably once been black, faded from many washings and time spent in the sun. Sonny noted the man's muscular forearms. Not the type of muscle a bodybuilder might have—Burrell's muscle was the type associated with raw strength and power. His cargo pants were sand-colored, frayed at the bottom. He wore medium height lace-up boots, the lightweight type the military was issuing special ops soldiers nowadays.

Sonny watched as the receptionist over at Alfa stepped into the conference room. "Your application is being processed, señor. Would you like something to drink?"

"No, thank you, ma'am."

"C'mon, Abi…where the hell are you?" Sonny grumbled.

The murmur had barely passed through his lips when his phone buzzed. It was her. He touched the screen.

"I've been trying to raise you for a half-hour," he griped.

"I've been busy working on the next mission," Abi Mikkelsen replied unapologetically.

"Well, you've got a candidate in your offices. We checked him out. He looks good…damn good. Nailed ninety-nine percent on the skills test. You've been after me about needing another man."

"Person."

"Excuse me?"

"I never said '*man*.'"

53

"Whatever. Anyway, about this candidate, he was U.S. Army Special Forces. Your human resources interviewed, tested and fingerprinted him, then sent everything over here to Lupita who confirmed his record. She said his fingerprints match the Army's records and all his dates and training match."

"What else?" Abi asked.

"He got out of the service about a year ago and says he's been doing contract security work. Says he heard about Alfa from some pals at Fort Bragg."

"Doesn't that concern you?" she asked.

"Nah," he answered. "Alfa is a known quantity. It's the Alfa and Nuestra relationship that, if mentioned together, might concern me."

"Family?"

"Nope. Parents and sister deceased. Never been married."

"That's convenient," Abi remarked.

"Such people do exist," Sonny replied, eyeing his teeth in his hand mirror. "I'm in the same boat."

Turning his eyes back to the monitor, Sonny noticed that Jeff Burrell was now staring directly into the camera. His face showed no emotion at all. He obviously knew he was being watched.

"Do you want him?" Sonny asked.

"If everything checked out, and you approve of him, then I'd like to physically test him. See how he reacts."

"La Merced?"

"It washed out the last two," Abi said. "Once he's been out there for a while, we'll see how badly he wants to work for us."

"My only concern is drawing an immediate line between Alfa and Nuestra."

"It's harmless. If we don't want to keep him, all he's done is helped guard one of Nuestra's Arabica plantations. What could be more innocuous? To him it's just a contract job that Nuestra renews annually."

"I'll go along with it, again," Sonny breathed. "But you know how I feel about new hires. I don't like them to know the truth until we've had them here for a few years. Until we fully trust them."

"I'll make sure it's no problem."

Sonny glanced again at the live feed of Burrell. "Won't Simon try his best to kill this American?"

"Simon better do as he's told," Abi replied. They were referring to Simon Winterbourne, the chief guard of the sprawling La Merced Arabica plantation.

"Regarding Simon," Sonny said, "I'm close."

"Close?"

"Close to...to discarding him."

"He's vile and crass, sir, but he's no risk."

"He's junk."

"Anyway, I'll do some additional background on the candidate. What's his name?"

Sonny eyed the sheet. "Burrell. Jeffrey Knight Burrell."

"Thank you, sir. Anything else?"

"We need to meet, soon. About the next job."

"Yes, sir. I'll be in touch tomorrow."

Sonny hung up the phone. He walked to the large, fireproof file cabinet and, after punching in a code, opened the second drawer. He removed a file and dropped it on his desk, flipping it open with his fingernail. The file was full of pictures, all of Abi Mikkelsen. Sonny used his pinkie to spread the photos around. There were pictures of her jogging. There was one of her buying groceries. One of the investigators even managed to get a shot of her at home, topless. She'd not been aware that the photographs were being taken.

Despite his deep tan, Sonny felt the reddening flush of his cheeks and neck as he stared at her pert, upturned breasts. Breathing deeply, he scrutinized each photograph, occasionally whispering her name.

"Abi. Oh, Abi."

His fixation bordered on obscene. For whatever reason—maybe it was her constant military bearing—she made him feel flagellant. He wanted her to punish him.

In the bedroom, of course.

Rarely did Sonny allow personal desire to get in the way of business. He had many misgivings about Abi—professionally. Yet, he continued to employ her. She was certainly good at the tactical portion of her job, but less than willing to acquiesce to, or overlook, the numerous gray areas in which Alfa and Nuestra operated.

But Sonny was obsessed. Utterly obsessed.

FIFTEEN MINUTES later, after entering the rear door of the single-story, basic Alfa Seguridad building, Abigael "Abi" Mikkelsen logged into her personal security system. She clicked the button for camera two, focusing on the man signing a stack of papers that would officially make him a contract employee of Alfa Seguridad. With a few deft clicks of the mouse, she engaged the audio and zoomed in on the man as he politely conversed with Maria, their office manager who genuinely believed Alfa was made up of a group of glorified security guards.

Abi dragged the man's scanned application to her other screen, perusing it as she listened to the Spanish conversation. Burrell's Spanish was passable and, based on the little bit she heard, had a characteristic intonation and timbre that would suggest he'd spent significant time in Spain.

Reading his application, she noticed that Jeffrey Burrell printed his letters in all caps, making the letters that were supposed to be capitalized twice as tall. His handwriting was nearly illegible. He listed himself at 6'1" and 210 pounds. For 44 years of age, he looked to be in excellent shape. She reviewed his medical history where he listed three gunshots, seven broken bones and five surgeries. He claimed to have no allergies and no conditions that would prevent him from performing a strenuous job.

His test scores were as good as Abi had seen, although the test had only been given to about a dozen people. The 200 test questions were pulled randomly by a computer program from a battery of 800 questions Abi had personally chosen. The questions covered everything from weaponry to basic infantry skills to escape-and-evasion to first aid. He missed only three questions. She viewed them, understanding why he might have answered each one the way he did. Abi turned her eyes back to the screen.

Burrell was saying something about a house he'd just rented in the Lurigancho area. "...and I hate that I have to pay rent on it while I'm gone. Will I be coming back here at all?"

Maria scanned the email in her hand, the one that Abi had sent as soon as she'd gotten off the phone with Sonny. "It doesn't say, sir. In my experience, guards like you who are sent on a first assignment like this usually only stay a month or so. Maybe even less."

It seemed something was weighing on Burrell's mind as he visibly struggled with this decision. He nodded after a moment, his face still mildly troubled. The remainder of the meeting was unremarkable. Maria provided him with an address for tomorrow's physical and vaccinations.

"Assuming your physical goes well, on Wednesday you are to be at this address at six in the morning," she said, handing him a sheet of paper. "You will travel by truck to La Merced. You can bring a small personal bag but you really only need bring toiletries, underwear and a second pair of boots. There is no cellular service in La Merced, and your uniforms and food will be provided." She paused for just a second. "The conditions there are difficult, Mister Burrell."

"Have you been there?"

"No, but I've been in the high jungle before." She gave him a practiced smile as she extended her hand, welcoming him aboard.

As Burrell gathered his things to leave, Abi lifted the radio, calling the Peruvian guard at the main entrance of the Alfa building. "Delay Jeffrey Burrell, the man who just interviewed. He'll be at your desk in less than a minute. Just tell him to wait, then pretend to call Maria to make sure she gave him the address for his physical. Okay? When you see my Ford Focus across the street, then you can release him. *Don't* be obvious, got it?"

Abi Mikkelsen snatched her ring of bump keys from the drawer, along with the set of car keys for her company vehicle. She hurried out the rear door of the building and screeched the narrow tires of the Ford as she raced around the block.

MARIA DIRECTED Gage—Jeffrey Burrell—on which way to go. While there were a number of cubes, offices and desks, Gage didn't see any other people in the building. When he reached the front entrance, where the guard sat who'd initially welcomed Gage upon his arrival, he unclipped his visitor's badge. After sliding the badge to the guard, Gage signed out. When he did, the guard, a Peruvian in a black suit with a security emblem on the pocket, politely asked "Mister Burrell" if they'd scheduled his physical.

"Yes," Gage replied. "It's tomorrow."

"Very good, but will you please wait here just a moment?" The guard dialed a few numbers, staring out the broad expanse of windows as he waited. Shook his head. "No answer. Let me try one more person," he murmured, hanging up and punching another extension. He continued to stare out the window, humming an indecipherable tune.

Keeping his eyes on the guard, Gage noticed the man's eyes briefly widen. He then spoke in rapid Spanish that Gage could barely follow. "Ah, *hola*, Maria. Did you provide Mister Burrell with the address for his physical?"

While he spoke, Gage casually looked outside the glass. The entrance to the Alfa Seguridad building was a flat driveway that bisected several adjacent parking lots. Scanning the entry drive and the parking lots, Gage noticed nothing out of the ordinary.

The guard hung up the phone and said, "Sir, the address for your physical, it was given to you?"

Gage lifted the company folder. "Yes, I have it, thank you."

"Good," the guard smiled. "I simply wanted to make sure. They sometimes forget to provide that to applicants. I hope you have a pleasant day."

Nodding, Gage exited, making sure he acted natural. That phone call was an obvious, poorly-acted delay tactic and Gage expected to pick up a tail as soon as he hit the street up ahead.

So, the question is, how difficult do I want to make this for my tail?

Gage viewed the question as twofold. He needed to ascend at Alfa—and quickly—which meant they needed to think of him as capable. So, being a pain in the ass on day one might hurt his cause. But, along those same lines of thinking, he didn't want to be a pushover, either. If they viewed him as some dumb lug, what motivation would they have to keep him around long enough for him to encounter Sonny Calabrese?

It only took a moment for Gage to decide on the best course of action. If they'd assigned him an amateurish tail, he'd burn them. He'd have to. If he were so aloof that he couldn't spot a sloppy shadow, they'd never respect him. But if the person operated with proficiency, he'd pretend they weren't even there. And if they were following him, they'd almost certainly search his apartment.

Besides, as he reminded himself, if he were coming here to innocently apply for this position, he should have little reason to be suspicious.

Suddenly, Gage was struck by an inspiration. For once he'd been outfitted with the proper gear. All he had to do now was set the trap.

At the top of the entry road, he turned left on the sidewalk beside the busy thoroughfare in Lima's San Borja district. If someone were tailing him on foot, it would be easy to follow him since the street was packed with pedestrians.

But, if they were tailing him by car, they'd have to wait at the traffic light, making things more difficult. Gage walked ahead at a normal rate of speed, staying out at the edge of the sidewalk, close to the frenetic traffic.

He was making himself easier to be spotted.

ABI MIKKELSEN was no dummy. She'd eased to the top of the drive as Burrell made his way down the sidewalk. When the light finally turned green, she bulled her way into the stream of cars on the far side of the six-lane street, getting into the flow of traffic which wasn't much faster than the speed of a person on foot.

The Lima bus system was often described as chaotic. For a woman hailing from Copenhagen, home of a near-perfect public transportation system, Abi felt "chaotic" was far too generous a description for whatever it was Lima was operating. She didn't even have a word to describe what they had here, other than the Danish word "*lort.*" When Burrell passed by the first bus stop, Abi realized he would likely continue on foot. She whipped the car into the narrow median, snatched up the parking brake and left it there. After a quick call on the radio to tell the front desk guard to retrieve the car, she deftly followed the American on foot, staying approximately fifty meters behind him.

A petite woman, she disappeared easily behind the dozens of people on the sidewalk. And Burrell was quite easy to follow, since he was much taller than the average local. He strolled like any person might in a new city, glancing all around with curiosity.

The beginnings of a plan coming to her, Abi phoned one of her local contacts, Polo, as she walked. Not only was Polo reliable, he was also trustworthy. Sometimes Abi did things she didn't want anyone at Nuestra knowing and, when she did, she enlisted Polo, a local private detective. He didn't answer but called her back within minutes. Abi told him where she was headed and asked him to drive to that general area and stand by. Polo, on a sizeable retainer, dropped his current task—which involved tailing a wife for a cuckolded husband—and sped to the Lurigancho area.

Abi continued to follow Burrell. He was still headed east by northeast, staying on the left side of Avenida Javier Prado. His pace was average if not a bit quick, especially considering the crumbling sidewalk and the teeming foot traffic. Abi studied her mark during breaks in the pedestrian traffic. He made no eye contact with others and walked just as the locals did, ignoring traffic signals and crossing when there were either gaps in the traffic or too much congestion for the cars to move at a deadly speed.

After about a kilometer, Burrell entered a café. Abi lowered her sunglasses a tad and plastered her phone to the side of her face to provide enough camouflage to her features. Burrell didn't yet know what she looked like, but why give him a clear picture that he might associate later? She slowly passed the restaurant, pretending to talk on her phone as she leaned down to view the menu. There he was, queued at the counter behind a line of locals.

Five minutes later he took a seat near the window, reading *El Peruano*, the local newspaper, and wolfing his food. He was obviously fluent enough to comprehend the written Spanish of the newspaper. Fifteen minutes later, Burrell was on the move again, carrying a small sack of food along with his

Alfa Seguridad folder. Abi followed him as the road tracked east with the Rio Rímac.

How far is he going to walk?

On they went, walking for well over an hour. Thankfully the streets were crowded the entire way, giving Abi cover. It was one of the benefits of living in a metro area that was populated with nearly ten million people.

Burrell eventually turned north on a narrow street that crossed the heavily-polluted Rio Rímac. There were no other people on the street. As the overhead sun burned down on Lima, Abi slid into an overgrown recession near the river, watching as her mark continued forward, climbing the street where it transitioned to gravel and dust. When he'd walked out of sight, she moved forward, following the road at least a kilometer past the river, eventually coming to an older, two-story home set back in the scrub brush next to a dry creek bed. The home had once been painted white and a set of rickety stairs on the side of the house told Abi that it was likely now used as a duplex. Abi found good cover behind a dense thicket, seeing no sign of Burrell. There was, however, a pickup truck parked beside the duplex.

Abi was carefully scanning the surprisingly secluded locale when she heard a door slam. She turned to see Burrell hurrying down the rickety stairs. He'd changed into a t-shirt, shorts and tennis shoes. Leading Burrell, on a sturdy leash, was a dog.

My scent!

Abi crouched there, perfectly still, trying to feel the breeze on her exposed skin. If there was a breeze, it felt as if it were whispering from the north. That meant, if Burrell followed the road back out, the dog would probably pick up on her scent.

No! No! No! What an amateur mistake this'll be. Abi cursed herself inwardly, mortified that she was going to get burned before this man had worked a single hour for Alfa Seguridad.

"Wanna see what's up there?" Burrell asked the dog, riling the pup. "Wanna go? Huh? You wanna?"

After the dog had relieved himself on the closest tree, revealing himself as a male, Abi heard Burrell say something about "let's climb to the top of the hill." Herself not a "pet person," she briefly wondered who talks so much to their dog. More important, she knew the hill he was speaking of was Lomas de Mangomarca, a small mountain directly to the north that, during clear weather, afforded the finest Pacific views in Lima. Burrell and the dog were off, headed up the hillside. If they were going to the top of Mangomarca, they'd be gone an hour at minimum.

From her vantage point behind the bushes, Abi phoned Polo again, telling him where her target was headed. She instructed Polo to take the access road into Mangomarca and pick them up there.

"Call me when they're headed back," she said.

After Burrell had disappeared into the scrub brush, Abi walked to the rickety stairwell of the home, climbing them without trepidation. If someone happened to be in the lower unit, she didn't want to seem suspicious. On the small landing at the top, Abi checked the lock brand. After choosing the correct bump key, she defeated Jeff Burrell's deadbolt in less than fifteen seconds with several good whacks.

Inside the small duplex apartment, she rifled the former Special Forces soldier's sparse belongings.

Abi had no idea she was being videoed.

THAT EVENING, as a worn-out Sheriff slumbered in the middle of the floor, Gage read the report that had been sent back to him by Falco. The report had arrived encrypted and was a one-time, read-only page that briefly appeared on the iPad Gage had been issued. The page was only available after Gage pressed his thumbprint into the toggled fingerprint scanner. The scanner also detected his pulse and body temperature, preventing someone from accessing the encrypted data through the use of a lifeless thumb. For the second layer of security, Gage spoke several sentences, watching as the security app turned green when it recognized his voice. The report immediately appeared, the notation over the report informing Gage that he had 75 seconds to read, after which the report would permanently vanish...

> **Eleven minutes after you powered the camera on, your quarters were accessed and searched by Abigael "Abi" Mikkelsen, Alfa Seguridad's Chief of Security.**

Mikkelsen's picture followed, the same one Gage had seen last week as he and Falco had made their plans. It was a corporate pose, showing a woman of approximately thirty years of age. Her sandy blonde hair was pulled back severely, making her seem the no-nonsense type. It almost seemed like a picture of someone trying to appear stern. Her face was youthful and unlined with no trace of a smile. Other than her obvious solemnity, Gage would certainly describe her as attractive. He continued to read the report, noting the timer at the top right of the report...47 seconds remaining...

She was in your quarters for fourteen minutes and seemed to find nothing remarkable. It was also obvious from her actions that she didn't suspect that she was being filmed.

Summarizing the briefing you received on her last week, intel says that Mikkelsen has been with Alfa for four years. Prior to coming to Peru, she was notable for her failed lawsuit against the Danish government. A soldier in the Royal Danish Army, Mikkelsen lobbied repeatedly to join the Huntsmen Corps, the Danish Army's special operations branch. We have a file on her due to her suspected involvement in the 2009 hijacking of a yacht in the Gulf of Oman. According to shared intel from the Danes to the US, she's known for her prowess with weapons, her extreme physical fitness and her superiority in high-level navigation. NOTE – just because she searched your quarters, it doesn't mean they're suspicious of you. Mikkelsen planted no cameras or bugs. The search was likely SOP for the type of job you applied for. Take standard precautions going forward and do nothing to arouse suspicion. Your moment will come soon. EOM.

The timer ticked down...4...3...2...1. The report vanished and the encryption app closed, appearing onscreen like a commonly-used e-reader app. Gage removed the scanner toggle and navigated to one of his email accounts.

There was only one message there, from a detective in the Fayetteville Sheriff Department. Gage had served with the man in the Army. The detective had taken the Diet Coke can from Linda DeLand and run her fingerprints. He told Gage everything about her background checked out, including her deceased son who'd once served in the Navy.

Gage had felt she was the genuine article but he'd simply wanted to make sure. Now he felt the slightest bit more secure about what he was doing here. He closed the iPad's cover, putting it to sleep.

After making sure all his devices were off, Gage found his personal scanner and swept the apartment for anything sending a signal. There was nothing other than a faint signal coming from the center of the floor—that would be Adriana's cell phone, downstairs. True to what Falco had said, Chief Mikkelsen had planted no listening devices.

Gage stretched out on the floor next to Sheriff, ordering his mind for tomorrow. Sheriff, no longer panting, nestled in next to his master. Overhead, the rickety old ceiling fan churned away. Gage tucked his arm behind his head, focusing.

Foremost on his mind was finding a boarding home for Sheriff. While Lima seemed a decent enough city, Gage had no idea how the Peruvians treated their pets. Bringing Sheriff to Lima had ignited a debate between Gage and Falco, but Gage had the trump card and calmly told his handler that not being allowed to bring the dog would be a deal-breaker. That shut Falco up. Besides, Gage reasoned that having a dog would make him appear less suspicious. To his credit, Falco agreed and relented.

So, tomorrow, after searching for a kennel in the morning, Gage would undergo the Alfa Seguridad physical at noon. They'd told him to plan for two hours. After the physical, he planned to buy a handful of prepaid cell phones. Then he'd stash them along with his communications gear and scanner— there was no way he could safely take any of it with him. Besides, he'd need cellular or secure Wi-Fi service and didn't expect to find either out in the Peruvian jungle.

No, Gage planned to go to this La Merced place to perform his job, and perform it well. It was the only way he knew to impress his superiors and ascend to a regular position with Alfa Seguridad. Doing his best to ignore the pit of dread in his stomach, Gage dozed.

The pit of dread was there because, deep down, he knew what was coming in La Merced.

Chapter Five

LIMA, PERU is located approximately 800 miles south of the equator. Being in such close proximity to the equator means the daylight differences are quite minor month-to-month, with only about an hour's variance over a full year. While many locales so close to the equator are blazing hot, Lima's weather is tempered by the cool waters of the Pacific Ocean lapping at its shores. July and August are Lima's coolest months, with high temperatures averaging in the upper 60's. And the current month, February, is typically one of the hottest months of the year, even though the average highs are only in the low 80's. With the mild Pacific breezes in the summer, it usually felt perfect, as it did on this night when Sonny Calabrese dined on the westward patio of his San Isidro home.

As is common in Latin America, the average workday begins and ends late, especially in comparison to the United States and Europe. It's not at all unusual to see shops and businesses open "around" 11 a.m. and remain open until 7-something. With siesta as their midday break, many white-collar workers don't finally leave their offices until mid-evening, and supper often rambles on until midnight. Sometimes even later on the weekends. While Sonny was fine with these customs, he had one pet peeve about many of the locals. Put simply, Sonny was obsessive about people arriving early for meetings. Much like a drill sergeant, Sonny believed if a person was just "on-time" they were actually late. If any Nuestra employee made Sonny wait more than once, they might find themselves making one of his famous choices of punishment. Sonny's employees, and anyone who was familiar with him, knew better than to test this pet peeve. Thankfully, no one was late on this night.

Another of Sonny's passions was the complete utilization of food, especially animals. While Sonny had no problem eating meat and fish, he felt it wasteful that many edible parts of animals were ignored. Tonight he'd ordered a full lobster, methodically devouring the crustacean, right down to the tiny amount of meat located in the arachnid-like legs. As he picked out the last toothpick of succulent meat with the tong of his fork, he read a briefing relaying the facts of the upcoming cartel heists. Chief Mikkelsen was due in fifteen minutes—meaning she would be there in five. Sonny sucked the slender piece of meat as he eyed the briefing.

The most recent haul of cocaine—from the Garcia Cartel—was due to be shipped out on Friday. The aircraft would make one stop in the United States before continuing on to Germany, where the buyer would take possession and distribute throughout Europe.

An Asian shipment would depart next week. It would first fly to California before proceeding to Japan.

Each shipment was worth millions.

Sonny eyed the levels of stock. They were perilously low. Depending how large each take happened to be, Sonny preferred to keep several shipments in reserve. He and his team stepped on the drugs as far as they dared, but never so far that they might lose their premium designation.

Premium cocaine is among the world's most valuable commodities when measured by weight.

Because of the low stock, the upcoming Manolo Cartel hit was critical.

Pedro appeared. "Can I get you anything else, señor?"

"No, Pedro. I'm fine."

"Your guest is here."

Sonny peered beyond Pedro, seeing Abi Mikkelsen standing at parade rest in the house. "Well, tell her to quit hiding in the shadows and come out here."

Pedro motioned with his right hand and Abi marched onto the patio. As he did whenever she was near, Sonny appraised her head to toe. She wore a tasteful dark skirt that draped to her knees. Her shoes were flat and form-fitting. While appearing somewhat dressy at first glance, upon closer inspection they seemed to be deftly-camouflaged athletic sneakers. Her light gray blouse appeared as if it had been freshly pressed only minutes before. Other than a runner's Timex, she wore no jewelry whatsoever. In fact, the only identifying peculiarity of her person—besides her alluring face—was a narrow tattoo that circled her ankle.

Years before, at his first glance, Sonny thought the tattoo to be an image of a vine of some sort. It had aroused him. However, he had later learned, through the aid of a cleverly placed camera, that it was actually a wrap-around Danish phrase done in a cursive script. Translated, it read, "No matter what, and at any cost, I shall only climb."

Someday, Sonny would drag his slick tongue over that tattoo.

Abi stood at the other end of the six-person table, her hands behind her in her preferred parade rest position. "Please sit," Sonny said, nudging the adjacent chair with his foot.

"No, thank you, sir," she replied. "I'm here to report on our new contract soldier. If you'll recall, his name is Jeffrey Burrell and—"

"Whoa," Sonny interrupted. "Slow down, will you?"

"Where should I begin, sir?"

"How are you?"

"I'm fine."

"You look *fine*."

Abi said nothing.

"Won't you eat something?"

"No, sir. I've eaten."

Sonny clasped his hands on the table, frowning. "Fine. Tell me more about Burrell."

"We confirmed more about his time in Special Forces. He was in Tenth Group, the battalion in Germany."

"Böblingen," Sonny added, flexing his intellect. "Go on."

"We dug all around in his background and everything checked out. As we discussed, we hired him temporarily and we're sending him to La Merced for a shakedown."

"I remember."

"And I did the search of his home."

Sonny lowered his hands. "*You* did the search?"

"I did," she replied with a note of indignation, coming out of her parade rest stance. "And I'm perfectly *capable* of handling such—"

"That wasn't an indictment," Sonny interrupted. "It just seems mundane for someone of your level. Continue."

She smoothed the sides of her skirt as her irritation melted away. "There was nothing remarkable about his quarters, sir, except the fact that he chose an isolated locale. He seems to be a bit of a loner. His apartment was clean. The only curious thing I discovered is that he owns a dog."

Sonny studied her as she spoke. Her accent, like so many northern Europeans who spoke English regularly, was rather mild. Her blue eyes never swayed from his face as she relayed the facts. She was robot-like, which made her all the more scrumptious. In bed, could he melt away all that ice? Could he eventually corrupt her, making her call him at odd hours, begging for a rendezvous that would bring them both to an inflamed—

"His personal effects are simple and exactly what I'd expect to find from someone who's been in special ops," she said, interrupting Sonny's licentious train of thought. "Later, I did a deeper background check and, once again, found nothing that stood out. He did twenty-two years in the U.S. Army, seventeen of them in Special Forces. He's credited with six combat tours and, like most who've served in the United States special ops, no useful information is stored in records that we can access. He's getting his full retirement benefit and, according to what we uncovered, he has $34,000 in regular savings. No dependents. No real estate. No debt."

"What else?"

Abi finished the précis. "While we've received walk-ins before, even with backgrounds such as Burrell's, such an arrival without any recruitment makes me instantly distrustful of the man. That's why I want to send him to La Merced. He'll guard the coffee fields and will take Simon's best shot." She ended abruptly, saying, "That is all." Then she straightened slightly and stared over Sonny, due west, to the orange line on the Pacific horizon.

Sonny ran his finger through the lobster's juices. He slurped the juice from his finger, turning eyes back to Mikkelsen. "How do you predict this playing out?"

"I couldn't say, sir."

"Why?"

"Predictions are reckless and useless. Real life is what matters."

"Humor me, then."

She was unable to hide a brief flash of annoyance. "First off, we need this man, Burrell. Desperately. Five qualified soldiers are not enough. Six will barely suffice, but will be an improvement. And I'd prefer it if you'd allow me to keep at least four more in reserve. Further, whatever discipline that's meted out against my team should fall under *my* purview. In the past year I've lost DeLand and Schneider. Neither deserved—"

"Noted. Now, please, go ahead with your prediction," Sonny interrupted.

Mikkelsen pulled in a breath through her nose. "If Simon does what I suspect he'll do, I predict this American will eventually respond with violence. He'll have to. Out there, in the high jungle, there is no other recourse. My instinct tells me the American is a bona fide warrior—the sort of man people want on their side. To me, at first blush, he seems morally upright but I have suspicions that he will not hesitate to respond if provoked, especially more than once."

"Interesting. Who will prevail?"

Frowning in thought, she said, "Simon is talented—no debating it. He's also an alcoholic. And he's ruthless and impetuous. He was kicked out of SAS after multiple warnings."

"And?" Sonny asked.

"The American will likely prevail if a showdown occurs. I'd favor the American with seven to three odds."

"Handicapping our soldiers," Sonny said with a chuckle. "I like it." He lifted his finger. "When the new soldier goes to La Merced, I want a word with Simon."

"Yes, sir."

"I want him to know that I'm nearing the end of my rope with him."

"Roger, sir."

"How about a glass of wine? Perhaps a coffee?"

"No, thank you, sir."

Sonny sipped his wine, pondering his best course of action. He'd tried every angle with this ice queen and had yet to make any progress whatsoever. Countless man hours of surveillance had revealed nothing about Abi Mikkelsen, other than her penchant for extreme exercise and clean living. Most important to Sonny, she'd never been discovered to take a sexual partner since coming to Peru. And the collective surveillance he'd ordered didn't encompass some tiny slice of time—it amounted to several hundred days and, frustratingly, not one instance of sex had taken place. As people often do with women who have no known partners, many at Nuestra and Alfa speculated that Mikkelsen was a dyke. But that was wrong, at least according to evidence. As far as Sonny knew, she was asexual. A beautiful woman without a desire for a lover.

How's that even possible? Sonny thought. *It just doesn't compute. Well, tonight I'll just be direct. And I shall enjoy watching her reaction.*

"Mikkelsen...Abi...to be quite frank, I'd like to share a fine bottle of wine with you, to talk to you, to get to know the things that are truly important to you." She opened her mouth to speak but he wagged his finger. "Then, Abi, when we're both quite comfortable, I'd like to take you to my bedroom and make love to you."

"I know you would," she replied.

"You do?" he asked, leaning back and plopping his linen napkin on the table.

"Of course, you would. You're an alpha male and I'm generally thought of as attractive. I'm single. I'm your subordinate. And in all your considerable surveillance of me, you've never uncovered anything in the sexual realm." Mikkelsen narrowed her eyes. "You, sir, are the very definition of predictable. And that, sir, with all due respect, bores me to tears."

Her final words were spoken with more edge than he'd ever heard from her. Without asking, she turned and stalked away, her tight little rear end swaying with each step.

Sonny Calabrese felt the flush of his cheeks at having been called out so bluntly. When he glanced down, he realized he was excited.

"Abi Mikkelsen," he whispered reverently. After he hurriedly finished his bottle of Los Vascos Sauvignon Blanc, he rang for Pedro. Inconsistent with his typical order, tonight he requested a petite European, blonde with blue eyes. Even though it took some time to fulfill the specific request, the Belgian hooker eventually arrived at the Calabrese estate.

And when he ravished her, Sonny didn't last long. Not at all.

TWO DAYS LATER

WHEN GAGE HAD first arrived early in the morning for transit to La Merced, he had a momentary flashback of his ride to Berga prison. Just as in Spain, he was departing a seaside city to head to what would become his veritable prison. No phones. No emails. No contact with anyone back in the States. It would just be Gage and his new "friends," whoever they happened to be. Gage's flashback, however, was truly the only similarity to that fateful Spanish drive that now seemed so long ago. It also stirred up memories of Justina, which he quickly tried to shake from his mind.

This time he rode up front, in the crew portion of a large straight truck that was lightly loaded. The two men in the front seats informed Gage they drove this route six days a week. They seemed grateful for Gage's presence— probably a welcome break to the monotony. Unlike most Peruvians Gage encountered in Lima, who spoke with an accent he could easily understand, these men spoke with rural Andean accents; it took Gage a full hour to adjust. Despite Gage's hesitance to converse, the men continued to pepper him with questions, forcing him to speak. In the end he felt it was good practice. According to these men, most of the people who worked at the La Merced facility spoke with the same accent—he'd have to learn it sooner or later.

The trip itself took about ten hours, marked by poor roads, sporadic heavy rain and hours of slow climbing. The Peruvian coastal area is arid, similar to Southern California. Halfway into their trek, lush vegetation began to appear and, by the time they closed in on La Merced, Gage guessed the area was regularly soaked with downpours, as it was today. Mountains surrounded the valley road with low clouds hovering a thousand feet above. Gage spied numerous colorful fruits growing in the wild, many of them hanging over the roadway in colorful canopy. At one point, a waterfall cascaded down on the right side of the road, rushing underneath at a small bridge. Gage craned his head to the left, seeing a bevy of children playing in the pool at its base. The area here was lush, perfect for growing coffee.

Or other highly sought-after plants.

In the ride's final two hours, both drivers were beset by weighty eyelids.

Gage asked if he could drive before both men weakly objected due to company regulations.

"Come on guys," Gage cajoled in Spanish. "I'm a good driver. And this way, you guys can get a little nap."

It didn't take much convincing.

For Gage, those final two hours were blissful. He was mentally exhausted from all the Spanish and, as the two men snored loudly, he was able to reorder his mind prior to arrival. Gage had been told the conditions at La Merced were harsh. The climate seemed nearly perfect so, of course, that had to mean the working and living conditions. Gage expected long hours and probably arduous physical labor. He also expected the guards to be inhospitable. Gage knew, if his background had held up, Alfa was interested in him becoming an operator. And this trip was almost certainly a way to find out just what kind of man he was.

So, Gage, what are you willing to do? Alfa wants company men. Men they can trust. And, though Gage was guessing at this point, he'd wager they wanted men who will readily kill yet remain loyal to the "company." Namely, to Sonny Calabrese's cause.

The physical exam he'd endured yesterday hadn't been all that rigorous. It was roughly the same type of exam a person received upon volunteering for the military. Blood work was done, probably to make sure he didn't have a life-threatening or communicable disease. His heart was given a full stress test, likely to make certain he wouldn't drop dead during heavy labor. And his urine was examined, almost certainly to make sure he wasn't a secret doper. Otherwise, the exam was cursory, although Gage did notice the doctor studying Gage's shoulder tattoo.

The other major activity yesterday had been aimed at finding a suitable kennel for Sheriff. After checking with several pet boarding facilities, each of which catered to the very wealthy—making them unaffordable, especially for Gage's cover—a pleasant worker at the last facility suggested he ask around the area where he lived.

"Most people here love dogs and will treat yours as their own," she'd told him.

The worker had been correct. Gage asked the woman who lived downstairs from him. Her name was Adriana. She was in her mid to late twenties and told Gage she actually worked for the landlord.

"I do all his paperwork and sometimes help him show houses and apartments to people."

Dressed simply in jeans, a plain blue top and flat sandals, she was a pleasant-looking girl. Her long, straight black hair framed her tan face. Most distinct was her wide smile, made all the more attractive by her large white teeth and full lips. Her teeth were slightly crooked—suggesting that she hadn't worn braces. Somehow, her teeth added to her character and good looks.

"Aren't you uncomfortable living way out here in the woods by yourself?" he'd asked.

"Not really," she'd replied. "My papa taught me to bird hunt when I was only six. I like the woods."

"Do you still hunt?"

She shook her head, a flash of pain registering on her face. "Not since he passed away."

"I'm sorry."

Adriana brightened. "But having a dog around will make me feel much, much safer." Within seconds, she was frolicking on the floor with Sheriff, laughing and letting him lick her face. Sheriff was in heaven.

"I love dogs," Adriana said, speaking excellent English. She'd massaged Sheriff's ears, baby-talking him for a moment. "My last dog lived to be fourteen…I got him when I was so young." After she convinced Gage she would only walk Sheriff on a leash and, in the end, knew far more than Gage about caring for a dog, Gage gave her money for food and for any veterinary care Sheriff might need. When he tried to pay her for her services, she shook her head.

"You can pay me when you return, Mister Burrell."

"Please, call me Jeff."

"Jeff, it is." They shook on their deal.

Last night, when Gage said goodbye to his pup, he'd had a tremendous pang of melancholy over Justina. Sheriff had bridged the gap after she'd left him, and now Gage was headed into the unknown all alone. Again.

Gage had caught Adriana watching out her window as he'd trudged up the stairs. He waved goodbye and made his final preparations. At his door, he looked down at her window. She was still looking up at him.

Last night, Gage had managed a few hours of sleep and now the only thing keeping him from being drowsy was the adrenaline over what awaited him. Fortunately, as Gage drove, those last two hours seemed to move quickly. In short order, sprawling fields of *coffea* plants extended away on both sides of the truck. Row after serried row, the Arabica plantation went on as far as Gage's eyes could see. He stopped and woke his new friends, climbing into the crew seat again. It took ten more minutes to reach the main gate, protected by two gun-wielding guards. The men appeared to be locals.

Inside the compound, the truck ground to a halt beside numerous pallets of cardboard boxes. Gage hopped out and glanced around. He was standing in a broad yard. The yard had been covered in gravel but mud had oozed over the gravel, making the far-reaching surface look like a huge sheet of peanut brittle. In the center of the yard was a guard shack and up on the hill, at the edge of the fields, were a number of cinderblock buildings and huts. One of the huts had smoke coming from its fluted chimney. All in all, it appeared like many jungle outposts Gage had seen in his past. A place to eat. A place to sleep. A place to store the guns—and nothing more.

Gage was then greeted by a large man in olive drab clothing. The man had curly blond hair and a ruddy complexion, dotted by numerous sunspots on his overly-tanned skin. With knowing blue eyes that squinted at Gage, the man spoke heavily-accented British English as he introduced himself as Simon, chief of the guards at La Merced. He extended his hand and squeezed Gage's with a bone-breaker grip. As he did, he measured Gage's eyes, looking for pain or surprise. Gage let the man play his little game, only gripping back with enough force to prevent his own bones from being ground together.

Once Simon's little alpha male game was over, he pointed up the muddy hill. "That's yer shack up there, on the right. Ya lucked out and got yer own, mainly a'cause mosta these locals go home at night."

"That one?" Gage asked, pointing.

"Yeh. Now head up there, drop your shit, take a wiz and change into the uni that's on yer bunk. Meet me back here in five so we can bust yer cherry, proper."

Gage did as he was told, arriving back in four minutes. Simon handed Gage a battered AK-47. "Clear it." Simon eyed Gage's movements as he complied with the request, removing the magazine and clearing the chamber.

Simon spoke with hands on his hips. "You'll walk on full-safe with no round in the chamber."

"Where am I walking?"

"I'll ask the fockin' questions!" Simon barked. "You see an intruder, you give one shouted warning in any language you like. They don't obey, ya fire on 'em—man, woman or child. If'n it's a man, yer within yer rights to shoot to kill. Ya folla?"

"Whoa," Gage said. "I need to know more than that. What if it's just some—"

"Do as I said, shitbird. Any human on these grounds is taking their life in their hands. And believe ya me, these little shit-eating Peruvians'll steal a handbag of Arabica faster than ya can pull on that stubby little pud o'yers. A few handbags full'o beans and they can trade that for enough food to last 'em a week." Simon crooked a finger at Gage's face. "You'll ask no more questions, shitbird. It's time ya start hoofin'."

Simon turned, gesturing to a muddy path that began down the hill from Gage's hut. "That's the main trail, goes clear around the entire fockin' plantation. You'll cross the main road two times, the first at kilometer thirteen, the second at kilometer thirty-one. Round trip's forty-two kilometers—essentially a marathon," he said, grinning savagely. "Average Joe takes about thirteen hours whilst pushin' hisself to the limit. You, mister nancy-boy Green Beret, better do it in *nine*." Simon consulted what looked to be an expensive diver's watch, clicking one of the timers. "1600 hours right now. If ya ain't back on this spot by 0100, yer booted from my force and you'll find your own fockin' transpo back to Lima. Oh…you'll do the trail without a light, and with no food or water. Hope ya drank well on the drive in." Simon aimed his crooked finger to the trail. "Go."

Jamming the magazine back into the AK, Gage fought the urge to ask another question. Instead, he turned and jogged, silently yelling at himself to buck up, to accept the situation and grind through it.

As Gage soon found, the trail was a muddy mess.

BECAUSE HE'D begun the forced trail march at four in the afternoon, Gage knew he had about three-and-a-half hours of light remaining. Sunset occurred shortly before seven in the evening and twilight lasted, at most, for thirty minutes afterward. Probably less with these heavy clouds. Based on what he'd seen of the mud-covered trail thus far, the speed Simon was demanding was a lot to ask—and that was probably the point. If he had any hope of making the round trip in nine hours, he'd better abide by the old saying and "make hay while the sun was shining." Though the sun was obscured by the heavy clouds, the daylight certainly aided Gage's progress.

He'd been at it now for ninety minutes and seemed to be at the highest point of this side of the plantation. The fields drew out in a lush panorama below him, running as far as the eye could see. Gage's goal was to make the first road crossing—which, according to Simon, occurred at 13 kilometers— at no later than six in the evening. That would mean Gage had averaged 6.5 kilometers per hour—about 4 miles per hour—during his first two hours. On the uneven ground of a narrow trail, that's quite fast. It would also mean he needed to average slightly higher than 4 kilometers per hour over the balance of his forced march. After the first road crossing, he'd still have another hour and a half of daylight. If he could maintain his 6.5 kilometers per hour pace during that period, he'd only need to average slightly more than 3 kilometers per hour once darkness set in.

All those numbers sounded good in theory, but the heavy clouds were going to obscure any moon that might otherwise help Gage to see. He chided himself for his laxity: *Why didn't you check the moon phases or the weather forecast before you left? Stupid! Stupid! Stupid!*

Assuming he'd have to deal with the worst, Gage picked up the pace.

Ten minutes later, the clouds burst.

A SHORT WHILE later, Simon Winterbourne stood at the first crossing and eyed the sky. The rainstorm had been fierce but quick, blowing by and leaving sparse clouds in its wake. To the west, sunlight beamed through the trees, probably providing rays of hope to that American bugger. Simon reached into his cargo pocket and grabbed the bottle of whiskey, taking two searing nips before replacing it. He sucked cool air through his teeth, feeling every bit the part of a real man. Jabbing the half-smoked Davidoff cigarette in his mouth, he squinted at the chronograph on his Breitling Super Avenger, chuckling as lacy smoke enveloped his head. After flicking the cigarette into a muddy puddle on the roadside, hearing it hiss, Simon pressed one of the presets on the satellite phone.

As the phone made its series of connections, the hulking former SAS man climbed onto the hood of the Land Rover, stretching out with his back against the windshield. The satellite phone was still initializing, so he indulged himself about this evening. After he'd dispatched with this arsehole Yank, Simon would head into the town of La Merced for a king's meal, copious amounts of drink, and five or six runs at the tipsy tourist gals who always found him, a true bushmaster, so damned interesting. Simon loved the adventurous tourists that made their way this far inland. Trying to get a glimpse of the jungle and how the real Peruvians lived, they still found it in themselves to go out at night and get smashed. Most of the tourists in La Merced were American or Japanese. But there were also the stray encounters with Germans, Chinese and even the occasional Brit. Simon preferred the American women. So phony and gullible. Hell, many were so stupid that, upon hearing his accent, they thought he was Australian! If Simon had a quid for every American scrubber he'd taken out behind the pub, he'd—

The phone chirped.

Lifting the device to his ear, he could hear the ringing. He was calling Sil, Alfa's team leader. Swiss by birth, Sil was Simon's direct boss and kept him updated on the goings-on back at headquarters.

When Sil picked up, Simon started right in. "This yank they sent out here ain't so damned tough. Real good hire the head twat made, wot? I'm standin' here at the first bloody crossing and the yank ain't so much as passed yet and he's already three hours in! Must'a been made'o sugar, he was, pussy-out like he did over a little squall. Bet that wanker, Sonny, had a hand in his hire, too."

"Er..."

"When this yank bolos, they gonna put me back on the team, wot?"

"I, um...I dunno, Simon."

"Why ya actin' pusslike, boyo? I catcha with the twat hoverin' over ya? Sounds hollow, you don't have me on speaker, do ya?"

"Uh, no. Hang on." There was a pause and a scraping sound. "Rain stop, yet?"

"Yeh. Quite nice now, actually. Gonna be a prime night for beavering."

"I can see you on the hood of the Rover."

"See me?"

"Look up and to your left."

Simon did as he was told, searching the canopy of the trees overhanging the trail that spilled out from the hillside above.

"Lower, just above the corner of the fence."

Eyes sliding downward, Simon spied the camera, looking no more conspicuous than a stubby limb. Done in light green and brown, it was mounted on the side of a Chuchuhuasi tree. Simon watched as Sil must have wiggled the joystick, activating the servo motors and making the camera buzz as it moved.

"When'd we slap that up there?" Simon asked.

"Few months ago."

"Fockin' Nuestra," Simon lamented. "Wish I had a quarter'a the quid that shit for brains Sonny pisses away."

"Simon?"

"Yeh."

"What time did your new guy set out?" Sil asked.

"'Bout sixteen-hundred." Simon lit another cigarette. "I'm tellin' ya, we're speedin' to shit 'round here and that twat and Sonny are steerin' the bus right into it. This yank is a pillock. Focker's still on the upper trail, or got hisself lost. Hah! The Green Berets just dropped ten pegs in my fockin' book."

"Well, given the conditions, what would have been a fast time for him to cross the road?"

Simon grunted as he did the math. "A damn good time woulda been quarter after six, and that'd only have been barely possible if we'd had no rain.

But it pissed good. I got here around then and now I been sittin' for damned near forty-five minutes. He ain't gotta prayer in hell'a makin' it by my deadline."

"You sure?"

"Yeh, I'm sure. Why?"

"Burrell crossed the road in a fast trot at seventeen-forty-two."

"Wot?"

"Seventeen-forty-two."

"That's bloody well impossible! That scammer hadda cut across the fields."

"He didn't, Simon, because we kept tabs on him. He's already seven kilometers down the trail from you."

Hopping off the vehicle, Simon glanced around as his mind struggled with the simple math. "That means he's almost halfway done. I ain't never heard'a the likes."

Silence.

"Wait," Simon said. "You just said 'we'."

"I know."

"Who's *we*?"

A woman's voice. "I'm here, Simon. I believe you referred to me as 'the twat'." It was Chief Mikkelsen.

Simon's mouth fell open.

"And I'm here, too, Simon. I guess you know me as shit-for-brains."

Simon's blood ran cold at the voice of Sonny Calabrese.

"Or wanker," Sonny added. "Which is it?"

Bloody hell, Sil! You're a dead man! Why did you let them listen to your phone?

Simon cleared his throat. "Listen, Sonny, Chief Mikkelsen…I'm, uh, I'm sorry about—"

"What did you just say?" Sonny roared.

Simon squeezed his eyes shut and grimaced. He knew better than to say he was sorry to Sonny Calabrese. "What I meant, sir, is I was stupid to say what I said."

"I agree."

Mikkelsen's voice was next. "You're probably wondering why Sil let us listen in."

"Er, yeh, I mean, yes'm. Crossed my mind."

"Sil's concerned about your viability, Simon, and your future with us.

He doesn't believe in you anymore. If you have any prayer of getting back in our good graces, then you'll put the *yank* through his paces, and do it correctly."

"Yes'm."

"We need another good soldier, Simon," Sonny said. "It's you or him."

"I'm your man," Simon replied, his chest swelling.

"We're watching you," Chief Mikkelsen said. The line clicked dead.

Simon glanced sullenly up at the camera, wanting so badly to make a vulgar gesture. Instead, he flicked the cigarette away, cranked the Land Rover and drove into town, cursing the entire way.

AT EXACTLY midnight, Gage pushed his way into the slick wet brush on the side of the trail, searching for more of the bushes with the cup-shaped leaves. Thankfully, after the storm the half-moon had been in and out and provided him with enough light to, at times, make what he felt was decent progress. He'd made his second road crossing, which was alleged to have been at the 33rd kilometer, around 10:15 PM. If what Simon had told Gage was correct, and Gage's calculations were accurate, he had to be nearing the end of the trail.

Despite aching hunger that seemed to grow worse by the minute, Gage's biggest problem was his thirst. Earlier, after the heavy shower, Gage had stumbled across a bush with cup-shaped leaves. He knelt by the bush, tipping each leaf to his mouth, taking what probably amounted to a quarter ounce of water with each one. Not all of the cupped leaves held water but, on his three previous occasions, Gage had managed to ingest 15 or 20, probably amounting to 4 or 5 ounces of water each. He'd ignored the bugs he'd also swallowed. Gage knew he'd probably shed five pounds in sweat. He also knew from numerous prior experiences that even small amounts of water can prevent the body from preemptively shutting down as a measure of self-protection. Each little sip effectively "tricked" the body into thinking that it was getting enough. Of course, physiology would eventually take over as full-blown dehydration set in. Once Gage was back at camp, he intended to rehydrate himself as quickly as safely possible.

After tantalizing himself at the bush, he pressed on, jogging up the trail. Despite the speed he'd moved with tonight, Gage felt his age. He'd made this trail with mind power and thankfulness that an out-of-shape man like Simon thought nine hours was impossible. Gage knew, however, that some young buck could run the same trail in a much lower time. There was always someone better.

In the distance, Gage thought he could see the glow of lights. It was ten minutes past midnight.

THE PHONE ON Simon's nightstand buzzed. On reflex, his large hand tapped around, sending the empty tequila bottle clunking to the floor of the hut.

"Yeh?" he croaked.

"Señor, he's coming up the western hill."

"What time is it?" Simon asked, rubbing his face and moaning.

"It's just after midnight, señor."

Simon bolted upright, flinging his legs over the side of the bed. "That cheating arsehole!" He jabbed the phone with his thumb, pulling on his boots and sliding his shirt on, leaving it unbuttoned. Still drunk and appearing quite disheveled, Simon swayed to the screen door and kicked it open, stalking his way across the main yard.

He didn't give a damn if anyone was watching by closed circuit.

"There's no damned way that yank did the full trail in less than nine bloody hours," Simon grumbled, hitching his thumb at Jose, the night guard who'd phoned him. Jose hurried away with no more coaxing.

Simon lit a cigarette, the nicotine quickly hitting his alcohol-saturated bloodstream. He sucked greedily on the cigarette, finishing it in only a few minutes. Then he posed with his hands on his hips, standing under the harsh yellow light of the center pole's light, squarely in the middle of the main yard. He made sure his scowl was pronounced.

Less than a minute later the American, soaked from head to toe and covered in the rusty jungle mud, burst from the trailhead and marched in Simon's direction. His gait suggested pain and exhaustion.

"I know ya cheated!" Simon bellowed. "That'll be yer end, fella, a'fore ya ever got fockin' started!"

The American kept right on coming.

"Didn't ya hear me, boyo? I gots no room for cheatin' fockers in this here guard platoon."

With a stony, unaffected face, the American trudged straight to Simon, stopping two feet away. He popped the magazine on the AK, clearing the weapon and clicking the mechanism. He offered the weapon and magazine to Simon. When Simon didn't take them, the American leaned both against the light pole. He then began slogging up the hill, headed straight for his cabin.

"Just where the fock you think you're going?" Simon bellowed.

"To sleep."

"Th'hell you say!" Simon ran as fast as he could with unlaced boots. He passed around the American, reaching his arm out to stop his progress.

The American, Burrell, stopped short and narrowed his eyes at Simon. "I'm going to tell you this once. I *didn't* cheat. You sent me out there with no food and no water in shit conditions and I got the job done." He pointed up the hill. "I'm going up there to get some water, and there better be some food around here for me, or you and I *are* going to have a problem."

"You didn't make that ruck without cheatin'!" Simon persisted, violently shaking his head. "Couldn'ta happened."

"For the last time, I did. And for your information, Simon, nine hours is nothing special. I'm not Superman. So, either you're just really slow on the trail, or no one else you've brought in has had the guts to tell you that your little test, while a helluva physical endurance test, isn't all that tough." Burrell took another step and stopped again. "Oh, yeah…I'll tell you something else, I saw two locals inside the wire and I didn't shoot them. I ran them off and I didn't confiscate their bags." Burrell gestured to the fields. "There must be a hundred-thousand acres of beans out there. I don't believe we should promote theft, but killing isn't the answer, either."

As he'd done earlier in the evening, Simon crooked a finger at Burrell. "Tomorrow'll be worse, boyo. That's my promise. You're gonna pay for this cheek'a yours and, if'n you don't watch it, you might leave this here hill in a bodybag."

"I learned a long time ago to worry about tomorrow tomorrow." The American turned and walked away, checking the small buildings until he found *la cocina* at the top of the hill.

Simon lit another cigarette, watching Burrell emerge from the small kitchen hut with an MRE and a gallon jug of water. He sat on a split log at the top of the hill, hurriedly devouring every calorie in the MRE and chugging the water. Twenty minutes later, the American retrieved another jug and retired to his hut.

What bothered Simon the most was the fact that he'd told the American to be outside at 0500 hours and the American hadn't protested. Now Simon would look soft if he wasn't outside then, too.

Cocksucker!

Simon Winterbourne vowed to kill Jeffrey Burrell. He'd do it in such a way that would get him back on the team and off the hook with Sonny.

Oh, how Simon would relish that killing.

Chapter Six

GAGE HAD SET his Timex alarm for 0445. He was so exhausted that the irritating beeping nearly didn't wake him. Though his bunk was nothing more than a foam pad on top of taut wire bedsprings, at that moment it was a heavenly cloud and he had no desire to leave it. When the alarm did finally wake him, Gage considered quitting this job. Any man would have. At that very moment, he wondered where his life had taken such a turn to find himself waking in a Peruvian hut after expending more energy in a day than most men spend over two weeks.

It will get better. It always does. Have faith. This is a valley. The peaks loom ahead.

Gage knew his best course of action was to stand quickly and deal with the pain and exhaustion. He did, moaning as he attempted to stretch. He was acutely aware of every portion of his body, all of it aching. The scar tissue of nearly every injury he'd ever endured sent desperate signals to his brain, each area demanding immediate rest and relaxation. The portions of his body that had taken the brunt of the load on the fast hike—his ankles, his knees, the muscles of his legs, buttocks and back—screamed even louder than his old wounds.

Gage felt like he'd been backed over by a bus. Twice.

Making matters worse, he *really* had to take a leak. He'd ingested a gallon-and-a-half of water last night, knowing much of it would be absorbed into the tissues of his dehydrated body. Despite the large amount of water his body had used, there was still an excess and it was currently creating painful pressure in Gage's midsection. He grabbed his shaving bag, clean underwear and his only other uniform, trudging toward the cinderblock latrine located between his hut and *la cocina*. He grunted with each step but eventually made it. Several men, the locals who stayed on the plantation, were shaving and brushing their teeth. They nodded to him but said nothing. Gage spoke Spanish, asking the group if there was a shower.

"*Afuera*," the closest one responded. He was shaving, his eyes squinted due to the hand-rolled cigarette pinched between his lips.

After hurriedly shaving and brushing his furry teeth, Gage labored his way outside, looking all around before he found it. Behind the latrine on a concrete pad was a simple metal frame with a garden hose wedged at its top. A check of his watch showed he had nine minutes before he was due. He hurriedly stripped and stood under the chilly water, rinsing first then soaping his entire body. With no towel, he used his hands like squeegees, removing as much excess water as he could.

When he'd been soaping himself, he learned that his feet were badly blistered. Nothing he could do about that now but it sure demonstrated to Gage how soft he'd become since leaving Colonel Hunter's team. Once dressed, Gage felt much better, though he was still thirsty and already famished. There was no telling how many calories he'd burned yesterday. Oh, what he would give for a gallon of apple juice, a hearty breakfast and four glorious Advil.

Stop…weakness!

After hurrying back to his hut, he straightened his bunk and personal items, setting his soaked boots under the lean-to porch to dry. That done, Gage grabbed his water jug and rushed down the hill, expecting some sort of formation call to occur at 0500. It was 0459 and all Gage found were four guards, the ones he'd seen in the latrine, already dozing against the small guard shack at the main gate. Simon was nowhere to be found.

There was another guard there. He was older, the hair of his temples flecked in gray. The guard opened his left eye at Gage. He shut it and spoke Spanish in a sleepy voice. "Might as well relax, *cúmbila*. There's no telling when Chief Simon will be out here."

"So, you show on time, but he doesn't?"

The man's chest hitched. "Oh, *we* don't dare be late."

"Is he sometimes late?" Gage asked.

Though their eyes were shut, most of the men chuckled. The same one responded again. "It's the way things have always been since Nuestra bought this plantation. With Simon, and the chief before, and the chief before him."

"Well, who's out guarding the fields now?" Gage asked.

"The night shift was there but they're probably already home."

Gage frowned. "Okay…so, shouldn't we just assume our positions even without our chief? I don't know where I'm supposed to go but I'd imagine you could direct me. That's what a normal guard shift would do if their leader was AWOL."

The older gentleman stood, massaging his face vigorously. He produced a pack of Laredo cigarettes, offering Gage one. When Gage declined, the man lit his, inhaling deeply before exhaling through his teeth. Like many locals, he was shorter than Gage by a full head. His chest and arms were muscular, despite his protruding belly which indicated he fed himself well.

The guard's face was affable and his dark eyes keen and knowing. He led Gage twenty yards away.

"I'll tell you what I know...but I never told you anything, get it?"

Gage nodded.

"Nuestra owns five Arabica plantations," he said, showing five fingers. "This one, La Merced, is the largest. They farm the beans, harvest them and sell them, right?"

"Yeah, I suppose."

"The thing is, even though coffee is incredibly popular around the world, farming coffee beans is extremely competitive."

"Lots of competition. I get it."

"And all that land you walked around yesterday grows beans, yes?"

"If you say so."

"It does," the man said with a nod. "But...here's the important part...those beans *aren't* what the world wants. They're poor quality. So Nuestra has no choice but to sell them very cheaply, almost always to an American company. Every three or four months we get visited by someone from our government and usually some official from some American food administration." He dragged on his cigarette and glanced around. "The thing is, I've heard these men saying that Nuestra has to be losing money on this Arabica or, at best, breaking even."

"Why?"

"It's not that hard to grow Arabica, *amigo*," the guard said, "if you have the right conditions, like we do here. My cousin is a grower, a good one, up in Pucallpa. He's paid very well and is in charge of many fields. He told me, like I've told you, that growing Arabica isn't difficult, but growing *good* Arabica is incredibly difficult...and expensive."

"So, who from the United States buys our beans?"

The guard waved his hand as if shooing away a fly. "Different companies buy bad beans for commercial use. But they can't sell their coffee for much, so they don't pay much for our beans."

Crossing his arms, Gage said, "So, what are you trying to tell me?"

"I'm not implying anything. All I'm saying is this entire operation is not all that important. Nuestra uses contract farmers and harvesters and they don't pay much for them or for the chemicals...it's as if they don't even care about improving."

"Well, if all this coffee is worthless, why guard it?"

"Not worthless, amigo, but probably not worth more than it costs to grow. As far as guarding the land, Simon is my third chief in four years and he's just like the ones before him. He comes to our region to give orders, to drink heavily and to impregnate our women. His job, in my opinion, is an afterthought to Nuestra."

"Are you a Nuestra employee?"

"No, señor. We work for a contract security company. Don't you?"

"Alfa Seguridad."

"Sí. Us, too."

After pondering this for a moment, Gage extended his hand. "My name's Jeff."

The guard accepted it, shaking with gusto as he said, "They call me Abuelito."

"Grandfather?"

The guard smiled. "I'm forty-eight…the oldest guard by a decade."

"Well, I'm right on your heels."

Abuelito made his dismissive motion again. "You won't be here long."

"How do you know that?"

"Men like you…"

"Gringos."

Abeulito smiled. "Men like you get sent here occasionally, usually only for a few weeks or maybe a month. This is like a proving ground."

"What happens to them?"

Shaking his head, Abuelito said, "Simon happens to them."

"Bad?"

"Watch your back."

Gage nodded and glanced around. The others were now sleeping soundly and there was no sign of Simon. "Abuelito, is there a chance someone could be growing coca out in these fields?"

He shook his head. "No, amigo, there is no coca in these fields. It would be widely known if there was. Just Arabica that could be so much better if effort was put into its care." Abuelito eyed Gage. "Simon made you walk the entire trail yesterday?"

"Yeah."

"How long did he give you?"

"Nine hours."

Abuelito sucked in a sharp breath. "And you made it?"

"Eight hours and change."

"You're like a mustang!" Abuelitio laughed, clapping his hands on

Gage's shoulders.

"Maybe I was yesterday. But today I feel like a broken-down old nag. There was a time when I could do a long, hard march without too much difficulty. But now I'm not used to it, especially my feet."

"You have blisters?"

"A bunch."

Abuelito flicked the nub of his cigarette into a barrel and walked to a building below Gage's hut. He returned with a battered first-aid kit. "Take care of your blisters, Jeff. There's plenty of time."

Gage removed his boots from his swollen feet. "How much time?"

Abuelito stared up into the sky, divining his answer. "I'll wager we won't see Simon before eleven this morning."

Gage thanked him and went back to his hut, pulling a crate into the good light of the doorway. After lancing his three blisters, he emptied them before adding a small amount of antibiotic gel. Then he covered each deflated blister in zinc oxide tape—thankfully, it was the thin variety—before adding talc to his boots. Satisfied, Gage laced his boots and stood. The tape on his blisters felt secure. It was now 0545 hours.

Washing his uniform and boots was easy at the concrete shower pad. He used shampoo and cleaned everything thoroughly, hanging the clothes in his hut. There was still no sign of Simon. Gage walked back down to where Abuelito stood, next to the slumbering trio of guards.

"Do you have a family?" Gage asked.

"I do, amigo," Abuelito replied proudly. "A wife, six children, and now two grandbabies."

Gage nodded. "Nearby?"

"Two of my boys are in Lima. They own a fishing boat. The rest are very close."

"How did you get this job?"

"I retired from the military and this is home. It was a natural fit."

"What did you do in the military?"

"I was a truck mechanic."

"Like it here?"

"It's a job."

"Do they take care of you?"

Abuelito shrugged.

Wanting to press about this break-even operation, Gage decided to let it rest. It was only his second day. "Eleven in the morning, you say?"

Abuelito was finishing another cigarette. He flicked it expertly before making a satisfied sound when it banked off the guard shack and into the barrel. With a smile he turned and said, "Sí, amigo, eleven at the earliest."

His personal work done, Gage ate another MRE before he joined his new platoon mates in leaning against the small guard shack. Though it wasn't as comfortable as his bed, he was soon fast asleep. But that wasn't before he tried to guess the reasons for owning an enormous coffee plantation that made little or no money.

Though the problem was intriguing, exhaustion won out.

SONNY CALABRESE had just finished reviewing the most recent profit & loss statement, known simply as the P&L. He'd reviewed the printed version; Sonny despised reading on computer screens. The statement he'd just gone over was not the official P&L associated with the company's above-board dealings. No, that P&L, which covered revenues and expenses, centered around Nuestra's legitimate products and showed an operating budget of nearly $100 million. The bottom line displayed a net income of less than $7 million—respectable numbers, but nothing that would set anyone's hair on fire. The above-board finances of Nuestra were managed by an accounting team that had no idea whatsoever of the activities that occurred under the cloak of the secret Narcotics Division.

The Narcotics Division's separate P&L, protected by a sophisticated encryption program that was believed to be unbreakable, displayed an organization with a budget nearly as large as Nuestra's legitimate business. But the real value was in the P&L's bottom line, the net income number.

$51 million last year. An increase of seventy-eight percent. And that didn't even take into account all the money that was secretly funneled into Nuestra to create a profit. Without the slush income, Nuestra would probably lose $10 million a year, minimum. Regardless, the Narcotics Division created obscene earnings with very little expense. And the only way to create such high margins is to provide something illegal—something illegal that's *highly* sought after.

Other factors come into play with such high margins. Even the world's greatest drug cartels had significantly higher percentages of expenses than Sonny Calabrese's organization. Those cartel's largest expenses, even with slave labor, centered around production and distribution. Half of their money went to operations, salaries and overhead.

But Sonny's group spent less than thirty-five percent.

Oftentimes it takes a newcomer, someone who hasn't grown up in an industry, to come in and revolutionize an industry with a radical idea. When Sonny had first arrived in Peru, immediately sensing the growth potential, it had taken him only four days to hatch the basics of his master plan. And the cornerstone of that plan revolved around a simple question: Why spend millions transporting relatively lightweight items such as drugs when someone else might do it for free?

Well, nearly free. But Nuestra's transportation costs were negligible.

Cartels typically spend millions shipping their product, with good reason. Drugs can't be shipped freight like coffee – they must be sailed or flown to their destination. The shippers take significant risks to avoid getting caught, and the price is high. When a shipment is seized, there's no insurance company to step in, either. The whole load is written off as a loss.

Transportation costs the drug cartels a fortune.

It had all come clear to Sonny when he'd been having a refreshing glass of ice water on an unusually hot day in Lima. As mentioned, it was his fourth day. He'd spent the first three speaking to a number of his contacts, all of whom were former Air Force PJs, with ideals similar to Sonny's. The primary difference between him and them was Sonny's expansive mind. Like many entrepreneurial types, Sonny despised the word "cannot" in all its despicable forms. If someone wanted to send Sonny into a fit of rage—and perhaps find themselves making a difficult "choice"—they would shoot down one of his ideas by dismissing it and saying it couldn't be done.

No one said "can't" around Sonny. Period.

So, like many who've come up in the aviation world, the expat PJs in Lima preferred an open air bar near the Jorge Chávez International Airport. Airplane after airplane rumbled through the sky almost directly overhead, into the warm, sea-level atmosphere. Like many airports near third-world countries, Lima's welcomed all manner of aircraft. Sonny knew the world's aircraft well, and had spotted no fewer than twenty in less than an hour while perched on that barstool. Sonny's friend had been giving him a mind-numbing history of his time in Lima, working as a glorified security guard. As the ex-PJ droned on about his wealthy employer, Sonny's eyes rotated upward as a medium-gray aircraft roared into the sky overhead. It was slightly louder than the commercial aircraft he'd seen up to that point. The airplane was decked out in a subtle U.S. Air Force paint scheme with what appeared to be Travis AFB markings on the tail.

Interrupting his friend, Sonny pointed up and asked, "Our C-17s land in Lima?"

"Huh?" Shading his eyes, his friend spied the stout aircraft, banking around to the north. "Oh, yeah. I see 'em every now and then. Maybe a coupla times a month."

Not having spent much time around the Air Mobility Command, Sonny sipped his water and watched the C-17's wings slowly rotate back to level. The cargo jet continued its steady climb to what would probably be 35,000 feet on its way back to the United States. He continued to stare at the jet till it was a speck on the horizon.

Sonny never heard another word his monotonous friend said that day. One phrase kept ringing in his mind, again and again. *C-17s...coupla times a month...*

C-17s...coupla times a month...

C-17s...coupla times a month.

Extending his stay in Lima, Sonny had rented a moped and lingered around the airport for eighteen hours a day. Nine days after seeing the original C-17, Sonny's heart raced when he spied another of the large Boeing aircraft on final approach to Lima's runway 15. The big craft landed beautifully, its jet engines roaring as the thrust-reversers were applied. Sonny watched the aircraft taxi to the southwest portion of the airport, to the cargo zone. Following an hour of paperwork and offloading, he spied a white van come to a stop near the big aircraft. A number of people in olive drab jumpsuits got out of the C-17 and entered the van before it drove away, puttering only a mile to the Hilton Lima Miraflores. Sonny stayed behind the van the entire way. When the crew of five exited the van, their mood collectively jovial, Sonny burned each of the faces into his mind.

Predictably, after quickly changing clothes, the four men and one woman were back in the lobby and headed in different directions. One of the pilots, a major, along with the crew's only female, a staff sergeant—both of them attractive—headed southwest on foot, toward the beach. Sonny chuckled...*those fly-boys*. The other pilot and the man Sonny guessed was the loadmaster were overheard asking the concierge about directions to the closest casino. Once they knew where they were headed, they hurried away as if the building were on fire. *Degenerates.* The last of the crew, the grizzled old fellow who'd been wearing senior master sergeant stripes, trudged off the elevator wearing tattered khakis and a faded button down. He headed straight into the bar.

Bingo.

Within a half-hour and four beers, Sonny had heard the soon-to-be-retiree's life story. A lifer, twice divorced, he'd essentially been put out to pasture by his unit and now hitched rides on their birds in search of new places to get smashed. Back when he was a PJ, Sonny had seen old buzzards like this one before. They were too close to retirement to be motivated to do anything. So their commanders assigned them mundane tasks in the hope that they'd just disappear.

R.O.A.D.: Retired On Active Duty.

"So you just hopped a bird down to Lima, huh?" Sonny asked.

"Why not?" the master sergeant countered, his voice already slurring, making Sonny wonder if he'd been nipping the whole way down. "Damned pilot brought his little contraband girlfriend along. This was only s'posed to be three-man crew."

"What's a C-17 doing in Lima, anyway?"

With sleepy eyes, the old master sergeant shook his head. "If you knew how we piss away taxpayers' money." He smacked his empty bottle of Pilsen Calleo beer on the bar, getting the bartender's attention. Once the bartender acknowledged him, the master sergeant continued. "Make runs all the time to places like Lima and Quito and frigging Aruba and every other damned place you can think of."

"Why?"

"Hell, all kinds'a reasons, friend. Embassy support, mainly…so they say. On this load we had a shitload'a Kentucky bourbon." He winked. "Also had food. Sodas. Medical supplies. Friggin' computers. You wouldn't believe how those embassy pukes live."

"Fly back empty?" Sonny asked.

"Yeah, nearly empty. They'll put some cursory bullshit on the bird but essentially we'll go back light."

The two men enjoyed several more beers. Sonny sensed his opening and played it slyly.

"Sarge, I was gonna ask you for a favor but I think you might have had one too many. I don't want to take advantage of our new friendship."

The big man's bushy eyebrow cocked. "Ask it."

"You sure?"

The man tilted his beer up, guzzling all of it before smacking it down and yelling "Uno more!" He belched and repeated, "Ask it."

"When do you fly out of here?"

"Tomorrow, zero-nine."

Sonny reached into his pocket and thumbed through his American money. It was nearly all he had to his name. He found his only fifty-dollar bill and laid it on the counter, his palm on top. "Tomorrow I'll bring you a package. It's small, about the size of a hardcover book. I'll also bring you another fifty for your trouble. Will you carry that package back for me and mail it once you're in the states?"

The old master sergeant eyed the ends of the fifty. He let out a loud, regretful breath. "Shit-ass customs hits us soon as we damn land because'a them dumb shits up at Dover who was runnin' ecstasy on their birds. If I get caught importin'—"

"The package is hermetically sealed. After it's sealed, it's sprayed with vinegar. There is no odor whatsoever of what's inside. A drug dog could stick his wet snout right on the package and he wouldn't smell a thing." Sonny's eyes bored into the sergeant's.

It was later in the afternoon by that point and the hotel bar had grown crowded. For a full minute the only noise came from the patrons. Finally, the sergeant's right hand slid over. With the fingernails of his thumb and index finger, he liberated the fifty, tugging it out and placing it under his sweaty bottle of beer.

"I'm in 817. You'll be my wakeup call...knock on my door at zero-seven. Got it?"

"I'll be there."

The next morning, Sonny delivered the package along with the extra fifty. He'd provided the master sergeant with a pre-addressed label and another five bucks for postage. One week later, when he was back in Texas, Sonny Calabrese found the package in the mail slot at his seedy apartment complex. The package was full of common sugar and nothing else, but the very fact that the old, underpaid master sergeant was willing to risk a brutal stretch in jail for a measly hundred bucks told Sonny all he needed to know.

From that day forward, Sonny's plan was in high gear.

Chapter Seven

TEN DAYS LATER

FEBRUARY GROUND on at La Merced Arabica plantation. The only mirror Gage had found on the entire complex was the wavy sliver of tin tacked to the wall in the latrine. Despite its poor reflectivity, Gage was able to see enough of his face to know that he'd shed five, maybe even ten pounds. While he'd been gorging himself when he could, he was burning mega amounts of calories with all the activity. Despite his frustrations with the hazing he was receiving courtesy of one Simon Winterbourne, Gage had convinced himself that all this activity was helping him get into better shape.

He'd been made to do all manner of things. Of course, he'd been forced to walk the trail four more times since that first day. Gage believed the trail march was Simon's default. When he was too hung over to think of more creative trials by fire, he always seemed to lapse back to "old Betsy." Simon probably hated marching the trail so, naturally, he thought others despised it just as much. Unsure of the SAS selection process, Gage thought back to his own selection for Special Forces. For a time, heavy rucking was about all they did. While Gage was much older now, he could still convince his body to reenter the needed mode of forced marching. He'd managed to do the trail in less than nine hours on each round trip and now felt he had the routine down to a science. The key was managing daylight and knowing the areas of the trail where he could move quickly.

In addition to the trail, Gage had also singlehandedly constructed two squat single-man towers, both about fifteen feet high. All Simon had done was pointed to the lumber and the tools, then showed Gage on the map where he wanted the towers built. Both towers were located on the upper ridge of the plantation, about a half-mile from the central facility. There were no plans for Gage to go by, only a tattered picture from a magazine page.

"And those towers'd better not fall down," Simon warned. "If they do, yer a dead man." Immediately after giving Gage his instructions, Simon drove away in the Land Rover—he wasn't seen again until well after midnight. The other guards were out on the range so Gage had been left to pack-mule all the items to the two construction sites before he set to building.

Despite the arduous labor, Gage had enjoyed the solitude, especially once he'd finished lugging the materiel to the two sites. If only he'd had a small radio with some good music. Regardless, working with his hands in mild weather wasn't the worst thing Gage had ever done. The towers took Gage three full days to build and the second tower was aesthetically far more pleasing than the first. Both were fully functional and stout.

On the third day of building, when Gage pronounced the towers finished, Simon had attempted to conceal his displeasure. With nary a word, he lumbered the trail to the towers and climbed all over them, tugging at the timbers with his meaty arms.

"Why dincha use nails?" he demanded. "A stupid waste of time to screw all the wood together."

Gage had his reasons—mainly due to the high humidity—but he offered no response other than a quick shake of his head.

"Gotcha an attitude, I see," Simon had said, dropping down to the ground and putting his hands on his hips. "Well, I'll break that outta ya, boyo. Just ya watch."

It had been early afternoon on that third day and, predictably, Simon made Gage get his weapon before sending him to walk the entire trail.

Gage would have been disappointed had he not.

Then, yesterday, on Gage's ninth day at La Merced, Simon never showed at all. Eventually, when midday passed, Gage and the guards decided to take it upon themselves to find something to do. Gage had wanted to tweak a few things on his guard towers so, along with his weapon, he carried a small bag of tools up to the top of the range.

Several hours later, smack dab in the middle of the time traditionally observed as siesta, Gage heard at least ten full minutes of automatic gunfire in the distance. Flattening himself on the tower, he'd chambered a round in the AK and peered into the hazy distance. The hills and mountains made it difficult for him to estimate range and exact direction, but he knew the gunfire was coming from the north. The shooting went on and on, punctuated by a number of faint yells and screams. Eventually, the gunfire ceased. Then, after about five minutes, several more shots rang out. They were spaced by twenty or thirty seconds, five of them in all.

"Executing the remaining living," Gage whispered solemnly. After that, there were only the sounds of the jungle.

Last night, at the end of their shift, Gage had returned to the main yard and asked Abuelito about the gunfire he'd heard.

"Where did you say the shots came from?" Abuelito asked.

Gage pointed north. "I was up at the top of the range, on the high ground, and it sounded farther north. A big gunfight."

"Ah, yes, we were on the south side and moving. That's why I didn't hear it."

"Any idea what was going on?" Gage asked.

"You mentioned coca before," Abuelito said soberly. "*Mucha* coca north of here. Probably the cartels warring with each other."

"How far north?"

Abuelito had glanced all around before lowering his voice. "I don't even like talking about such things, *amigo*. But it's close by. Very close. Some of the guards believe that's why we have a job…to keep the cartels away from our fields."

"Have you ever had a skirmish with any of the cartel people?"

"No," Abuelito said. "Thank God."

Gage turned his head north for a moment. "Sounded like a helluva firefight. Went on for quite a bit. Then there were single shots at the end. Executions?"

"Very possibly. Blood is spilled in the Peruvian jungle every day. That will not be the last time you hear such things." Abuelito had clapped Gage on the shoulder before ambling away. Gage watched him go, all the way to the main gate before turning to the left and disappearing behind the foliage.

So, on this, his tenth morning, Gage finished shaving his lean face at 0430. He retrieved an MRE, eating nearly all of it. Since he'd gotten up early, he even made a cup of instant coffee with the provided packet and a propane torch he'd discovered several days earlier. Afterward, Gage felt as good as he had since arriving and decided to change tack with Simon. Today would be different. Gage had put in his time and proved his mettle.

Enough was enough.

Abuelito was smoking a cigarette and standing where he normally stood, along with the resident guards who were snoozing in their regular places. The Peruvian tugged on the brim of his hat as Gage approached, bidding him good morning. Walking a short distance away from the others, Gage beckoned Abuelito over.

"If what I'm about to do makes things difficult for you, please know that was not my intent," Gage whispered, his eyes on the Land Rover.

"What do you speak of?"

"It's just something I have to do." With that, Gage turned and marched up the muddy hill, headed straight for Simon's hut.

Abuelito removed his hat, crossed himself and whispered, "*Dios mío.*"

SIMON WINTERBOURNE was in the middle of a pleasant, yet frustrating, dream. There was a young woman in La Merced who he'd pursued for months. Like his own personal white whale, she always seemed to appear whenever he was least expecting her, usually showing herself at his favorite watering hole when he was either too drunk to stand or already well into the courtship of another, lesser, female. Despite the fact that they were in the mountainous jungle, the woman could have come straight from the finest Peruvian clothing store, what with her colorful short skirts and tight tops that accentuated her firm bust. Simon felt she was probably in her early twenties. Whenever she appeared, she'd make brief eye contact with him, curling her lips upward before disappearing into the crowd.

The woman had become the target of all Simon's desires. Oh, how badly he wanted her! And now, in his dream, she'd disrobed but held a towel over herself, tantalizing him, teasing him.

"Please!" Simon begged in his dream. "Please!"

Each time he'd lunge for her, desperate to pull that damned towel away, the woman would take a deft step backward—a dancer's step—laughing and taunting. She knew what she was doing.

Then, it happened.

Opening his crusty eyes, Simon gasped several times, aware of his own rancid breath. Dull light filtered into his hut, puncturing the optical portion of his brain like shards of glass. But it was the banging, the clanging, that was causing him the most pain. What the hell was it?

Rubbing his eyes, Simon sat up, coughing. The clanging continued. When he'd cleared his vision, Simon nearly couldn't reconcile what he was seeing.

Standing there, just inside the hut, was that American plonker, Burrell. The prick had lifted two empty AK-47 magazines and was clacking them together.

"Are you fockin' mad?" Simon roared, his own voice splitting his head wide open with the effectiveness of an expertly-swung axe.

"If you want us out there at zero-five, then *you'll* be out there at zero-five."

The cheek on this bugger!

Despite his condition, Simon automatically reached for his mission belt, flipping the holster open and snatching out his Sig P-239. No sooner had he liberated it than his right arm smashed into the bedpost, sending the pistol clattering across the wooden floor. Simon was still drunk so it took him a moment to realize he'd been kicked.

"You're actually gonna draw on me for waking your drunk ass up?" the

American asked, far too calmly for Simon's taste.

Simon rolled off the bed, trying to tackle the American at the knees. Instead, the American stepped backward, using Simon's momentum to propel him facedown into the floor. Crying out as his arm was wrenched behind his back, Simon had no choice but to stand.

"You're a dead man," Simon growled, mustering as much bravado as he could between his chirps of pain.

The American was in his ear. "Any weapons in here other than the AK and that Sig?"

"Like I'm gonna tell—argh!" The American torqued Simon's right arm so far up his back that he swore he heard his tendons popping like ukulele strings. "That's all, dammit! No more weapons!"

Shoving him out the door, Burrell went back into the hut, coming back with the Russian rifle and the Swiss pistol. He spoke mechanically, pointing his finger to each location as he said, "You have fifteen minutes, Simon. Eat something. Clean your teeth. Take a piss. Then you're dressed in your gear and down at the guard shack with us."

"You don't give me orders!" Simon spat, working his right arm. It hurt like hell but maybe the tendons hadn't quite snapped.

The American took a step closer. "Look down the hill. See all your guards staring up here? They just saw me drag your ass out of that rack and, if you keep objecting, they're going to see you get your ass whipped in extremely embarrassing fashion. Now, why don't you save face and just do what I said?"

"I won't do it," Simon said. "Kill me now."

The American shook his head. "No."

"Kill me, you pussy!"

"No. You're going to do your job, for once."

Simon eyed the others as they watched in a combination of fascination and horror. The situation was bad and Simon could think of only one way to restore his dignity. Lifting his chin in an effort to appear noble, he turned to Burrell.

"Burrell, I challenge you to a duel."

"A duel?" Burrell laughed.

"You heard me. High noon, in the fields. A duel. Yank versus Brit. Special Forces versus SAS. We'll start at the red center marker post and walk three hundred paces out each. Then we'll have a go at one another." Simon smiled. "The one who walks out is the victor."

The American turned and looked at the guards before turning back to

Simon. "I don't have any desire to go to jail for shooting you, Simon."

Despite his condition, Simon managed a smile. "The others'll vouch for us. They'll say some cartel boys came here and killed you."

"Killed me, huh?"

"Yeh. 'Cause I ain't dyin' today."

"Rather than work, you want to have a duel."

"Time someone put you outta your misery," Simon countered.

"Noon?"

"Yeh. Leave here at eleven-thirty hours."

Burrell scratched his chin. "Then I want a condition."

"Wot?"

"One rifle and one knife. No other weapons."

Simon shrugged. "Fine by me."

"Ten rounds."

"No."

"You can't make do with ten rounds? Are you that poor of a shot?"

Simon rolled his eyes. "Whatever."

"Can I trust you till eleven-thirty? You're not gonna shoot me in the back in the meantime?"

"I'll relish killing you during the duel, boyo. Till then, enjoy the fact you're breathing."

A flash of something passed over Burrell's face. It almost looked like sadness. He walked down to the guards and said a few words, then passed by Simon on his way back to the huts. Burrell replaced Simon's weapons. Then Burrell retrieved another MRE and munched on it as he field-stripped an AK-47, meticulously cleaning each of the parts.

Now that the adrenaline of the moment had passed, Simon wondered if this was his last day on earth. The languor this plantation encouraged had finally come home to roost. He went back to his cot, hoping he could sleep off his hangover.

But there was no more sleep for Simon.

AT THAT MOMENT, 234 miles away on the back porch of her small Indepencia hillside home, Abi Mikkelsen sipped the strong black coffee she'd ground and prepared in her French press. Leaning back in the chaise, she swiped her finger across the screen, watching the curious scene replay for the third time. She wished it were accompanied by audio.

In the greenish video, aided by the camera's night vision, the American could be seen stalking up the hill in the main yard at Nuestra's La Merced plantation. He disappeared into Simon's shack for a moment before reappearing with Simon in an arm-lock. Despite the absence of sound, it was obvious what was happening. Abi was actually surprised that it had taken ten days. She watched the American go back inside the hut before coming back out with Simon's rifle and pistol. Then, after a long and apparently heated exchange, the two men went their separate ways.

Coming back to real time, she watched the American as he cleaned a rifle on the picnic table. Normally, they'd have gone out on a guard rotation. But the American seemed to be preparing for something.

Closing the app, Abi switched to the text feature, sending a brief message to Sonny.

> Our new soldier has done what we wanted in La Merced and challenged Simon. Simon is probably going to seek revenge. If the American survives the day, let's bring him to the team. Agree?

Abi lowered the iPad and took a large sip of the strong, *laekker* coffee. As the sun came up behind her, she surveyed the beauty of the morning city sprawling before her. Stretching luxuriously, Abi had a momentary pang of weakness as she remembered the sensation of intimacy in the morning, her favorite time to make love. But Abi was disciplined. She'd sworn herself to celibacy until she achieved her goals, and put the thoughts out of her head as quickly as they'd appeared.

Until her goals were met, her snippets of memories of lovers past would have to suffice.

Abi's iPad chirped. She smiled as she read Sonny's expected positive response.

Alfa Seguridad's formidable spec-ops team was gearing up for a new member. Now, it was up to her to create a plan of action. Her own plan of action.

Abi's goals were in reach. They didn't involve Alfa or Nuestra—and they especially didn't involve Sonny Calabrese.

Chapter Eight

AFTER CURSING himself for taking this ridiculous job in the first place, Gage spent the morning making preparations.

"A duel, Gage?" he whispered to himself as he slipped away, walking far into the fields. "You think you're Aaron freaking Burr? Are you insane?" Gage shut his eyes for a moment, trying to imagine Justina's face and how disappointed she'd be with all of this.

If you're to ever have any hope with her, start by making it out of La Merced.

When he was near the center of the sprawling plantation, Gage placed a handmade target on two stakes in front of a berm of soft dirt. He then walked 25 paces away, drawing a line in the rich earth. Gage took his time, firing five shots at the target, satisfied with the tight grouping high and left of the bull's-eye. He then used the zeroing tool from the cleaning kit to adjust the iron sights on the Soviet-era rifle. After two adjustments, he was peppering the center of the target with lead.

Satisfied, Gage used his knife to scratch the settings into the iron sights before walking back to the red center post. The main path through the center of the plantation ran east and west. Glancing around and seeing no one, Gage hurried to the north. There, he removed the rope from his cargo pocket and set to work with his knife.

At 10:30 that morning, as Gage returned from the fields with his paper target, he saw Simon leaning back in a chair against his hut. Simon brayed laughter, chortling that it would take more than a zeroed rifle to walk out of that field today.

"Indeed," Gage whispered.

ABUELITO WAS THE de facto judge. Standing at the red center post, he searched each duelist, pronouncing both as carrying items within the stated rules. Each man carried one knife, one rifle and ten bullets. As sweat poured down from the brim of his gaucho hat, Abuelito removed a shiny whistle and swallowed as if he were trying to get his words out.

"You will each walk three hundred full paces away. Jeff, you go that way," he said, pointing east. "Simon, you go that way," he said, pointing west.

"I'm going west," Gage replied.

"Th'hell you say," Simon snapped.

"The USA is west of Britain," Gage countered. "You go east and I go west."

Sneering, Simon shrugged his agreement.

"This is very important, gentlemen," Abuelito said, the other guards behind him, listening intently. "You will not commence until you hear this whistle." He pointed to the high ground near the berm where Gage had zeroed his rifle. "We will be up there, watching from the hill. Please make sure you don't shoot us." Abuelito displayed a roll of orange tape. "Each of us will have orange around our hats."

Gage nodded his agreement. Simon said nothing. He was eyeing Gage much the way a fighter eyes his opponent before the opening bell.

"Don't walk until we reach the hill and I lift my arm," Abuelito said. "Then turn and walk three hundred paces and wait for my whistle. After that, you must move toward each other. You have to stay north of the creek and south of the hill. Agreed?"

"Yes," Gage said.

"Agreed?" Abuelito asked Simon.

"Fock yeh, I agree. I'm comin' right at this here wanker."

Gage didn't reply and showed no emotion.

As Abuelito and the guards scurried away to the hill, Gage extended his hand to Simon. "No matter what happens, no hard feelings?"

Simon's upper lip curled so high it touched the bottom of his nose. "Go to hell! And I ain't touchin' your nasty dick-beater, either."

Gage pulled his hand back and gripped his AK-47 at port arms. The two men stood in silence. Simon stared at Gage, quivering with rage. Gage looked all around, occasionally chuckling when he joined eyes with the enraged Brit. Several minutes later, Abuelito and the guards reached the summit of the fifteen-foot hill. Below them, the lush green Arabica plants swayed in the gentle noontime breeze. Abuelito's arm went straight up and the two men set out, Simon to the east, Gage to the west.

Counting his paces, Gage steeled his nerve and recalled the exact location. He was going to have to get this just right...

On they marched.

*

UPON ACHIEVING his 300 paces, Gage turned and slid the fire selector down two notches for semi-automatic fire. He chambered a round and eyed Simon in the distance, more than half a kilometer away. Simon was a big sonofabitch, the Arabica bushes not even reaching his chest. Simon raised his AK-47, aiming at Gage.

A 600-meter shot with an AK-47? Difficult but not impossible.

Gage's heart thudded as he awaited the whistle. To his credit, Simon also waited on the whistle.

As soon as the shrill sound reached Gage's ears, he saw the slight blast of gray smoke from Simon's AK. As Gage dropped to the soft earth he heard the round zing by.

Too close for comfort.

Popping his head back up, Gage saw Simon charging boldly. He was headed right for Gage.

Staying in a low crouch, Gage scurried to the northeast, headed toward Abuelito and the other guards.

SIMON INTENDED to run back to the center pole. He held the AK at the ready as he ran, just in case the Yank decided to show himself. While Simon knew blatantly running in was a risk, he also knew he needed to be inside 300 meters to effectively use the AK. Decorated for his rifle prowess back in the SAS, Simon liked his chances against Burrell. Despite wasting a bullet, Simon had planned the opening volley for two reasons. First, he knew it would probably make Burrell duck into the cover of the bushes. And second, there was a small chance Simon might hit him with the long shot. Simon had added the proper amount of elevation and a bit of windage due to the breeze. Despite the round not hitting home, it had definitely put the American on the defensive.

When Simon reached the center pole, he was able to see down the wide center row where Burrell had been. Predictably, the American was no longer there.

Simon partially hid himself behind the pole, aiding his aim by resting his left hand on a long nail that protruded from the massive piece of round wood. Making an educated guess that Burrell would be heading north—the high ground—Simon waited, ready to swivel and fire at the first sign of movement.

Sweat beaded on Simon's face as he waited, listening, watching.

THE ARABICA bushes were thick and fragrant, smelling vaguely like jasmine. Gage had to be highly selective when crossing each row. The gaps between bushes were small, and if he moved too fast, he would shake the bush. Simon had nine rounds remaining and could easily blanket the shaken bush with lead, killing Gage or leaving him disabled so Simon could come and finish him off with the knife.

Having passed eight rows, Gage knew he had eight more to go. Occasionally he was able to spy Abuelito and the guards. Due to the angle, they wouldn't see him unless they knew exactly where to look. But based on where some of them were looking, Gage knew Simon was back to the east.

Playing this most dangerous game, Gage continued to slither to the northeast, to his homemade device.

"DO YOU SEE the American?" one of the guards asked Abuelito.

Puffing his cigarette, Abuelito scanned the fields and shook his head. "No. He's gone to ground." Turning his head, Abuelito lowered his voice. "Listen, when you do see him, don't react and don't point. Simon knows we have the high ground and he's watching our reactions."

"I don't think he is," the youngest of the guards said.

"Oh? Watch this," Abuelito replied. He turned around and waited a moment, then suddenly pointed back to the east, behind Simon. Simon immediately swiveled around the center pole, frantically searching the field in the direction he'd come.

"You see," Abuelito replied in a sibilant voice. "He's going to try to hit Jeff when he raises his head. So, if you *do* spot Jeff…our friend…don't react. Not unless you want him dead."

The group of guards drew solemnly quiet as the gravity of the situation descended upon their hill.

"WHAT THE FOCK?" Simon growled when he saw Abuelito pointing to the east. Could Burrell have switched rows and gotten by him? Sneaky little bastard.

Simon swiveled the AK back to the east, seeing nothing. After a moment he turned his head to the guards, shrugging animatedly with his right hand.

The guards were motionless, other than that prick Abuelito sucking on his cancer stick.

"Dickheads," Simon muttered. He turned the AK back to the west, considering a change in tack. If Burrell eased up through an Arabica bush unseen, Simon would be a large, perfectly still target.

Making up his mind, Simon dropped to the rich Peruvian earth. After a moment's thought, he grinned to himself as he popped the magazine from the AK-47. From the inside of his left boot, Simon produced a full magazine brimming with 30 rounds. He pocketed the duel-legal magazine, just in case he needed the extra rounds. Simon clicked the selector on the AK to full automatic, then began crawling between the bushes.

He was headed due north.

GAGE WAS ALMOST to the row. Without realizing it, he snagged the base of a bush with his scabbard, making the bush shake.

Oh no.

Several shots rang out from Simon's AK, making Gage flatten himself into the soft earth. A small limb fell from the bush Gage had shaken. The shots had missed him by no more than two feet and the sound of the rifle couldn't have been more than 50 meters behind Gage, and back to the east.

Simon Winterbourne was very close and was far more skilled than Gage realized.

Doing his best not to rattle the bushes again, Gage hurried across the final two rows, fearful that Simon might be too close for this plan to work.

I GOT HIM! I know I did!

Simon broke stealth by poking his head up and staring at Abuelito and his men. There was no reaction from the Peruvians as they stared back, their faces stony.

I heard him shake the bloody bush!

Frustrated, Simon dropped back to the earth, holding his breath as he listened. Fear began to creep into his chest, making it tighten. The bush could have been shaken by a bird or a rodent. Burrell might be somewhere else entirely, tracking Simon rather than Simon tracking him.

No. Simon was certain he'd come this way.

Go with your instinct.

Simon continued to prowl to the north, ready to unleash his nearly full magazine on the Yank.

GAGE FINALLY reached the row. He looked east and west, trying to get his bearings. Taking a risk, he came to his knees, carefully peering through the nearest bush. He saw the hill where Abuelito and the guards stood fifty feet to the north and slightly east. That meant Gage's spot was slightly to his east.

Off he went, using a standard military low-crawl. His face and body was covered in mud, his sweat mingling with the dirt to make a rich paste that smelled of sour jasmine and manure. After a minute of crawling, Gage saw the faint outline of his rudimentary device. He'd concealed it with some of the wispy weeds—known locally as *totora*, a species of cattail—that grew between the plants. Once Gage reached the device, he situated himself under the southern bushes and began vigorously digging with his hands.

Using a motion similar to a dog's—wouldn't Sheriff be proud?—Gage scooped twin handfuls of dirt and slid it backward. Thankfully, the rich soil was soft down to a depth of ten inches, making it easy for Gage to dig a trench to conceal himself.

That done, Gage moved to the north side of the row and gathered the branches he'd broken earlier, placing the leafy Arabica around his concealment trench.

There were four things left to do: get in the trench; cover himself with soil and branches; shake the bushes...

And pray.

SIMON HAD now scuttled ten rows to the north. He'd begun to get unnerved at the lack of anything from his opponent other than the one shaken bush. Simon began to get the sneaking suspicion that the American was lying in wait like a patient snake ready to strike. Such a strategy wasn't bad, considering the circumstances. That's why Simon was being so careful to move with stealth and not reveal his position. If the American were aiming straight down a row, he'd have to wait until Simon's body emerged through a gap in the bushes. But Simon believed he had an advantage. Along with the contraband magazine containing 30 rounds, Simon also brought a telescoping mirror.

With a flat black finish, the only shiny portion of the mirror was the reflector itself, and even that had been coated with a dulling agent. Such a mirror was standard equipment for insertion teams and it had fit nicely in Simon's boot next to the illicit 30-round magazine.

When Simon reached a new row, he would simply extend the one-meter rod through the gaps and check the reflection both ways. If he didn't see the sneaky American crouched in a shooting position, Simon would proceed. But when he did find the American, he was going to cut loose on full rock-n-roll from the AK. Let Abuelito claim that Simon had used more than 10 rounds. What would it matter? The Yank would be dead and as long as Simon policed up his brass, how would anyone be able to—

What was that?

Simon whipped his head to the left, to the west. There'd been another rattling in the nearby bushes. This one had been much more pronounced. Simon didn't breathe, willing his heart to stop pounding. It could have been a crow or a rodent.

Desperate to pinpoint where the sound had come from, Simon waited as the hot sun beat down on his back.

GAGE KNEW HIS strategy could be catastrophic. That's why he'd attached the brown string to the bushes diagonally across the row. But if Simon sprayed the entire area, Gage could easily catch a stray bullet or two.

The first shakes had yielded nothing. It was time to do it again.

A soldier who has been in battle eventually gets a sixth sense about things. While Gage had no idea who would emerge victorious, he did have a sense of one thing, at least in regard to one of the combatants...this would soon be over.

He grasped the string, wincing instinctively.

Here comes the pain.

SIMON HAD FINALLY begun to breathe again. Just when he thought his ears had played a trick on him, he heard the rattling again. At first it was a scrape, then a shake.

That focker is crossing a row!

Springing to his knees, Simon unleashed nearly all of the magazine on full auto, cutting an arc in the direction the shakes had come from. The bullets pumped from the AK, cutting down branches and sending dust and debris flying. Simon couldn't help but laugh maniacally at the damage he created.

That should do it, he thought, releasing the trigger.

As soon as the sound of the gunfire had faded, he heard the anguished yells.

Got him!

AK at the ready, Simon lurched to his feet, seeing the guards looking in horror to a spot a mere ten meters from Simon.

Crashing through the two rows, Simon turned west toward the yells, ready to finish the Yank off.

GAGE YELLED for a good ten seconds, making his cries full of agony. He quit as soon as he heard Simon crash through the second line of bushes. Gage was nearly fully buried and watched as the big Brit now thundered toward him. The cheating asshole had switched magazines—Gage knew that for certain. If Gage been crouching by the bushes across the way, marked by broken branches from the 7.62 rounds that had ripped through seconds before, he knew he'd be dead.

But Gage wasn't dead.

And Simon was in for a mighty big surprise.

THE FORMER SAS man was quite proud of himself. Yes, he'd cheated by carrying more rounds than the rules had allowed. But a man does what he has to do to survive—particularly a man in special ops. Simon had heard it a million times, especially from the Yanks. "The rules are, there ain't no rules." Simon could just envision some redneck American saying this with a line of tobacco spittle dribbling down his chin.

The cries had now stopped. Maybe Burrell was already dead. Simon plundered on, ready to shoot Burrell, dead or alive, on sight.

As he rushed westward, Simon couldn't help but briefly think about tonight's celebration. While he got drunk every night of the week, he rarely treated himself to fine liquor. But tonight he would. Simon could already taste the silky Don Julio tequila. He'd share it with La Merced's most expensive—

Interrupting his licentious train of thought, Simon felt a jerk across both his shins. It almost felt like a high tripwire, but it gave as he moved forward.

A loud whoosh startled him, as though he'd flushed a ground-dwelling pheasant. He jumped back, and then felt his feet being yanked out from under him.

Before his body had completed the violent half-turn that slammed him down to the ground, Simon knew what had happened. He'd been trained on rolling snare triggers and had even used once while deployed with the SAS to Brunei.

What a dirty fockin' trick!

As Simon was snatched into the northern Arabica bushes, he tried to engage his AK-47. But the sudden jerking movement had dislodged Simon's trigger hand. As he clambered to get the AK back in his grip, Simon felt Burrell pounce on him.

Covered in dirt and mud, Burrell had his knife out and held it to Simon's throat. Simon thrust upward with the rifle and his free hand but it was no use. Burrell was in a full mount and Simon had no prayer of getting him off.

Simon's right hand shot to his side for his knife.

"Ah! Ah! Ah!" Burrell yelled, pressing the blade against Simon's larynx. "You unsheathe that knife and you'll suck your last breath from your sliced-open neck."

Simon gritted his teeth, angered at the crafty Yank's device that had upended him. He cut his eyes to the left, seeing the thick and pliable bush that Burrell must have tied down to create such pulling force. The snare had lassoed Simon's feet and yanked them north, hammering Simon's head into the dirt as it had snatched him away.

"You cheated!" Simon growled.

"I cheated?" Burrell laughed. "How many rounds did you bring? Just a second ago, you let go at least twenty."

Abuelito and the guards crashed into the dusty row. Abuelito laid a gentle hand on Burrell's shoulder.

"Jeff, what are you going to do?"

"I don't know," Burrell replied, keeping steady pressure on Simon's throat.

"Don't kill him, Jeff," Abuelito implored. "You won."

"But he tried to kill me."

"And you cheated," Simon grunted.

Burrell tensed the knife again before giving a small shake of his head. Keeping his focus on Simon, Burrell said, "Abuelito, take his rifle and count the rounds in the magazine and chamber."

Abuelito complied, slowly ejecting the rounds. "Seven, señor, including the one in the chamber."

"Seven, huh? He shot one at the beginning, a few more when I got snagged on that first bush and then about twenty just a few seconds ago."

"I agree," Abuelito said.

"Good," Burrell answered, continuing to hold the sharp blade against Simon's neck. "Grab his knife and rifle, then search him." Burrell tensed the knife. "Don't you move, you sonofabitch."

Abuelito complied and began carefully patting Simon down. "Here's another magazine." He used his thumb to eject the rounds into the dirt. "Nine more rounds, señor."

"I cheated?" Burrell asked. "All I did was prepare. You broke the rules."

Simon wanted to curse the Yank but he knew he'd been defeated. Instead, he remained quiet as Burrell rolled him over. The American used the rope from the snare trigger to tie Simon's hands behind his back, attaching them to his ankles. There was barely enough slack to walk. Escape was out of the question.

"Lead the way, Simon," Burrell said, poking him in the back with one of the AK-47s. "And I wouldn't try anything if I were you. Thanks to you, I've got two Kalashnikovs…and plenty of rounds."

Simon lowered his head and walked.

IT WAS MID-AFTERNOON when they arrived back at the main yard. The gathering clouds threatened rain. As Gage loosely held the rope behind Simon's back, he idly viewed the tops of the swaying trees. Definitely a storm brewing.

"What am I going to do with you, Simon?" Gage asked, slinging the two rifles. He truly had no idea what to do with the chief of the guards. If he disarmed Simon but let him resume life in La Merced, Gage wouldn't be able to trust him. Simon had already demonstrated his willingness to kill Gage.

On the other hand, he couldn't exactly kill the SAS man, either. That would be a murder in cold blood. If it had happened out there, Gage could justify it. Not anymore.

Gage guessed he'd have to imprison the big man and somehow reach out to Alfa Seguridad and explain what happened.

Just as Gage turned to consult with Abuelito, several strange things happened. Gage noticed Abuelito staring past him, eyes wide. Like Abuelito, the other guards were all looking beyond Gage. Just as Gage wheeled back around, he heard a thumping sound, like the rush of compressed air. His ears were spot-on, because the sound was followed immediately by stinging pain in Gage's left rear shoulder.

As he went for his slung rifles, he was gripped by several sets of hands. Freeing his right arm, Gage instinctively reaching back, like a person would when stung by a bee. He snatched the projectile from his shoulder, examining it in the waning sunlight. It was a .50 caliber dart and Gage immediately knew it'd been fired from what is known as a capture gun. When he twisted his head to see who was holding him, he saw a man he didn't recognize along with Chief Abi Mikkelsen. They were holding him steady, preventing any reaction. The dart tumbled from Gage's hand.

Here it comes...

The onset of the symptoms was brisk but actually quite pleasant. As exhausted as Gage already was, and despite the drug flowing into his bloodstream, his thoughts were quite lucid. He was aware that he'd have no chance at fighting whatever he'd been injected with. He also didn't think that whatever he'd been shot with was fatal. If it was, why not just shoot him with a rifle or shotgun? Why go to the trouble of shooting him with a much less reliable dart gun?

Chief Mikkelsen and the man lowered Gage to the ground. As he lay there, staring up at the low clouds, Gage's muddy mind threw up a last-second alarm. If whatever drug he'd just been injected with had psychoactive and hypnotic properties, he could seal his fate if he revealed who he really was. Gage screamed to the corners of his brain to reveal nothing if questioned.

But another part of Gage's mind knew that such precautions were futile.

It won't matter, he thought. *It's going to happen the way it happens.* Feeling dreamy and serene, Gage knew that he was now under the complete spell of whatever drug he'd been injected with. No amount of willpower would change the course that had been set for him.

And with that acquiescence, and the pharmokinetic response taking place in his recently-depleted body, Gage Hartline fell fast asleep.

Chapter Nine

THE CLÍNICA DE CIRUGÍA Distrito de San Borja had multiple treatment rooms, including one with two hospital beds, and was staffed 24 hours a day by a rotation of physicians' assistants and nurse practitioners. One of Lima's largest hospitals was less than a mile away, in the event a specialist doctor was ever needed. This outpatient surgery clinic was particularly "friendly" to Alfa Seguridad, and was used for nearly all of its injuries and medical needs. Alfa's large cash payments ensured special treatment from the clinic's staff.

Although the clinic was small, it was immaculate and well-stocked. Major surgery had been performed here before, despite the grumbling of the attending doctors. Today's day-shift nurse didn't know the background on the American who lay in bed number one, nor did she ask many questions. Señorita Mikkelsen, the clinic's top customer, had left instructions that they should call when the American awoke. At that time, the nurse was to answer no questions of his other than requests for water or the usage of the bathroom.

Regarding the American's usage of the bathroom, catheterization had not been necessary. Because the dimethylheptylpyran, known far more simply as DMHP, had not been administered in an extremely heavy dose, it had acted only as a powerful sedative. If too much had been administered, not only would the American have lost control of his bladder, he'd have also needed to be intubated. But, combined with his exhaustion, the DMHP had simply put him into a deep sleep. When he'd arrived at the infirmary late last night, the nurse and the guard had managed to rouse Burrell enough to get him to relieve himself. Since then, he'd slept heavily. In fact, he didn't begin to stir until the nineteenth hour of his medically-induced slumber.

"Señorita Mikkelsen," the nurse said into the phone. "He is beginning to awaken." She listened for a moment before agreeing and replacing the receiver.

"Where am I?" the American grunted.

"*Mi English es muy malo,*" the nurse said apologetically.

After blinking several times, the American asked the same question in Spanish.

"You're in a medical clinic, señor," the nurse replied.

"Where?"

"Lima, Peru."

"Lima? How did I get back here?" he asked, rubbing his eyes as he slowly sat up.

"I'm not exactly sure, señor."

They spoke for several minutes before the nurse asked, "Would you like to use the restroom?"

"That'd probably be a good idea." The American stood, steadied himself, then slowly shuffled to the restroom. Barefoot, he was still wearing his utility pants and a brown t-shirt. He'd left dirt stains all over the white sheets. While he was in the restroom, Abi Mikkelsen appeared and told the nurse to leave for at least a half-hour. When the American exited, he glanced at Abi and continued his shuffle to the bed.

"My head's killing me," he said. "And who are you?"

"My name is Mikkelsen, Mister Burrell, Chief Mikkelsen. I'm the Chief of Security for Alfa Seguridad."

Burrell frowned at what she said before glancing all around the room.

"Do you need something?" she asked.

"Water. Or, better yet, a Gatorade."

Abi went to the clinic's refrigerator and came back with two bottles of water as well as a Coca-Cola. She placed them on the table beside his bed. The American eyed her before cracking open the top on one of the waters and guzzling every bit of it. He took several deep breaths before tousling his own hair.

"Do you remember what happened in La Merced?" she asked.

"Lady, I just woke up from…how the hell long was I out?" He grabbed the clear plastic bag that was hanging on the end of the bed, spiriting his Timex out. He whistled as he looked at the time.

She spoke as he fastened his watch. "You were asleep for quite a while."

"Where are the others?" Burrell asked. "Where's Abuelito? Where's Simon?"

"They're fine," she said.

"Are they here?"

"They're fine, Mister Burrell. I know what happened yesterday. I know about the duel and I know you spared Simon, even after he cheated and tried to kill you."

"I have another question."

She arched her eyebrows.

"Why was I tranquilized?"

"I didn't want the situation to get out of hand."

The American snorted. "You were a little late for that."

"I agree."

He pointed to the small bandages on his forearms.

"IVs. You needed them."

Burrell cracked open the Coke. He took a large sip and stifled a burp. "IVs or not, I'm going to need some food…*soon*. This sugar won't cut it."

"I'll see that you're fed."

He reached over his shoulder and rubbed his upper back. "What did I get knocked out with, anyway?"

"It's known as DMHP. It's a derivative of—"

"Cannabis. Yeah, I know what it is. Why would you choose *that*?"

She shrugged. "It's safe. It's common. It's non-lethal in a dose like you received." She took a few steps toward the door. "What would you like to eat?"

"Breakfast…pizza…a burrito…I don't care…anything."

She opened the door and instructed the nurse to go to the café on the corner and get enough breakfast for two men.

"Nice Spanish," he remarked.

"It helps when one lives in Lima."

"Where are you from?"

"Doesn't matter," she said.

"You're not German and you're not from the Netherlands."

Ignoring his assumptions, she crossed her arms.

Burrell stood again, steadier than before. He walked to the end of the bed and inspected his boots and his web gear. "Did someone grab my other things?"

"I gathered the effects from your hut, yes."

He walked to the room's only sink. After rummaging through the cabinets above, he grunted with victory when he found a packet containing a disposable toothbrush and a small tube of toothpaste. Using a fresh bottle of water, he took his time, liberally brushing his teeth. Afterward, he soaped the washcloth and cleaned his face and neck.

"I'm filthy. Gonna need a serious shower after I eat," he said, walking back to the bed. Then he began to stretch, starting with his upper body. His joints popped loudly, making him groan with satisfaction.

The nurse came in. "I figured he was hungry so I purchased what they had ready-made."

Burrell clapped, rubbing his hands together with gusto. He took the sack of food and bottled orange juice, placing them on the tray table. When he managed to get a huge mouthful of bread and egg partway down, he sipped his orange juice and asked indistinctly, "Where's Simon?"

"Elsewhere."

He swallowed. "Exact location, please."

"He's being evaluated."

"He's an alcoholic. He's unstable. He's too violent. And he's a cheater."

She said nothing.

Burrell peeled a banana and bit a third of it, speaking with his mouth full. "You gonna keep him with Alfa?"

"Doubtful."

"Why was I sent out there, anyway? Nothing to guard there but Nuestra's average coffee beans."

"Nuestra pays us well to guard those beans."

"That doesn't make the beans any better."

She shrugged. "You were sent to La Merced for evaluation, Mister Burrell. Nothing more, nothing less."

"Did I check out?"

"Thus far."

"What now?"

"You have the sort of background, the sort of training and the sort of determination we seek."

"I hope so. After I retired from the Army, I did a few contract jobs…hated 'em. Then I heard about Alfa Seguridad. Good pay. Interesting locale without any cold weather. It didn't take me ten minutes to decide to come down and try to get hired." He pushed the food tray aside and took a few deep breaths. "But, in my experience, Chief Mikkelsen, companies like yours do not hire high-paid special operations types just to man guard shacks in parking lots, or to walk muddy trails around unprofitable Arabica concerns."

Abi tilted her chin upward. "The work at La Merced is a good example of what we do."

"I suspect you do more?"

"We do. That's why we use locals at La Merced, other than Simon. For true soldiers such as you, we have other jobs."

"Like what?"

"Mister Burrell, you will be limited in what we divulge to you. In fact, our clients are fervent about limiting what *we* know. Oftentimes we don't know who we're working for."

"Would you mind explaining what it is you do? What I'll be doing?"

"Before I do, the question is, are you willing?"

"Willing to do what?"

"Kill on command, Mister Burrell."

He looked away, a strange expression coming over him. "I'm not an assassin."

"And no one is asking you to become one. What we are asking, Mister Burrell, is you to comply with our client's requests."

"Mind giving me an example?"

"Certainly. A client of ours might engage me to send my team to a drug manufacturing site in the jungle. Our mission would be the destruction of that site and the elimination of its workers."

"The elimination?"

"We have a stipulation, Mister Burrell. We don't kill innocents. Significant scrutiny goes into each job and cartel members are the only ones who are eliminated."

"These sound like scorched-earth missions."

"Oftentimes, yes." She stood. "If you'd like, I can show you some examples of how the cartels operate."

He shook his head. "I've seen enough of what they do in Mexico. I don't have a problem with it, provided we aren't killing slave workers, children, women."

"The cartels occasionally employ women shooters. And they'd slice off your balls and feed them to you."

"You know what I mean." Burrell slid fingernail clippers from the shaving bag beside the bed. He used the pointy file to extract dirt from under his fingernails. "Who will I be working with?"

"I'm the chief and there are five other principal operators."

"Was Simon an operator?"

"Yes."

"But he's not anymore?"

"Correct."

"Mind telling me about the others?"

"They're men like you, Mister Burrell. Four Americans. A former Marine from Force Recon. A Navy SEAL and two from the Army. One from the Army was in Special Forces and the other was a Ranger."

"And the fifth man?"

"Swiss…he was parachute recon. He's the most experienced and is my team leader."

Burrell drank all this in and nodded. "What do you want from me, in regard to the team?"

"You'll be no more and no less important than the others. We've got a demo and engineering soldier. We've got two snipers. We've got a commo expert. We've got a medic. And everyone, including you, is HALO certified."

"Will we ever jump?"

"Possibly."

"So, what's my role?"

"You're the utility man. Based on what we read in your records, you've got a little bit of everything in your background."

"Guess so."

"Good. Be ready to prove that." She gestured around the room. "Relax here as long as you like. The rest of your things are just outside with the nurse. Your first paycheck is tucked into the side of your bag. Take today and tomorrow to recuperate. Then come back to Alfa on Wednesday, ready to train and assist in planning for a strike that will occur in short order."

She thrust her hand forward. Burrell showed the fingernail clippers.

"Uh, my hands are kind of dirty."

With a perfunctory smile, she shook his hand anyway. Abi departed the clinic, satisfied that she now had a quality sixth man.

SEVERAL MILES from the clinic, in one of the windowless back rooms at a quiet warehouse facility, Simon Winterbourne sat in a chair. The chair was wooden, with no arms, similar to the chairs used when he was made to sit in the corner at school. This punishment, however, was far more unsettling.

Upon leaving La Merced, Ortiz, Simon's fellow Alfa Seguridad solider, had allowed a securely shackled Simon to sleep on the drive back to Lima. Once in town, as the sun came up, Ortiz called someone and followed their directions to this warehouse and this room. He re-cuffed Simon's arms and legs to the chair and walked to the door.

"He's in the seat and secure." Ortiz listened to the phone. "Yes, sir. Will do." He slipped the phone in his pocket and eyed Simon.

"No matter what happens, sit quietly."

"Who were you talking to?"

Ortiz's eyes went up and to the corner of the windowless room. Simon followed the gaze and saw a small black bubble. A camera.

"Simon…no matter how long it takes, just sit quietly. Got me?"

"How long?"

"Just sit quietly." Ortiz dipped his chin and whispered without moving his mouth. "Just be cool and maybe you'll get outta here." Raising his voice back to normal, Ortiz said. "I'm leaving. Again, no matter how long it takes, stay in here and remain calm." He flipped the light switch off and left, pulling the door shut. The only light in the room was a rectangular sliver of yellow around the edges of the door.

What the hell?

Simon waited. And waited. And waited. He could have really used a drink. Not a big one. Maybe just a beer. Something to smooth out his nerves.

What was it, an hour now? Maybe two? At one point Simon thought he heard voices, toward the front of the building. Simon had been blindfolded when Ortiz had first brought him into the building. But, through the gap at the bottom of the blindfold, he thought he recognized the gray linoleum flooring consistent throughout the Nuestra facilities.

Simon opened his mouth to yell but halted himself. Ten more minutes.

But what if they'd forgotten about him? Who had Ortiz been speaking with? Probably Sil. It had sounded like a man's voice, based on the snippets Simon had heard.

Other needs began to gnaw at Simon, eventually clawing at his will. The need to piss. The need for water. The need for booze that went far beyond the craving of a single beer. That damned duel had taken it out of him and now his body yearned for rest and nourishment.

Oh, to be resting in a cool bed with a pitcher of ice water at arm's reach. And my flask. Heaven.

Where the hell are they?

I'm going to yell. I have to. Have to! What if they've left me here? Could I smash this chair?

Just wait fifteen more minutes. You've endured worse, boyo.

Simon felt his chest hitch, aware that he was on the verge of tears. They'd be quiet, private tears. He didn't let others know he sometimes cried.

Life had turned years before.

There's so much anger…and pain.

Just so much…

A scrape.

Simon watched as the hallway light went out, throwing his little dungeon into complete darkness. He stiffened.

Is this it? Is there a silenced bullet coming my way?

"Bah, just kill that big lug," Simon envisioned Sonny Calabrese saying. "If we don't, he'll wind up getting sauced and flapping his gums to the wrong person."

Simon knew that Sonny was the puppet master. No one had ever admitted it, per se. But after a while, it had become obvious. Alfa was to Nuestra what the SAS was to Her Majesty's Armed Forces—a highly skilled extension. It didn't take a Rhodes Scholar to figure that one out. Spend enough time here and pay attention and one eventually learns who the master truly is.

Another sound.

The door whispered open and shut with a click. Footsteps scraped across the floor. A slight breeze from the bodily movement.

Then, silence.

"Hello?" Simon asked. "Who's there?"

Stillness.

Simon swallowed thickly. "C'mon, mate…show yourself. Gimme some light, willya?"

Nothing.

Simon sniffed, the temporary blindness amplifying his sense of smell. It smelled like lotion or fine soap. It was the scent of a man. Halting his breathing, Simon attuned his ears. He listened. No other breathing. No other sound.

Am I focking losing it? Did someone really come in?

"Ya there? Who is it? C'mon, friend…don't do this."

This went on for more than an hour, with Simon eventually screaming his queries. By the end of the hour, Simon was wailing in tears of hysteria, the chair attached to his back and ankles as he slammed it against the wall, trying to break it in an effort to free himself. As he did this, he shrieked, screaming unintelligible phrases about spiders and snakes.

"They're everywhere, eating my flesh!"

Simon had gone mad.

Then. Without fanfare. Light.

As if all sanity came rushing back with the illumination of the single bulb, Simon stopped in mid-smash. He rediscovered himself hunched forward, the chair dangling against his massive backside, his arms bloody from the numerous strikes and the chafing of the cuffs. The cross support that the leg shackles had been cuffed to had broken, peppering Simon's calves with splinters. His mouth was open from the scream that had been cut off, a long strand of thick saliva still hanging. His eyes were nearly squinted shut from the sudden light but he didn't cower or move at all. Other than his heaving chest, he was suddenly still, frozen in that awkward position.

Staring at the man.

In front of Simon, at the light switch, stood Sonny Calabrese. He wore a fine blue suit with the faintest of chalk stripes and stared quizzically at Simon, as if he were some freshly-discovered species.

Despite the mania that had just consumed Simon, now he felt ridiculous. Here he was, filthy, crying, losing his mind. And in the same room, in an extreme juxtaposition, stood a man who was the image of calm and affluence.

It embarrassed Simon. How far he'd fallen.

Then, in a strange choice of word, Simon heard himself say, "Oh." He said this as if he and Sonny had been having a conversation. Simon followed it with, "And my arms hurt."

"I'm sure they do," Sonny replied. "I think the chair will still hold. Please sit back down where you were."

Simon obeyed.

Sonny glanced at his watch, tugging on his lower lip afterward, as if he were choosing his words before he spoke. "Simon...do you know why I'm here?"

"No...no, sir."

"I'm here for a little experiment."

"Experiment?"

"Indeed. I find the Brits to be a fascinating people...so industrious and hard-nosed, yet with some inner desire to appear proper to the rest of the world. Even the punks and rebels, for whatever reason, live by a uniform code and conform to their own. All this is done with great zest."

Uneasy, Simon cleared his throat and nodded.

"One hundred and twenty-six minutes, Simon. That's what it took to break you." Sonny gestured to the floor and walls. "Do you see the snakes and spiders?" Closed his eyes and shook his head. "Two hours, Simon, and you were screaming like an adolescent. Wailing phrases of feebleness. My, my, my..."

"I'm sorry."

"Oh, how I despise that word."

"Excuse me. I regret my actions."

"I've had others make it more than a day in these exact conditions. Same room. Same chair. Same darkness." Sonny tsked three times. "What would the SAS think?"

Simon dipped his head. "I'd like to get back to the man I once was."

"This particular experiment is one of my favorites, Simon. I watched a forty-one-year-old Peruvian in these same conditions for two full days. He never made a peep. I had to end the experiment for fear that he'd sit quietly until death claimed him."

"Well...I guess I'm just impatient, sir."

Sonny laughed warmly though his repartee was biting. "Impatient? Is that it? Do we all have paranoid delusions due to our impatience? Should I just leave a smoking crater over at Nuestra because I'm impatient?"

"My life's turned, sir," Simon said, dipping his head and trying to stifle a sob.

"Simon," Sonny crooned. "Siiiiiiiimon."

The Brit raised his head. He watched as Sonny removed two small envelopes from his breast pocket, arranging them on the floor at Simon's feet. The first envelope, at Simon's left foot, was printed with the word PRODUCTUS. The second envelope, inches forward of his right foot, read CITO.

Stepping backward, all the way to the wall, Sonny removed one of his trademark Cohibas, preparing it meticulously. He made a great show of spinning it as he set the tip aflame. Once it was lit, Sonny clamped it in his teeth and stepped outside the door. He came back with a small table and situated it ten feet in front of Simon. Then, stepping outside again, he came back with three items and placed them on the table.

This first item Simon knew well: a Walther P22 pistol with silencer. The second item was a large syringe loaded with a golden liquid. The third item was a large digital timer like a person might see at a sporting event. The red letters displayed 00:00:00.

With a majestic flourish, Sonny smiled with the cigar in his mouth—the consummate master of ceremonies—waving both of his hands over the envelopes before removing the cigar and uttering the one chilling word every person dreaded hearing him say.

"Choose."

Simon feared his heart might explode. He'd never felt it beat this way, even at moments of physical exhaustion. It pounded audibly against his massive chest.

"Simon...choose."

"Choose what?" Simon choked.

"An envelope...a destiny..." Sonny pulled in a deep breath through his nose before dramatically saying, "...a conclusion."

"Sir?" Simon asked, aware of the tears on his face.

"Choose *your* conclusion."

"From those envelopes?"

"Yes, Simon, in those envelopes are two conclusions. Denouements, if you will."

After eyeing both phrases again, Simon lifted his head to the pistol, syringe and timer. "Sir, are those items involved?"

Chuckling, Sonny held up his palm. "No hints. Others have taken this...*challenge*...so I'm quite curious how you will perform given the same conditions."

"What do those phrases mean?"

"That's the point, Simon. No more talking," Sonny said, drawing deeply on the Cohiba.

Taking deep breaths, Simon attempted to focus his racing mind. He looked down and reread the first envelope, the one that read PRODUCTUS. Simon thought the word seemed Greek. He tried to think of related words, but could come up with nothing other than "product." His eyes flicked right.

CITO. Simon racked his brain but could think of no related words.

"Ten more seconds," Sonny said.

Productus. Cito. Productus. Cito. Productus. Cito.

The completely unknown or the mostly unknown?

"Answer now, Simon."

"I...I choose..."

Sonny pointed the cigar at the gun and syringe. "I need your choice or I'll choose."

Wincing and turning his head, Simon reached out with his left foot, stamping down on the first envelope: PRODUCTUS.

Silence.

Simon raised his eyes to Sonny.

"You choose productus?" Sonny confirmed.

Simon nodded. Sonny placed the cigar on the table. He appeared to stifle a grin as he bent down, ripping the envelope open and placing the paper on Simon's lap. It read the following:

Productus – *Latin,* adjective: lengthened; protracted; drawn-out

"I don't understand," Simon mumbled.

"This is what you chose."

Simon shook his head. "I know, sir, but I don't understand what it refers to."

Sonny lifted the other envelope: CITO. "Would you like to see this one, just for curiosity's sake?"

Shuddering slightly in his misery, Simon nodded.

Sonny ripped open the envelope and placed the thick paper on Simon's knees.

Cito – *Latin,* adjective: swift; quick; rapid

Simon shook his head. "No. I change my mind."

Ignoring him, Sonny flipped both pieces of thick paper over. The cito paper read the following: *Lethal injection by phenol directly into the heart. Death should occur within fifteen seconds.*

Simon's eyes flicked to the productus paper: *Eleven hollow point rounds into various parts of the body. Rounds will be fired at one-minute intervals starting at the feet and working up.*

Leaving the productus paper on Simon's knees, Sonny took the cito paper—the one promising a swift death—and tore it in pieces, tossing the pieces in the air. He was, once again, the master of ceremonies.

"Interesting choice, Simon," Sonny said melodiously. "I'm curious to see if you can hold out past eleven minutes."

Simon shrieked.

Sonny put the cigar back in his mouth and touched a button on the timer. Sonny puffed until the timer reached ten seconds. He cocked the hammer of the Walther and spoke as smoke escaped his mouth. "So, Simon, shall we begin?"

With his left eye shut, Sonny carefully aimed at Simon's left foot.

AFTER LUNCH, Abi was summoned to Nuestra. She entered through the private back entrance and was taken to Sonny's office through the rear hallway. Sonny and his assistant—*La Bruja*, the witch—were the only people with access to the rear hallway, meaning Abi's visit was completely confidential. Sonny welcomed her and gestured her to take a seat in front of his desk. Once Abi had declined La Bruja's offer of water or coffee, the sour woman quietly took her leave and shut the door.

Sonny wore a starched white shirt and tie, his chalk-striped blue suit jacket hanging on a mahogany coat hanger over by the wet bar. An unlit cigar sat at the ready in a clean ashtray on his massive desk. Abi despised cigar smoke and assumed that he'd deliberately set the Cohiba out to annoy her.

"Long night?" Sonny asked, his tanned forehead wrinkling into three distinct horizontal lines.

"It was."

"How is your new soldier, Burrell?"

"He's fine. He's also ready. Did you watch our exchange at the clinic?" Abi asked, referencing the hidden security camera in the room with the beds. While it had been furtively installed primarily to keep an eye on the care of Alfa employees, the camera had turned out to be an excellent eavesdropping device on more than one occasion.

"I did," Sonny replied. "He's a bit taciturn."

"I'd go so far to say there's something slightly *off* about him."

"In what way?" Sonny asked, frowning.

"Can't exactly put my finger on it. It just seems he's distracted, or guarded. Almost like he has other agendas."

"Interesting. That gives me reservations about you bringing him onboard."

"I don't think he has bad intentions. What I'm doing a poor job of saying is he's just different. But he's also skilled and we need him. Besides, at this stage, he's harmless."

"Do you want him on the Manolo hit?"

"Absolutely," Abi answered firmly. "And I have other concerns about the hit itself."

"Expound."

"The weather."

"What about it?"

"The forecast doesn't look good. If the weather is poor, we should postpone."

"Special operations teams don't postpone over rain," Sonny said, shaking his head.

"It's not because we're made of sugar," Abi retorted. "It's because I don't like using external intel. If you want us to be fully self-sufficient, allow me to build a proper intel team that we own and control."

"Perhaps in the future, Abi. For now, we do it the way that's always worked."

Abi said nothing.

The two sat there for a moment. Finally, Sonny slapped his knees and stood. "Well, you've been up all night. Get some rest and tomorrow we'll hash out the structure of the Manolo plan." He walked her to the door.

Abi turned. "Where's Simon?"

Sonny was impassive. "He's gone."

"Where?"

"I had him shipped out after he was debriefed," Sonny said with a shrug. "He's being taken to a medical facility in Panama where he'll be dried out. Afterward, Sil will go and debrief him again and let him know what will happen to him if he ever utters a word."

Abi screwed up her face. "He's *already* left?"

"He tried to duel one of our own men. Yes…he's gone. Ortiz is accompanying him—by private jet on my dime, I might add—to Panama. And I don't want to hear another thing about it." Sonny smoothed his silk tie. "Now, unless you'd like to go have a late lunch and a few bottles of wine, I'd suggest this discussion end."

A red-faced Abi Mikkelsen turned on her heels and departed without escort.

Sonny slammed the office door and phoned Silvan "Sil" Zobrist, the strike team leader. "Sil, you tell Ortiz and Desgreaux that nobody better ever find that hunk of shit who was once named Simon, got it?"

Sonny listened for a moment.

"You just tell Ortiz to stick with the Panama story. And if someone ever finds that corpse, I'll make Ortiz and Desgreaux wish they had the death Simon had." Sonny jabbed the red button on his phone screen.

At that moment, Ortiz and Desgreaux were headed out to sea on a large fishing boat. They reassured Sonny that they would properly weight Simon so he'd never surface again. And unlike they'd done with Jimmy DeLand, when they'd only gone out a few miles, this time they were going out fifteen miles and dumping the body in the northwestern current.

Satisfied with the stimulation he'd enjoyed in the first half of his day, Sonny opened a folder on his computer and perused pictures of Abi Mikkelsen.

Chapter Ten

BY THE TIME many of the locals had begun siesta, Gage had arrived at his secluded duplex and retrieved Sheriff. The dog seemed to be in excellent condition and, after greeting Gage ecstatically, he sprawled out on the floor while Gage spoke to his neighbor, Adriana.

"He's exhausted because we went on a very long walk this morning," she said, kneeling and scratching Sheriff's belly. Sheriff showed his appreciation by thumping his tail on the floor.

"And he ate well?"

"Never missed a meal. And he might have had a treat or two—hope that's okay."

"No prob. Did he ever show signs of abuse?"

She cocked her head. "Not really, but he's jumpy around loud noises."

"I hope that eases over time," Gage replied.

"What happened?"

Gage told her about how he'd come to own Sheriff, editing the story slightly.

"I'm glad you rescued him," she said, stroking Sheriff's neck.

Gage handed her the money for watching Sheriff. "Do think you'll be able to watch him again? Looks like I'll be traveling every now and then."

She tucked the money into her pocket. "I don't have plans to go anywhere anytime soon, Jeff. Other than working, I'm studying to get into nursing school."

"Good for you," Gage said. He glanced outside. "Say, you didn't see anyone come up here to my apartment while I was gone, did you?"

She shook her head. "Not that I can recall. Were you expecting someone?"

"No, but I, uh, know a few people here in Lima and they may not have known that I was out of town."

"If anyone visits and I see them, I'll be sure to get their name."

"Don't trouble yourself with that...just let me know if you ever see anyone."

"I will."

"Also, I shopped at the little grocery up near the intersection but they didn't have a lot of things I need. Is there a larger one nearby?"

"Much larger," Adriana said, pulling her hair back and expertly making a pony tail with a thick elastic hair band of some sort. "If you go back down to the intersection and turn left, there's a large supermarket about five blocks away, in Campoy."

"Will they be closed for siesta?"

"No. They're open all day and night." With a part grin, part grimace, she looked Gage up and down. "Want me to go for you?"

"That's not necessary."

"It's okay. I'm not doing anything right now and I suspect you'd like to take a shower?" she said, wrinkling her nose.

"That bad, am I?"

She smiled.

When he realized she wasn't going to take no for an answer, Gage made a quick list and sent her on her way. He watched as her compact pickup truck disappeared into the scrub brush at the bottom of their drive. Without waiting for the water to warm, Gage showered, shampooing his hair three times. He utilized two washcloths, replacing the first one after two washings, scrubbing his skin until it was bright pink. Finished, he eyed himself in the mirror and estimated that he'd lost at least fifteen pounds. He dressed in shorts—having to wear a belt just to hold them up—and an old t-shirt and continued to rehydrate by hurriedly drinking a full bottle of water. Despite the big breakfast he'd had earlier, he was already feeling pangs of hunger.

Gage went back to the mirror, staring into his own eyes…

What are you doing here? You do realize, dumbass, that you took an assassin's job. That you fought a duel yesterday. That you'll be lucky to ever come in contact with Sonny Calabrese, much less make it out of here alive. Get on that iPad's secure email and tell Falco you're out. Tell Falco, when he objects, that you'll come after him if he makes trouble for you. No matter what you tell him, pack your bags and get the hell out of here.

Backing away from the mirror, Gage used his towel to mop the perspiration from his face. He calmed himself the way he typically did when struggling with anxiety; he took deep breaths and made a conscious decision against knee-jerk reactions.

He'd jumped into this job without thinking. He didn't want to make the same mistake twice.

Stick with it a little while longer.

Gage peered through the brittle slat blinds. Adriana was nowhere to be seen—she'd only been gone about twenty minutes. Estimating it would take her at least a half-hour and probably longer, Gage used a knife to open the new bag of dog food, slicing the glue along the slit. Although he had never fed Sheriff from this bag, he'd carefully opened it once before, resealing it with the thin strip of Elmer's Glue, making it appear to have never been opened. Gage fished down into the dry kibble, finally placing his hands on the Ziploc bag that contained his iPad and implements. He removed the iPad from the airtight bag, flipping the cover open. The device still held a strong charge. Gage went through the process of checking his encrypted messages, finding only one. It was from Falco, requesting that Gage report in when he was back from La Merced.

No knee-jerk reactions...

It didn't take long for Gage to generate a brief message detailing what had happened at La Merced. There was no point in going into detail. He relayed that he'd allegedly passed muster and had been approached by Alfa's chief, Abi Mikkelsen, about some sort of action that would take place in several days. He also told Falco that a reliable local had said the Arabica at La Merced wasn't good quality. And, of course, he told Falco there was no sign of Sonny Calabrese. Keeping the message brief and factual, Gage informed Falco that he would check his messages again tomorrow morning for further instruction.

Afterward, Gage used his frequency scanner to sweep the apartment. This time there were no signals at all—Adriana had obviously taken her cell phone to the grocery store.

That done, Gage powered the iPad on again and decided to check his Gmail account. The few people that had the email address knew not to use his name and certainly knew not to transmit sensitive information. There were hundreds of messages, many of them junk mail. As Gage browsed to the second page, his heart lurched when he saw a message from Justina. She'd used her Yahoo account that had no identifying name. Smart girl. Gage also guessed she would have used her mobile device that gave no identifying IP address.

Justina!

What might she have to say?

Heart thudding audibly, Gage took a deep breath and started reading.

> Hi.
>
> After I left, I felt bad about how I broke the news to you. You didn't deserve that. So, I want you to know how appreciative I am to you for bringing me out of the hole I was in when you first met me. I will always be grateful to you for what you did. But,

over the past months, I've faced facts and I realize (and I think you realize) we are not right for each other. In fact, even though I wish happiness for you, and I hope you might even find a woman someday, I truly think you're destined to be alone. I don't say that in a nasty or spiteful way. It's just that I believe you're a lone warrior, like the Ronin we saw in that old movie back in the summer. You were put here on this earth for one thing, and it's not to be a father and a husband.

Gage closed his eyes and massaged the bridge of his nose. This felt like punches to the gut from a pro boxer. He continued reading...

I've decided to go home. In fact, I'm in Vancouver writing this in an airport coffee shop. My flight leaves in three hours. Things are better in Poland, now, and my brother is doing well. I'm sure I can get a job and it will be nice to be around my family again. I just need some time to reset my life and start fresh.

Believe it or not, a few nights ago I actually thought about coming to Fort Bragg. My friend was out on a date and I was drinking bad wine and not thinking straight. But the next morning, when I sobered up, I knew that all I would find was you preparing for some job, if you hadn't already left. You were supposed to have three months off. Supposed to. But I know you, and three months, even with the one you love, would drive you crazy. As strong as you are about certain things, I don't think you could do it. Your strength is your weakness. You will continue to be a warrior until it kills you. And, even though you love it, it kills me every time you leave—because I know you might come home in a coffin. So, as you can see, I chose not to come back. Nor will I <u>ever</u> come back.

Please know I will always love you. I hope knowing this makes you feel a little better. But I also want you to know I cannot ever be with you again. We are headed in different directions and, as I said, I will always be grateful to you for putting me on the right path. But that path leads me away from you, and I am certain I will never change my mind.

Do not worry about me, okay? Someday, and it may be a year or two from now, I will check in again. Please don't write back in the meantime because I won't read it.

Oh, in case you were wondering, Ranger is fine and is flying to Poland with me. The airline assured me he'll be safe. I've renamed him Kochanek. Honestly, I think he likes that name better.

Now, go be who you are and forget all about me.

Goodbye.

Forget punches to the gut, Gage wished one of Simon's bullets had pierced his brain. He squeezed his eyes shut, trying to glean the good from the email.

"I will always love you…"

That was the best part. His eyes flicked back up to the section about her considering a trip to Fort Bragg…

"I knew that all I would find was you preparing for some job, if you hadn't already left."

He shook his head. Boy, did she ever know him. In fact, Gage wasn't sure that she didn't know him better than any person on earth. Well, except for Colonel Hunter. But Gage was more of an extension of Colonel Hunter. He never judged Gage for who he was—to him it was like looking in a mirror.

His hands tensing on the edges of the iPad, it was all Gage could do not to fling the device against the wall. But he didn't. He maintained his cool and found a tiny sliver of solace in her profession of eternal love for him.

"You're right back where you started," he murmured to himself, replacing the items in the dog food. Gage sat at the kitchen table, shelling sunflower seeds with his tongue and teeth while he absently petted Sheriff.

"Renamed my dog," he mumbled. "Kochanek." Gage continued to eat the seeds, spitting the shells into a paper cup.

It was at moments like these that Gage wished he still drank.

WHILE GAGE awaited his groceries, Abi Mikkelsen planned the upcoming assault on the Arequipa-based Manolo Cartel. Her table was clear other than several Sharpie pens of different colors, high-quality photographs and her iPad with a maps application open. Also on the table were a bottle of Evian water and an open bag of trail mix, heavy on nuts and seeds.

The Manolo Cartel was relatively new, even in Peru. Peru's cocaine business had exploded over the past decade with the rapid decline of production in Colombia. Since Peru's growing conditions were ideal, some cartels simply moved into Peru. But other new cartels sprang up, like the one created by Oscar Manolo, the fanatical ex-politician/now ruthless drug kingpin. The latest intel Abi had commissioned ranked the Manolos ninth among the "big 11" Peruvian cartels. Despite being ninth, they were apparently fifth in revenue, having recently passed the teeming yet inefficient Garcia cartel. She wasn't surprised at the growth because, according to her information, the Manolo cocaine was absolutely transcendent.

Two weeks before, Abi's local private detective, Polo, had confirmed her intel by performing a taste test of sorts. He'd taken four types of cocaine to several wealthy and discriminating users, allowing them to "ski" with each one. All four remarked that the Manolo product was vastly superior. As Sonny had taught Abi, in the top markets of the world—places like Dubai, Hollywood, West London, Tokyo and especially Moscow—a kilo of cocaine sells wholesale in a range as low as $50,000 to upwards of $200,000. Purity, current demand and total quantity determine the final price. The Manolo cocaine, to the right dealers, could easily be wholesaled at $250,000 per kilogram. There is always room at the top of a market for a premium product, especially when it comes to glorious "studio fuel" such as the white powder Abi planned to steal from Oscar Manolo.

During her tenure at Alfa Seguridad, Abi had not allowed a single witness to survive an ambush. This was of critical importance. Thus far, the cartels assumed the hits were performed by other cartels. Such hits had been going on for decades, dating back to Colombia. And, despite the windfall gained by Nuestra, the quantity typically stolen probably didn't amount to much at all to a man like Oscar Manolo. It was a week's pay.

In order to eliminate all possible witnesses, Abi followed a tight protocol system. First, she needed immaculate intel regarding the transport. Second, the ambush had to take place somewhere remote—she would not partake in killing innocents. And third, the operation had to be flawless. This was why Nuestra would only hire veterans of special operations.

And some country's soldiers need not apply. Special operations soldiers are almost always elite, but certain militaries' qualification parameters were far too lax for Abi. Yes, she sued the Danish for not allowing women. But Abi was under no illusion that *any* woman should be allowed to serve. The standards should welcome a warrior who is well inside the top few percent of soldiers, regardless of sex. And Abi had been at the top of the top *one* percent. The only thing that had held her back was her gender.

Shaking the weak thoughts from her head, she continued to mark on the aerial photos taken from the ultra-quiet Cessna 152 outfitted with a special prop and suppressed exhaust. Though Abi only had 240 hours of flight time, she was extremely comfortable flying the small aircraft while manning the special, high-powered camera system. On ambush days, Abi quarterbacked the entire operation from the sky, her transponder pinging away as she stayed in the good graces of the Peruvian Air Force.

The biggest problem with this particular ambush was the Manolo's route to the sea. There were three possible paths between the manufacturing location in the Yanama District and the drugs' destination at the coastal port of Chimbote. When she'd first arrived, Abi wondered why the cartels didn't just fly their drugs out. She soon learned that the Peruvian government, despite its sporadic corruption, fought vigorously against the drug trade. And the easiest place to fight such corruption was through the spotting of aircraft departing the mountain regions. Few aircraft operated there, making the patrol of air traffic quite easy.

But the prolific farming in Peru of coffee, grains, nuts, beans, as well as a host of other products, made for tremendous transport traffic on the winding roads. It was impossible to police the drug distributors effectively. In fact, the cartels had taken to sending the occasional shipment of "drop"—cocaine that was flawed in production—with patsies in the hopes that they would get caught. Provided the police and drug enforcement agencies were making enough arrests and netting enough product, they didn't feel the pressure to create task forces to precipitate greater seizures. Plus, Abi had found numerous evidences suggesting payoffs to prevent the legal disruption of transit. The cartels offered up the occasional sacrifice and otherwise enjoyed free legal reign of the snaking roads that led from mountains to coast.

Free reign—except when they were ambushed.

Abi had chosen three chokepoints for the Manolo ambush. She had no intel as to which route the small convoy would take, so she picked an ambush site on each possible one. If the Manolos had any sense, they'd pick their route at the last second – giving informants less chance to spill the beans.

Instead, Alfa's hit team would be on a chopper, hovering at treetop level, equidistant between the three routes. Yes, the Peruvian Air Force patrolled the inland skies in their Cessna Dragonflies. But Sonny Calabrese had greased those skids long ago, showing the commander-in-chief of the Peruvian Air Force the distinct Alfa Seguridad Huey, painted in a nighttime camo pattern, along with the stealth Cessna 152, one of the world's most common civilian aircraft.

"We've contracted Alfa to run military-like security and surveillance operations at our many coffee plantations, general," Sonny had explained. "You're free to visit all of my properties if you like, because you will find no evidence of drugs whatsoever." He'd then asked the general to make his pilots aware of the Alfa chopper, and to leave it alone.

"We hate drugs as much as you do, general," Sonny had boasted. "And I'm not ashamed to tell you that we've fought off many a drug-runner, leaving them to spill blood on our coffee-growing soil." Sonny then, of course, had given the general a generous "donation", telling him to give it to the cause of his own choosing. Since that day, Sonny made it a point to dine with the general each year, always smoothly buying himself another year of inaction.

Despite his crass behavior, Sonny was a smooth operator.

After her reconnaissance flight, Abi had visited each of the ambush sites by vehicle. As she'd thought, they were indeed remote. Only one of them was somewhat close to a village. But the village was far enough away that, even if the locals did hear the gunfire, it's doubtful they could arrive before Abi and her men were long gone.

With each of the ambush sites marked, all that was left for Abi to do was brief her professionals. Then, on Thursday morning, they would seize what Abi believed to be more than 100 kilos of premium-grade Manolo cocaine. And Uncle Sam, that benevolent old man, would blithely fly all that cocaine around the world for Nuestra's distribution.

Abi filed her photographs in three different envelopes. One thing she'd been carefully watching was the weather. All trustworthy weather agencies were forecasting a large low-pressure system to move into Peru in less than 48 hours.

Her heart rate increasing, Abi dialed Sonny, once again requesting that he postpone in the event of a low ceiling.

"Negative," he replied without hesitation. "I've already alerted our spook friends that we may need them. They'll assist if the skies don't cooperate."

"I don't like using outsiders," she persisted. "It increases our risks."

"I know you don't." His tone essentially said, "I really don't give a shit."

"Sir, I'm asking you to reconsider."

"Why? We've never had a single issue when using them."

"It's one less thing we can control."

"Just relax, Abi. You'll be fine." He hung up.

"*Pikhoved*," she hissed in her native tongue.

Abi put her things away and tried to put her frustrations out of her mind. She'd done all she could do for now, so it was time to go for a long run. Once she'd changed into her running clothes, she went back to her work folder on her iPad. She'd forgotten to do something. In her files was an enlarged, enhanced photo of Jeffrey Burrell's upper right arm. On his arm was a beautifully-rendered tattoo of the goddess of justice, Themis. Abi knew who the Goddess was from her classical education.

But what Abi didn't know, and had made a note to look into, was whether or not that tattoo had any meaning beyond the obvious. Was Burrell just another macho man who'd thought he'd display his penchant for meting out deadly justice? Or did the tattoo signify his membership in some sort of faction or council?

It was probably nothing.

She fired off a quick message to a private "information think tank" located in Alexandria, Virginia. In all actuality, they were a mash-up of rogue lawyers and ex-law enforcement. Their specialty was tough-to-find information, especially in regard to human intelligence. Sonny often bitched at Abi for using them, saying they were too expensive. But Abi knew the kind of money Nucstra was making, and she didn't have a problem taking an ass-chewing over something that could turn out to be critical.

In the email, she explained that the tattoo was on the arm of Jeffrey Burrell, formerly of 10th Group, United States Special Forces.

"Does the tattoo have greater significance?" she typed. "Need ASAP."

Abi closed her iPad and set out for her run, just as the sun threatened the ocean in its nightly plunge. Tonight she would do 15 kilometers.

THE GROCERY TRIP wound up taking Adriana nearly an hour. After the bitter pill of the email from Justina, Gage was happy to have another human being in close proximity. He met Adriana on the small porch and took several bags from her as she came inside.

"I hate that you had to do my shopping for me," Gage said.

"It's nothing," she replied, handing him his change.

"No. Please, keep it."

She placed the money on the counter. "Are you okay?" she asked, tilting her head as she studied his face.

"Yeah. Just tired, I guess. Had a long trip."

"Where were you, anyway? When I first met you, you said you were headed east."

"Yeah, I was in the Chanchamayo Province."

She made a face. "Why were you *there*?"

"Just some training for work," he said with a shrug. He began removing the cold items from the bags. "Thanks again for shopping and watching Sheriff."

"You're welcome," she replied, lingering.

Gage continued to stow away his groceries.

"Jeff?"

"Yes?" he asked, turning.

"Would you like to…" She cleared her throat. "Would you like to have dinner with me tonight? We can go down to the waterfront and bring Sheriff along."

"Adriana, I dunno. I'm not sure I'll be the best company for you right now."

"But you're new here. You need someone like me, a local, to show you around, show you where to go. And, if it makes you feel any better, I'd really like to get out. I'm tired of staying home."

"Surely you've got lots of friends."

"Well, I'm not exactly a true local," she said, smiling. "My mother lives in Chiclayo. That's where I grew up. I only moved here a few years ago. So…"

Sheriff looked up at Gage with pleading eyes, almost as if he understood what she was suggesting. Gage thought about Justina's words to him…

"No, Adriana…I can't go. It wouldn't be fair to get you mixed up in my life."

"Just having dinner is mixing me up in your life?"

Gage tried to explain in Spanish, telling her that his life was complicated and not all that appealing.

"Why…are you married?" she asked.

"No."

"Do you have a girlfriend?"

He paused for a moment before answering truthfully. "No. Not anymore."

"Then, it's okay."

"Yeah, but…"

"Jeff…I'm a big girl, okay? We're not getting married, we're not doing anything other than having dinner."

Gage thought about it for a moment. "Tell you what, I slept last night, but it wasn't exactly what I'd call good sleep. Let me try to grab a nap and when I wake up, I'll come down and let you know."

"I don't want to wait on your answer," Adriana replied, maintaining eye contact a moment longer than normal social interaction would dictate. "We can go late. It'll allow you plenty of time to rest beforehand."

Swayed by her persistence, he nodded. "Okay. Let's go to dinner.

Sheriff and I will come down at…"

"Sleep as long as you want. I'll be ready when you are."

When Adriana had left, Gage lay on the bedspread with Sheriff sprawled out beside him. He stared at the ceiling fan whirring slowly above him, wondering if he would always be alone.

Though it took him some time to fall asleep, he slept surprisingly well.

DINNER WOUND UP being extremely pleasant, far better than Gage would have imagined. It's not that he didn't think he would enjoy spending the evening with an attractive young stranger; his reason involved his current state of mind. But, once they were on their way, Adriana's manner was both disarming and charming. They'd taken her old truck, which she explained had belonged to her father before he died.

"He didn't leave any money, but I do have this truck to remember him by."

Despite her pleasant personality, Adriana was a surprisingly aggressive driver. She cursed like a sailor, in English and Spanish, but transformed instantly into a sweet and attentive companion when she turned her attention back to him. Gage felt there were many layers to Adriana.

The restaurant, as she'd promised, was just off the ocean in an area known as San Miguel. The neighborhood where they'd parked seemed to be low-income, despite being adjacent to what had to be prime ocean property. Gage soon found that this particular beach area was vibrant but not ritzy. It was fronted only by low-rise buildings and populated with a teeming young, and young-at-heart, crowd. There were numerous street performers consisting of musicians, painters, mimes and sketch artists. While the performers worked on pocket change and tips, they weren't aggressive at all. The result was a relaxed, thriving and colorful community with the sunset-splashed Pacific as its breathtaking backdrop.

Taking Gage's hand and Sheriff's leash, Adriana led them to a restaurant called La Paz and insisted they sit on the patio. The hostess informed her that there would be a thirty-minute wait for a patio table. Adriana gave her name and walked Gage into the restaurant's adjoining bar. She asked him what he would like and ordered for both of them. When the bartender quickly produced their drinks—a bottle of water and a Peruvian beer called Cusqueña—Adriana slid the frosted mug back to the bartender.

"I was a bottle baby," she said. After Adriana clinked Gage's water with her beer bottle, she chugged more than half of it. Covering her mouth, she laughed after she stifled a burp. Then she chugged the rest of the beer, holding up her finger for one more.

"Thirsty?" Gage asked, amused.

"Very. Work and studying have been hard the past few weeks."

"Glad you can relax tonight."

She touched Gage's hand. "Before we eat, know that I'm paying and I want no argument."

"Adriana," Gage said, shaking his head.

"I just recently got a very nice bonus and I *insist* on paying. You won't win this argument."

Based on her tone, she wasn't going to take no for an answer. Gage reluctantly shrugged.

The bartender slid her another Cusqueña. She took a mighty pull and let out a satisfied breath. "There…I feel a little better. So, Jeff, how do you like Peru?"

"Well, the weather's fantastic. It's nice having summer rather than winter this time of year." He gestured around. "Lima seems okay but I'm not really a big city guy."

"And what kind of guy are you?"

Gage couldn't help but be slightly thrown by her forward nature. "I'm a soldier by training. At least I have been for most of my adult life. I'm happier in a more natural setting, like where our duplex is situated."

"Which military were you in?"

"The Army."

"Did you like it?"

"Yeah," he replied, drawing the word out, the way someone does when there are many layers inside such a simple answer. "Like anything, it had its drawbacks." Gage wanted to get the conversation away from him. "You know, you certainly have good command of English."

"I had eight years of English in school. It's a pretty easy language, especially with all the American TV and movies I watched as a kid."

"You mentioned your father had passed. But you said your mom is nearby?"

"In Chiclayo, about two hours away."

"Brothers and sisters?"

"Three brothers. I'm the baby."

"Bet you can hold your own."

She took a big slug of her beer, stifling another burp. "I can…but sometimes people think I'm just one of the guys."

You don't look like one of the guys, Gage thought to himself. "Are any of your brothers here?"

"Nope. I'm the only one who ran off to the big city. Just me, all alone, happy to be here with you."

Feeling his physical attraction growing, and wanting none of it, he decided to throw cold water on their night by asking, "Do you have a boyfriend?"

"Nope...no boyfriends. That's another reason I moved here. Back home, I dated a guy for a long time. When we broke up, I had no desire to stay in Chiclayo."

"Like it here in Lima?"

"I guess. I always enjoyed coming here when I was growing up," she said, leaning down and petting Sheriff. He was doing quite well in the crowded bar, having wedged himself between their two stools as he fervently watched all the action.

"Earlier you told me you don't have a girlfriend *anymore*."

"Yep. Not anymore..."

"Wow, look at those sad eyes," she said, playfully ribbing him.

Gage gnawed on his tongue. How was it that he could be so vicious when out on a mission, but completely helpless when matched with a straight-talking woman?

He decided to be honest and, like Adriana, straightforward. "It ended just a few weeks ago, although I suspect she'd been ready to end it for a while. I was a crappy boyfriend to her. In time, she'll be fine, and so will I."

Seeming impressed, Adriana again clinked her beer with his bottle. "You know...I think you're right, Jeff. You're gonna be just fine. You seem like the kind of guy who doesn't mind being alone."

"Ouch."

"I'm not saying that in a bad way. It's a compliment. What I mean is you're confident in your skin...and I like it."

Despite the fresh tan on his skin, Gage felt his cheeks flush.

The conversation went on that way straight through the meal. Gage quickly learned that there was nothing off limits with this young woman. She brought the conversation back to money on several occasions, mentioning how she'd just paid off a host of bills.

"So, you got this bonus for doing good work?" Gage asked.

"Yes. We had a big year last year."

"Really? When I first came to your main office, they said they had plenty of vacancies."

"Oh, yeah," she said, waving her fork in a dismissive manner. "They always say that to keep new renters interested."

Adriana ate grilled fish along with three more beers—making her total five—Gage counted them aloud. She told him she was going for the six pack, but she backed off halfway through her fifth. Gage had a wonderful Argentine steak with mashed sweet potatoes and a local vegetable medley. The restaurant's bread was homemade and he ate three pieces with his meal. He'd brought Sheriff's food and bowl and fed him below the table. The waiter brought out a bowl of water—Sheriff was in heaven. After he'd wolfed down his food and had a brief growling session with another dog, Sheriff sacked out under the table, his body touching the feet of both Gage and Adriana.

Adriana occasionally asked questions about his new job. Gage dismissed them with quick, bland answers.

"Do you know when your next trip will be?" she asked.

"In a few days, I think."

By the time their plates had been cleared away, it was dark and chilly with a stiff breeze blowing off the ocean. La Paz had large heaters on the patio but, with the growing breeze, the temperature had grown uncomfortable. Adriana sat with her knees pulled up to her chest. She was shivering.

"I'm kinda drunk," she said, laughing heartily.

"Want me to see if they have any blankets?" Gage asked. No sooner than the words had left his mouth, Gage spotted Chief Mikkelsen, running on the beachfront sidewalk. Wearing the nighttime gear of an avid runner, she was moving at a good clip. She eyed Gage and Adriana as she passed. She did not wave, nor did Gage.

"Jeff?" Adriana asked.

"Yeah?"

"Did you hear me?"

"I'm sorry…what did you say?"

"No need to ask for blankets. We probably better get back," she replied. "I need to be up early tomorrow."

"I'll drive us back," Gage said, holding out his hand for the keys.

"No argument from me." She tossed the keys to him. "Who was that who ran by?"

"Just a woman I work with."

"Hmmph," Adriana uttered, using the universal tone of a person who didn't quite believe what they were just told. The server brought their check.

"What exactly do you do, Jeff?"

"Just security work…nothing special."

"Is it dangerous?"

"Not really," he answered. "I guess it could be."

"I have a feeling you're important."

Gage cocked his head. "Why do you say that?"

Something passed over Adriana's face but she shrugged it away. "I think I'm just tipsy. What are you doing tomorrow?" she asked, leaving the money under the salt shaker.

"No real plans. Back to work on Wednesday."

"I'll be home all day. Pop down if you're bored."

"I'll do that. Thank you for dinner. You didn't have to pay."

"I invited you," she reminded him.

When they left the restaurant, Adriana took his hand again. They hurried to the truck and, at her often tardy direction, Gage managed to get them back to their two-story converted duplex. He bade her goodnight at the base of the stairs.

"Please kiss me," she said.

"Adriana…I don't think I'm—"

Grabbing his lapels, she pulled Gage down and kissed him. It was a warm, soft, enjoyable kiss on the lips. Gage opened his eyes to find her staring at him as she kissed him. After a moment she released him, smiling impishly.

"It was just a kiss, Jeff. Sleep well."

Adriana petted Sheriff, keyed her lock and disappeared inside. When the door was shut, Gage could hear her humming a tune.

Despite his puzzlement over her mild advance, and something else he couldn't quite put his finger on, Gage hurriedly climbed the stairs and went inside. He and Sheriff were asleep in minutes.

Chapter Eleven

WEDNESDAY

IT WAS TIME. Finally. The day when Gage would become a part of Alfa Seguridad's team of operators. No one had told him exactly what to expect. He only knew a mission was scheduled to take place at some point in the near future. Having been instructed to be at Alfa by nine, Gage arrived at just a few minutes past eight. The facility was locked so he waited out front, standing in a misty rain, deliberately stretching his muscle groups as he ordered his mind for what lay ahead.

While he'd interacted with Adriana yesterday morning, asking her to watch Sheriff, Gage had purposefully made himself scarce. The kiss she'd planted on him Monday night had been nice but also made him uncomfortable. So, yesterday Gage spent much of the day nosing around town, eyeing Nuestra from a safe distance. To him, it looked like any other factory with a set of gleaming front offices. He never spotted Sonny Calabrese.

When he'd returned home late yesterday afternoon, Adriana was cooking dinner and insisted he join her. She'd instructed Gage to shower and to come downstairs for an early meal. The food was delicious and afterward they went on a nice walk with Sheriff, winding their way down the hill by the dry creek bed. At the end of the evening, thankfully, Adriana didn't try to kiss him. As he was leaving, she grabbed his arm, rubbing the bicep and tricep as she said, "I like your muscles."

There are certain phrases men like to hear. And while Gage knew he was no bodybuilder, he couldn't help but enjoy the flattery. As he and Sheriff had climbed the stairs to their apartment, Gage saw Adriana move the curtain aside and give him a little wave, watching him as she always seemed to do. Needless to say, he slept quite well.

Doing his best to repel the allure of Adriana, and the painful memories of Justina, Gage cleared his mind and thought about Sonny Calabrese.

What if he showed himself today? Gage had several ideas about how to kill the man, but he wasn't ready to proceed just yet. Despite everything Falco had told him about Calabrese, Gage planned to confirm the facts for himself. If and when that happened, then Gage could put a plan into motion.

For now, he was simply Alfa Seguridad's newest soldier and his job was still to gain trust. And the best way for a soldier to gain trust is through prowess.

After a half-hour of waiting, a silver Ford Focus eased into the parking lot. The driver stepped out and grabbed a duffel bag from the back seat. He was rather small and wiry with a deep tan. He wore cargo pants, a black t-shirt and lightweight boots.

"You're Burrell," the man said, slinging the duffel over his shoulder. His face matched the rest of his body. Lean and tan and heavily lined, but sharp with quick, intelligent blue eyes that looked Gage up and down.

"Yes, sir, that's me," Gage said, offering his hand. They shook but the man didn't introduce himself. After finding the key on his ring, he unlocked the door and punched in a code on the alarm.

"C'mon in," he said, holding the door for Gage.

"Does everyone else who works here always come in so late?" Gage asked, glancing around at the nothingness.

"Admin staff comes in at ten. And my name's Silvan...most here just call me Sil," he said. "Coffee?"

"No, thanks," Gage replied, recalling that Sil was a native German speaker. His accent was faint, as if he'd been away for many years, but Gage knew German accents better than any other. He followed Sil to a commercial coffee maker where he set about making a pot.

"Everyone's glad you're here, Burrell," Sil said, filling the carafe from a bottled water dispenser. "Needed a sixth man badly."

Gage wanted to ask what happened to the previous men, but bit his tongue instead.

"I hear you and Simon got acquainted," Sil chuckled as he poured the water into the commercial coffee maker.

"That's one way to describe it."

Sil's smile faded. "Simon's off the team, just so you know. And, like I said, we really need you."

"It's good to be needed," Gage responded. "And I'm hoping you can give me some idea about what to expect."

After sliding the loaded filter basket into the slot, Sil flipped a switch, waiting until the machine made a hissing sound. He let out a satisfied grunt and took a few steps backward, leaning on the back of a chair.

"Chief Mikkelsen give you the broad strokes?"

"I guess," Gage replied. "Actually, she didn't tell me much, sir."

Sil wagged his finger. "No need for 'sir,' Burrell. You can call me Sil, Silvan or Zobrist, my family name."

"You're Swiss, aren't you?"

"Yes, from Schaffhausen. Heard of it?"

"I have. I was stationed north of there, in Böblingen," Gage lied, thinking back to the time he'd sunken a motorcycle in a pond and hid out in Böblingen with his good buddy Kenny Mars.

"You speak German?" Sil asked, having switched to his native tongue.

"I do," Gage replied in German. "I'm nearly as comfortable with German as I am with English."

Gage was doing his best to be engaging, but Sil seemed to be a neutral sort. It was almost as if he was struggling to be pleasant.

Sil retrieved a cup from the cabinet and snuck a half-cup from the still-brewing coffeemaker. "C'mon in here." They walked down the darkened hall into an office on the right. Sil hit the switch and spun the blinds to display a view of the dusty La Molina hills to the east. He sat behind his desk.

Gage glanced around, not seeing too much identifying paraphernalia other than an award on the wall from Fallschirmaufklärer Kompanie 17, from Sil's time in Switzerland's esteemed Parachute Recon unit. Sil followed Gage's eyes.

"Ever work with FSK-17?"

"In training several times," Gage replied honestly. "We did a joint exercise in the Netherlands early in my career and then served side-by-side in Saudi Arabia much later."

"We're the absolute best in the world."

Gage maintained his poker face. He'd heard similar bluster from soldiers of all backgrounds. Making such claims was ridiculous, in Gage's mind. Each organization had its strengths and weaknesses.

Sil sipped his coffee as he eyed his citation. "Unlike most of the guys here, I wasn't in the service all that long...just six years. But it gave me all the foundation I needed." His icy eyes came back to Gage. "Been in South America more than twenty years now. This is home."

Gage had guessed Sil's age as about 50. Seems he was right. He eyed Sil. "Have you been doing this kind of work the entire time?"

"Yeah, believe it or not, I have. I managed to survive fifteen years in Colombia, doing all manner of things." Sil shook his head. "Did a few years after that in Paraguay and now here I am."

"You're the team leader?"

"I am. And, frankly, I'm expecting a lot from you, Burrell."

"About that, would you mind giving me specifics about what we do?"

"I don't mind, because you need to know up front. And I need to know if you're okay with it. If not," he said, motioning to the door, "then we're done before we've started."

Gage nodded. "I've already been quizzed by Chief Mikkelsen and I agreed to her terms."

"I can be more specific."

"Let me have it."

"We do dirty work for the cartels or for entities that hate the cartels. Plain and simple. We hit facilities and transports for them. Sometimes we're out to destroy. Other times we're out to take." He stabbed the desk with his index finger as he said, "Every job involves spilt blood." Sil shrugged. "Helluva way to make a living…but, if not us, someone else."

"That's essentially what she told me. But, when you say, 'we do dirty work for the cartels and entities that hate the cartels'…you don't know who you're working for?"

"Never," Sil replied, maintaining eye contact.

"Who owns Alfa?"

"Good question. Chief Mikkelsen has a few bosses. Investors…whatever," he said, dismissing their identity with a wave of his hand. "Those people, whoever they are, communicate with her through dark networks." Sil killed the rest of the coffee and let out a satisfied breath. "All that matters is we follow orders and we get paid damn well for it."

"She told me we only hit cartel personnel. No innocents."

"Damn straight. That's rule one. When she gets wind of a job, she recons it, sometimes with my help, then she reports if the job is doable. If it is, we do it, then we get paid. Make sense?"

"Yeah. Perfect sense."

"So, I'll ask you again. Are you okay with it? You will kill people, Burrell. They're drug-runners, and they know all the risks. They made the career choice—so did we." He leaned back and clasped his hands behind his head. "These people have chosen to manufacture and run drugs. Don't get awash in sympathy for them thinking they're trying to feed their families. Got it? They're complicit as hell."

Gage nodded. "I understand and I don't have any problem doing the job as you described."

"Good."

"But I won't kill innocents."

"I already covered that."

"I just want to emphasize my stance."

Frowning, Sil said, "That's why we recon. We've knocked over several manufacturing facilities that had a sort of slave labor working. We usually clear them with CS gas or come up with another plan." Raised his finger. "But, occasionally, you'll find a woman shooter, Burrell. Not often, but it happens."

"If she's an enemy soldier then I'll treat her like I would any soldier."

"You have it in you to kill a woman like that?"

"If she's trying to kill me," Gage replied. "Chief Mikkelsen covered this, too."

"Then it sounds like we're all set," Sil answered, the concern on his face dissolving. "We do a mission or two a month. We've got an ambush laid on soon, in a day or two. We need you on this one."

"I just need to get dialed in on weaponry."

"That'd be a great idea. In fact, I want you to do that today. You're fine doing it alone, aren't you?"

"A day of shooting by myself sounds perfect. Where do I go?"

Sil removed several keys from his ring and placed them on the desk. He walked to the other side of the office, coming back with a laminated, accordion-style military map, flattening it before Gage.

"We're here, got it?" Sil asked, stabbing the Lima map at the San Borja district. "You're going here," he said, poking the map again, about thirty kilometers southeast of Lima, in the mountains. "The Relleno Sanitario is there. You'll pass it and continue on a few klicks. After that, you'll see a razor wire fence. Come to the first gate and hit the buzzer. We'll let you in from here. Follow that road up to a small house...a shack, really...and then you'll use these keys," he said, separating two of the loose keys.

"Once inside, you'll go down into the basement. There's a vault-style door down there. Hit the button next to the vault and we'll let you in again."

"Armory?"

"Yep. Get whatever you want and go back outside. About two hundred meters north of the shack you'll find the range. Zero in and feel free to personalize any weapon you want, other than the ones marked with colored tape. Each person has his own color." Sil went into a drawer and came back with three rolls of flat-colored tape, each with colors found in various camo patterns. "Pick."

Gage took the brown tape.

"The vault has damn near every accessory you could want. Gunfighter grips. Optics. Lasers. Once you've zeroed and gotten each of your weapons set up the way you want, mark it. After that, it's your baby. You'll clean it. Maintain it. Keep it zeroed. And make repairs, if need be. If you pit one or deadline it too badly, we just chuck it and buy a new one. Got it?" Sil asked, speaking quickly without giving Gage much time to process all the information.

Gage felt the fast instructions were deliberate, probably to determine if he could handle information overload. Fortunately, Gage recognized the tactic—Colonel Hunter used it, too. Thankfully, Gage's mind was clear and he absorbed the information like a sponge.

"I'm ready to go."

"Good. When the team arrives, we'll square things away around here and come up to meet you. Later today, we'll do a mock-up of the ambush. Until then, get prepared."

"Understood."

"The rain's supposed to clear out, but there's more on the way. Take care of that little Ford. It isn't mine."

"Whose is it?"

"Company car."

"Roger."

One hour later, Gage was out on the hilly, dusty range with a bevy of weapons and crates of ammunition. He had an M4A1 and an M16A2 that was mated with the M203 grenade launcher. He outfitted the M4 with a scope and a visible laser. Gage had been surprised to find a rack with gleaming new Heckler UMP45's—he grabbed one. He also took a Heckler USP-Tactical in .45 caliber. Sil had told Gage not to worry with any long-range rifles, at least not for the moment.

"For now, just get squared away with the assault rifles," he'd said. "If we need you to reach out and touch someone, you'll have ample time to get ready."

Gage sent lead downrange for a full two hours. The range itself was rudimentary, but contained everything he needed to zero his new weapons and, in general, have a complete blast. Several times Gage reminded himself that he wasn't here for fun, but damned if this morning didn't plaster a big grin on his face.

He continued to shoot, preoccupied, never paying heed to his growling stomach.

BY SUNDOWN, Gage's weapons were zeroed, outfitted and marked with his brown tape. He'd also met his new team and, as a group, in true spec-ops style, they'd hashed out their plans for each of the three ambush sites.

Tomorrow, if there was time, they would do a physical walkthrough for each of the sites while they waited on specific intel regarding the shipment. Based on what they currently expected, the shipment was supposed to be made tomorrow after lunch. Sil made it a point to emphasize that the plans might change.

"It's happened before, it'll happen again," he warned. "This could take several days." That was just after Gage learned that the team typically received three days off per week. Typically. They were also subject to working seven days a week. It all depended on the workload. Thus far, Gage felt like he was back in the Army—plenty of uncertainty.

His team members were a mixed bag as far as personalities went. He'd already met Sil and classified him as a pragmatist and a bit of a shape-shifter. A career mercenary, Sil seemed the type of man who'd probably lost his way years before. Working in a tainted industry like the Colombia drug trade, on either side of the fence, will do that to a man—Gage had seen it too many times. Overall, Gage's instinct told him that Sil was a solid operator and most likely dependable in action. But as far as being an ally, Gage wouldn't trust him one bit.

The former Marine sniper from Force Recon, named Griffin, was the youngest of the bunch. He was a big, poster-worthy Marine with a beach tan and white blond hair. Griffin oozed confidence as he'd gripped Gage's hand, giving it a slightly harder shake than necessary. Such a first meeting with a Marine was commonplace—they were always ready to one-up their brethren. Other than the handshake, Griffin didn't say much. Gage guessed he was the newest of the bunch and was probably ten years younger than anyone else on the team.

The Navy SEAL, Ortiz, who doubled as the team medic, hailed from Long Beach California and was the oldest of the bunch, not counting Sil. He had a twitchiness about him, mating perfectly with his narrow, darting eyes. Slightly shorter than average, he was muscular and had a mouth of squared-off, straight teeth. When he smiled it seemed to come off as a challenge, almost as if he knew something no one else did. Gage's first instinct told him that Ortiz was a highly-capable soldier with a suitcase of insecurities. Otherwise, Gage didn't really know what to make of him.

Of the two Army soldiers, Gage was mildly surprised to like the Ranger more than the one from Special Forces. The Ranger's name was Dinkins, the team's commo specialist. Dinkins had dark skin and didn't seem to have an ounce of fat on him. In their short time together, Dinkins talked to Gage more than any of the others. He even cautiously expressed a bit of guilt for making a living in this manner. Gage guessed Dinkins was probably in his mid-thirties. He didn't really seem the type to work for Alfa Seguridad, but Gage knew his first impression of the man could be off the mark.

The former Green Beret, Desgreaux, was the team's demolition man. He was a brooding and swarthy character, long and lean and sneering. Though it was like pulling teeth, Gage learned Desgreaux was from backwoods Louisiana. He was exactly the type of person someone might expect to find killing drug runners in Peru. Killing drug runners anywhere, for that matter. In fact, unless Gage read him wrong, Desgreaux would probably slit his own brother's throat if the price was right. Gage had expected a bevy of Special Forces questions from him but, after a quick handshake and fifteen-second bio, both of which seemed to pain the gloomy sonofabitch, Desgreaux subsided into silent, ominous stares.

Sil, who also counted as a trained sniper, had walked them through the ambush using the aerial reconnaissance photos and the plans laid out by Chief Mikkelsen. Gage had to give the group credit. Based on the intel Sil presented, Gage felt the plan—no matter who designed it—was about as good as it could be.

Two of the chosen sites were ideal. Both winding mountain roads, cut through the steep hills, narrowed and ran through what amounted to shallow ravines at both sites. The team would execute an L-shaped ambush at these locations, with four men firing from the higher side of the road, and two men firing from the low side of the road, slightly ahead of the others. This would prevent cross-fire and would also assist in eliminating anyone who tried to take cover on the opposite side of the vehicles. The four-person squad on the high side would fire first, leaving Sil and Griffin, the two men with the most sniper training, to clean up the mess.

The third site was a short bridge over a river. Their method here would be a variation of the L-shaped ambush, but there were no raised areas to fire from. This, in Gage's mind, made the bridge the most precarious of the three sites. Because of the layout, most of the team would fire from the forward area of the bridge, shooting into the windshields of the convoy once the forward vehicle was stopped. The sixth man would be positioned on the far side of the bridge, well off the field of fire. He was, in effect, a one-man security team, intended to keep vehicles from hastily backing away when the ambush was identified. Gage volunteered for this job, in the event the third route was chosen. Sil seemed to want to use Griffin, who'd also volunteered.

"You're new," Sil said to Gage. "You should stay with the team on this first one."

"I'm also more experienced," Gage added. He turned to Griffin. "No offense."

Griffin leered at Gage, his nose breaths sounding like those of a bull.

Sil eyed the two men, sucking his teeth as he pondered the decision for just a few moments. "Alright, Burrell. If it's the bridge, you've got rear security. Don't fuck it up."

While Gage wouldn't typically attempt to aggravate a teammate in a situation like this, Griffin's red face and heavy breathing were too much. Gage looked at the Marine and gave him a wink and a big grin.

The Marine balled his fists.

A direct hit.

When the planning was finished, when all the questions were asked, Gage asked one of his own. "Do we have any sort of backup?"

All eyes were on Gage. Griffin snorted. Ortiz cut his eyes back and forth—the way he always seemed to do. Dinkins arched his eyebrows, as if Gage's question were a good one. Desgreaux sneered. Sil simply shook his head.

"No backup. We've got each other and a dust-off. That's it."

Gage nodded his understanding. "Is there any chance this cartel knows we're going to hit them?"

"No chance," Sil replied crisply. "We're airtight. And, of the thousands of drug shipments that take place each month in Lima, we might hit two of them."

"Don't other shipments get hit sometimes, by other cartels?"

"Sure."

"So won't they be on guard?"

"Oh, they'll be on guard," Sil said. "But they'll also be driving on a day-long journey with about fifty possible ambush sites. And these runners do this three or four times a week so, despite the need for caution, they're human and they get bored. As I said before, our intel tells us they'll have three vehicles. The front and rear are security vehicles, containing two or three shooters each. Counting the transport truck itself, they'll have a maximum of eight men, all armed with assault rifles or submachine guns."

Gage nodded his understanding. "Which cartel are we hitting?"

Again the snorts and sniggers. Sil answered, "We have no idea. In fact, Burrell, we don't even know where these sites are." He shook the photographs. "Chief Mikkelsen doesn't share that until we're in the air. These jungle roads you see here could be a million places in this country."

"So, they keep us in the dark till the end?" Gage asked. "How do we know the sites are remote?"

"They'll be remote," Sil answered patiently. "They always are. I realize this is a bit unnerving the first few times, especially after being on an A-team when you usually get an overload of intel. But you'll soon see, this is a tight operation despite the cloak of secrecy."

Ortiz jabbed a soaked, unlit cigar in his mouth and spoke with his teeth clamped down. "It's all about OPSEC, new guy. Even though each of us here trusts each other when the lead is flying, there's no way to have leaks about things we don't know."

Keep prodding, Gage told himself. Even though you know Nuestra is the puppet master, they don't know you know that. And you're a pro. When faced with potential death, any pro would ask these things.

"One more question?" Gage asked.

"We've got all night," Sil replied.

Licking his lips, Gage said, "How do we know we're not getting sold out? If we get these jobs blind, through emissaries, then how do we know at some point we might be the ones getting set up for an ambush? I'm sure having us out there on the street is bad for business for many cartels. A lot of people probably want to get rid of us. Can you imagine what the cartels, as a group, would probably pay someone to make us go away?"

Sil nodded. "I asked the same question, Burrell, six years ago. Dinkins asked it. Desgreaux asked it. All of us asked it. But we're still here, and it hasn't happened yet. I've been assured by Chief Mikkelsen, who's been assured by our principals, that we're protected, locked down as tight as a frog's asshole. Whoever it is who owns us must be making a fortune because the intel is always spot-on. We do our jobs, and we won't get double-crossed."

Scratching his chin in contemplation, Gage relented, nodding.

They ran through the plans one last time.

"The chopper departs Los Olivos tomorrow at zero-seven, gentlemen. Gonna be a day raid unless something changes. We'll fly eastward from Los Olivos, eat some chow and then do our walkthrough while we wait. Any more questions?"

There were none.

"Load your weapons and ammo on the truck and let's go home."

GRIFFIN DROVE THE men to Sil's car and dropped him off, before they all made their way back to Alfa Seguridad in Lima. Per protocol, they placed their weapons in the specially armored room and would retrieve them in the morning at 0630 before heading to the private airfield at Los Olivos. After taking the bus back to Lurigancho, Gage retrieved Sheriff around nine that evening. Though Adriana seemed to desire his company, Gage told her he had an early day tomorrow.

"I've got to leave here around five in the morning," he said, feeling bad for the constant imposition. "I hate to ask you this…"

"I'll watch him anytime you want," she said. "Don't feel bad about asking."

"Thank you," Gage replied, relieved.

"Where are you going tomorrow?"

"I don't know yet. Just some work out of town. I'll find out tomorrow."

"Sounds mysterious."

Gage shrugged. "Not really. It'll probably be boring."

"Will you be back tomorrow?" Adriana asked.

"I should. But, in case I need to stay over, can you watch him tomorrow night?"

"It's no problem."

"Thank you," Gage replied, thankful his neighbor was so flexible. "Do you want Sheriff to stay with you tonight so I don't have to wake you in the morning?"

"Oh, no. Just knock. I'll be up."

"Thanks, Adriana." He paused at her door. "Say, can I ask you something?"

Adriana was curled up on her sofa, reading with the television muted. She tilted her head. "Of course, you can."

"If something were to happen to me, if I didn't come home…would you keep Sheriff, take care of him?"

"Why do you ask that?"

"Just a thought."

"I've asked you this before, Jeff…is this security job of yours dangerous?"

"It can be," he breathed.

"In what way?"

"I don't want to give you the wrong idea. It's not a big deal. Pretty boring job, actually," Gage lied.

She narrowed her eyes. "Are you sure?"

"Yes. Forget I said anything."

"Dinner when you get back?" she asked.

"Absolutely." He bade her goodnight.

"See you in the morning," she replied.

Gage hated lying to Adriana but there was no sense in worrying her over his job. The less she knew the better. But Gage was worried. His job was dangerous, very dangerous, compounded by the fact that he was working undercover, doubling his risk.

Because of such risk, sleep came scarce on Wednesday evening.

And he was right to be worried.

EVERYTHING HAD gone to plan on Thursday, other than the weather. They'd departed Los Olivos right on time in a Huey painted with a modern, nighttime camo pattern. Having flown on many Hueys in his day, Gage pegged this one as well-maintained. Though he didn't speak to the pilot, Gage heard him several times, guessing he was American and probably in his mid-forties. He was tall and handsome and had the stereotypical pilot look about him, all the way down to the mirrored aviators. Like most helicopter pilots, he flew from the right seat. Chief Mikkelsen sat in the co-pilot's seat and seemed to be in constant communication with the pilot and Sil, who also wore a headset. Gage watched her as she changed frequencies on occasion, speaking to someone who wasn't onboard.

Trying to relax and occupy his mind, Gage thought back to early this morning. It had been dark when he'd dropped Sheriff off. Adriana had obviously just showered, due to her wet hair and fresh scent. As far as he could tell. she wore only an oversized t-shirt, and after taking the dog, she gave Gage a very tight hug that lingered as she planted a long kiss on his cheek.

"That's for good luck," she said when he gently pulled away.

Gage didn't quite know what to make of Adriana. A bit of turbulence brought his mind back to the mission at hand.

After leaving Los Olivos, they flew east for what Gage guessed was about fifty miles. They weren't flying all that fast due to the rapid altitude gain. Overall, it took a bumpy half-hour to get to their first destination. After landing at what appeared to be a well-worn landing site, Sil assured Gage that this site was secure due to its lack of access roads. To Gage it just looked like a large chunk of scrubby land, right on the edge of several cliffs. After a quick briefing, Chief Mikkelsen led the team through three walkthroughs. Just as he had been with Sil, Gage was impressed by this woman's skill, her knowledge and her tactics. Gage also noticed that Mikkelsen was on her satellite phone in between each of the scenarios. After the second simulation of the bridge ambush, she told the group to eat quickly and get ready.

"We fly in twenty and we may be airborne for a long time," she said. Across the shallow valley, Gage noticed the pilot fueling the helicopter from a large fuel tank with sling-load straps. Every person ate alone and Gage made sure he took a leak just before climbing aboard the freshly-fueled aircraft. He knew from experience that a bone-shaking Huey combined with tense nerves could quickly fill a bladder painfully full.

Once aloft, the helicopter had pushed on eastward and that's when the weather deteriorated. The clouds were thick and, in short order, Gage felt the pilot descend below the ceiling, flying very low over the jungle hills in intermittent rain. Gage sat next to Sil on one of the aft-facing web seats, directly behind the pilot. Chief Mikkelsen was over Gage's right shoulder, frequently talking to Sil over the headset, both of them referring to a map and gesturing to various landmarks. It was easy to see that the two leaders were very concerned by the limitations that the weather might add.

Making the conscious decision to detach himself from worry over the weather, Gage studied his other team members. Typical of any group of professional soldiers faced with battle, there'd been precious little chit-chat today. Had anyone been talking heavily, Gage would've been instantly wary of them. Such behavior is typically a sign of nerves, and also a sign of someone who's not experienced in combat. Thankfully, however, the entire group had been quiet.

As the helicopter banked to the north, Gage eyed each man. Ortiz, the SEAL, rested in the middle web seat, facing forward. His eyes were closed, his head bouncing lightly against the rear bulkhead that housed the transmission. If Ortiz wasn't sleeping, he certainly looked the part. This was just another notch on the belt for him and it appeared he prepared himself for action through rest.

Griffin, the big Marine from Texas, looked mad as hell, like a fighter who just entered the ring. Sitting on the floor with his feet on the port skid, he went through a constant routine of checking his gear. Gage watched him methodically touch every item he'd brought, checking each one thoroughly. He went over his SG 550, removing the magazine and tapping it on the floor to seat the rounds before jabbing it back in. He checked the selector lever before placing the long-range assault rifle across his lap. He repeated this process with his sidearm, a 1911, and then checked all his ammunition. Next he checked his radio and his headset, then set about silently going through what must have been a mental checklist as he touched his fingers one by one, his lips moving the entire time. Finished, he repeated the process. Gage turned his attention to Dinkins.

Sitting directly across from Gage and next to Ortiz, the former Ranger seemed completely focused. His lips were knotted tightly, his head tilted backward as he stared at the fabric headliner. He was taking deep, controlled breaths, the way a person does when meditating. Dinkins looked like he could chew nails.

Turning his eyes to the starboard door, Gage eyed his fellow Green Beret, Desgreaux. Easily the most relaxed of the bunch, he sat languidly, his body swaying with the movements of the helicopter. It looked like one good jolt of turbulence would send him flying. Desgreaux's Heckler 416 bounced around, lightly held by Desgreaux's right hand. Lounging against the aft frame, the Louisianan turned his brown eyes to Gage. Gage watched as Desgreaux's mouth slowly transformed into a lazy smile, the chewed piece of grass in the corner of his mouth tilting upward. He looked more like a man on a relaxing vacation than like someone who might meet his death in the next hour.

This was Gage's team. Though he wasn't truly a part of their long-term plans, he was certainly on their side today. He needed them every bit as much as they needed him, at least for the moment. Soldiers understand the kinship that develops when serving side-by-side. It's a kinship that far supersedes socioeconomic background, skin color, religion and sex. During his time on Hunter's team, Gage often heard the word "paraclete", derived from the Greek paraklētos. Often used by Christians in reference to the Holy Spirit, the word is derived from Greek warriors who desired another warrior, their paraclete, to cover their back in times of close fighting. Another form of the intention is the modern question, "Who would you want in your foxhole?" In a regular military line unit, there are usually a few soldiers who wouldn't fit that bill. People who others feared might tuck and run. But on a small, elite team like this one, each man was the others' paraclete. Inherent trust must exist between soldiers and mercenaries, especially in the special operations field.

After 52 minutes of flying, Sil touched his headset, listening intently. He nodded and yelled to the group that they were now green, displaying three fingers—thumb, index and middle—meaning ambush site number three.

The bridge.

In Gage's estimation, the bridge was the worst of the three sites.

Damn.

Chapter Twelve

PER THE PLAN, the team watched Sil for hand signals. He made a flattening motion and showed five fingers—five minutes till landing. From that point on, time moved rapidly. Though Gage had no idea where they were, he did make a point to view the cockpit during their final approach. The GPS displayed several rivers with distinct patterns. They were traveling north between the convergence of the two rivers. Gage burned the image into his mind and committed himself to match what he saw on the moving map with the terrain he would soon be treading on.

After the fast descent and landing, the team exited and rallied in a nearby wooded area. As a security perimeter was quickly established, commo checks were performed. All green. The team began to move tactically to the north, encountering no resistance along the way. The canopy was sparse, allowing the sky to bleed through. It wasn't raining at the moment but the low-hanging gray clouds appeared full of moisture, as if they might burst at any time.

Thus far, everything had gone as planned. The team continued northward in their wedge formation, slowed only by the vines of the lush vegetation. After approximately fifteen minutes of northward movement, the river appeared to the west. They continued on. Following ten more minutes of movement they arrived at Gage's break-off point. If they were under any sort of surveillance, this would be a critical moment. Sil spoke to Gage over his headset, making sure he was prepared and clear on his mission. Gage indicated he was and promised a commo check once he'd cleared the small river.

Off he went.

They'd chosen this spot as a crossing rather than have the helicopter deposit Gage on the far side of the bridge. The closest village was on the river's western side, and flying the helicopter in such proximity could have alerted the locals who might somehow warn the small convoy. Such worries were low-percentage, but crossing the river alone seemed a far better risk to take, and was left to the new guy.

The river crossing, despite the rain, was simple and went without incident. Gage had been prepared to cross the river using a number of methods. Upon surveillance, however, Gage and Sil both declared the river free of surveillance. Down below, a number of large rocks connected by small, handmade bridges allowed Gage to make the crossing without ever having to step foot in the rushing water. As he crossed, his team provided security behind him. When he'd cleared the river and ascended the western bank, Gage checked in before continuing his solo movement northward.

It took less than five minutes to reach the western edge of the old, truss-style bridge. The road that the ambush would take place on curved in from the north just before it turned east over the bridge itself. The long approach road would allow Gage an excellent vantage point to call out the convoy's arrival. It had also been decided, since the bridge was definitely an ambush site that even an inexperienced tactician could identify, that the team would approach with maximum stealth and remain on the south side of the road until just before the convoy's arrival.

Sil informed the team that the convoy was at least twenty minutes out. Gage set about placing his anti-transport mines. During their walkthroughs, Sil had been emphatic that these mines were only to be used in a critical situation. Since Alfa Seguridad's client was obviously after the cargo, the last thing they wanted was supersonic spall ripping into the precious white powder. Gage had been instructed to position the mines for what is known as "tire splatter", meaning the directional mines are aimed at an angle, down at the roadway. The desired effect would hopefully only cripple the vehicle.

It was far more important that each of the marksmen made clean shots on the drivers. If that happened, the remainder of the ambush should be like shooting fish in a barrel.

Gage's position was set inside of ten minutes. During that time, two cars passed, both of which he warned the remainder of the team about. When he was satisfied in his preparation, Gage radioed his readiness and settled in, reminding himself that these men he was preparing to shoot were drug runners.

Gage conjured images of all the lives he'd seen destroyed by illegal drugs. Then the other side of his mind started in…

Do you actually believe that these men transporting the drugs, so far down the totem pole in whatever cartel they work for, have any clue of the far-reaching damage they're doing? They're probably peasants, making a living in the only way they know how.

"Weak thoughts," Gage whispered to himself. "These men are drug-runners."

You don't know their true intentions…

Read and react, the most sensible area of his brain shouted, essentially ending the cerebral debate.

"Convoy is five minutes out," Sil's voice pronounced in Gage's ear.

"Security, give us the call when you have a visual."

"Roger," Gage replied, pushing all sympathetic thoughts from his mind and focusing on the approach road. He couldn't help but feel a small frisson of excitement.

FOUR MILES AWAY, Abi Mikkelsen sat with the pilot in the idling Huey. She'd plugged her headset into the hand radio that she was using to communicate with her intelligence asset—the group she'd complained about to Sonny. Because of the weather, the intel team had been forced to track the convoy from a distance, using a five-vehicle rotation. While Abi had no desire to use outsiders, they'd performed well for her on previous occasions. Best of all, they had no idea who Alfa Seguridad was or where the ambush site was located. They were far enough back that Abi had halted them long before the bridge. The intel team was now turning around and driving the other way.

After hearing the final location, Abi lifted the tactical radio, speaking to Sil. "Five minutes out. The lead and trail cars are white and muddy and the actual transport is a blue Isuzu straight truck."

She listened to the silence for nearly five minutes before Sil called back. "We have a visual. Stand by."

Abi took a deep breath and waited, listening to the final bit of chatter before the bullets began to fly. Sitting on the sidelines was one of her least favorite activities. She despised it.

DESPITE GAGE'S fears, the security transport personnel working for the Manolo drug cartel were not peasants supporting their families. Every one of the six men had killed in cold blood, many of them having killed someone in the past thirty days. Six hours into their eight-hour drive, the men were already discussing their plans for tonight in Lima. In the tail car, the passenger, sitting with an AK-47 across his lap, was detailing a recent sexual experience he'd had at the hands of a young prostitute in the San Borja district.

"She squeezed my balls really, really hard right at the end, *sapo*. Even though it hurt like a mother, I spewed like an angry volcano!"

The driver laughed maniacally, just before the 5.56 millimeter round entered his head just below his right eye. The supersonic round had been slowed by the damp atmosphere and the glass of the window, but was still traveling well in excess of 1,500 feet per second. Due to the high speed of the impact with bone and soft flesh, the NATO round eventually fragmented as it passed through the driver's zygomatic bone. The effect was, of course, catastrophic.

The driver never felt a thing. One second he was cackling—the next second…blackness.

It took the passenger several seconds to realize what had happened. He first saw the spidering of the windshield, his wide eyes eventually turning to the red frothy mess that had been his friend's head just a moment before.

Well, they actually weren't friends. Just a week before the two men had threatened one another with switchblades in a drunken, pisco-fueled rage. However, cooler heads had prevailed that night and they'd managed to set aside their differences long enough to make this ride in relative peace.

Well, until now.

The Chevrolet continued on diagonally, thudding dully into one of the steel girders of the old bridge. Now realizing that they were under attack, the passenger struggled out the door, impeded by the bridge's girder, leaving him only a small space. When he'd wedged himself between the car and the bridge, he brought his AK-47 to his shoulder, searching the backside of the bridge for a shooter.

He finally saw the man. Actually, he only saw the distinct muzzle flash from the shooter's M16A2. The birdcage flash was cut in half with the newer model flash suppressor, designed to prevent barrel rise.

The reason the passenger saw this was because the first round impacted him just below his sternum. It wasn't an immediate kill shot.

Compared to the driver's death, this man's death took a veritable eternity. It was nearly a minute before his heart stopped beating.

"THE REAR IS green," Gage said into his headset. Only a few seconds after he dispatched the passenger, Gage watched the car at the front, an Opel sedan, explode from the impact of the rocket from the trusty M72 LAW. Ortiz, the SEAL and medic, had fired it, striking the car in the windshield. There was no way anyone in the car could have survived, Gage quickly decided, watching the gray smoke billow from the blown-out windows.

Unlike what is shown in movies, a weapon like a LAW doesn't often cause a fiery explosion. This particular LAW had fired the High-Explosive Dual-Purpose round, giving it a similar, yet far more powerful effect of a hand grenade. The fragmentation and shock wave were enough to kill anyone inside the effective radius.

So far, so good. Gage felt that old familiar detachment one feels after the bullets have started flying. Those questions he'd had before were gone, replaced by the cold decisions and confident maneuvering of a professional soldier. He moved on to his second task and, in his mind, the trickiest portion of his assignment.

Tasked with rear security, Gage had several key responsibilities. First and foremost, he was responsible for keeping the transport vehicle from escaping. With the ambush having gone perfectly to plan thus far, Gage felt an escape by the transport vehicle was highly unlikely. Even if the driver were to back away in expert fashion, he wouldn't be able to clear the tail Chevrolet cleanly. In an old, underpowered Isuzu straight truck, he'd almost certainly get stuck.

Gage's second responsibility, and one that he hoped didn't require any action, was the patrol of the road that the convoy had come in on. It was entirely possible that another vehicle could approach. Chief Mikkelsen's scout team had reported that the road had been clear between them and the convoy, but a car could have easily entered the roadway after the surveillance had ended. Strange things like that often happened, especially at the worst possible moment. The other end of the road was to be watched by Griffin, the Marine, but Gage couldn't concern himself with that. His worry was his stretch of road. For now, it was clear.

Then Gage watched as something highly unexpected happened. Because of the restrictive angles of the bridge, and the resulting smoke from the explosion of the lead car, the remainder of the team's vision was briefly obscured. And rather than make a suicide run for escape, the two men from the Isuzu truck clamored from the vehicle, neither of them armed, both with their hands raised high. The thunderous boom of the LAW had passed and Gage could clearly hear the drug runners' yells.

They were screaming for mercy.

Prior to leaving, during their walkthroughs, Sil had been clear. "We shoot to kill and we leave no one alive." But, in Gage's experience, a situation like this one exposed several factors to be considered on the fly. In Gage's instant opinion, these men weren't a threat at all. Of course, Gage understood Sil's reasoning for not wanting to leave anyone. It could be potentially catastrophic if the cartels learned that the ambush team was comprised of non-cartel members. Additionally, valuable time would be lost in the disarming and safeguarding of the men. Such a delay could be disastrous. Could ruin the mission.

But Gage wasn't a part of this team, was he? He certainly didn't give a shit about Alfa Seguridad's—and, therefore, Nuestra's—mission.

Gage found himself conflicted.

With his sights trained on the driver, Gage spoke. "The two from the transport truck are out with their hands up. They've surrendered."

Sil's response was immediate and crisp. "Kill them."

"Say again," Gage responded, buying time.

"Kill them, *now*."

Gage delayed.

"Copy?" Sil snapped.

"Roger."

Grudgingly deciding to go through with the order, Gage paused his breathing for a moment, applying eight pounds of pressure to his M16A2. His range was approximately 70 meters. Even for a weak shooter, it was an easy shot.

The first round caught the driver in his chest. He went down in a heap. Gage turned the rifle to the other man, estimating the range as 65 meters. Just as the man began to run, Gage fired, missing him.

"Damn it," Gage growled. The man kept coming, zig-zagging toward the rear of the bridge. He was surprisingly fast.

Gage sighted him, watching as he grew in the scope. Suddenly, Gage noticed something. The man was preparing to throw something.

A grenade!

Changing his gait for the toss, the man pulled his arm back. By this point, he was only thirty meters away. Gage squeezed off two shots. The first struck the man in his shoulder. The second missed the man as he tumbled backward.

Gage hadn't seen the grenade's arc. He flattened himself.

The explosion came a few seconds later—the grenade's delay had felt like an hour. No shrapnel reached Gage. He lifted his head, realizing that the grenade hadn't left the man's hand. Gage eyed the remains. A mess of shredded beef.

"Both targets are down," Gage called just as something yellow caught his eye. He whipped his scope to the right, peering through the girders across the bridge.

Standing in the brush on the eastern side of the bridge, not fifty feet from Dinkins and Desgreaux, was a young man. He wore a yellow t-shirt and ragged pants. He was very thin and was peering with wide eyes at the carnage. In his right hand was a fishing pole.

Gage instantly marked him as a local who'd been angling under the bridge

Had Gage been on a normal alpha team, he'd have reported the sighting. But Gage wasn't on a normal team, and despite all of Sil's bluster, Gage didn't believe him for one second about his unwillingness to kill innocents. Gage continued to stare at the young man as the team discussed extracting the drugs from the bridge.

Hey! Gage wanted to yell. *Go back down to the river! Hide under the bridge.*

He heard a snippet of Sil speaking on the radio. "…think the truck will easily push the car out of the way. We need to be gone in less than…"

"Break! Break! Break!" Desgreaux yelled, cutting Sil off. "We've got a man north of the road, watching everything."

Desgreaux described him.

IN THE CHOPPER, Chief Mikkelsen covered her headset with both hands. "Is he a threat?"

"Negative," the new guy, Burrell, replied. "He's probably eighteen and has a fishing pole."

"Then let him walk," Mikkelsen said.

"You got him, Desgreaux?" Sil asked.

"Negative!" she yelled.

"I got him," Desgreaux drawled, ignoring her.

"Sil, you sonofabitch, stand down on the fisherman!" she shouted.

"Green light," Sil said, ignoring her, his voice eerily calm.

GAGE LISTENED to the strife.

Before Chief Mikkelsen had gotten her next objection out of her mouth, Gage watched in horror as the man's head went pink and he crumpled unseen into the foliage.

"Status!" Mikkelsen yelled.

"He dead, 'dat d'status," Desgreaux drawled. "I'd done shot a'foe I heard ya, chief. But he ain't no threat no mo."

"What the hell!" Chief Mikkelsen yelled. "Sil, damn it, you know better than to allow a shooting on an unknown."

Silence.

Gage saw red as he growled into his headset. "He wasn't an unknown, he was fishing...we just killed an innocent!"

"What?" Sil snapped.

"He was a peasant, holding a cane fishing pole. Desgreaux killed an innocent and you ordered it."

"You saw him?" Sil demanded.

"I saw him just as Desgreaux murdered him."

"Sheeeeeit!" Desgreaux laughed. "Innocent my ass."

"Was anyone with him?" Chief Mikkelsen asked.

No one saw evidence of anyone else.

"Complete the mission," she said, her voice dripping with disgust. The ambush continued.

Gritting his teeth, Gage continued to perform his job, though it revolted him to no end. He did all he could to keep his mind in the mission, although a recess of his brain told him to forgo this job and blow the whistle on the entire Alfa Seguridad and Nuestra operation.

Sonny wasn't the only murderer in this group. Gage wanted to burn them all.

Desgreaux and Dinkins made their way onto the bridge, clearing the three vehicles for threats. That done, Gage listened as they discussed what to do about the forward vehicle. They were charged with driving the Isuzu across the bridge but the lead car was in the way and inoperable. Its front tires were both flat. Sil asked if the lead car was a manual. When it was discovered that it was, Desgreaux leaned through the smashed window and yanked the shifter to neutral. Although the front of the car sagged, he felt they could push it off the bridge through the use of the Isuzu truck.

"Let's hustle," Sil said. "We're supposed to be gone by now."

Remaining where he was, Gage continued to cover the approach road. The road rose up from his position, ascending for quite a distance prior to the turn and the bridge. Gage was able to see at least a kilometer. The road was clear.

Then it wasn't.

Gage's blood ran cold.

Coming down the approach road at a high rate of speed were three pickup trucks, each of them jacked-up 4x4s. They skidded through a turn at the top of the hill and accelerated, the sound of their big V-8s roaring through the valley as they sped down the long approach hill.

Three identical trucks, racing to the bridge. He could see people in the back of each one.

These weren't innocents.

Gage's voice was a razor. "Three trucks approaching at high speed." He eyed the trucks through his compact binoculars, aware of his pulse. "There are multiple gunmen in the bed of each truck."

Chapter Thirteen

CHIEF MIKKELSEN'S voice cut in. "Three trucks?"

"I say again," Gage replied. "I've got three four-by-four trucks approaching at high speed. Shooters in the back. Twenty seconds until they reach the turn at the bridge."

"Sil?" she asked.

"Are those three trucks your intel team?" Sil asked.

"No," she answered.

"They're still coming!" Gage said. "This has to be deliberate."

Sil's voice was resolute. "There's no time to pull back. We have to hit them."

"I'm repositioning the mines," Gage said, not waiting for an answer. He slid forward on his stomach, knowing he had precious few seconds. Using both hands, he grasped the edges of the first mine, tilting it upward. The trucks roared onward, nearly to the turn. There was no time to reposition the second mine. He'd have to use it on one of the truck's tires and hope for the best.

Sliding backward, Gage found his two detonators. He grasped the first one, watching as the first truck sped to the curve at what had to be 80 miles per hour.

He's not going to make the turn, Gage realized with a spike of fear. If the truck didn't make the turn, it would lurch into the brush and flatten Gage along with the saplings that concealed him. Then, just before the first truck reached the turn, it braked rapidly, the massive rubber tires scrubbing over the damp macadam.

Wait...wait...wait...

The truck just barely negotiated the turn, nearly flipping as it briefly went to two wheels. The occupants in the back held the roll bar for support.

Gripping the detonator in both hands, Gage prepared himself for the shockwave. As soon as the first truck began accelerating out of the turn, he mashed the trigger detonator three times, momentarily stunned as he was shoved backward several feet. Clawing his way forward again, Gage grasped the second detonator, eyeing the mine to make sure it was still in place. It was. He also saw the remains of the first truck. Still right side up, the truck was shredded, its roof peeled upward like the lid of a tin can.

All occupants were very dead.

Three seconds had passed since the trucks had reached the turn.

Still trying to figure out what these guys were after, Gage turned his attention to the two trailing trucks. Gage counted no less than eight men, armed to the teeth. With one driver in each cab, there were three gunmen in each cargo bed. Wearing green camouflage, the men were firing over the roofs of the trucks, aiming across the bridge. Surprisingly, none of the shooters had turned their fire to the area where the first mine blast had originated.

Gage twisted his head to the right, seeing his team's return fire coming from across the bridge. Gripping his M16, Gage aimed at the nearest shooter and put his finger on the trigger. Before he could shoot, he watched through his scope as the man's face instantly disfigured, making him tumble off the side of the truck.

Someone made a nice shot.

Sliding his scope to the right, Gage sighted his second target just as the second truck roared back into motion. It was blocked by the truck Gage had destroyed with the mine. The driver whipped to the right and the truck thundered up into the brush where Gage lay.

The saplings slapped down as the truck plowed straight at him. He could see every feature of the undercarriage, including the red boots and logos on the Skyjacker shock absorbers.

There was nowhere for Gage to go.

He would be crushed.

SIL HAD REPOSITIONED himself after making sure Griffin still guarded the eastern approach. If these people were bold enough to bring three trucks of shooters from the west, why wouldn't they bring a second set of shooters from the east, pushing the Alfa Seguridad team down into the river? Then it would be nothing more than a turkey shoot. Thus far, thankfully, no other aggressors had been identified.

Suddenly, one of the trucks revved its engine and bounced up into the brush where Burrell had been concealed, its front end lurching high like a monster truck before thudding back down, possibly flattening the new operative.

"Shit!" Sil yelled. "Burrell, you copy?"

Nothing. The truck ground to stop, sitting on higher ground as its passengers blanketed the area behind Sil in lead.

"I think they ran him over," Griffin remarked, able to see both front and rear from his distant position. "That truck crashed down right where he was. I was able to see him as the truck came down on him."

Sil turned his eyes to Dinkins and Desgreaux. They were sitting idle in the Isuzu straight truck, their backs to the aggressors. Because of the precious cargo, the shooters hadn't sent any bullets their way. In fact, because all the shooters could see was the back of the truck, Sil wasn't so sure they knew anyone was even in there. When Burrell had blasted the first truck with his mine, Sil had instructed Dinkins and Desgreaux to lie in wait.

Now, for the moment, the shooters were just wasting their ammo, firing blindly across the river. Sil had knocked down one of them with a head shot and, after that, told Ortiz and Griffin to be selective with their shots, and to provide cover fire before adjusting positions.

There were no clean shots available, so the three men waited.

BACK IN LIMA, at the Lurigancho duplex, Adriana was curled on her bed, Sheriff beside her. The dog obviously knew she was upset. He'd nestled close to her and was studying her face. Earlier, as she'd cried, he'd licked her hand.

The tears had now stopped. All that Adriana was left with was an awful, horrid premonition that she'd done something terrible.

At first, the offer had seemed harmless. A nice little payday for reporting on someone's comings and goings. What was the harm? She'd planned to use the money to pay off her credit cards. But did the man have to come back and threaten her, telling her he'd have her brutalized if she did anything at all to mislead him?

Why had he changed like that?

At first, the man had been slick but pleasant—flattering, even. Telling her how pretty she was. Offering plenty of cash for her moving in next to Jeff and keeping an eye on him.

But Adriana would never forget the way the man had acted once she'd agreed and the exchange of information had begun. "I'll bring men, savages, to rape you until you cry for death," he'd whispered, hungrily eyeing her up and down.

Although Adriana didn't believe he would follow through with his threats, the very notion frightened her. The man was small and full of fake bravado. In a pinch, she felt she could kick his ass. But still, such wicked threats…

And, earlier this week, when Jeff had told her he had to go away again, Adriana had phoned her contact. He'd been so intense, so demanding, wanting every little scrap of information. He'd called back three times, demanding more. Asking how Jeff's voice had sounded. Asking if Jeff had seemed nervous. After that, when Jeff admitted his job was dangerous, Adriana had been left with the awful feeling that she'd put him in more danger.

All of this for a little bit of money. If only she hadn't been such a spendthrift.

And the worst part for Adriana was the fact that she'd grown to like Jeff. Really like him.

"I just want to know he's safe," she moaned into her pillow, her premonition of dread growing worse by the minute.

"I just want to know that I didn't kill him."

WHEN THE JACKED-UP truck had roared up onto the rise where Gage lay hidden, he had quickly repositioned himself so the truck would straddle him. Unfortunately, the truck had bounced at an odd angle. Gage had tried to adjust himself again but it had been too late. Now, the front right tire of the idling behemoth lay on Gage's left arm. He was trapped.

Making matters worse—and excruciating—the driver was leaning out the window and firing. He must have been using the steering wheel for leverage because every time he moved it caused the steering wheel, which led to a powerful power-steering unit, to grind the tires a few degrees in each direction.

The twisting ground his wrist into the Peruvian earth.

Agony.

From his darkened position, Gage stared at his trapped arm. Everything beyond the elbow was trapped under the massive tire. He tried to wiggle his fingers and almost yelled out from the spike of pain.

All sorts of unpleasant scenarios ran through Gage's mind. Being stuck in such a position was bad enough, but if the truck moved, he could easily get smashed by the rear tires. Worse, Gage feared that Ortiz might let loose with their second LAW—they'd brought three. That'd be the end of Gage, for sure.

The team's Motorola Saber-R radios were "always on," meaning the team's secure channel was open to anyone on the team without having to key the mic. Because of the idling truck rumbling inches above his head, Gage couldn't hear anything in his headset. He hoped, however, that they could hear him above the constant roar of the truck as he called out his position and predicament.

Hopefully they knew he was alive.

There was nothing else Gage could do now but wait. Though the big tire blocked much of his view, Gage was able to see the hood of the other truck which was still out on the road. Gage didn't dare squirm or even move because the shooters in the back of that truck might see him.

Frustrating him nearly as much as his pinned arm, he couldn't hear a damn thing on the radio. And with his arm smashed and trapped by three tons of truck, there would be no getting away.

THE TEAM HEARD Gage's radio call. The idling engine squelched some of the transmission, but Sil was able to make out what was being said.

"Burrell's trapped," he repeated.

"If he's trapped we should return fire!" Griffin shouted.

"They don't know where we are," Sil snapped. "I don't want to give up our positions. You just watch our six."

"I can pop that driver from where I am," Ortiz said.

"And get return fire from five others? No!" Sil demanded. "The way I see it, we lay down controlled cover fire while Desgreaux and Dinkins drive the truck out."

"But what about Burrell?" Dinkins asked from the Isuzu.

"He's S.O.L.," Sil replied, using the military acronym for Shit-Out-of-Luck. "We go for him, then everyone dies and we lose the prize."

"That's bullshit!" Dinkins objected. "We can't just leave him."

"The fuck we can't," Ortiz chimed in.

"And what if they take him alive?" Dinkins asked. "OPSEC is blown because you know they'll torture him."

There was a long pause as one shooter from the truck that trapped Burrell continued to send bullets blindly across the river. On the bridge, the Isuzu idled quietly. The front car that had been hit by the LAW barely smoked by this time, with only a lacy wisp drifting from its smashed rear window. Behind the Isuzu, men lay dead across the bridge, their crimson blood mingling and diluting in the rain puddles. At the other end of the bridge, the first bandit truck, the one that had been hit by the mine, somehow still idled, albeit roughly. Its tires were flat and its right side was completely mangled by the blast. Behind it was the third truck, its occupants crouched down and discussing their plan. And, to the right of the two trucks on the road was the second truck, also idling. Its massive BF Goodrich tire held Gage Hartline hostage. Gage still couldn't hear anything over the engine.

A new voice broke the radio silence—English, with a strong Cajun accent. "T'hell wid Burrell. He ain't one of us. I say you guys blanket th'far side wid cover fire while we drive dis sumbitch off th'bridge. Ortiz, you wait to see if dey follow and den smoke each truck on th'bridge with your remaining LAWs. If Ortiz does get to hit dem, everyone piles into th'back of dis truck and off we go. If dey don't give chase we call in th'dustoff, load th'chopper and then pull back and load in a safe and secure military manner. What are your questions?"

"That's some cold-ass bullshit man…leavin' him like that. He's your fellow Green Beret," Dinkins replied, sitting in the same truck as Desgreaux.

"He ain't my fellow nuthin'," Desgreaux responded.

Griffin spoke next. "We can't leave him behind if he's still alive. It could blow our cover."

"Well…who say we gotta leave him alive?" Desgreaux asked, sounding as if he had a smile on his face as he said it. "Once we clear of dis here bridge, we blast dat truck he trapped under wid a LAW round and he ain't no problem no more."

"That dog hunts," Ortiz added. "It solves everything."

"It's bullshit!" Dinkins yelled.

"I don't like it, but it does solve the problem," Griffin muttered.

"Then it's settled," Sil replied. "We hit the trucks with the two remaining LAW rounds and blanket the area with cover fire in the event of survivors. As we do, they drive the goods off the bridge. Nice and neat and everyone goes home happy."

"Nobody is leaving anyone or firing another LAW round," cut in another voice. The voice was strong but feminine.

Chief Mikkelsen.

UNDER THE IDLING truck, Gage had pressed his left ear to the damp earth and covered his right ear with his free hand. This had allowed him to finally hear the radio, despite the rumble of the truck that held him captive.

He heard every word.

"BURRELL IS STILL alive, we're *not* leaving him and we're not sacrificing him," Mikkelsen reiterated. "Shut down the chatter for a moment so we can hear his next—"

"I don't know if anyone's reading me 'cause I can't hear a damn thing," Burrell said, cutting the chief off. "This truck has exhaust cutouts and it's loud as hell. If you can read me, I'm trapped but I've got a plan. Give me a tone if you acknowledge."

Without waiting, Dinkins complied with a one-second RAT tone—loud enough to be heard over even a revving engine.

"Roger," Burrell said. "I've got you. My arm is still pinned tight and this truck is right over top of me. From where I'm trapped, I can shoot my pistol right up into the tub and hopefully catch the driver in his ass. On my call, can you blanket the topside of this truck in lead? Then use the LAW to hit the *other* truck—the one out on the road. I'm far enough away that I should be good. If my truck reverses to the road, I can still fire the other mine because it's still upright. Gimme one tone for yes and two for no."

"Chief?" Sil asked, disgust evident in even his one spoken word.

"Can you guys get shots on his truck?" she asked.

"I got the three assholes in the back," Griffin said.

"Me, too," Sil grumbled. He and Griffin clarified who would shoot who. Then Sil said, "Ortiz, can you pop the road truck with the LAW?"

"Gonna be tight because I have to snake the shot through two bridge girders."

"Can you do it?" Sil roared.

"Yeah."

"Desgreaux...when we fire, you hit the gas," Sil said. "Can you push the lead vehicle clear?"

"Dis is a shit plan," he replied. "If anyone misses..."

"No one asked your opinion!" Chief Mikkelsen snapped.

"We *can* do it," Dinkins interjected.

"Desgreaux?" she demanded.

"I guess."

"Give Burrell the tone," Chief Mikkelsen said.

One long, squawking RAT tone jolted everyone's ear drums.

*

WHILE A .45 ACP is a renowned bullet for stopping power, it's not known for its penetration abilities. Gage's pistol was loaded with full metal jacket rounds, which would help the bullet's penetration. Gage was also concerned with the numerous layers of material the bullet would have to breach to do its job. He would have much rather been able to use his M16, but there was no way to get an upward shot from his trapped position. It was the .45 or nothing.

Taking a few seconds as one of the shooters in the truck above him started firing again, Gage thought about the construction of a truck cab. Of course, there was the floorboard. He could see the ribbing and indentations in the metal that gave it rigidity. Above that would be insulation, carpet, the metal frame of the seat, then springs, foam and vinyl.

A lot to travel through.

Gage decided to put several rounds straight up, aiming to send them through all the layers, then he would adjust and shoot several forward, toward the driver's legs. If the seat stopped his first rounds, maybe he'd get lucky and shatter some legs and ankles.

Setting aside his anger, Gage spoke into the radio. "My shots coming in three, two, one...*now!*"

He opened fire, sending three bullets into the area where he guessed the seat was. Then he adjusted forward, sending three more between the seat and the pedals. Gage had no idea if his shots were hitting home or if the others were accomplishing their duties.

Until he heard—and felt—the explosion.

The LAW round struck the rear truck on the road, hitting it in the cab and certainly killing anyone inside. Gage had no time to take inventory of the damage because, suddenly, the truck above him roared and lurched backward, the four-wheel-drive spitting Gage's shattered arm out from under the tire.

Despite the intense pain, Gage slid to his right, pulling his limp left arm to his body. The truck straddled the mine on its way back down the slight slope, just forward of the smoldering first truck.

After unclipping the safety on the firing device, Gage grasped it and squeezed one-handed, knocked backward as the lower side of the truck that had trapped him was riddled with supersonic spall and shrapnel.

When the truck had backed away, the massive tires had spit Gage's M16 elsewhere. Gage palmed his .45, watching as the driver stumbled from the truck. He was wearing olive drab clothing and combat boots. His head was bleeding and, giving Gage the most satisfaction, his left lower leg appeared to be injured—probably from Gage's ankle shots. But the driver's leg wasn't so bad that he couldn't stand.

In the driver's hand was a gleaming, long-barrel revolver. Despite having been shot and taken a mine blast, he was lucid enough to know Gage was in the brush and, though Gage couldn't hear, he knew enough to know he was being viciously cursed as the driver stepped away from the door.

Gage steadied his arm by putting his elbow on the ground. He thought he had two rounds remaining—he'd had seven in the magazine and one in the chamber. As soon as the driver's arm began elevating, Gage fired.

The shooting position hadn't been optimal and the kick from the .45, especially when firing one-handed, was extreme. It jolted his body, sending lightning pain down his other arm.

But the shot had been true, hitting the driver in his chest and dropping him. Gage continued to hold the .45 on him, waiting for movement.

There was none.

After a moment, Gage found his M16 and remained trained on the remnants of the trucks. No other shooters emerged.

In spite of the blasts, the radio still worked. It had taken a few minutes for Gage's ears to begin working again. He listened as Ortiz and Sil made their way over the bridge, headed for his position. Through it all, Gage didn't look at his arm. He didn't need that distraction right now.

Soon after his teammates arrived, Gage lost track of the time. Perhaps he passed out. His next recollection was a thudding sensation followed by the unmistakable, whipping wind a person feels when flying in an open helicopter. And the steady tattoo he heard—*whomp-whomp-whomp*—was the unmatched audible signature of a Huey.

High on morphine, Gage surveyed the faces. Ortiz gnawed on his bottom lip as he diligently worked on Gage's arm. Dinkins was kneeling over Gage, lightly tapping Gage's chest and speaking some sort of encouragement. Griffin, the stoic Marine, was behind Dinkins, sitting in front of the transmission box, peering at Gage. When Gage caught his eye, Griffin turned away.

Turning, Gage saw Sil speaking to Chief Mikkelsen. The chief eyed Gage and gave him one rueful shake of her head, followed by the hint of a smile. It was the visual equivalent of saying, "That was wayyy too close for comfort."

Sil turned to Gage and smiled. It was a mouth-only, humorless smile. It was the smile of a man who'd not gotten his way and was now trying to act the part in front of his boss.

His vision dreamy and blurry, Gage turned his head back the other way, looking beyond Dinkins and Ortiz. There he was, Desgreaux, the man who'd been so eager to blow Gage to smithereens. Desgreaux was sitting in that signature aft space of a Huey, the transmission box to his back as his feet dangled out of the starboard side of the chopper. Somehow, he'd managed to get a cigarette lit.

He wasn't looking at Gage, wasn't looking at anyone. Just sitting there, smoking as the jungle slid by like a rippling green sea. Gage continued to stare until Desgreaux finally turned. He didn't fake-smile, didn't nod, didn't do anything other than narrow his eyes at Gage.

Fighting the powerful urge to drift back into unconsciousness, Gage continued to hold the former Green Beret's eyes. Though Gage didn't speak, he gave Desgreaux a knowing look. He wanted Desgreaux to know.

He wanted him to know that he *knew*.

For the moment, Gage had forgotten the reason he was in Peru— forgotten all about killing Sonny Calabrese. For the moment, all Gage could think about were the assholes he was surrounded by. Other than Dinkins and Chief Mikkelsen, the rest of the team hadn't valued Gage's life at all. Griffin had seemed somewhat apathetic. Ortiz had been okay with Desgreaux's plan. But it was Sil and Desgreaux who were the true psychopaths.

In Gage's opinion, they didn't deserve to live. They were just as bad as Sonny Calabrese.

Maybe it was the morphine, but as Gage rested on the floor, he felt it was time to rethink the mission.

Maybe come up with a new one.

Chapter Fourteen

BLACKNESS TO DIM. Dim to bright. Gage's eyes fluttered open. He squinted under the stark white lights, his right arm coming up to rub his eyes.

"He's up," he heard a man's voice say. Gage lifted his head, watching as two men exited the room. Then Gage's memory kicked in and he remembered being in this exact same room just several days before, courtesy of a compressed air dart fired by Chief Mikkelsen.

No sooner had Gage thought of Chief Mikkelsen than she appeared, looking as if she'd just walked out of a band box. Her uniform-like outfit was starched and freshly pressed, making swishing noises as she moved.

"What day is it?" he asked.

"It's still Thursday," she replied, checking her watch. "Sixteen-hundred hours. You've been here less than three hours."

Gage lifted his left arm, seeing the blue, water-safe cast that went to just below his elbow. When he attempted to twist his wrist inside the cast, he was jolted by a sharp pain, making him hiss.

"Your ulna is fractured," she said. "Mid-forearm, also known as a nightstick fracture." She gave a little shrug. "The doctor said it wasn't all that bad. Not even bad enough to require surgery. They sedated you for the x-ray and while you were out he manipulated it straight. You've got extremely heavy bruising and some nasty abrasions under there, too."

Gage gingerly lifted his arm again, eyeing it. "Prognosis?"

"Cast for four weeks. Elevation. Rest. Drink lots of milk." Her smile was fleeting, so quick that Gage questioned if she'd even smiled. "Maybe your *little* girlfriend will take care of you."

Eyeing the chief, Gage asked, "My little girlfriend?"

"You have one, don't you? The local I saw you eating with by the beach."

"She's just a friend."

"Well, this setback shouldn't affect things. In the meantime, not a word to anyone about what happened. Clear?"

Things began to come back to Gage. He felt his heart rate increase.

"Burrell...clear?"

He licked his lips. "Yeah, clear."

"We always try to give R&R after a good job. Sil will speak with you about your schedule," Chief Mikkelsen said, turning and leaving. He heard her outside speaking to someone.

Turning his attention back to his arm, Gage wiggled his fingers, feeling the stabs of pain when he moved them in certain directions. He thought back to being pinned under the truck. In the numerous incidents and firefights Gage had found himself in over all the years, he'd never been trapped before. It had been unsettling. Thankfully, the men they were fighting this time were unskilled and, more than anything, untrained. If they had stopped to ponder the original ambush setup, or been curious about the origin of the mine blast, Gage would be dead.

Like morning fog being defeated by the heat of the midday sun, the haze of Gage's mind began to clear. Who *were* the men in the three trucks? Where had they come from? Who did they work for?

And how did they know?

Gage listened. Outside the room, the light timbre of the chief's voice stopped, followed by her footsteps. She was leaving.

"Chief!" he bellowed.

The footsteps stopped for a moment then hurried back in his direction. "What's wrong?" she asked, walking into the room with a severe expression. "Are you in pain?"

"Yeah, I'm in pain...lots of it...but that's not why I called you." Using his good arm to push himself up, Gage groaned as he swung his legs over the side of the bed. He worked his neck in circles, flexing his jaw at the same time.

"Did you call me in here to watch you stretch?"

Gage stopped and stared at her. "Who were they?"

"Who?"

"You know who. The men in the three trucks. Were they your so-called *dependable* surveillance team?"

Chief Mikkelsen's pink lips knotted into a tight little walnut. She casually walked across the room and shut the door. "No," she replied, walking back. "I've used the surveillance team on numerous occasions. They're clean."

"Maybe someone on that team was talking to whoever hit us...giving our location."

"There's always the possibility."

He shook his head. "Lie down with dogs..."

"Excuse me?"

"It's an old saying... Lie down with dogs and you'll wake up with fleas."

"It's frustrating to have to use anyone," she admitted. "If the clouds hadn't been so low, I'd have done the route surveillance from the air. We'd have been independent."

"But they *were* low, and we went anyway."

"We had no choice."

"Said who?"

"Said me."

"No...said our *client*," Gage countered.

"Said me," she repeated, her voice steely.

"Where I come from, we'd have postponed until we had the weather we wanted."

"That wouldn't work," she replied. "The shipment was moving regardless of weather."

Trying his best not to be an armchair quarterback, Gage halted himself before he gave an admonishing shake of his head. "Chief Mikkelsen, I'm sure I'm not telling you anything you don't already know, but by using an external organization for surveillance, you increased our risk tenfold."

"We don't know that the hit team found us because of the surveillance group."

"It was an unnecessary risk," he said, purposefully badgering her.

Her cheeks flushed. "You don't know all the factors. We had no leeway. The ambush had to be done this morning."

"I fail to believe that you, an experienced soldier, would have made such a poor decision unless you were pressured."

She pulled her head back a fraction. "Look, I realize there's no place for pride in my position—special operations organizations are built upon the foundation of zero ego and constant improvement. That said, the F.N.G. has no place in questioning my judgment."

"Whether I'm the F.N.G. or F.O.G., I know enough about risk assessment to know that, by allowing a third party to do our route surveillance, we screwed up. Royally."

"We?"

"Yeah, we. I'm not trying to castigate you. But if we're to improve, we have to be brutally honest."

"We had to do it today."

"See," Gage said, raising his index finger. "We *had* to do it. Why? Who forced you?"

"You're out of line."

Earlier, on the chopper, Gage had decided to blow this mission to hell. The anesthesia had clouded his memory for a bit but now it was all clear. This would be the beginning.

"Something's amiss here, Chief Mikkelsen. You're either not telling me the truth, or you're not very smart." He paused for effect. "And I believe you're smart."

"What are you implying?"

"I'm not implying anything. I'll just say it. I don't believe that you...that *we* have numerous clients like you told me when I was hired. I think Alfa Seguridad works for one client, and one only. The risks of working for multiple clients are far too great. You'd have shit happening all the time." Gage reached beside the table and lifted the insulated cup, sucking gloriously cold water through a straw. "The cartels can't be trusted. But one cartel, or some other sort of organization that could benefit from the drugs we steal, could use us like the pawns we are."

She seemed to be searching for a response as she rapidly blinked.

"I can look around that crappy Alfa office building and guess that they probably pay thirty, forty grand a year for it. Based on what you're paying me, salaries annually for the six mercenaries aren't too much over a million. Great pay for soldiers, but nothing compared to the value of even a *single* haul of cocaine. They probably pay you two-fifty, maybe three a year. Give you a little bonus at the end of the year and pat you on your butt."

Her nostrils flared as her breaths came in huffs. "Burrell, I'm warning you..."

"They pay for quality weapons and ammo. Pay for some surveillance and an old Huey. Maybe have a few other incidentals like the use of this clinic and the locals out at La Merced. And for all that..." he smiled, "...they steal hundreds of millions of cocaine each year." Gage nodded. "Young lady, that's what I call a helluva business."

"Stop!"

"Why?" He looked around, eyeing the ceiling. "Is our *only* customer listening, chief? Watching, even? They got the room wired? You scared of them?"

She made no movements, no sound. She *was* scared.

"I'm no threat, chief. However, I am good at my job. And if whoever we're working for wants to do it right, they'll let us operate the correct way—and not force us to go when the conditions aren't ideal. You can do stuff like that with a regiment, but not with a small alpha team. You can't stick to timetables when you're hamstrung with tiny numbers – you'll end up in deep shit." Gage glared at her. "Like we did today. And you know it."

"Are you finished?"

"No. There's one other thing."

"What?"

"The innocent who was murdered." Gage believed he saw genuine sorrow on her face.

"I didn't want that to happen," she breathed.

"But it *did* happen. And that little shit Sil assured me we don't kill innocents. Hell, it was like they were fighting to see who could get off the kill shot."

"They've been debriefed. It better not happen again."

"Oh, good. A debriefing should do the trick. That'll make that fella's wife or mother feel better, won't it?"

"I'm as upset about it as you," she said, eyes glistening.

"I should hope so." Gage stood, wobbling for a moment.

"Where are you going?"

"To take a leak. That okay or do I need to ask *them* for permission?" he said, gesturing upward.

She began to leave.

"Chief?"

She stopped at the door.

"One other thing…I quit. You tell our client, whoever they are, that I said they can shove this job straight up their ass."

"I realize you're upset," she said. "So take a day or two to rethink what you just said."

"I don't need a day or two."

"I insist." Abi Mikkelsen stepped out and pulled the door shut.

After Gage relieved himself, he eyed himself in the mirror and gave a small shake of his head. He wondered if he'd live to see the sun rise again.

If he did make it to tomorrow, he'd use the day to plan his next moves. For now, Gage shuffled to the shower and turned it on, making the water extremely hot.

JUST AS HE'D done on Monday, Sonny Calabrese reviewed the footage of the wounded sixth man, Jeffrey Burrell, at the clinic. After swiping his finger across the iPad numerous times to speed the video forward, he finally arrived at the tense exchange between Abi Mikkelsen and Burrell. Sonny watched the exchange four times, replaying it in a louder volume each time. Finished, he sat quietly for a moment, letting what he'd heard settle in. Then he phoned Chief Mikkelsen.

"You did a good job today," he said, without preamble.

"Thank you. It wasn't easy but it turned out okay."

"It was a success. That's what matters."

She didn't respond.

"How's your man who got hurt…Burrell?"

"He'll be fine. Broke his forearm. Nothing serious."

"I heard he almost bought it."

"Who told you that?" Abi asked.

"Did he?"

"He's fine."

"Did he say anything?"

"About what?"

"Is he upset about the fisherman getting shot, or getting trapped under a truck…about getting hit by an unknown third party?"

"I have no idea. He's drugged at the moment." She paused for a moment. "I'm the one who's upset."

"Why?"

"The local who was shot bothers me. But my biggest concern is that hit squad. Who were they? Who leaked our ambush?"

"Believe me, I'm making inquiries. But for now, it's done. You made it out."

"I'm not using an outside party again. If you attempt to make me, I'm gone."

"Calm down, Abi. Besides, how do you know it was them?" Sonny asked, keeping his tone reasonable.

"Who else could it have been? Someone had to spill our location."

"Perhaps they were following the convoy."

"Our surveillance team would have seen them."

"Maybe one of your men talked."

"Didn't happen," she said flatly. "And I say again: no more outside surveillance."

"I've noted your objections and we will deal with all that in due time." Sonny brightened his tone. "I have an idea. How about we take a drive up to Playa Hermosa, tomorrow? The weather's supposed to be warm and sunny. Do a little walking on the beach. Enjoy a fancy meal. Maybe stay at a beachside inn for the weekend?"

"No, I'm not *at all* interested."

"Why not?"

"Are we done, sir?" Abi breathed. "I'm exhausted."

"Abi…just like today, life is unpredictable. So many things could happen. I can help you. I can make things better for you. Much better. Won't you just get close to me? We can do great things together."

"I don't want to do *anything* with you."

Without another word, he stabbed the button on his phone and hurled it against the wall, smashing it. "Nasty little bitch!" Not only was she resisting his advances, and being rude about it, but she was also hiding the critical conversation she'd had with Burrell.

His desk phone buzzed. It was *La Bruja*. "You okay, sir?"

"I'm fine!" he roared. "Piss off!"

The witch clicked off.

Sonny crossed the room and picked up the pieces of his phone. He buzzed *La Bruja* again, telling her to load his contacts in a new one. "I need it within the hour."

She knew the drill. He broke a phone at least once a month.

Leaning back in his chair, Sonny closed his eyes and took a series of deep breaths. *You just displayed great weakness. You're a gifted and critical thinker…act like it.*

Sonny carefully scrutinized Abi's covering for Burrell. Why didn't she reveal what Burrell had done at the clinic? Sonny guessed Abi was simply trying to contain the issue, to handle it herself. She needed a quality sixth man—maybe that's why she didn't want him to make waves.

And what of him quitting? Did she not take it seriously?

And most importantly, where the hell did Burrell get off spouting off the way he did? Sonny paid soldiers to fight, not think.

Or was there more to it? Was Burrell as green as everyone thought? Or did he arrive with knowledge that no one realized? Sonny made a notation on his legal pad and moved on to the next subject…

Who the hell were the mercenaries in those three trucks? Where had they come from and how did they know about the ambush? They'd obviously been smart enough to wait until Alfa Seguridad's ambush was complete, when they were at their most vulnerable, before storming in to steal the cocaine.

But how did they know?

And who were they working for?

Sonny shut his eyes again, tugging down on the skin of his face.

Though he'd attempted to downplay the significance of the mercenaries, Sonny was shaken by their presence. Who talked?

He listed the name of every person who knew about the ambush. Then he thought about how much those people knew. One name stuck out. One person knew the whole story – and had been stationed conveniently far from the firefight. Sonny used a Sharpie to make a thick red circle around the name…

Abi Mikkelsen.

THE REST OF the day had been sheer torture for Adriana. It was now nearly six in the evening. Jeff had told her, twice, that he might not be home for a day or two. As the day had worn on, her intuition had terrorized her with frightful thoughts as she stared out the side window for hours, Sheriff by her side, waiting for Jeff.

What have I done?

Then, when he'd finally come walking up the curved dirt road, Adriana had yelled her thanks to the heavens. She and Sheriff burst through the door to greet him. As she ran out into the tree-covered area around the duplex, she noticed him walking with a slight limp and saw that his left arm was casted and resting in a sling.

"What on earth happened to you?" she asked, knowing she appeared horrified. Sheriff had jumped up on Jeff and was actively sniffing the cast. Overcome in his joy, the dog began to lick his master's fingers, which were still tinged in some sort of iodine solution.

"I had a little accident," he said with a shrug. "Broke my wrist. Hey, easy, Sheriff, easy. Don't lick that!"

Adriana scrutinized Jeff top to bottom, noticing numerous cuts and scrapes on his face and neck. Feeling a pit of dread in her stomach, she realized she was instinctively covering her mouth with her hand as she said, "You look like you were dragged behind a truck!"

He chuckled. "Close…but, really, I'm fine."

"You're limping, too."

"Just twisted my ankle," he said with reassuring tone. "It's all good—I'm okay."

"Well, what happened?"

He gestured to their duplex. "Let's go inside."

She took his small bag and led him into her bottom apartment, sitting on the sofa next to him. "Now, please, tell me what happened."

"I can't really get into it," Gage said. "My job involves…security. Sometimes things go a little haywire. It's done. I'm fine."

Adriana took his good hand. "Look at me." He did. "Believe me when I tell you, I'm here for you. And I need to know the truth, for my own peace of mind. Please…what happened?"

He eyed her for a moment. "It doesn't matter. It's over, okay? Please, don't trouble yourself with worrying about me."

She began to cry.

"I'm fine," he reassured her. "Don't be upset."

Adriana took his good hand, rubbing it, massaging it. "I feel so bad."

"Why? I'm really okay. Believe me, I've had far worse injuries than a broken wrist."

Despite her tears, she leaned to him, kissing him. The kiss was hot and passionate. Her face hovered inches from his as she stared at him lasciviously.

Gage pulled backward, shaking his head. "I don't think now's a good time to—"

"Why?"

"Please…let's don't do something that—"

"Wait," she said, cutting him off and wiping her eyes. "You've had such an effect on me. At first, I thought you were just like all the other men I've known. But, after getting to know you, finding out what's in your mind…and, now, seeing you injured…" She bit her lip and turned away, her eyes welling with tears again.

"I appreciate your caring," he said. "I appreciate it, and your words mean a lot, but don't jump to conclusions about me. I'm nothing special."

"I just feel so bad."

"Why? It's just a broken wrist."

"What happened, Jeff?"

"Ade…"

Her hand moved up to his chest. She flattened it over his heart, applying just a touch of her fingernails. For whatever reason, her guilt made her want to repay him.

He touched her hand, gently pulling it away. "Seriously, I better go."

"I want you," Adriana breathed. "I need you."

His lips parted as he gaped back at her. "Ade…no. I can't."

She leaned over to kiss him again but this time he turned his head. When she pulled back, he stood. "I really better go. Thanks for watching Sheriff."

"Don't leave."

"I'm exhausted." Jeff and Sheriff walked to the door.

Reading his troubled face, she called out to him as he stood in the doorway. "Jeff, did I just mess things up between us?"

He smiled. "Not at all. I'm just not ready and it's got nothing to do with you."

"I'm glad you're okay."

He nodded his thanks and pulled the door shut. She watched through the window as Sheriff rocketed up the wooden stairs with Jeff's feet trudging behind.

Tossing her head back on the couch, Adriana wondered what exactly had happened to him today.

And she knew she was the cause.

INSIDE HIS upstairs apartment, Gage immediately checked the three markers he'd left to see if anyone had been inside. The hair he'd left on the lip of his top dresser drawer was still there. In the bathroom, his zipped shaving tackle bag was at 1 o'clock, exactly where he'd left it, right down to the scant dusting of talc he'd deposited on the teeth of the zipper. In the kitchen, the stack of papers he'd left out were just as he'd left them, with the alternating pages ruffled in a telltale pattern he'd used for years.

Gage checked his watch and took three ibuprofen, chasing them with bottled water from the fridge. When he'd quenched his thirst, he walked to the window, staring at the hills to the north, remembering when he'd taken Sheriff there after first arriving. As he eyed the landscape, not really seeing anything, his mind pondered what had just happened downstairs. Why had Adriana acted that way? It didn't seem natural.

What she'd done reeked of desperation. It didn't fit her character. It also didn't come off as desperation for love or sex. She was quite beautiful, and getting either shouldn't be an issue for her.

No, she'd been in a state of panic since he'd walked in the door.

But why?

Shaking his head at the puzzling questions, Gage retrieved his iPad and communication items. While he was arranging his things, Gage thought about the ambush, and the secondary ambush of the three trucks.

Who were they and how did they know?

Before doing anything else, Gage fired up his frequency scanner wand and searched the apartment. The wand's LED readout had green and red lights, along with a signal meter. When it eventually initialized, the light displayed red along with a relatively strong signal strength.

Adriana's phone, Gage realized. *She's right downstairs. But it wasn't this strong last time.* He shrugged. *Maybe it's not in the same place it was before.*

He began to walk his apartment with the device, watching as the strength grew past ninety percent each time he passed his sofa. Gage stopped, twisting his head as he pondered the layout of Adriana's apartment. The floor plan was nearly the same and, as Gage recalled, her cellphone normally rested on the coffee table. Her coffee table was underneath his sofa.

There was a knock at the door. Gage slid his items under the throw blanket and looked out the window. It was Adriana. He opened the door. She stood there, wringing her hands in front of her.

"I feel weird about earlier."

"Don't. It's fine."

She raised her eyes. "You promise?"

"I do weird crap all the time."

She laughed. "What would you say to me picking up some dinner?" She displayed her palms in a show of innocence. "Just friends."

"That'd be great," he said. Although he was hungry, he was mainly acquiescing just so he could complete his tasks.

"Do you have a preference?"

"I'll eat anything," he replied. They chatted for just a moment and she said she'd be back in twenty minutes. Gage eyed her out the window as she crossed the wooded yard to the pickup truck. She had her purse on her shoulder and, in the way so many people do nowadays, she was carrying her cellphone in one hand and her keys in the other.

Gage lifted the homing device and resumed his sweep. The meter was still red, the detected signal strength as strong as ever.

What?

Walking to his sofa again, he slowly waved the device all around. The signal was strongest near his pack. Opening the pack, he removed his soiled clothes, watching as the readout reached 97 percent when it passed by his utility shirt.

It only took a few seconds to find it. In his left breast pocket was a tiny metal rod no larger than a stout watch pin. Gage lifted it, holding it next to the homing device.

100 percent.

Aware of his heavy breaths, Gage lowered the tracking bug to the floor and, with the heavy heel of his boot, smashed it until the percentage on the homing device dropped to nil.

Gage had been wearing the utility shirt at the ambush.

His breaths still coming rapid-fire, Gage turned his head as he thought back to the second ambush—the mystery had been solved.

The men in the three trucks knew where we were because of me.

Holy shit.

AROUND THE same time Gage discovered the homing beacon, Abi Mikkelsen arrived at her hillside Indepencia home and immediately popped a beer. She chugged it in several swigs, opening another as she began to feel marginally better. Despite the welcome feeling of alcohol hitting her bloodstream, Abi was disgusted. Burrell had been right about a number of things, but the one that bothered Abi was the imputation that she was somehow reckless.

He was correct. That's what was bothering her.

Flopping down on her sofa, she took another slug of her beer, replaying the second firefight in her mind. Although she'd not wanted to use them, she didn't think the surveillance team had been behind the attack. Each time she'd employed the team, they'd been professional and capable, tracking the convoy with a rotational five-car team. They used advanced techniques like trigger cars and cheating vehicles—the cheating vehicles actually drive ahead, rather than follow—and they'd never burned their cover. Not once. Up until today, Abi had never had anything from them other than spotless intel. Regardless, she'd always objected when she'd been forced to use them.

But each time, Sonny had overruled her.

Burrell had been correct. If Alfa couldn't have handled everything independently, then the mission should have been aborted. Zero tolerance. That's how a good special ops team would have done it. You don't use outside surveillance when you're dealing with a prize worth many millions.

Money like that gives people ideas.

Setting her beer down, Abi rubbed her face vigorously. What had happened to her? Where did it all go wrong? Oftentimes she'd catch her own eyes in the mirror and ask those questions aloud.

The youngest of three, Abi had dealt with high expectations all her life. So very high, which was typical for a Danish family. Abi's only brother, the oldest, was a mechanical engineer living just outside of Copenhagen in the rather dull suburb of Glostrup. With a wife and two kids, he was about as milquetoast as a man could be. His life matched the work he did: highly-structured, methodical and with little risk whatsoever. Abi often wondered how he'd managed to reproduce—had he and his wife planned that, too? *A meticulously planned insertion, aided by sterile petroleum jelly, at an entry angle of 172 degrees...* Back in school her brother had always received incredibly high marks. He'd just never had a personality. Abi hadn't spoken with him in more than five years.

Her sister, the middle child, floated about on life's unpredictable breezes. She couldn't have been more different from their older brother. The most intelligent of the three, Abi's sister had discovered psychedelic drugs during the summer before her freshman year in college. After that she'd learned the pleasure of boys, then girls, then boys and girls—and who knew what else? She'd run off to Mallorca, followed by Brazil, then Austin, Texas, where she'd waited tables while shacked up with whatever band she was currently following. Most recently it was a "newgrass" band from Boulder, Colorado. Oddly enough, the band consisted of two Canadians, an American and a Namibian. Quite a quartet. Her sister had been on a Texas tour with them at her last update, three months before. She and Abi spoke occasionally, usually through the help of the Copenhagen bank where Abi left her some money each month.

"And then there's me," Abi said, closing her eyes. "Killing people because the world didn't give me what I want." A sour, mirthless smile spread over her face. The smile evaporated when she thought about the local who'd been killed this morning.

He'd been fishing and heard a commotion. He died because of it. Because of me.

Though no one else knew it—because she'd never openly defined it— Abi operated under her own personal rules of engagement. Yes, she'd cut her teeth in the criminal world by architecting the pirating of a yacht on the shallow blue waters of the Gulf of Oman. The group she'd assembled had done it without permanently harming anyone—something Abi was quite proud of. Besides, the owners of the yacht were pirates in their own right, trafficking women throughout the Middle East. She didn't feel at all remorseful about what she'd done, executing the operation with concussion grenades and rubber bullets.

Now, working for Alfa, Abi was nothing more than a glorified thief and killer. She knew it. But she also knew that the men they took down were experienced drug runners. No cartel in their right mind would leave drug transportation to some impoverished local. Only the most trusted associates were charged with carrying such a cargo, trusted associates who would kill at the drop of a hat.

But the man today, the fisherman…

After being rejected by the Danish Huntsmen Corps, Abi Mikkelsen had adjusted her life sights. Everything she did was well thought out. Everything. That's why she'd not been romantically involved with anyone since arriving in Lima. What Abi was missing, and she knew this, was an ultimate goal. Since she'd left the military she'd been operating without direction—without a compass. If she had remained in the Army, or been accepted in the Huntsmen Corps, Abi would have sought to achieve rank and leadership. Such a path in the military is quite clear. Now she was floating about rudderless, amassing money with no direction. And no goal.

Abi knew enough to know that she had no desire to be like her brother—he probably scheduled his bowel movements to the minute. Nor did she want to be like her sister, either, drifting along through life without a plan for even her next meal.

Though Abi knew she didn't want her siblings' lives, she was also aware that she wasn't happy with her own.

In fact, she hated it.

She'd spoken to Griffin after the ambush. He described the fisherman as a young man of perhaps twenty. He said he was thin and poorly dressed, maybe even catching fish to feed his family.

Abi knew he'd once been someone's baby, someone's pride and joy. Perhaps he'd had a child of his own. She curled up on the sofa, racked by tears. The young fisherman shouldn't be dead tonight. He should be at home with his family, with people who love him.

He didn't have to die.

She cried for a half-hour.

When she'd somewhat recovered, Abi popped her third beer and finally acknowledged her growing hunger by boiling water for pasta. As the water boiled, she opened the safe under one of her kitchen cabinets. Inside, next to a special pistol and a brick of emergency money, rested her private mobile phone. She removed it and powered it on, waiting until the message feature blipped. Once she'd poured the noodles into the boiling water, she placed her thumb on the fingerprint scanner and unlocked the device. She saw one message that caught her eye, dragging it to the decryption application and providing the dual password that would allow her to read the report from the firm in Washington, DC.

The report was in reference to Jeffrey Burrell, her man who'd just quit. She'd inquired about him with the photo of his tattoo to the investigative think tank that specialized in running down hard-to-find leads.

Abi read the brief communique, her lips parting.

While the pasta cooked far too long, she sat there, thunderstruck.

Chapter Fifteen

GAGE HAD REMAINED quiet about the tracking bug during dinner. He wanted to learn more before saying anything. But Adriana had been the one who planted it. Gage could think of no one else, and it also explained her earlier behavior. A guilty conscience can be hell to hide.

It had to be her.

Throughout their meal, Gage continued to glance out the window.

"Are you expecting someone?" she asked.

He shrugged. "Old habit."

What do you think, Gage, that they'll come knock on the door when they kill you? Oh, and great idea leaving the curtain open. It'll give them a nice clean shot at your big melon. Hey Ade…do me a favor and duck when you see a red dot dancing on my head. It'll keep you from having my brains splattered all over that pretty face of yours.

Fortunately Gage didn't die during dinner.

Adriana went downstairs around ten and Gage set his alarm for two hours later. Shortly after his alarm, Gage slugged a glass of ice water to wake up. He followed Falco's previous instructions for phone calls, walking several miles from the duplex house in order for his conversation to transmit through a different cell tower. This was the first time Gage had used this particular prepaid mobile phone, another burner he'd purchased upon his arrival in Lima. He eventually came to a horse park loaded with bleachers and picnic tables, sitting atop a table and making the call. Gage would be sure to avoid certain keywords in the event one might trigger an NSA recording.

He also planned to play Falco along.

The phone rang. "Yeah?"

"I'm back from the first job and I'm lucky I'm alive."

"What happened?"

"Well…after we made the hit, another group appeared out of the blue and hit *us*."

"Who were they?"

"I wish I knew," Gage said flatly.

"Wild west down there," Falco replied. "But you guys did make the snatch?"

"Yes. Based on what I heard, we took several hundred of the units. Top quality. The brass here should be happy."

"Do you know where the units are now?"

"What?"

"*Where* did they take the units?"

I knew it. "What does that matter?"

"It matters!" Falco yelled.

Gage held the phone away from his face, staring at it for a moment. "Sorry, sir, but I didn't realize that was an objective."

"I'm paying you. If I ask, it's an objective."

"I'm not your bitch," Gage replied.

There was nothing but light static for a few moments. "What's wrong? Your tone has changed."

"I almost got killed in a very suspicious double-ambush. And a civilian died, too. The whole situation reeks."

"Reeks of what?"

"Reeks of a shit."

"All the more reason to wrap this up so we can get you out of there."

"It was...very...suspicious," Gage maintained.

"What are you implying?"

"Well, my first job with them goes to shit when some unknown group tries to hit us and take what we'd taken. Remember, they'd made hundreds of hits before me with no problem. Then I show up, and something like this happens."

"Are you suggesting I was behind it?"

"The thought has certainly crossed my mind."

"Look, you either trust me or you don't. We're working for those families who lost their sons, nothing more. If you don't trust me, then just stay on that team and be a soldier of fortune...or come home, I don't care." Falco paused. "If you do trust me, then let's finish the damn job."

"What do you want me to do now?"

"Have you seen the objective?"

"Not once."

"Heard about him?"

"Just a little bit...idle chat here and there."

"You need to get to him ASAP."

"The team is off for a week. It's going to be difficult getting to him anytime soon."

"You're off for an *entire* week?"

"Yes."

Falco cursed. "Then let's use that time wisely. I want you to do two things. Find out where they process the units you took and, concurrently, get eyes on your target."

"Which is priority?"

"Your target."

"Why do you want to know where those units are?"

"I have a secondary plan to bring down the target. I can't get into it over the air but, if you can't pull off the primary mission, we can use the secondary intel to bring him down."

"I'll think about it," Gage replied.

"What?"

"I don't know if I want to work for you anymore. So…I'll take a few days and think about it." Gage clicked off without another word. He couldn't help but smile as he envisioned the tantrum Falco was throwing at this very moment.

Then, just as he'd done with the tracking beacon, he dropped the phone to the dusty earth, bringing the heel of his boot down and smashing it. Gage lifted the pieces, separating the battery just to be certain. He dropped the battery in a park trash can and, on his way home, tossed the remainder of the phone in the already polluted Rio Rímac.

An hour later, Gage was still wide awake, staring at the blue shadows of the ceiling.

Falco…

Was this entire mission a setup just to get someone on the Alfa Seguridad team? Someone who would blithely carry a tracking bug to an ambush? Someone who would lead a hit team to tens of millions of dollars in pure cocaine?

Was it?

Or am I just being paranoid?

And even though Gage's mind was nearly made up, he needed to be 100 percent sure.

AFTER HIS MORNING tennis game, Sonny Calabrese was whisked to Nuestra in his armored Mercedes. As always, he was driven into the safety of the underground garage before he exited. Sonny then strode through the antiseptic hallways of Nuestra's noisy manufacturing facility. He was jovial. On both sides of him, behind thick Lexan walls, was the pristine manufacturing environment. Dozens of workers in special clothing, complete with hair nets and booties, created medical supplies and casings that Sonny hardly concerned himself with. He left that to others.

When Sonny first founded Nuestra, he'd initially focused on the manufacturing—the "smokescreen," as he often referred to it. Because he had no desire to put his energies into the smokescreen, Sonny had been bright enough to hire local professionals as senior management. He'd also been wise to incentivize them with enough bonus potential that they *would* care enough to do a good job. Then, once the smokescreen was up and running, Sonny had turned his attention to his true love: narcotics. This morning, one shipment of narcotics was making him particularly happy.

The Manolo cocaine.

At the end of the hallway, on a recessed keypad, Sonny tapped in an eight-digit alpha-numeric code. A small green light and a satisfying magnetic click granted him access to open an innocuous-looking steel door. Inside, with the pungent aroma of vinegar hanging in the air, he descended a steep set of steel grid stairs to another door, this one resembling a watertight oval door a person might find on a ship. Entry here was a bit more involved. First, he swiped a keycard. Then, Sonny had to place his eye over a retina scanner while holding his left thumb to the adjacent fingerprint reader. Once the computer was satisfied with his identity, another lock clicked, allowing Sonny to unseal the ovoid door.

If the earlier smell of vinegar had been strong, the smell of vinegar in this room was overpowering. This, even after the room had been showered with scalding brine from the four ceiling nozzles. In the room's center, packaged, sealed and awaiting drying and boxing, were 720 light brown packages with the familiar acronym M.R.E., for Meal-Ready-to-Eat. Had the packages been the genuine article, Sonny might have curled his lip. He'd eaten more than his share of the unappetizing meals during his time in the Air Force. Known, among other things, as Meals-Requiring-Enemas, the MREs did their job of providing basic subsistence. But, as anyone who's eaten them over prolonged periods will testify, skipping a meal or two soon becomes a worthwhile and appealing alternative to simply subsisting.

These "MREs," each weighing 18 ounces, the same as an actual MRE, were more valuable than if they were each filled with 24-karat gold. Each of them, of course, was filled with packages of highly-sought-after Peruvian cocaine. After being packaged and sealed in special interior packages, then treated, the exterior was also sealed and treated again. In the narcotics industry, it's widely believed that drug-sniffing dogs cannot be fooled. However, the lead-treated plastic packaging that Nuestra had pioneered had proven, time and time again, to be sufficient around an entire pack of the world's most sensitive drug dogs.

Each interior packet was filled with a precise amount of cocaine, then packaged by sterile machinery that contained no trace of the illicit powder. After a test for integrity, the interior packets were bathed in vinegar and dried. The entire process was repeated as the outside packaging was applied and, like the inner packets, bathed in vinegar before being washed clean and dried. The final test would be performed at another facility, this one near the airport. A team of four drug-sniffing beagles would be brought in to test the pallets of MREs. Provided no trace was discovered, the "meals" were ready for shipment and would be flown from Peru at a cruise speed of 515 miles per hour, courtesy of the United States Air Force.

Three people were charged with the sterile packaging process and had labored throughout the night to prepare the illicit MREs. The foreman, a Peruvian, was nearly 70 years old but highly skilled, having spent most of his professional life in cleanroom packaging for a Japanese micro-electronics manufacturer. Under his employ were his two middle-aged daughters. The women were unmarried and lived together in a small villa next door to their father, whom they doted on. The trio was well paid and, in Sonny's opinion, the three most proficient people who worked for him, Alfa Seguridad included. The family was invaluable.

The two daughters stood demurely by the far end of the room, near the sealed clamshell loading door. Their heads were bowed as they waited subserviently. Their father, however, stood proudly, his bird chest puffed outward as he awaited his master's questioning.

"Any problems, Señor Camara?" Sonny asked, making his voice hearty and booming.

"No, patrón," the older artisan answered, his chin tilting upward. "The packages are secure and every gram is accounted for."

"Excellent. You're confident they will pass the smell test?"

"I'd wager one of my girls," the man said, his brown eyes twinkling. "In fact, I'd wager them both."

"That won't be necessary, Señor Camara," Sonny said, smiling at the daughters. "Your two lovely offspring are safe for now."

The two women, despite their supposed inability to speak English, giggled like schoolgirls.

"When will the pallets be moved?" Sonny asked.

"After dark, patrón," Señor Camara said. "At eleven."

"Very good." Sonny waited until the women lifted their eyes again. He gave them a little wave, setting off another round of sniggering and giggling. With a nod to Señor Camara, Sonny turned and exited, chuckling to himself. For whatever reason, Sonny always enjoyed giving the Camara spinsters a little thrill. It probably had something to do with his mood whenever he saw them, which was directly correlated to the transcendent payday that awaited him.

As he departed through the ovoid door, Sonny again calculated the windfall on the hit the Manolo Cartel had netted. Though he'd hoped for 300 kilos, Sonny had been thrilled to find the ambush had netted a hair over 367 kilos, now equally dispersed in the 720 MRE packages. The 367 kilos would bring in slightly under 14 million U.S. dollars. Not counting overhead at Nuestra, which was mostly taken care of by the smokescreen medical products, Sonny estimated that he would net approximately $13.5 million on this shipment alone. $13.5 million—and all he'd had to do was pay for a little intel and employ special ops idiots who were too stupid to realize they were doing all the work for pennies on the dollar.

In celebration of his latest haul, Sonny had booked a Gulfstream for an early evening flight to Cali. There, he'd dine famously before being whisked back while enjoying the "services" of several beautiful women.

The good life.

Though he whistled while he climbed the stairs, Sonny's good cheer slowly evaporated. Until now, he'd not allowed the hit team that had tried to steal his cocaine to worry him. When he'd made a list of the people who could have been behind the hit, he'd theorized that Abi Mikkelsen made the most sense. But something else was niggling at Sonny, making him uneasy about the situation as he knew it.

Sonny's instinct told him there was an undercurrent in his organization that he wasn't yet aware of. Something nefarious.

It was time for Sonny to change tack.

A CLOUDY SKY hung low over Lima, Peru. Though it was the middle of summer, a damp chill had settled in with the promise of a storm. People hurried along the street, their collars pulled tight, their eyes squinted in the misting rain. Regardless of the obvious South American setting, Gage couldn't help but be reminded of Germany. The cool, damp air, one day after such summer heat, had an intensely German characteristic.

You just miss being there, he told himself. He missed Justina, too – and spent the next few minutes struggling to get her out of his mind, How had he screwed that up so royally? Despite their age difference, their time together was almost always perfect. Their senses of humor complemented each other's, their tastes were the same, they ordered their lives in much the same way, and they even made love in complete synchronicity.

Again, how in the hell did he screw that up?

Hopefully, today's activity would distract him from his morose line of thinking. After leaving Sheriff with the uber-willing Adriana—the tracking bug planter—Gage carried the high-powered scope in a gym bag and walked from his duplex, down the winding dirt road toward Lurigancho. When he passed a copse of trees, he looked back, seeing Adriana watching him through the window. Further down the road, he removed his scanner wand and made sure he wasn't wearing a new bug. He wasn't. Then he boarded a teeming city bus at the nearest stop in Lurigancho. This bus would take him into the heart of the city. No one boarded the bus at his stop and, unless they were highly skilled, no one followed. While on the bus, he popped more Advil for his wrist, which seemed to have improved slightly.

At the Estacion Monserrate stop, near the city center, Gage hopped off the bus and transferred, taking another bus to San Borja. The buses were on time today—a miracle. Gage walked into the small bus station in San Borja and used his calling card to dial Colonel Hunter on one of the old payphones.

"Hunter."

"Colonel, how are you, sir?"

"I'm fine," Hunter replied. "How the hell are you?"

"A little banged up but I'll live. Sir, I'm sorry for the way I left."

"No need to be. I know what drives you."

"I'm still sorry."

"Thanks, son."

"Well…you were right."

"About?"

"It's dirty, sir. The whole situation. And I'm pretty certain my handler's dirty, too." Gage gave a thumbnail sketch of all that had happened, including Falco's bizarre behavior and the tracking bug Gage had found.

"You gonna pull out?" Hunter asked.

"Sort of."

"What's that mean?"

"I think I'd like to cause a little trouble before I leave."

"Son, I feel like all I've been doing lately is warning you, but…"

"I'll be careful, sir. And believe me, if you were here, you'd do the same. A few of these guys need to be erased."

"Are you all alone in this?"

"Pretty much."

"That's not good odds."

"I know. I need to learn some things, first. Some intel that will give me the advantage. I also may have an ally or two that I need to speak with."

"Do that cautiously. The more people who know, the more risk you take on."

"Will do. And, sir, I may need a favor or two."

"Anything...you know that."

"Roger that, sir. Stand by, will you?"

"Wilco. Be safe, son."

"I'm not in danger...yet. But in about ten minutes, I will be."

Hunter chuckled. "I'd bet a grand that I'm hearing a big, shit-eating grin on your face."

"You'd win that bet," Gage replied. "Keep your phone on."

He hung up the payphone and took a deep breath as he walked outside.

Colonel Hunter was right about the grin. This next conversation was going to be fun.

Gage headed toward Alfa Seguridad.

GAGE TOOK HIS time as he rehearsed what he planned to say. He found himself outside the front doors of Alfa Seguridad fourteen minutes later. The team had been given the week off, meaning this trip might end up a fool's errand. But something told Gage he'd find Sil here. Maybe Desgreaux, too.

He knew he'd probably pay for this later. But for now, he just planned to enjoy the moment. It's not every day a person gets to tell their employer exactly what they think about them.

The local guard at the front desk greeted Gage normally.

"Anyone from the security team here?" Gage asked in Spanish.

"Sí, Chief Mikkelsen is here and I believe Señor Zobrist and Señor Desgreaux are here, also."

Gage nodded his thanks and strolled down the hallway. He passed Chief Mikkelsen's office, hearing her chair move when she saw him. She was probably surprised, especially after he'd "quit," but Gage wasn't here to see her. He continued on, walking toward the rear of the building. Sure enough, Sil's door was shut. Without knocking, Gage tried to open it.

Locked.

"What?" Sil roared from behind the door, obviously angered that someone had tried to open the door without knocking.

"Open the damn door," Gage commanded.

The lock clicked before the door opened a fraction, revealing one of Desgreaux's eyes and a sliver of his bearded, scornful face. "Th'hell you want, Burrell?"

"Sil in there?"

"Mebbee."

Using his good arm, Gage shoved his way in. Desgreaux didn't resist. He stepped to the side, his upper lip curled into his trademark mocking sneer.

"Why are you here, Burrell?" Sil demanded. "You're supposed to be off and convalescing."

"You're supposed to be off, too," Gage replied, stepping into the center of the room.

"Brassy all'a sudden," Desgreaux remarked from Gage's flank.

Gage turned, aiming his finger inches from Desgreaux's nose. "Why don't you shut the hell up?"

Despite his bravado and nasty nature, Desgreaux couldn't hide his surprise. He recovered quickly, however, when he lifted his middle finger, displaying a dirty fingernal.

Ignoring him, Gage turned back to Sil. "Yesterday."

"Yeah?"

"When I was trapped under the truck..."

"We helped get you out," Sil finished.

"Was that *your* decision?" Gage asked.

"You're the one who came up with the plan to shoot up into the truck," Sil countered.

"Wuttn't my plan," Desgreaux muttered.

"And it wasn't yours either," Gage said to Sil.

Sil nodded knowingly. "You could hear us."

"Damn right I could hear you," Gage replied.

"I'll be da first t'say I wanted t'leave yo ass," Desgreaux chuckled. "And I still wish we'da left yo ass."

"Not leave me...you wanted to *kill* me," Gage corrected, continuing to face Sil. Gage hitched his thumb at Desgreaux. "I'd expect such an idea from a lowlife piece of shit like this, but I guess I misjudged you, Sil."

Sil shrugged. "Battlefield decisions aren't always pretty, Burrell. But we got you out in the end. I was thinking of the group. Thought you were already a goner. So, don't take it personally."

Gage shook his head. "No...you *knew* I was alive. You knew that with some effort, you could get me out. But you were ready to walk on a teammate. So, in my book, you're a piece of shit."

Gage turned, aiming his finger at Desgreaux again. "You, too. You hear me, Desgreaux? You're even worse."

Desgreaux smiled.

"So, that's it?" Sil asked, pouting mockingly. "You came to tell us we hurt your feelings?"

Gage backed to the door. "I came here to tell you that I'm off your team. I don't want anything to do with you two. I've got no beef with the others. It's just you."

"Then haul ass," Sil said.

Don't do it!

Gage ignored his inner voice as he said, "And I'd suggest you two watch each other's backs. Because I don't forget when people try to kill me."

Gage pulled the door shut and headed back the way he came. As he passed Chief Mikkelsen's office, he heard her yell his name. He kept going. She caught up to him just as he stepped outside into the light rain.

"What are you doing here?" she demanded, the rain dotting her light blue blouse.

"I told you, I quit."

"And I told you to take a few days to think about it."

"I quit. And I wanted those two pieces of shit to know it's because of them."

"You're just angry."

"No." Gage pointed towards Sil's office. "And I'm warning you, if they come after me...if your bosses from Nuestra come after me...if you come after me...I'll bring a war to Lima, Peru."

"Really, *Gage*?"

She knew.

"Yeah," he replied. "And I'm not scared just because you know my name."

"I'd just like to know what you're up to," she said.

"Look, lady, I've got no beef with you. You played that ambush the right way and got me out." He pointed to the building. "But those two pricks poked the wrong hornet's nest."

"I'm not against you," she said. "And, even though you might not fully trust me, perhaps I can help you."

"I'll let you know."

"But why did you join our team under a false identification? And yours wasn't some simple fake ID...someone created fake government records."

"You should haul ass, Chief Mikkelsen. I'd say you've got a few days or maybe a week. Then this whole place is coming down." Gage turned and walked away.

Abi Mikkelsen stood there, watching her former employee limp up to Avenida Javier Prado. He turned left and disappeared into the teeming foot traffic.

"Kneppe mig," she muttered, using her native tongue.

BACK IN SIL'S office, Sil crossed one arm across his body and used his other arm to massage his face. "Let me ask you a question," he said, pausing afterward. "Do you think Burrell, in his current state, is a danger to you or me?"

"Even though I ain't scared of him...yeah."

"Agreed. And would you have a problem taking down your fellow Green Beret? Your brother in arms?"

"Dat sumbitch ain't my brother."

"That's what I thought."

From his pocket, Sil produced his key ring. He opened the third drawer in the heavy, fireproof file cabinet in the corner. It took him a moment to piece together the partial stacks of bills. He turned and handed Desgreaux the wad of wrinkled money, American dollars.

"That's twenty grand. Go take your week off as prescribed. When you come back, Burrell has vanished, and no one knows what happened. Got it?"

"Oh, I got it. Dis gone be fun. You ain't gone tell Chief or Sonny?"

"Not Chief...no way. I'll float it to Sonny later. You let me worry about all that."

Abi walked in. "What'd Burrell say?"

"Ah, he's just pissed off," Sil replied. "Said he was quitting. He'll be fine after a few days."

"That's it?" she asked. "That's *all* he said?"

Desgreaux was digging dirt from his fingernails with his knife. He glanced up and nodded.

Sil spoke up. "Yeah, that's all he said. Why? He say something to you?"

"No. Just seemed angry."

"Want me to keep an eye on him?"

Abi didn't answer. She turned and walked away.

"Think she know what we up to?" Desgreaux asked.

"Nah."

"What 'bout Sonny?"

"I'm gonna call him."

"Be sly," Desgreaux warned. "He d'chessmaster...he can see tru tangs."

"Don't worry." Sil phoned Sonny and had a brief conversation. When he hung up, he told Desgreaux to get going and not wait on him.

"Where you goin?" Desgreaux asked.

"I'm flying with Sonny to Cali...for dinner," Sil replied with a smile. "I'll use the trip to set the whole thing in motion. And by next week...you and I will be running this place."

"Member what I said 'bout Sonny," Desgreaux reminded Sil. "He slick."

Chapter Sixteen

GAGE RODE THE back into the heart of the city, taking a seat in the back so he could watch for tails. There were none. He assumed it would take Sil and Desgreaux a little time to get organized. Unless Gage was wrong, they'd be coming to kill him.

That's what he hoped for, anyway.

In the center of Lima, he crossed Avenida Arica and ducked into a large department store. In order to lessen his conspicuity, he'd eschewed his sling and tried his best not to limp. The walking motion of a normal gait, especially the swinging of his arms, had begun to make his wrist throb.

Having taken the escalator to the second floor, Gage perused a nearby rack of clothes. Two elderly ladies rode the escalator up, followed by a young woman of no more than sixteen. Gage knew, however, if someone was following him, they could be waiting on him downstairs. Continuing to keep an eye on his tail, he walked the floor, searching for an exit. At the far end of the lingerie section, Gage discovered an exit that led to a parking deck. He went outside, again watching to see if he was followed. When he wasn't, he walked down on the car ramp and hopped the wall on the opposite side of the exit. Gage found a taxi and instructed the driver to take him to a certain car rental facility in the wealthy district of Santiago de Surco.

The rental facility specialized in hard-to-find vehicles, including motorcycles. The stuffy gentleman at the counter first turned his nose up at Gage's initial request of a rental without a Peruvian driver's license or credit card. The rental, for one week, totaled 585 Peruvian Nuevo Sols— approximately $210. But after Gage discreetly promised to pay cash up front, in the amount of 1,000 Peruvian Nuevo Sols, plus a "tip" of five hundred American dollars, the starchy rental employee turned obsequious, happily renting Gage a very basic Suzuki GS500 motorcycle. The man even managed to find a full-face helmet for Gage, earning another fifty bucks in the process.

Riding the motorcycle was fine, but squeezing the clutch with his left hand was pure hell. Thankfully the Suzuki's clutch had a light spring and Gage managed with as few shifts as possible, able to do nearly everything in third gear. As he carefully obeyed traffic regulations—he might have been the only driver doing so—he thought about Falco's demands from last night.

Why did he want to know the location of the cocaine that had been stolen? How would that aid in the killing of Sonny Calabrese?

It was out of place. It seemed like the request of a man who'd hired a young lady to secretly plant a tracking bug on her new friend. It seemed like the request of a man who employed three trucks of armed locals in an effort to steal a truckload of cocaine from a group of pirates.

I don't know...for sure...that it was him.

Did Falco initially take this job with good intentions and then change his mind when he realized what was at stake? He couldn't just take over if Sonny was dead. But what about the shipment itself? If the coke was as good as Gage had heard, then he estimated its worth between ten and sixteen million dollars. While Falco assumed control of Nuestra, he could very well have had plans to steal the most recent cocaine haul. His expenses thus far were minimal—maybe fifty grand, tops. This single batch of cocaine could set him up for the rest of his life.

Gage had grown curious about the flow of information between Alfa and Nuestra. He was most interested to learn if there were any lines of communication back to Falco. That was part of Gage's reason for quitting— to see if Falco might react. Would he somehow find out what Gage had done based on the people Gage had talked to? Thus far, those who knew were Abi Mikkelsen, Sil Zobrist and that scumbag Desgreaux. Would Gage's plan smoke out Falco's collaborator? If so, it would give Gage a clearer path.

Time would tell.

THE MOTEL WAS old, probably built in the 50s or 60s, with external stairwells and walkways. It resembled an old, run-down Howard Johnson's. At the front desk, Gage learned that only a few rooms remained. None of those rooms were in a location with the vantage point he needed. So, carrying his helmet and the bag that contained the scope and his dinner, he'd gone to the third floor on the north-facing walkway and quietly rapped on several doors. One older lady had answered, quickly denying his request with an irritable wave of her hand and a slammed door in his face. Keeping his eyes on the backside of Nuestra, Gage waited a few minutes before knocking on the door of the corner room. He knocked again before the door was opened by a sleepy-looking man in his mid-twenties. The man wore baggy jeans and a soiled white t-shirt. Based on his bed-head, he'd been asleep.

"Yeah?" the man asked, eyeing Gage up and down and glancing at the motorcycle helmet in his left hand.

"Can I rent this room from you?" Gage asked.

"Go to the damned front desk for a room."

"Wait," Gage pleaded, removing a wad of bills and showing them. "I proposed to my wife in this room. And this is where we first…well…you know," Gage said, adding an embarrassing smile to his poorly-acted ruse. "Anyway, this is our fifth anniversary and I'd like to surprise her. I'll pay you double what you paid, and you can go downstairs and rent another room."

The man's eyes moved left and right as he pondered this offer. "What if you trash the room? It's in my name."

"I won't. And, tell you what, I'll pay triple. How long do you have it rented?"

"Through tomorrow night."

Gage shelled off Peruvian hundreds, rounding up and holding the bills out to the man.

The man packed quickly.

Five minutes later, Gage had opened the two windows to air out the musty room that reeked of sour alcohol breath. He'd moved the chair adjacent to the window with the best view, and watched the rear of Nuestra with the high-powered scope close at hand.

Knowing he might be chasing his tail, but having nowhere else to begin, Gage sat back and did what soldiers do best.

He waited.

SIL RECLINED IN the Corinthian leather seat of the exclusive private jet. With his and Sonny's stomachs full of Cali's *bandeja paisa, bollos* and two bottles of expensive Dominio del Plata Nosotros malbec, they now stretched out like overstuffed lions for the flight back to Lima. While the pilots focused on their duties, and as Sil and Sonny spoke of weighty matters, the two high-priced hookers in the forward compartment had their faces pressed to the port windows, watching as the early evening lights from Quito slid by. Guayaquil loomed in the distance, and beyond that, Lima. The pilots were cruising low and slow and had been instructed not to land without seeking Sonny's permission.

The hookers had come from Lima's premier escort service and were more taken with the view than they were the $60 million private aircraft. Neither woman—one was eighteen and one nineteen—had ever flown before. They had no idea that their first-ever flight was taking place on what was arguably the finest business jet on earth. Their awakening to commercial flying would be someday rude, when they eventually purchased a coach ticket on one of South America's many bargain airlines. They'd get crammed into the fuselage with the rest of the steerage and recall how pleasant that one night with the two gringos had been.

Due to their interest in the world that lay below them, neither woman paid a bit of attention to the silent, yet animated, conversation that was occurring to their rear.

Sitting aft of them, Sil and Sonny had swiveled their seats to partially face one another. They were continuing a conversation they'd had off and on over the duration of this brief dinner trip. Sonny sipped his sparkling water and shook his head over what he'd just heard.

"You know I respect your judgment. Right?"

Frustrated, Sil nodded.

"That said, your position feels *weak* to me. Frankly, I'm shocked you'd take it."

Sil might have been slapped across his face. Being Swiss, he prided himself on accuracy and precision. He hated to be associated with weakness. Smoothing his pants legs as he recovered himself, Sil said, "Perhaps, then, I should summarize the facts in close succession. In my earlier versions of the story, I was a bit long-winded, but if you hear the facts concisely..."

Sonny hungrily eyed the hookers. "Make certain you're extremely concise."

"Since Abigail Mikkelsen's hire, we've suffered numerous issues at Alfa Seguridad. We've had operators go AWOL. We've had addiction issues. We've had people with loose lips. And we've had them suddenly sprout minds of their own. All of this is an indication of *weak* leadership. Not—of—my—doing."

Sonny grinned fleetingly. "Go on."

"Yesterday's failure was nearly catastrophic, sir. While we eventually succeeded in netting the Manolo cargo, we were nearly overrun by three trucks of what appeared to be local mercenaries. As you know, a vicious firefight ensued." Leaning forward, Sil lifted his index finger. "Imagine, sir, what would have happened if that group of mercenaries had wiped out our team. Imagine the scene that would be found by the locals. The dead men from the Manolo Cartel, along with our dead—mostly Americans. Identities *would* be learned. The American government would push for an investigation. Eventually, some thread of evidence would link Alfa to Nuestra...to *you*, sir."

Sonny listened intently. When Sil had made his point, Sonny looked briefly away. "You're correct, Sil, about the potential catastrophe that, thankfully, *didn't* occur. However, you did manage to beat back the aggressors and—"

Hazarding another rebuke, Sil politely interrupted Sonny. "If I may, sir, I've one more piece of information." He made his tone grave. "It's something I've not yet told you."

It seemed Sonny deliberately controlled his temper over the interruption. Though his nostrils flared, he settled back in the chair and sipped his water. There was a note of exasperation in his voice as he said, "Go ahead."

Sil relayed what had happened when Burrell was trapped under the truck. "The best move was to blow the truck and escape with the coke. Tough decision, but it was the safest plan."

"I heard all about it."

"Chief Mikkelsen overruled us."

"I know all this, Sil. And I'm not going to castigate her because of it. I've heard all your points today, and I know you'd like control of—"

Sil leaned forward. "Sorry to interrupt again but, before you go on...Burrell came in this afternoon and quit."

Sonny's mouth was still open from the interruption. But his eyes widened at the revelation. He sat back and frowned. "Why are you just now telling me this?"

"I wanted time to explain everything. Believe me, there's more."

"What?"

"First, sir, when he quit, Burrell threatened me and Desgreaux. Told us to watch our backs."

Sonny waved his hand. "He's probably just pissed off."

"No, sir." *Here comes the ace in the hole.* It was all Sil could do not to grin. "And, second, sir, based on some things Desgreaux and I have seen in the past few days...I'm positive Chief Mikkelsen...well..."

Sonny sat forward. "Go on."

"We're positive she's..." Sil lowered his head, "...she's fucking Burrell."

The only sound was the dampened vacuum cleaner-like sound of the twin Rolls Royce jet engines. After a moment, the two hookers could be heard tittering through the glass. Sil raised his eyes. He couldn't decide if Sonny was sad or enraged.

"Sir?"

"What makes you think this?" Sonny asked evenly. "You and Desgreaux?"

"At first it was just the way they acted around each other. Flirting. Grinning. Then I saw them making out." Sil let out a breath, trumpeting his cheeks. "After the ambush, when he almost bought it, she was hysterical,

204

clinging to him in the helicopter."

Sonny stared at Sil through gun-slit eyes.

"Sir?" Sil asked.

"It's peculiar," Sonny said, sucking his teeth.

"What is?"

"I watched them in the clinic via closed-circuit, after the ambush, and they didn't seem amorous at all. If fact, he told her he was quitting and when I spoke to her, she brushed it off."

Sil shrugged. "She knows there are cameras in there, sir. I'm sure she warned him. She's very intelligent. Don't underestimate her."

"She is that." There was another spate of silence.

"Sir, do you think Chief Mikkelsen could have been behind the hit team?"

"No."

"You don't sound very sure."

"The thought crossed my mind, but I don't see how that's possible." Sonny turned his head to the window. "You're sure about her and Burrell?"

"They're screwing, sir."

Sonny sipped his water. "I want you to bring Burrell to me."

"But he quit, sir."

"I don't care. Find him and bring him to me."

"Wouldn't you rather we just eliminate him?"

Sonny sat forward. "Did I say to eliminate him?"

"No, sir."

"Then do as I say."

"You do believe me, don't you, sir?"

Sonny smiled with his mouth only. "I believe you. And I'm looking forward to chatting with Burrell."

Sil knew his hand had been forced. He could feel a slight sheen of sweat on his forehead. He'd simply have to follow through with his plans that were already in motion and deal with Sonny's blowback once Burrell was dead.

"You okay?" Sonny asked, arching an eyebrow.

"Sure," Sil replied.

"Telling me the whole truth?"

"Absolutely," Sil replied with a trace of heat.

"Good. Anything else you've been 'holding back?'"

"No."

"Then call them in." Sonny adjusted himself in his seat, unzipping his suit pants.

A minute later, the two men spoke in non-specifics about mundane, unrelated issues. As they conversed, the two women, peeled out of their skin-tight dresses, knelt on the floor in front of each man.

After some time had passed, a relieved Sonny leaned his head back into the plush leather seat. "Are you truly serious, Sil? You really think our Abi is involved with Burrell?"

"I do, sir."

"You wouldn't be lying, would you?" Sonny asked. "Lying so *I'd* bring the world down on a man who wants *you* dead because you wanted to kill *him* during a mission?"

"That's preposterous, sir."

"I certainly hope so," Sonny replied.

As the hooker continued to work on him, Sil shut his eyes, knowing he was in trouble. As Desgreaux had warned, Sonny was indeed the chess master and had ferreted out the scheme in mere minutes. And after they landed, it wouldn't take Sonny long to prove that Sil was lying.

That left Sil with only one move.

He had to kill the king. He had to kill Sonny Calabrese.

HAVING EATEN his dinner and taken more Advil for his arm, Gage was sleepy. He'd purchased a Diet Coke for the caffeine and drank it warm sometime past ten. There were no cars at Nuestra and the building was quiet. Gage began to wonder if he'd guessed incorrectly. Besides, if the cocaine was at Nuestra, maybe they'd move it during the day, with other shipments. That'd be the least conspicuous. But, on the other hand, who would handle the coke? How could they contain such a mammoth secret?

At 10:45 P.M., an old Ford Grenada with only a single headlight rumbled into the rear parking lot of Nuestra. Gage stood, eyeing the car through his scope. It was blue and had a distinctive rectangular patch of gray on one of the rear doors. He watched as a hunched-over old man shuffled into the rear of the building, pausing to disarm the alarm. Minutes later, one of the garage doors opened at the loading dock and, from inside, Gage could see the man use a pallet mule to tug two wrapped pallets to the edge of the dock. Gage was unable to discern what was on the pallets but was able to see the distinct day-glow yellow tape that had been wrapped around each one.

Shortly thereafter, a straight truck appeared, its back-up warning audible even in the motel as the driver backed to the loading dock. According to the logo on the side, the truck belonged to a local courier service. Gage watched the driver chatting with the old man and saw the old man sign the driver's clipboard. That was enough for Gage to see. He grabbed his helmet and made his way down to the Suzuki. Minutes later, after the truck was loaded, Gage fell in behind and followed it as the driver made three more nearby loading stops. After the third stop, the truck made its way to the northwest. Judging by the road signs, it was headed to the airport.

A half-hour later, Gage stood across the street from the industrial end of Jorge Chávez International Airport, staring at a busy cargo operation. Over the main building was a sign that read Lima Cargo City. The cargo area of the airport was fenced and highly controlled, so Gage viewed the operation from a convenience store across the street.

He'd followed the straight truck here, watching the driver produce the proper paperwork before the truck entered Lima Cargo City, crossing the massive lot and backing into one of the dozens of loading dock spaces. At that point, Gage eyed the customers at the busy, 24-hour convenience store. Purposefully acting nervous, Gage had approached three different workers who were there buying sodas, snacks and cigarettes, asking each one if they could check on a shipment for him. The first two brushed Gage off. The third, an older lady with a tired mien, told Gage she was on break and could possibly help him. In the pocket of her security badge that was clipped to her reflective coveralls, Gage saw a dog-eared photograph of two toddlers.

"Your children?"

"Grandchildren," she said flatly.

Gage produced 200 Nuevo Sols, about seventy bucks, and pressed it in her hand. He then described the shipment with the bright yellow tape, and explained exactly which truck it had come from.

"I need to know where and how it's being shipped," he said. "And I won't tell a soul you helped me."

The woman had eyed him, then the money, then him again. She walked outside and pointed to the row of old payphones and told Gage to wait there. She'd been gone for twenty minutes.

As a light rain began to fall, the drops streaking like neon with all the lights, Gage scanned the numerous gray aircraft outlines on the tarmac across the road. There were probably fifty jet aircraft sitting idle on the tarmac. Just as Gage turned his head to the right, eyeing the aircraft belonging to the Peruvian Air Force, he saw the woman approaching the fence with her industrial ear muffs over her ears. She said something to the gate guard, then stood inside the fence and beckoned Gage across the street. Gage jogged over.

"Two pallets?" she asked.

"Yes."

"They're shipping to…" She shook her head, producing a piece of paper from her pocket. "I can't pronounce that." The woman handed it to Gage.

"Spangdahlem AFB, Germany," Gage read aloud, suddenly aware of his thudding pulse. *Spangdahlem…what the hell?*

He looked up. "How is it being transported?"

"*La Fuerza Aérea de los Estados Unidos.*" Translated, it meant, "The United States Air Force."

Gage grasped the fence as water cascaded down his face. "Lady, are you sure?"

"Sí," she replied. "The pallets were already in queue for loading."

Taking measured breaths, Gage turned his head to the right again, to the Peruvian military planes. Parked in the far corner, between the civilian airplanes and the numerous aircraft of the Peruvian Air Force, was the hulking and unmistakable muscular silhouette of a United States Air Force C-17.

"Thank you," Gage said to the woman, finding another bill in his pocket and handing it to her. She nodded and ambled away.

Taking his time, Gage did a slow review of every single aircraft within sight. The C-17 was the only airplane he saw that belonged to the United States government.

"That's the one," Gage whispered to himself, staggered and exultant at the same time. "That's how they're moving their drugs. Sonofabitch."

Twenty minutes later, sitting in an all-night coffee shop in the Callao district, Gage opened his encrypted email. There was nothing from Falco about Gage's quitting. So, though he couldn't be sure, Gage was confident that neither Abi Mikkelsen, Sil or Desgreaux were associated with Falco. But Gage would bet his busted left arm that Adriana somehow was.

And Gage would know later tonight.

His next priority was finding another pay phone. He finally located one of the soon-to-be-extinct anachronisms in a dark strip mall and used his memorized calling card to phone Colonel Hunter's operations phone—the one he kept beside him at all times.

"Yeah?" Hunter grunted.

"Hello, sir. Sorry to call back so late."

"Wait one," the colonel replied in a whisper, having clearly been asleep.

Gage could hear him walking into the other room.

"Again, sir, I apologize for getting you mixed up in this and for taking this job in the first place."

"Yeah, well…ain't the first time you or me have made a stupid decision."

"And not the last?"

"Oh, hell no. Definitely not the last. I'm sure I'll make a crap decision before the sun comes up. Now, what can I do to help you in the middle of the night?"

Gage told Hunter about his own personal Gregory Harris identification he'd brought with him—one that Falco wasn't privy to. Gage needed Hunter to do something very special for Mister Gregory Harris. Hunter needed to act as a travel agent, of sorts.

"And I need it before sunrise," Gage added.

"Before sunrise, huh? You don't ask for much, do you?"

"Piece of cake, right?" Gage chuckled.

"I'll wake up some friends. Give me two hours and call this number again."

"You got it. Thank you, sir."

"You just watch your tail. Talk to you in two." Hunter ended the call.

After taking steps to make sure that he was, indeed, free and clear of tails, Gage sped back to the motel, still staggered over the U.S. Air Force connection he'd uncovered. He left his motorcycle at the motel before taking several late-night bus connections to the area north of his duplex. He planned to use the "back door."

IT WAS JUST past 1 A.M. when Gage approached the duplex from the north. He'd walked no less than five miles to arrive at his residence from this direction. Sweating the entire way, he realized it wasn't because of the heat or the pain in his wrist and ankle—it was pure anxiety. Would he find Adriana dead? Were Sil and Desgreaux that cold? When he was several hundred meters away, he finally saw the duplex in the clearing of undergrowth. Gage scanned the visible area with the thermal scope. He saw nothing.

Keeping the phone hidden, Gage dialed Adriana's number. She didn't answer. He dialed again.

"Hello," she answered groggily.

"It's Jeff," he whispered. "Listen to me closely and do exactly as I say."

He told her to completely power down her iPhone, to grab a bag and, without turning on any lights, to quietly open one of the two *north*-facing windows. She would help hand Sheriff through to Gage, then she'd climb through.

"Why?"

"Someone's watching the house, Adriana. They want to kill me."

"What?"

"I wouldn't joke about such a thing."

"Are you sure?"

"Positive. Don't turn on any lights, don't make any noises, and be ready in five minutes. I'll be outside the *north* windows. Don't give off any clues or we're both dead." When she agreed, he kept the structure between him and the road and used available cover to navigate to the north side of the duplex.

Getting Sheriff out was the most difficult part. Between Gage's bad arm, and the dog's wagging tail, Gage was sure they'd alerted whoever was out there. Once the threesome was out of the duplex, Gage told Adriana where he wanted her to go. It was due north, about a kilometer away, to a large tree they'd sat under one day after their walk.

"I'll be there in five minutes. Do not go left or right. Just go straight to the tree and try not to make any noise on the way there."

As Adriana and Sheriff made their way up the hill, Gage used the scope to peer around the duplex. Her truck was parked there, and beyond it the entry road. Gage saw nothing through the thermal scope other than some light phosphorescence from a few plants. He went to the western side of the building and repeated his actions. Again, he saw no one.

Just as Gage was about to leave, the thermal scope exploded in light. He continued to stare as most of the light quickly abated. However, there was still a small glow. It moved a short distance back and forth, and would grow in intensity every thirty or so seconds.

Someone had lit a cigarette.

Desgreaux.

Undisciplined bastard.

Gage didn't know for sure if it was Desgreaux, but he would bet on it. The Cajun was well down the road, with plenty of scrub brush between him and the duplex. He probably knew Gage wasn't home, so that was where he'd chosen to wait on him. While his body heat wasn't warm enough to show through all that foliage, especially on a muggy night like this one, the cherry of the cigarette gave him away. The explosion of light must have been from Desgreaux's lighter.

Gage wondered how Desgreaux had survived as a Green Beret. Any good soldier knows a cigarette is a beacon, especially at night.

He's underestimated me. Good. He thought I'd just come waltzing up the road. Score one for me.

Desgreaux's presence was huge. Gage now knew they were after him. He wasn't surprised, but knowing gave him a slight edge. He kept the duplex between him and Desgreaux and slowly made his way to where Sheriff and a flustered Adriana awaited him.

"I'm scared," she said, tears sparkling on her face.

"You should be. Come on." He took Sheriff's leash and led them away, walking farther north before turning west, to the district of San Juan de Lurigancho.

LEANING BACK against the earthen cut of the ravine, Desgreaux smoked without concern. He knew his actions weren't tactical. He also didn't think there was a chance in hell Burrell would be stupid enough to come back here.

Besides, Desgreaux had no plans to kill Burrell. Not yet, anyway. Not after the cash the Cajun had been paid today.

And what a day it had been.

Desgreaux thought back to his days as a soldier. He'd been straight infantry before he was invited to Special Forces Selection. Despite his psychiatric misgivings, he'd been blessed with an iron will, incredible endurance and keen weapons skill. It wasn't until after he'd been awarded his green beret that the leadership knew they'd made a mistake. But, by that time, Desgreaux was baked in. He did his five years before getting out and going for the real money.

Though he had no true plans beyond his current position at Alfa Seguridad, Desgreaux was always game for a shake-up. And today's shake-up, in his slanted opinion, could leave him in a far more lucrative position. The thought of so much cash – and so much potential debauchery – warmed his frozen heart.

Deciding to give it one more hour—for appearances only—the Green Beret arched his head backward, blowing smoke rings into the scant light of the night.

This wasn't the night to kill Burrell. No. But that night would soon come.

After Desgreaux had lined his pockets.

Chapter Seventeen

GAGE DIDN'T speak to Adriana as he led her and Sheriff over the hill and back down the northern face of Mangomarca. Once they'd crossed a footbridge, he told her to stay with him but continue to be quiet. Finally, when San Juan de Lurigancho was before them, he found a bus shelter on the side of the quiet road. He told her to sit.

"Do you know how scared I am right now?" she asked.

"I can imagine. And thanks for coming quietly."

"Why was someone watching the duplex?"

"I told you...they're trying to kill me."

Though her lip trembled, she didn't respond.

Gage sat down and told her to look at him. "What's wrong with you, Ade? I can tell you're scared of something *other* than people trying to kill me."

"I'm afraid," she croaked.

"I can see that. What are you afraid of?"

"You."

"Me?"

"You're going to want to kill me."

"That's ridiculous," Gage said, feeling acidic dread churning in his stomach. He knew what was coming.

She lowered her face into her left hand and said, "I haven't told you the truth."

"What truth?"

She began to sob. Although his heart was racing over whatever secret she was keeping from him, another piece of Gage was empathetic. He didn't mark Adriana as a bad person.

"Adriana," he said, turning her chin so she was facing him. "I can help you. Talk, please."

Sheriff had been lying between their feet but sat up at the sound of her cries. Adriana massaged his scruff as she spoke. "After you first came to the rental office to look for an apartment, a man came to me and offered me money to move in near you…to get close to you. He paid me to tell him what you were doing…to report on when you came and went. That's why I steered you to the secluded duplex."

"Who was he?" Gage asked.

"I don't know who he was."

"Tell me what you remember about him," Gage commanded.

"He was nice at first but then, when he came back and I told him no, he threatened me," she said, seeming to be on the verge of crying again. "He told me he'd bring other men, savages, who would rape and kill me if I didn't cooperate. Then he changed very suddenly, smiling when he told me I could be paid 500 Nuevo Sols a week for getting close to you and reporting on what you were doing."

Gage touched her hand. "Did he say why?"

"No," she cried.

"Was he Peruvian?"

"Yes, I'm almost positive he was from Lima. He was very slick. He drove a nice car and wore expensive clothes."

"When did he approach you?"

"Right after you first came in…then he came back the next day. He came back a third time after you came back from the east."

"Did he only have you tell him what I was doing? Did he want to know about anyone else?"

Adriana's face contorted as she began to sob, shaking her head at the same time. "Just you."

Though Gage knew the next answer, he wanted to hear her say it. "Adriana…what else?"

"He had me…he had me put a tiny transmitter in your clothes so they could track you." She broke down. "And that's when you broke your arm. I know it's my fault and I'm so sorry."

"You're *sure* he was a local?"

"Almost positive," she sobbed. "And each time he came to me I would see him call someone right after. And now he's been calling and trying to find you."

"When did that start?"

"Earlier today."

Despite the fact that she'd spied on him, Gage believed everything she'd told him. Whoever the man had been, he'd used intimidation as his leverage. How could she have said no? Purposefully softening his demeanor, Gage reaffirmed his grip on her hand. "I'm not angry with you, okay? But I want you to come with me. We're going to a motel room and you'll stay there till I tell you it's all clear."

"How long?"

"Days."

"But I have to go out. I have things I have to do. I have class."

"Not for a few days, you don't," he said with an emphatic shake of his head. "You're going to wear a big hat and big sunglasses to conceal yourself, and you'll take the dog outside and stretch your legs for a few minutes each day. Nothing more."

"Who was he, Jeff?"

"I don't know yet."

"Am I in danger?"

"Grave danger," he said bluntly. Something occurred to Gage. He changed his tone as he asked, "Adriana, why did you act the way you did, last night?"

She lowered her head.

"Did that man tell you to sleep with me?"

"No!" She looked away as she spoke. "I was just…well, I was sorry…sorry for what I'd done to you. And…"

"What?"

Adriana turned to him. "After spending time with you, after doing all the bad I'd done, I really just wanted to be with you. I like you, Jeff."

Embarrassed, Gage glanced around. "There won't be any buses this late." He eventually found a cab and had the driver take them to the motel. Ninety minutes later, after a trip to an all-night grocery store, Adriana and Sheriff were situated in the La Victoria motel. It was after 3 A.M.

Gage walked downstairs to the office, showed the clerk his key, and told him he wanted to prepay for three more days. The sleepy clerk didn't even question Gage about his name. The clerk took Gage's money and tapped a few strokes into the computer.

That done, Gage found another payphone and called Hunter.

"You're all set," Hunter said. "I'd like to tell you it was tough, but since your Gregory Harris I.D. is actually connected to a military I.D., pulling a few strings with the flyboys was a piece of cake."

Gage thanked the colonel and told him he would call with an ETA sometime tomorrow. Then Gage headed back up to the motel room. Adriana was sitting beside Sheriff on the bed.

"Do me a favor, Adriana. Power up your phone."

*

ALFREDO NIEVES had been awake for nearly twenty-four hours straight. The American man he was working for had been insistent—fanatical, even—about locating the local gringo, Burrell. Alfredo hadn't known what to do, other than continue to harangue the girl, Adriana. And, for the balance of the day, she'd had no news. What else could he do? However, just as Alfredo had just begun to doze off after his second bottle of wine, his phone rang.

Aleluya!

It was Adriana. She was cryptic about the details but told Alfredo to hurry to a specific area of La Victoria. "I followed him," she said.

"Burrell?"

"Yes, and I don't know how long he'll be here!" Her voice trembled with excitement. "I'm hiding in the alley next to the Japanese restaurant."

"Sí…I know exactly where!"

Weaving, Alfredo rushed out to his rose-colored Cadillac and squealed the tires as he pointed the two-and-a-half-ton Detroit product toward downtown Lima. With all the wine, combined with a lack of sleep, he was in no condition to tail Jeffrey Burrell. But he had no choice, because Alfredo wanted the $5,000 bonus his American employer had promised him.

The Cadillac thundered toward the La Victoria district, weaving in and out of the sparse nighttime Lima traffic.

GAGE HAD GIVEN Adriana an explicit set of instructions. She was to meet Alfredo in the small alleyway directly across from the motel. Halfway down the alley were two dumpsters. Gage hid behind them, crouched in the alley's feculence. Adriana would tell Alfredo that Jeff Burrell was in one of the rooms of the motel across the street. She'd suggest they wait in the alley until the American showed himself.

And Gage would take it from there.

"Here he comes," Adriana said over her shoulder.

"Act excited but nervous. And no more talking."

Gage could hear the roar of the big V-8. He watched sparks fly as the colossal Cadillac bottomed-out, skidding onto the curb and past the alley. A crash followed. The engine of the Caddy was shut off, the resulting hissing sound followed by a torrent of Spanish curses.

When the curses ceased, Alfredo said, "Where are you?"

"Over here," Adriana whispered.

Gage watched as Alfredo unsteadily made his way into the dark alley. He was wearing a shiny purple suit. His white silk shirt was buttoned only halfway up his chest, the wide pointy collar resting over the lapels of the suit jacket. The getup reminded Gage of the leisure suits during his childhood back in the 1970s. Alfredo was rather small and, despite his disheveled and inebriated appearance, he fit Adriana's "slick" description to a tee.

"How'd you find Burrell?" Alfredo slurred at Adriana.

"I spotted him earlier and followed him there," she said, pointing to the hotel. "He's in one of the first-floor rooms near the end."

"Bueno," Alfredo said, trying to pat her on her butt. She backed away. Gage watched as the man fumbled for his phone. He swiped the screen one time before holding the phone to his ear. He was swaying so heavily he had to lean on the wall for support.

"Señor, sorry to wake you…oh, you were awake? Good news…I found him," Alfredo said proudly, speaking accented but fluent English. "He's in a motel here in Lima." He listened for a moment. "Before I tell you, I want the money sent by Western Union." Alfredo's face contorted as he pointed at the phone. "Go to hell, *cojudo*! Not another word until I get my money."

He covered the phone and switched to Spanish. "You're absolutely positive Burrell is in there?"

"Absolutamente."

Gage eased away from the dumpsters.

Alfredo lifted the phone to his ear and stared at the hotel. "Listen to me or I'm hanging up."

Gage was in motion.

"This will probably be your only chance to get Burrell, señor," Alfredo hissed into the phone. "As I've said repeatedly, he's a slippery—"

Gage whipped his good arm around Alfredo's throat, pulling the little man backward. Alfredo's phone clattered to the ground as his white patent leather shoes elevated six inches above the grime of the alleyway. Unable to use his left forearm as a lever, Gage wrenched Alfredo several times, seeking the best angle with his right arm. Gage was eventually able to grasp his left upper arm and apply enough pressure to restrict the blood flow to Alfredo's brain.

Adriana stared wide-eyed.

When Alfredo was unconscious and limp, Gage lowered him to a seated position, leaning him against the wall. Gage gave Adriana the signal for silence. She nodded. Gage lifted Alfredo's phone, holding it to his ear.

"—the hell is happening? What's all the commotion? You there?

C'mon, Alfredo, dammit…don't play damned games with me! I'll get you the money but I need that fucking location!"

Falco.

Fighting the urge to levy a warning that would make Falco shit his pants, Gage decided to play it smart. He dropped the phone to the ground and, like he'd done with his own phone, smashed it with his boot. Then Gage lifted the already stirring "Alfredo" and found his keys.

"Here," he said, tossing the keys to Adriana. "Assuming it's drivable, move his car a few blocks away and come straight back to the room."

Spinning Alfredo around, Gage held the little man nose-to-nose and growled, "You make a sound…you die. Understand?"

"Sí," Alfredo replied, nodding enthusiastically.

Gage hoisted the little man over his shoulder and carried him to the motel room, fireman-style. A lone man in the parking lot looked curiously in their direction. Gage purposefully staggered and sang a drunken tune as he carried his "friend" up the stairs. The person seemed unfazed by what he saw as he cranked his car and drove away. And Alfredo remained quiet the entire time, hanging limp over Gage's back like a shiny purple possum.

So far, so good.

NOW THAT GAGE had confirmed it was Falco who'd hired Alfredo, things began to cement into place in Gage's mind. But before he could do anything about it, he needed to clean things up on this end. After patting him down, Gage wrapped Alfredo's mouth, wrists and feet with duct tape and placed him on the bed closest to the bathroom. Thus far, Alfredo seemed content to lie there while Sheriff bathed his face with licks and kisses. Adriana arrived within five minutes, telling Gage she parked the Cadillac five blocks away.

"There was steam coming from the engine," she said.

"It'll quiet down as soon as it cools," Gage replied, shooing Sheriff off the bed.

"What about him?" she asked.

"If I remove that tape, will you keep quiet?" Gage asked Alfredo in Spanish. "And, before you answer, I know you threatened this lady with rape. Screw with me once, just a little bit, and I'm gonna come up with an extremely creative, and painful, way to end your life."

Wide-eyed, Alfredo nodded. Gage yanked the tape off, noticing a few dots of blood on the man's lower lip.

"Thank you," Alfredo gasped, breathing in huge lungfuls of air.

"Who was the man on the phone?"

"I don't know his name and I've never seen him."

"Never?"

"I swear. He pays me through Western Union."

"What does he call himself?"

"Mister Smith."

Gage narrowed his eyes. "How did Mister Smith find you?"

"Through another man I've done work for."

"What did Mister Smith initially hire you to do?"

"When he first called me, he told me about a man—you—coming to Lima for a job. He told me to follow you and to devise a scheme to track you anywhere you went. That's how I came across her," Alfredo said, cutting his eyes to Adriana.

"What else?"

"After I'd set Adriana up with you, Mister Smith told me you were going away for a while and to relax. Then, a few weeks later, he told me you were back and that's when I gave her the tracking device to put in your clothes."

"How did you get the tracking device?"

"He shipped it to me."

"Where did it come from?"

"The U.S., but I didn't note the return address."

"You're sure?"

"Yes."

"What else?" Gage asked.

"That was all, until today."

"What happened?"

"Mister Smith…he went crazy insisting I find you. He offered me five thousand more dollars to track you down."

Gage produced his folding Tanto knife, flicking the blade open. He didn't have time to mince words with this little prick. Pressing the blade into the soft nerve area behind Alfredo's right ear—raising a pinhead of blood—Gage said, "This is your final chance to tell me everything, or I go digging for brain."

Alfredo began to cry. "I've told you everything, señor! Mister Smith hired me to follow you and track you. Everything else, planting the tracking bug…her," he said, glancing at Adriana, "were of my doing. I swear, señor, anything else I tell you will be a lie."

"What about threatening to bring men to rape Adriana?" Gage growled.

"It was just to get her to cooperate, I swear! I would never hurt a woman. I have two daughters."

"You have two daughters, but you intimidated this lady with savagery."

"I'm sorry." He turned his glistening eyes to Adriana. "I'm truly sorry…please…I needed the money. If you'd have resisted I'd have just moved on."

Gage eyed Adriana. She rolled her eyes and nodded.

"Stop crying," Gage said, pulling the knife away from Alfredo's head. "I sure hope no one's looking for you, because you won't be going anywhere for quite a while."

"What do you mean?"

Adriana looked at Gage. He nodded. She stood over Alfredo. "It means you'll be staying here with me. And if you give me the least bit of trouble…" She lifted the pistol Gage had given her.

"No one will be looking for me," he said, smiling weakly. "My wife left me and I only get my daughters two days a month."

"Friends? Clients?" Gage asked.

"This is my only job at the moment." Alfredo smiled obsequiously. "I promise to be a good guest." On cue, Sheriff jumped on the bed beside his new friend and began to lick Alfredo's face.

Adriana turned to Gage and curled her lip. "How many days will you be gone?"

"At least two or three."

She closed her eyes and rubbed them, muttering Spanish curses.

WHILE ALFREDO snored cheap wine fumes on the bed, Gage began his travel preparations, starting with the buzzing of his hair. He'd purchased battery-powered clippers at the grocery's pharmacy, allowing Adriana to do the honors. Gage decided against shaving it to the skin, feeling his scalp would be too white and it wouldn't look natural. The job only took a few minutes as Adriana used a "two guard," leaving him with a quarter-inch of hair. Nodding his approval in the mirror, Gage retrieved the brand new hand saw from the bag.

This part was going to suck.

At 4:35 A.M. Gage set the blue, waterproof cast on the sink. He wiped his sweaty right palm on his shirt. Though his broken wrist had begun to feel marginally better when elevated, the day's activities had taken their toll. His wrist currently throbbed and Gage knew it would soon get worse.

Much worse.

He lowered the saw to the wrist joint area, eyeing the cheap saw's teeth as they rested over the cast they would soon bite into.

"Don't do it, Jeff," Adriana said, holding the door jamb for support.

"Got to." Gritting his teeth, Gage's right arm went into motion. Sawing. Sawing. Levering. Sawing. Wrenching. Sawing. Tugging. Sawing.

It took twenty agonizing minutes to remove the cast. Adriana helped with the last part, spreading it open while Gage cut the last little stubborn connection. He'd only nicked himself a few times and, thankfully, the bruising wasn't so bad.

But the wrist hurt like hell.

His entire body covered in sweat and dust from the cast, he took a cold shower and settled in for two hours of sleep.

Closing his eyes while his arm throbbed, Gage did his best to put his mind at ease. Adriana kept her distance, staying on the other side of the bed. In the other bed, Alfredo continued to snore as Sheriff had nestled in next to him.

When the alarm went off after what felt like mere seconds, Gage swallowed four Advil and chugged a full bottle of water. He dressed and stepped into the bathroom as he prepared to leave. Seconds later, Adriana opened the door to the small bathroom and apologized for the trouble she'd made for him.

"It's okay," Gage replied. "I'm the one who started the trouble by taking this ridiculous job."

"Still…I want you to know I'll stay here and wait on you even if it takes you two weeks."

"Thanks, Adriana. I'll be back before that."

Her eyes went to the floor. "You don't like me."

Gage lifted her chin. "I do like you. I'm just not ready for a relationship. I've been honest with you about that."

"What if I hadn't betrayed you?"

"It's not about that at all. I'm honestly not mad at you and I know you had no choice."

Her lips trembling, she attempted to smile.

"You'll feel better when this is all over," he said.

Gage finished gathering his things and gave Adriana precise instructions on what to do, including no phone calls and leaving the Wi-Fi feature of her phone and iPad off. He left plenty of money for food and, if necessary, more nights in the room. Then he woke Alfredo, threatening him again.

"She will slice off your balls if you make a peep," Gage said, pointing a finger at the man's midsection.

Alfredo's arms and feet were still bound. He managed to give dual thumbs up. "I promise, señor, I will be an asset to her. Just wait and see."

Gage bade Adriana and Sheriff goodbye, carrying his items to the motorcycle. After dropping it at the rental facility and sliding the keys into the night drop, he took a taxi to the back side of the airport.

After showing his fake Gregory Harris credentials, he was told to wait at the main gate. The military personnel would be along shortly.

Chapter Eighteen

YEARS AGO, an Air Force pilot lamented to Gage about a group of people the pilot had termed "MAC rats." Back then, MAC stood for Military Airlift Command. That acronym had since changed to AMC, Airlift Mobility Command, probably so some junior congressman could brag that he'd changed a good acronym to a poor one. According to the pilot, MAC rats were military retirees who did nothing but hop MAC space-available, or space-A, flights all around the world.

AMC space-A flights are open to active duty personnel and their dependents, to government officials, to military retirees and a few other narrow segments of governmental society. Regular AMC routes are available all over the world. Some of the more popular routes are Travis AFB, in California, to Hawaii; Joint Base Lewis, in Washington to Christchurch, New Zealand and Joint Base Charleston, in South Carolina, to Rota, Spain. From what Gage remembered, popular routes like these were often teeming with qualifying personnel, so many that a priority list was often formed. In true military fashion, there was a hierarchy involving delineators such as official duty, rank and so forth. And once all of the passengers had boarded by hierarchy—official business, active duty and dependents with orders—the retirees traveling the world on Uncle Sam's nickel were finally granted access, among them the grizzled old MAC rats.

While Gage had never officially met a MAC rat, he remembered the pilot's lamentations over them. "They just won't freaking shut up!" the pilot had complained. "Flying on our birds is their life. They never take into account that, while they're hopping all over the world, I'm at work on that airplane. I'm doing my job and it's not all fun and games. All I want to do is step down into the cargo bay and stretch my legs while having a cup of joe and, before I get two sips in me, I've got some crusty old retired master sergeant with a scraggly beard latched onto me, asking, 'dude, where's the coolest place you've ever flown to? Ever declared an emergency? Ever caught any old timers with a joint on them? Know any mind-blowing locales I should hop to next?'"

So, as soon as Gage was escorted out to the ready-to-depart C-17, he immediately began to pepper the loadmaster with questions. As they boarded the C-17, the loadmaster finally found a pause to speak. He briefed Gage on the basics, laconically informing him that he was the only space-A passenger for this flight.

"You got this whole area here, okay? You can stretch out and snooze once the seatbelt light goes off. You can take a leak at the john there," he said, pointing. "You can walk anywhere you want between those two yellow lines," he said, moving his fingers to the painted stripes on the cargo deck. "I'll have some coffee going in a bit. Otherwise, just stay in your area and enjoy what should be about a seven-hour flight to Charleston."

"You think the pilots will let me come up on the deck?" Gage asked, showing a toothy grin.

"No, sir. That's against regulations. Now, if you don't mind, I really need to—"

"I flew to Guam last month. Hot as hades. Been there?" Gage asked.

"Yeah. If you don't mind, I need to go up and brief—"

"Gonna try to catch a hop into Africa after this trip. Think my best bet'll be to get to Ramstein and wait it out. What's the best place in Africa to go where I won't get assailed by kids lookin' for a handout? Any ideas? I'd like to see some elephants and giraffes and crap like that."

"No idea," the loadmaster snapped. "Not to be rude, but I *have* to work. We have a departure window we have to hit. Stay *inside* the lines. Good day." He stormed away, shaking his head as he headed for the flight deck.

Gage suppressed a grin, certain that he'd just bought himself a guaranteed seven hours of peace and quiet. He craned his neck to the flight deck, seeing through the small elevated window as the loadmaster crouched between the two pilots, going over paperwork. Gage was certain the loadmaster was warning both pilots about the MAC rat, or whatever the modern term was, that was currently infesting the cargo hold.

All alone in the belly of the cavernous aircraft, Gage stepped from his seat and surveyed the cavernous interior of the transport aircraft. C-17s are extremely large, especially in terms of girth. Unlike an airliner, where passengers are relegated to the space at the top half of the fuselage, the C-17 has only one large cargo compartment. This allows the operators to take on incredibly large loads, including an M-1 Abrams tank. Painted mostly light gray, the interior of the big bird had non-skid floors and olive drab webbing everywhere. Two rows of seats were installed for this aircraft. Gage lifted the arm rests on his row, happy that he'd be able to stretch out and get some sleep.

Earlier, when he'd been escorted to the airplane, the loadmaster had expressed surprise that Gage had managed to get on this flight. "We had six space-A flyers on the way down, but they told me they were staying in Peru.

We don't usually get space-A *out* of an abnormal locale like this unless it's one of the embassy workers or someone that rode down with us."

"What were you guys hauling down here?" Gage had asked.

"Normal embassy stuff," the loadmaster had replied. "We even brought them a brand-new black Yukon. Sweet ride. Those embassy pukes get all the nice gear."

"You carrying anything back?" Gage had asked as casually as possible.

"Very little. They're sending a couple of pallets of paperwork that'll make its way back to D.C." They'd been approaching the big airplane. "Also got a couple of pallets of MREs. Embassy sent 'em back. Their Marines probably've gotten spoiled, eating fish tacos from the locals."

Gage made a sour face. "MREs? They still make those things?"

"Unfortunately."

And that's when Gage had begun his irritating ruse.

Once his gear was stored, he eyed the cargo of the C-17. The pallets were wrapped in heavy plastic and secured by more of the olive drab webbing. The forward two pallets were the ones Gage had seen last night—the MREs—with the telltale yellow tape around each one.

Gently flexing his throbbing left hand, Gage plopped down in the seat and lightly buckled his lap belt. He occupied himself by reading, trying to keep his mind from racing. Fifteen minutes later, the loadmaster came by and gave Gage a quick safety brief which wasn't too unlike one a person might hear on a civilian airliner. He also offered Gage some orange foam earplugs, which Gage readily accepted.

Before long, the C-17 was roaring into the late morning sky over Lima, Peru. Although the sound inside was deafening, even with the earplugs, Gage lay down to rest.

Or, to *pretend* to rest.

He turned his head to the two pallets, eyes wide as he stared at them. Even Gage had to admit that packaging cocaine into MRE packets was ingenious. Especially when Nuestra's distribution system was the United States Air Force. Carrying MREs wouldn't even cause a raised eyebrow.

A diabolically clever scheme.

IT WAS NEARLY noon when Sonny reached Abi Mikkelsen's home. He'd hoped to arrive earlier but the traffic had been snarled down by the Plaza Norte. Since Sonny rarely drove, he didn't know the good shortcuts to take.

Despite being late, he believed he would find her at home, especially if her schedule was still as rigid as it had been back when he'd had her under full-time surveillance. An early riser on work days, Abi typically awoke later on her days off. If the weather was nice, she'd take her breakfast out on the back porch, surrounded by the lush vegetation of her steeply sloping back yard. According to the investigators, she preferred yogurt, fresh fruit and a single cup of black coffee while she read either the newspaper or a nonfiction book.

Afterward, as was her habit, Abi would normally engage in a long run. Occasionally, she would do plyometric exercises in a local park or, if the weather wasn't pleasant, she'd bisect her run with a stop at her health club where she would train alone. Abi typically finished with a jog back to her home, where she'd arrive anywhere from mid- to late-morning. While she was normally unseen during the lunch hour, she would head back out during the traditional time of siesta and do any number of things from errands to solo sightseeing to renting a small airplane and flying for a few hours. Her evenings were typically marked by a takeout meal at home and, often, another run.

In the end, an incredibly predictable woman.

"One who really needs to get laid," Sonny whispered as he pushed a breath mint into his mouth. He didn't believe what Sil had intimated about Abi—that she was screwing the new guy, Burrell. But Sonny was a critical thinker, even when blinded by a piece of ass. And it was entirely possible that he just didn't want to believe it.

So, today he intended to find out the truth. And if she was screwing Burrell, she probably wouldn't live to see the sun set. If she wasn't screwing him, then Sonny planned, one way or another, to introduce Abi to Sonny Jr.

Reminding himself that she was skeptical and oftentimes a cold fish, he rehearsed his lines one final time. Satisfied, Sonny exited the Nuestra company car and slid the nifty CZ Kadet silenced pistol into the rear of his trousers. He nearly buttoned his suit coat but decided against it, since the loose fabric would better conceal the small pistol loaded with rimfire hollow points. He hoped he wouldn't have to use it. Following a steadying breath, Sonny lightly climbed the stone steps that led to her tidy hillside home.

He rang the bell and straightened his tie in the reflection of the glass, mildly disturbed with himself that he was growing somewhat "excited."

He waited. Rang the bell again. Nothing.

Murmuring curses, Sonny turned his head both ways, glancing up and down the steep Indepencia street as if he might see her coming or going.

Had he known where to look, he might have spied Abi. She was across the street and above him, her right eye directly behind the adjustable sights of a Japanese assault rifle.

*

IT HADN'T BEEN critical that Gage stay awake during the entire flight. There wasn't much he could do on the C-17. In fact, he felt this entire trip back to the U.S. might turn out to be a fool's errand. Once he arrived in Charleston and been shuttled off the plane, it would likely be impossible for him to track the pallets. And he wasn't even one hundred percent sure that the pallets contained cocaine. So many variables. But, despite his lack of sleep, he was unable to even doze as the loud aircraft droned on.

Several hours into the flight, Gage watched as one of the pilots, a rather young-looking captain with dark skin and a shiny shaved head, came down into the hold to stretch his legs and relieve himself in the broom closet latrine. Gage closed his eyes to a squint, pretending to sleep. After coming out of the latrine, the captain glanced at the snoozing passenger before pouring a Styrofoam cup of coffee and heading back up to the flight deck.

Fifteen minutes later, the other pilot, this one a major, climbed down and followed the same routine. Coffee in hand, he strolled through the hold, walking slowly by Gage. Gage made sure his jaw hung slack as he allowed the requisite spittle to drool from his mouth. When the major had passed, Gage turned his head and watched the pilot reach the MRE pallets. The pilot glanced back at the flight deck and then he touched the webbing that covered the pallets, caressing it like he might a woman.

Bingo.

Gage stirred, sitting up and rubbing his eyes. By the time he was standing, the major was already heading back to the flight deck. Stretching, Gage stepped from the seats and, mid-yawn, said, "Hey there, major, you the pilot of this big buzzard?"

"Uh, yeah," the major said, trying to sidestep Gage and make it back to the privacy of the cockpit.

"Hang on," Gage said, affably, hoping to learn a little something about the pilot. He was approximately Gage's size but only in average shape. He had pale skin, green eyes and, like Gage, a closely shaved head—except the pilot had what looked like reddish hair. He looked to be in his mid-thirties. Gage was also able to tell that the pilot was based in Charleston, today's destination, due to the patch showing the 437th Airlift Wing. Over the pilot's heart was his nametag, displaying his name as Wolfe.

Major Wolfe the drug smuggler.

"You fly all over, don't you?" Gage asked.

"Yep. All over."

"How come y'all go way down to Lima, anyway? I'd been down in

South America for months and was tickled pink when my wing-wiper buddy stationed up at Eglin emailed me that there was a hop comin' down."

The major's shoulders sagged as he realized he was now trapped into answering. "You'd be surprised where we fly. Regular spots, typically, but we occasionally head out to just about anywhere."

"So, you live in Charleston?"

"Yeah." He started to edge away.

"I was TDY there, once. Too bad you're married, with all that young tail runnin' around. There's a college there."

"Yeah, I know, and I'm not married," Major Wolfe replied. "Enjoy the ride and excuse me, I've got to get back up there and run a checklist." The major didn't wait for a response.

Gage watched him go. After the door to the flight deck was shut, Gage stood by his seat, continuing to stretch. With great pain, he lifted his broken left wrist and twisted it to sharp pains in both directions. He wondered how he was going to pull this off.

Upon taking his seat again, Gage pushed up his left sleeve, rewrapping his wrist tightly with the stretch bandage.

Nothing to do now but wait.

He turned and eyed the MREs, recalling how Wolfe had caressed them.

ABI'S NEIGHBOR across the street was away at work. His quiet home had provided Abi an excellent vantage point. In the hundreds of days she'd studied her neighbor, a bank manager, he'd never once come home early. He lived alone and, judging by the visitors he occasionally entertained on weekends, he preferred the company of men over women. Due to his predictability and lack of a sophisticated security alarm, Abi had scoped him one day as he disarmed the alarm pad at his front door. This morning, when she'd broken in his house through the rear, she punched in the five-digit code, satisfied when the system beeped once and had since remained silent. Abi then hastily departed to hide in a nearby copse of tropical plants. She waited two full hours but the banker still didn't come home. She'd been cautious that his alarm company might have sent him a text that his system had been disarmed. Many of the better systems did that type of thing. But after two hours and no banker, Abi pronounced the home as all clear. She'd then gone inside and made her preparations.

This entire chain of events was due to an inkling Abi had that Sonny would come see her. After their tense conversation, Abi reasoned that Sonny would watch the video of the clinic exchange between her and Jeff Burrell, the man she now knew to be an imposter. And, due to slowly escalating tensions between her, Nuestra and even her own Alta Seguridad people—and the fact that she wouldn't give herself to Sonny—Abi predicted an intervention of some sort. Sure enough, she learned that Sonny and Sil took a Gulfstream joyride last night, and that's when Abi guessed they were discussing what to do about her.

Abi had never liked Sil. He was a weasel who would do anything to save his own skin.

Minutes before, even Abi was surprised to see Sonny boldly exit the company car with a silenced pistol on his person. What the hell did he take her for? Was he just an arrogant man who thought, just because he built a drug empire, that he was all of a sudden a skilled urban warrior?

Gently cinching the 5.56 millimeter rifle a tad closer, Abi thought about the ramifications of gunning Sonny down on her own porch. It wouldn't take the authorities long to realize where the shot had come from. To her knowledge, she'd left no trace in the banker's home, but she could have dropped a hair from the blonde mane she rarely let flow freely. Doubtful, but certainly a possibility. When questioned, the banker would insist she'd never been in his home. If Abi retained a skillful lawyer, she would argue that the hair probably came into the house via the banker's shoe, picked up out on the street that Abi regularly jogged. Despite the alarm having been disarmed—because there would be no proof who disarmed it—such a defense was reasonable and, without any other concrete evidence, would probably allow her to walk.

However, this was Peru, not Denmark. The culture here was far more misogynistic, and a woman on trial for shooting a man might be viewed by a mostly male jury as a way to retain their dominance through a guilty verdict.

And, on the other hand, what if someone had seen her entering via the back door? Abi had no alibi, nor anyone that she'd trust to cover for her. She made these calculations, and more, in less than five seconds. Abi knew there were numerous other permutations of evidence that might conspire against her.

Her verdict: this was neither the time nor the place. She'd learned enough about Sonny's intentions to craft a far more elegant plan to dispatch of him.

Sonny walked back to the company car, glancing around again before he removed the pistol from his pants and tossed it onto the passenger seat. After executing a three-point turn, the tires on the underpowered company car chirped as he sped away. Abi gave him five minutes to double back. He didn't return.

Satisfied she could now leave, she placed the Howa Type 89 rifle back into the guitar case, rearmed the alarm, and let herself out the back door. Abi took the service road two houses down the hill before cutting through the alleyway back to her own street. She removed her surgical gloves, tucked them into her pocket and made her way back up to her own house. After loading the guitar case into her personal car—leaving the Alfa Seguridad Ford Focus at her house—she quickly grabbed her emergency bag, her stash of cash, her purse and two bottles of water. As she departed her house, she wondered if she'd ever see it again.

Abi drove away, pondering her best course of action. The first involved leaving Lima today, right now. The odds of Sonny Calabrese, or Sil—or the entire team—coming after her were fifty/fifty.

Someone would be coming.

The second option, one she didn't much care for, involved killing Sonny assassination-style. While gunning down the former Air Force PJ on her porch was fraught with complications, Abi felt confident that, with a day or two of planning, she could execute the Nuestra founder neatly and quickly in an anonymous fashion that would look like the handiwork of any number of worldwide assassins. At that point, the rats would scurry from the sinking ship. There'd be no more of an evil eye on her than on anyone else. And once the authorities discovered the dirt Sonny had been into, there'd be far less pressure to find his killer. The cartels would most certainly be suspected.

Still, Abi knew Sonny was somehow mixed up with American military officers—Air Force officers. In her mind, the American officers were the wildcard. She didn't need the most powerful country in the world as her enemy.

Abi felt that there was a third option – something in between the first two – but she needed time and space to figure out what it was. For a start, she felt that she needed to get in touch with the man whose real name was Gage Hartline. Abi also reminded herself not to underestimate Sonny in the coming hours. Despite his twisted ways, he was quite intelligent. If she'd figured out that Burrell was Hartline, then Sonny might find out, too.

If he hadn't already.

Her immaculate false identification in her purse, Abi drove to the Callao area and left her personal car parked in a busy lot. She took a taxi to Playa Waikiki, where plenty of blonde-haired, blue-eyed women, just like her, roamed the streets and beaches this time of year.

She secured an oceanfront room at a mid-level hotel, ordered room service and set about her planning.

*

THE WEATHER IN Charleston, South Carolina was a stark contrast to what Gage had grown used to in Lima. While Charleston typically experienced mild winters, this late afternoon was one of the coldest of the year, according to the civilian escort from the AMC passenger terminal. The sky was low and gray and the winds strong. The escort had met Gage in a golf cart. She was wrapped in heavy clothes and a scarf, telling Gage to stay warm as she drove him and his bag across the tarmac to the modern AMC Passenger Terminal. From there, Gage would have to take a taxi to the rental car facility. He lingered, trying to view the C-17 he'd just hitched a ride on. He couldn't see it from the runway-facing windows and he was unable to go back out onto the tarmac. Because of that, he wouldn't be able to see how the C-17's cargo was handled. Ten minutes later, Gage departed Charleston AFB in a taxi, making his way to the rental car facility several miles away.

Once he was inside an anonymous black Chevrolet, Gage found a coffee shop with free Wi-Fi and connected his iPad while enjoying a strong cup of java and a banana. It took him twenty minutes to finally locate Charleston-based Major Wolfe on the Internet. When he did find him, the fact that Wolfe's first name was Brody—a fairly unique name—helped with subsequent searches. Gage learned all sorts of things, most of them having to do with Wolfe's love of flying and fishing. In fact, he probably relished being stationed in Charleston, given the multitude of fishing opportunities he had in the surrounding rivers, bay and ocean.

Though Brody Wolfe's address wasn't listed in the white pages Gage searched, he eventually found what he hoped was his current address on a website advertising fishing charters. It seemed that Major Wolfe owned a 28' fishing boat, "perfect for bachelor parties, wedding parties or just a day of fishing and drinking beer." Wolfe had even given his boat its own page, displaying eight photos of the handsome craft. Gage highlighted the make and year of Wolfe's boat, doing another Google search—he found the same boat, used, selling for prices between $1.1 and $1.4 million. Gage let out a low whistle. Major Wolfe would have to be taking out a shitload of charters to make that monthly nut.

Or he'd have to do something else to supplement his income.

From his time in the military, Gage knew that pilots sometimes had things a bit easier than the common soldier—at least in regard to schedule. Though cargo pilots had an extremely demanding job, they often received a fair number of days off per month—but only because they had to fly round-trips to places like Afghanistan and Japan, leaving them gone for three and four days at a time. Trying to give the man credit, Gage assumed the major would have enough time to take out seven or eight charters a month. Maybe more. And, for all Gage knew, he might have people working for him who captained the boat when he wasn't around. Perusing the website, Gage found a gallery page.

In almost every picture, Major Wolfe could be seen at the helm or posing with his customers and their catch. Gage didn't see any photos of other employees. Though Gage had never even paid a mortgage, he knew enough to know that a person would pay a higher interest rate on a boat than they would a house—and probably do so in a shorter term. Looking it up for confirmation, Gage estimated that Wolfe's minimum monthly payment on the boat was around $7,500—assuming he'd not had a wad of cash for a big down payment. That's far more than an Air Force major could afford, unless he was doing an incredible charter business.

Then it hit Gage—having a fishing charter operation was the perfect cover, the perfect way for Wolfe to launder illegal income. Gage assumed that Wolfe flew to Peru occasionally, perhaps even exclusively. Maybe pilots had a bidding system that allowed him to be priority for that flight. Or, maybe Wolfe's commander was in on things.

Gage reminded himself that this entire bit of conjecture could be way off base. Maybe Wolfe actually did make a great living with these charters. Or maybe his parents had died and left him with enough money to buy that boat. There were any number of possibilities.

One of the photos on the website's gallery displayed a red-faced Wolfe helping two fishing buddies hoist a massive wahoo. Behind them, a bevy of beer cans littered the deck of the boat. Wolfe's green eyes gleamed in the photo. There was something in those eyes, a trace of guile, that cemented Gage's feelings: Wolfe was dirty.

After writing the major's charter address on a napkin, Gage flipped the cover shut on the iPad. "Screw it," he whispered to himself. "It's not like I'm going to kill him."

He tried the fingers of his left hand, sucking in a whistling breath due to the jagged bolts of pain he still felt. He'd need to find a pharmacy first—the wrist was a potential problem.

MAJOR BRODY WOLFE was one of four venal Air Force pilots who smuggled Nuestra's cocaine from South America. He suspected the other pilots' existence, but didn't know for sure. Anyway, he was too busy to care. In his rather complicated life, Wolfe served several masters, and served them well. First and foremost was his boat, his true passion. For twenty years, since he first piloted an airplane at the young age of fifteen, Wolfe had dreamed of owning his own airplane. At first, before his tastes grew more refined, he simply wanted a small Cessna to jaunt about like a carefree bird. Then, during flight school, the cadet dreamed of someday owning something a bit larger, like a Piper Seneca. And, just a few years ago, shortly before he'd begun running cocaine for his commanding officer, Wolfe's tastes had drifted to something far more advanced, like the Extra EA-500, so he could fly his buddies cross-country to Vegas for a few days of decadence.

But all that had changed when Wolfe had been stationed in Charleston and, on a whim, had rented a boat to take out into the harbor. It had been just after his wife had left him, after she'd found out about the nasty little affair he'd had with a civilian contractor while TDY in the south Pacific. After that sleazy period of his life had ended, Wolfe had been reassigned to Charleston AFB, vowing to live for himself and no one else. He quickly learned that boating rounded out his desires, especially since the flying portion was obviously covered by all the stick time he received with his day job. And since he'd been promoted to major, his life and schedule had grown a bit easier. He was usually able to get leave when he wanted it, and had more say in the routes he flew.

All that led back to his fishing boat and charter business. To Air Force pilot Major Brody Wolfe, there was nothing quite like taking a group of rowdy men out on a fishing trip. As the captain of the boat, he was already the de facto alpha male. But once his charter guests learned he was also an Air Force pilot, their male admiration always transformed to a form of hero worship.

Wolfe had all the tricks down pat. Take them out, get them rip-roaring drunk, find a few fish, then troll back up the Ashley and dock the boat at one of Charleston's numerous waterfront bars, where the women were often as drunk as his guests. While each trip was roughly the same, it rarely grew tiresome. And when the long day was over, Wolfe didn't even maintain his boat or have to clean up—he paid someone else to do it for him. By the time he arrived for the next charter, his service company had taken care of everything. His baby was serviced, gassed up and sparkling clean.

Ah, the good life.

Wolfe had just completed his three-day shift and was staring three days off squarely in the face. And the cold, hard cash on the seat next to him warmed him better than his GMC's heater. He viewed the low, gray clouds and the whipping wind carrying palm fronds skittering over the street. Yes, the weather was bitterly cold today—and depressing. But before he'd left his squadron, Wolfe had checked the latest met-data. Tomorrow would be an improvement and the day after was an indication of why so many northerners had migrated down south. The February 25th weather forecast called for blue skies, light winds and a high of 74 degrees. Happy at the prospect of the coming spring-like weather, Wolfe cranked his radio up as he wheeled into his rather affluent neighborhood, all done in stucco with palmetto trees and fine landscaping.

The very good life.

Wolfe didn't have a charter to take out this week, so he planned on calling in one of his standbys. His current flame—or, more accurately, fling—was the wife of an Air Force tech sergeant. That poor sap was currently deployed to Afghanistan and his young, not too bright wife was sitting home all alone. The only thing she had to occupy her time, other than Wolfe, was her job waiting tables at the Mount Pleasant sports bar, which is where Wolfe had met her. And damn if she didn't love his boat. Who wouldn't?

Wolfe chuckled as he thought about his boat's name, *Living Dangerously*. "Well, I am," he said aloud, winking to himself in the rear view mirror of his late-model Yukon.

The big SUV thudded as he whipped into his slightly elevated driveway. He had to brake rapidly because, for whatever reason, his electric garage door wasn't going up. Cursing, Wolfe continued to press the button on the rear view mirror. After jamming the selector in park, he opened the glove box and found the original garage opener—the one he'd programmed into the Yukon's convenience system. Aiming it at the garage, he continued to press the button.

"Piece of freaking shit," he grumbled, jangling his keys as he hurried down the walkway to his front door. Wolfe suddenly halted, walking back to his SUV and retrieving the small rip-stop bag from the passenger seat. No sense in taking chances, even for a minute, especially when he had twenty grand in cash in there. Despite his irritation over the automatic garage door not working, the weight of twenty grand felt damn good swinging in his left hand.

Two years ago, after being stationed in Charleston, Wolfe made his first two "MRE trips" in the fall. Last year, Wolfe had made five "qualifying" trips to South America. This year, he wanted six, or more. He'd have to work the colonel pretty hard to get it—if six was even possible. Pressure, as Major Wolfe knew, is a fantastic motivator. He'd been spending more than he'd made since the divorce. And this cash in his hand—it probably weighed five pounds—would tide him over for forty-five more days.

Wolfe keyed the door, an idea occurring to him. He'd invite the colonel out on the boat. Surely Wolfe's paramour had a slutty little friend she could bring along for the colonel. That'd do the trick. Get him out on the water and send him down to the cabin with a little waitress who didn't mind giving him some extra service.

The familiar smell of home greeted Major Wolfe as he walked into the entrance hall. He tossed the bag on the nearby sofa and walked around the corner to the door that led to the garage. He flipped on the light and yanked open the door, immediately seeing something out of place.

Squarely in the middle of his garage was some sort of wire rigging and, beneath the rigging, his short stepladder. Wolfe didn't have much of a chance to consider the peculiar scene, however, because he suffered a sharp blow to the back of his head. He wasn't even conscious as he fell forward, smacking the cold concrete of the garage floor and losing a canine in the process.

Chapter Nineteen

AN IMMEDIATE jolt of consciousness flooded into Major Brody Wolfe's brain, not unlike the bright pre-dawn barracks lights that were often flipped on during his time at the Air Force Academy. However, this sudden consciousness wasn't only the irritation of a rude interruption to his slumber. No, this one involved pain. Sharp, distinct pain inside Wolfe's mouth. He bit down instinctively.

"Ah, ah, ah," a voice admonished. "Too late."

Surprisingly lucid, Wolfe recalled the blow to his head. Whatever pain remained from the strike, however, was defeated by the agony in his mouth. Probing with his tongue, Wolfe felt the hole where his canine had been. He also felt something cold and metallic on the right side of his mouth, up near the gum line around his molars. It was accompanied by an awful, stabbing pain around his cheek. His eyes were blindfolded and his hands were snugly bound behind his back. He tasted blood.

"Aghh!" he yelled, the sound modulated by an excruciating tugging on his cheek.

"Stand up, dipshit," came that voice again, the same one that had admonished him. "If you'll just get up, you'll release the pressure…for now."

Wolfe staggered to his feet, tugging at the binds that held his arms.

"Listen to me," the calm voice said. "I'm *not* going to repeat myself. Stand there and don't yell, and you won't get your cheek yanked off your face."

"Who ah ooo? Whad ah ooo oing?" Wolfe sounded worse than he did when the dentist loaded his mouth with Novocain.

"I've jabbed one of your big fish hooks through your cheek. I've threaded it with some of your fishing line that's supposed to be good up to four hundred pounds. And, after I disconnected your garage door, I looped the fishing line over the door rails. You with me?"

"Liiiee?"

"Hang on…I can't understand you." The tension abated slightly. "There. Try that."

"Why are you doing this?" Wolfe asked.

"Because you're a piece of shit drug smuggler."

Wolfe froze. Despite his panic, he didn't breathe for several moments.

"Yeah," the man said. "I know."

Taking a few deep breaths, Wolfe attempted to think clearly.

Well, he's not a cop, that's for sure. If he was, I'd be under arrest. So, who is he? I'm just a middle-man…the guy who moves stuff from point A to point B. Why would he be interested in me and, more important, how does he know? According to the colonel, only a handful of people on the planet know about this operation.

"Thinking it through, aren't you?" the voice asked. "Wondering who I am…how I know…why I'm doing this."

"Yeah, I am," Wolfe said, adding a touch of attitude to his slurred voice. "Let me go now and I won't call the cops."

Silence. Long silence.

Wolfe tuned his ears. He couldn't hear a thing. Did the man leave? There'd been no footsteps.

"You still here?" Wolfe asked.

There was a slight scraping sound followed by more silence. Then there was a tug on his cheek before Wolfe was nearly snatched off his feet. He shrieked. The hook was pulling his cheek straight up. Wolfe tilted his head as far as he could and stood on his tiptoes, doing everything possible to alleviate the pressure.

"I wouldn't yell, if I were you," the voice chuckled. "If someone calls the cops, I'll be long gone and they'll find the note I left them inside the front door."

Wolfe ceased his shrieking, realizing he was whimpering like a puppy. The tension quickly ceased. "What note?" he cried, angry with himself for blubbering so quickly.

"I left them a note telling them about the drugs you just smuggled from Peru. You know, the cocaine hidden in MREs. I also told them about the money you've got in that little flight bag in the entrance hall. They'll put your dumb ass in jail forever. The queens at Leavenworth will just love to add an emotional flyboy to their harem."

Wolfe sobbed. His captor allowed it.

As the major again calmed down, he willed himself to think through the situation. When faced with an emergency, a pilot should never panic and never freeze. Both reactions can create or exacerbate already deadly circumstances. Major Wolfe forced himself to adhere to the same principles right now. *Don't panic, and don't freeze. Just calm down and think this through.* He steadied himself.

"What is it that's yanking my cheek so hard?"

"I found some weights out here in your garage. I attached a ten-pounder." The man paused for a moment before emphasizing the words he'd just spoken. "Did you hear me? A measly *ten* pounder. Imagine what's going to happen when I really add some weight."

"Okay," Wolfe said, still sticking to his principles. "You obviously want something from me. What is it?"

"You're recovering well, major. Good job. And, yes, I *do* want something."

"Money?"

"No. I don't want your drug money that you financed that boat with, smuggling in coke that kills people and destroys families."

Wolfe could hear his own pulse. *Ba-boom. Ba-boom. Ba-boom.* "What, then?"

"I want you to fill in some blanks for me."

"I can do that," Wolfe agreed.

"I already know a great deal, but I'm not going to clue you in about anything I know. So, make sure you remember that some of the things I will ask you will be solely to test you," the voice said. "Dick with me *one* time and I'm going to rip your mouth wide open. And then I'll just hook the other cheek and start over." A pause. "And if you think I'm blustering, just try me."

Wolfe felt himself sweating all over. His underwear was warm in the crotch. *Did I piss myself?* Whoever this guy was, he was very serious and very scary and Wolfe believed his every word. Still, Wolfe also felt he needed to get some sort of concession, anything, just to get the ball rolling. "Okay, mister, I believe you. But before I talk, I want you to release the weight."

"I'm barely pulling on it."

"Still…it hurts."

"Why should I?" the voice asked, amused.

"If you don't, then I'm *not* cooperating."

The line yanked and Wolfe screeched again as fresh blood flooded his mouth.

"Go ahead, keep yelling," the man said, releasing the pressure.

"Okay! Okay! Okay! I'll tell you anything you want to know. I just…I just thought you'd hear me better if you released all the tension."

"Now, see," the voice remarked, "that was a much better way to request a little mercy. I'll slacken the line…for now." All tugging suddenly ceased. "There. Ready to chat?"

Taking huge breaths, Wolfe swallowed a few times, clearing his mouth of excess blood and saliva. "Yes."

"What did you smuggle on that flight from Lima?"

"You said cocaine. I honestly don't know what it was but that's what I've always assumed."

"It *is* coke. How many trips have you made?"

"That was my eighth."

"How much per trip do you make?"

"Twenty grand."

"So far, so good, major. Who else in your flight crew is in on things?"

Wolfe pulled in a deep breath. "No one...that...that I'm aware of."

"Are you sure?"

"I swear! I've never spoken about it to my crew."

"Is it always MREs?"

"Yes."

"Don't people get suspicious that the embassy in Peru is always sending back MREs?"

Shrugging, Wolfe said, "I don't think so. Do you realize how much cargo flows through Charleston?"

"What happens to the coke once you get to Charleston?"

"It's usually transported elsewhere on another flight."

"Where?"

"You name it. Wherever we fly. Look, mister, I'm paid to fake the paperwork in South America, then get the stuff here and that's it."

The man paused. "Who do you work for?"

The blood in his mouth was suddenly accompanied by acid. "Mister, if I tell you that..."

"You're a dead man?" the voice asked, sounding amused. "Want to guess what happens if you delay for another breath?"

"Colonel Guidry," Wolfe said quickly. "He's the wing commander."

Wolfe heard a long, low whistle. "The wing commander's that dirty, is he?"

"Yes."

"How'd he approach you?"

"What do you mean?"

"Why did he pick *you*?"

"I'd had a few reprimands along the way. If he'd have wanted to, he could have ended my career."

"You were vulnerable, so he approached you."

"Yes. I could have lost my flight status and been booted from the service."

"So, you're a piece of shit all around, in other words."

Wolfe swallowed. The trickle of blood had slowed. "Yes."

"Tell me how the entire flow of this smuggling operation works."

"I don't know much, which I'd assume is by design. When we get flight schedules, and I see Lima, La Paz or Quito on mine, then I know it's probably a run. Within a few days, the colonel finds me and we talk, always in person."

"About what?"

"He just makes sure I'm still cool. He's pretty jumpy about things."

"Who else is in on it?"

"Obviously someone, but I have no earthly idea. None. He's compartmentalized me."

"Are there more pilots involved in this?"

"If there are, I don't think they come out of Charleston."

"Who's behind the drugs?"

"In Lima?"

"Yes."

"I have no idea."

"Who do you suspect?"

"I truly don't know. I fly there, spend one night, sometimes two, and fly back. All I know is the MREs are always at the cargo hub with the embassy's items. I fake the paperwork to match what's in Lima's paperwork and fly it back."

"Does anyone in your crew know?"

"The flight crews always change so I would assume not."

"Ever seen those MREs get sniffed by drug dogs?"

"Yes, and it scares me every time. Whoever packages them must know what they're doing."

"What's your cell phone number?"

"Why do you want that?"

"I'm so close to snatching that cheek open."

Wolfe relayed the number two times.

"Good. In the next seventy-two hours, if you see a number call you that you don't recognize, you'd better answer the phone. If I call you and you don't pick up...your asshole is going to hate Leavenworth."

"I'll turn the ringer all the way up and keep the phone by my side."

There was a long pause.

Then Major Wolfe heard the man step closer. "Let me explain something to you, Wolfe. When I leave here, you resume life as you knew it. If you tell Colonel Guidry, or anyone else, what happened today, I'll know. I *will* come back for you, and that's a promise, buddy boy."

"I believe you. I swear."

"Make up something about your cheek and your tooth."

"I will," Wolfe said, nodding eagerly and feeling a jolt of pain.

"When's your next drug run?"

"None scheduled."

"Then just get back to being the piece of shit you are, got it?"

"Yes."

"You know something, Wolfe? You make me sick. You took an oath. You're supposed to serve our country."

Wolfe didn't respond. He heard the clicking of something being wound.

"This timer will go off in ten minutes. When it does, you can get yourself loose."

"How?"

"You're a pilot. You must be somewhat intelligent. Figure it the hell out. But not till you hear the timer. I'm gonna be inside for a little bit and if I see you so much as tugging at that rope around your wrists, your cheek is coming off."

"I understand," Wolfe replied, again crying involuntarily.

True to what he'd been told, the timer buzzed ten minutes later. About ninety minutes after that, when he'd finally freed himself by sawing the ropes that bound his wrists against the metal housing of his lawn mower's blade, a shaky Major Brody Wolfe removed his blindfold and entered his house, guzzling a glass of water. As he did, relieved that his cheek didn't leak water, he noticed the faint aroma of smoke. It only took a moment to find out why.

On the low hearth of the fireplace he rarely used was the rip stop bag he'd carried the money in. And inside the once-clean fireplace was a small pile of ashes.

The money.

Major Wolfe lay on the floor in front of the fireplace, his mouth hanging open with no sound coming out. He desperately needed that cash. Twenty minutes later, as he remained on the floor, nearly catatonic, he wondered if he'd know who his assailant was.

AFTER LEAVING Major Wolfe's house, Gage headed back to Joint Base Charleston via Dorchester Road. He could use his fake retiree credentials to get back onto the base but, after just a moment's thought, he decided to pull into the Visitor Control Center. There, he should be able to casually gather a little more information on the wing commander, Colonel Guidry. Gage knew from experience that military visitor centers usually displayed pictures of the chain of command along with nifty bios for each person. Guidry's bio might provide critical information.

Gage eased the rental car into a parking space, having to use his right arm to hold the door against the whipping wind. Earlier, he'd gone by a pharmacy for a reload of Advil. He'd also purchased a Velcro wrist splint, which he tightly secured around his left wrist prior to his interrogation of Major Wolfe. Fortunately, everything had gone to plan and his wrist actually felt decent provided he kept the splint nearly tight enough to restrict bloodflow. As Gage crossed the small parking lot, he watched a C-17 roaring into the sky, the big craft buffeted by the northerly gusts. He entered the warm visitor's center, earning an obligatory smile from a young airman behind the desk.

"Help you, sir?" the young man said, standing.

"Just flew in on an AMC hop and wanted to look around."

"Anything in particular you want to know?"

"I've never been here before, so I'm just looking for info on Charleston."

"We have several kiosks with information," the airman said, gesturing around.

"Thank you."

"Please let me know if you have any specific questions." The airman sat down and turned his attention back to his mobile device.

Other than the attendant airman, the Visitor Control Center was empty. To the right, a flat-screen television ran a promotional video on a constant loop. Someone had muted the volume. Behind the television was a mural displaying a combination of Air Force photos and images from Charleston. An action photo of a C-17 was superimposed next to the famed Charleston Battery. Airmen running morning PT were shown next to the Cooper River

Bridge. There were pictures of beaches, festivals and stately southern mansions. The Air Force emblem dominated the center of the mural. Gage walked to the other side of the center.

Closest to the door was a recruiting table with all manner of pamphlets and brochures, explaining to the youth of America why the Air Force was the choice for them. Gage quickly thumbed through a few of the items. He moved to the right, toward the restrooms.

Bingo. On the short hallway that led to the restrooms and two snack machines was the Joint Base Charleston Chain of Command. Shown there were the base commander, the base command chief, and the numerous commanders of the various wings and detachments. Gage shuffled to the right, eyeing each one until he reached the commander of the 437th Airlift Wing.

Despite the many critical situations Gage had encountered in his life, very few times had he felt truly shocked. The last time he experienced klaxons in his mind, coupled with springs of sweat and knee-buckling panic, had been in Germany, when he'd learned his French enemies had found Monika's location. And that had turned out in the worst way possible.

So, standing in the short hallway, as a female airman exited the restroom, Gage had to lean against the back wall for support. The airman stopped and eyed him curiously.

"Sir, are you okay?" she asked.

Gage managed to nod and struggled through a very fake smile. "Fine, thanks."

She nodded, frowning at the same time as she walked on and took the seat next to her fellow attendant, who was still engrossed in something on his mobile device.

Gage staggered to the nearby water fountain, gulping water before letting it splash all over his face. He lifted his shirt, mopping the water away before walking back to the photos. He stared into the green and yellow crocodile eyes of the 437th wing commander.

A pilot…

The deeply tanned skin. The tight mat of gray hair…

Gage knew him.

Gage was, in fact, working for him.

Falco.

*

SONNY LISTENED to the computerized voicemail of Abi Mikkelsen's cell phone. It had picked up immediately as if her phone were turned off. Earlier today, after striking out at her house, he'd had a discreet private detective— one of the private detectives who had followed her before—break into her Independencia home through the back. The private detective quickly reported back to Sonny that she was not there, but the company car was in the garage.

Abi Mikkelsen had disappeared.

He then had the private detective search for Jeffrey Burrell. Same story.

Sonny's unease grew. Something was going on but, for whatever reason, he didn't fully subscribe to Sil's version of the story.

Reclining on the lawn chair next to his heated pool, Sonny lit a Cohiba and puffed thoughtfully. Though the cool had blown in with the evening, he was overheated from his activity in the artificially warm water. Pedro appeared, averting his eyes from Sonny's nakedness.

"Shall I prepare your table, señor?"

"I'm still not hungry. Maybe in an hour."

"Very well."

"Pedro?"

"Yes, señor?" Pedro answered, turning.

"What do you do when you have a feeling, a gut instinct that something is badly wrong?"

Pedro frowned in thought. "If it's serious, for instance something involving my family, then I thoroughly gather all the facts before making my judgment."

"And then?"

"Once I have all the possible facts, I make whatever suppositions I have to. Then I deal with the problem."

"Very well, Pedro. On the patio in one hour."

The dutiful servant dipped his head and walked away.

Knowing he was wasting time, Sonny snapped his fingers and spoke Spanish. The two women in the pool, one of whom was splayed on a float, ceased their activity.

"Knock it off…I've got work to do."

"But we've only been here an hour," the one in the pool replied.

"Pedro's got your money up at the *casa*. Get your shit and go."

Eyes shooting daggers, the two women gathered their bathing suits and sulked to the house. Sonny didn't even look at them. He was leaning back in the chaise, smoking and staring at the stars. Though he was perfectly still, his mind whirred at high RPM.

HOURS AFTER making the Falco discovery, Gage sat in a corner table at a nearby Mexican restaurant, the type that offer an endless supply of chips and salsa. He'd eaten—quite a bit—and still absently nibbled on chips as he scribbled on his yellow legal pad with a red pen. The polite server came by, refilling Gage's unsweet tea for about the tenth time.

"No more, thanks," Gage said, waving his hand over the glass. "I promise I'll get out of here soon and leave a nice tip." He looked around. There were still a few patrons eating and drinking. Massaging his left fingers with his right hand, Gage reviewed his notes.

Colonel Troy Guidry's biography—Falco's biography—listed him as having graduated from the United States Air Force Academy. The Air Force Academy's mascot was the Falcon. Cute. Guidry had served all over the map, spending a great deal of his time in Texas and Japan. Gage found nothing else pertinent in his bio other than the fact that he appeared to be single. All of the other biographies mentioned spouses and/or children. Before he'd departed, Gage snapped a photo of Guidry and his biography.

The Mexican restaurant had wi-fi, and Gage used it to try to ascertain Guidry's address. Thus far, he'd been unsuccessful. Earlier, when he'd first gotten there, Gage called the 437th Airlift Wing and asked for Colonel Guidry. Gage told the person on the phone he was Colonel Enright from McChord.

"Sorry, sir, but the colonel is on leave for the next week."

"Damn, that old buzzard didn't tell me that. Me and the wife are gonna be in Charleston this weekend. Did he say he was leavin' town?"

"Yes, sir," the youngish sounding lieutenant answered dutifully. "But he didn't say where he was headed."

"Driving or flying?"

"Uh…"

"C'mon, son, he and I were at the Academy together."

"He was flying, sir."

"Flying himself or taking a hop?"

"Neither, sir. He flew commercial. I know because he was griping about the restrictive flight schedules."

"But he didn't say where?"

"He didn't tell me but I'm sure he left that information with the command at the Eighteenth Air Force."

"Thanks for your help, son. Just leave him a message that I called." Gage hung up. Since the call, he'd been hypothesizing about all that had happened since he'd first accepted the job.

At the top of his first page, Gage had devoted a section to his "boss," Colonel Guidry A.K.A. Falco—the man behind the Air Force smuggling operation. This meant, obviously, that Falco worked for Sonny Calabrese. That was now known. But what Gage didn't know—for sure, anyway—is why would Falco hire Gage to *kill* Sonny Calabrese?

Option 1, in Gage's mind, was pretty straightforward. Falco actually wanted Sonny dead. Gage didn't think it had anything to do with the families of the Alfa Seguridad deceased. They were unknowingly part of Falco's ruse. Perhaps Falco wanted to take over Sonny's operation. Or maybe he owed Sonny a tremendous debt. Or perhaps he just wanted out, and killing Sonny was the only way. Regardless, in this scenario, Falco's intentions were essentially genuine—minus the revenge for the families.

Gage made a side note. He wouldn't be surprised if Falco planned to take money from the wealthy DeLand family, despite deceiving them. Gage scribbled a reminder to try to find out.

Option 2 indicated a grand ruse on Falco's part. The families, the hiring of Gage, the killing of Sonny Calabrese—all of it complete bullshit. The only objective in this mission was to interest Gage enough so that he'd take the job and get hired. Then, Falco's local contact would facilitate a method to get a tracking bug in Gage's clothing. That tracking bug would lead Falco's hit team to the ambush site where they'd steal many millions of dollars in cocaine. If Option 2 truly were the plan, Gage wondered how Falco planned to kill him? He'd have to. But Gage doubted this was the plan, unless the shipment was worth a fortune.

How much was the Manolo shipment worth? Gage scribbled.

While Gage believed Option 2 was far more realistic than Option 1— mainly because he had no idea how Falco could assume command at Nuestra—Gage also felt there could be plausibility in a combination of the two options. Perhaps Falco wanted to make a run at a single shipment of cocaine. Perhaps he aimed to do this several times in a row before Gage would eventually kill Sonny. It made sense. Kill the dangerous golden goose, but only after you've managed to snag a few of its priceless eggs.

Gage turned on the wireless feature of his soon-to-be-discarded mobile phone and dialed a number. It rang twice.

"Yes?" a voice trembled.

"Wolfe. You do know who this is."

"Y-y-yes."

"Why doesn't your boss just steal those pallets?"

"Steal them?"

"Why doesn't he take them when they arrive here?"

"Impossible. He couldn't do that without getting caught. And I'd also guess that whoever packages those MREs down in Peru wouldn't be okay with it."

"Why couldn't he just take them? I think they're worth enough that he could disappear afterward."

"He couldn't get away with it," Wolfe answered. "Years ago we used to bring back all sorts of things. Pineapples from Hawaii. Beer from Germany. But they cracked down on that after several shipments of drugs were found, unrelated to South America, and now U.S. Customs is extremely stringent about items that get pulled upon arrival."

"Then how can those MREs clear Customs as a genuine shipment?"

"Because they're in the system and they don't get as much scrutiny. But if someone tries to transport pallets of personal belongings, it gets searched in a major way, just like my own flight bag. Believe me, I'd know how to do it if it were possible."

"Wouldn't a wing commander have more sway?"

"He'd have to have people on the inside at Customs, but those people rotate constantly. I don't think it could be done and he would know that."

"Very good. That's all for now," Gage said. "Keep this phone on."

"Why did you burn up my—"

Gage ended the call and turned off the wireless. After a moment's thought, he left a generous tip and paid his bill at the cash register. Outside, he sat in his car pondering his next move. He thought about calling Linda DeLand, the mother of the dead Navy SEAL. But that wouldn't do him any good. She was on the up and up and had been deceived by Falco. Another option was to fire up Falco's iPad with encryption and send the sonofabitch a message that he was quitting and, oh by the way, he knew who Falco really was. Come after me, Falco, and you're dead. Go to ground – you're still dead. How do you like that?

Gage pondered that one for a few minutes.

No.

Falco had gone to Lima. Gage would bet his life on it. When Gage had disappeared, along with Adriana and Alfredo, that had turned Falco's little plan upside down, and now the bent Air Force colonel was headed down to try and clean up the mess.

Gage thought back to the ambush, back to the pricks he vowed to take down. Sil. Ortiz. Desgreaux. They'd all turned on Gage, and the Cajun had enjoyed it. That trio, along with Sonny Calabrese, needed to be exterminated. Gage was indifferent about Griffin, the Marine; he actually liked Dinkins, the former Ranger.

So Gage had to go back, because he had to liberate Adriana and Sheriff, who were holed up in a dinky hotel room with Falco's bagman.

Then there was Abi Mikkelsen—what to do about her? She'd saved Gage's skin at that ambush. Gage sort of liked her but didn't know which side she might take.

How could he get back to Lima quickly? He investigated commercial flights. The earliest flight wouldn't get to Lima until tomorrow night. Then he'd have to deal with customs, a taxi…

Worst of all, if Sil and Desgreaux had gotten wind that Gage had left, they could very well be watching for his return.

There is another way…

Squeezing his eyes shut, Gage gritted his teeth. If he played this card, he knew he was going to get roped in for another long stretch.

I've got no other choice.

There were four cell phones in Gage's bag. One was his normal phone—he hadn't used it in weeks. The second was the phone he'd used regularly in Lima. It was powered down. The last two were burners, one of which hadn't yet been used. Gage powered on his normal phone and made an international call to a satellite phone. It was morning where his previous boss was currently located and he couldn't have been chippier.

As Gage had predicted, the former credit card executive drove a hard bargain. He wished Gage luck in whatever his South American endeavors were and told him he'd see him on April 1st.

That done, Gage checked his watch and called Colonel Hunter. After Gage's litany of apologies, he asked the retired colonel a pivotal question.

"Would you want to fly to Peru with me?"

"Are you kidding?"

"No, sir."

"When?"

"Before sunup."

"For what?"

"A takedown, sir."

"A takedown," the colonel said flatly. "Of whom?"

"The group I was hired to work for."

Hunter whistled. "That all?"

"No, sir. We'll also take down the man who hired me."

"Why not just leave it alone?"

"Because I don't think they'll leave me alone."

"Are you asking me to come because you're hoping I will participate?"

"Absolutely, sir."

Hunter was quiet for a moment. "Is there a plan?"

"Nope. Just a hit list. I was thinking we could do our planning on the airplane."

"How many damned connections to Lima?"

"United has a direct from Houston."

"Yeah, but they don't have a direct from Fayetteville. I'll have to connect through Dulles or drive to Raleigh."

"No, you won't."

"Why's that?"

"Because we're flying on a private jet."

Hunter snorted. "How'd you pull that off?"

Gage told him.

"Hell, I was about to say no till I heard that. Will they feed me a ham sandwich?"

"I'll make it myself and even cut the crust off."

"I'll have to make up something to tell Alice."

"You can manage."

"When do we leave?"

The jet would depart Fayetteville Regional Airport at 0900.

Chapter Twenty

AS THE PRIVATE jet carrying Gage and Hunter crossed the equator on its way to Lima, Falco was already there. Gage had been correct—Falco had rushed to South America as soon as he'd heard about Gage's abrupt departure. In fact, when he was unable to raise his local contact, Alfredo Nieves—part private eye, part common thief and soon-to-be-dead-man if he didn't answer his phone—Falco had just finished ransacking Gage's duplex, along with Adriana's. The Air Force colonel found nothing useful in either domicile and was mildly panicked that neither of them seemed to have been there for several days. After flirting with the notion of torching the dilapidated old converted house, Falco thought better of it before speeding away on the BMW motorcycle he'd rented from the specialty dealer.

If he had time, he'd get the woman's previous address and see if that's where she was. If he found her, he'd brace her. But that couldn't happen until after his next meeting.

With his potential new partner.

The meeting was scheduled to take place in the city, at the famed Monastery of San Francisco. Since today's weather was due to be sunny and warm, the plaza and surrounding grounds would be teeming with sightseeing tourists along with locals from the nearby office buildings. Falco guided the motorcycle to a spot next to several rows of bicycles. Despite the warmth, he wore his leather riding jacket which nicely concealed his Walther P99. There were ten minutes remaining before his meeting.

Falco didn't trust this bastard at all—hence the meeting in such a busy place. If this man had gone to Sonny Calabrese after Falco's call, this meeting could quickly turn into an ambush. Falco could wind up dead or, if Sonny used his local influence, arrested by the police for all manner of trumped-up charges.

But Falco needed a new partner. The Air Force gravy train would be ending in less than six months. When Falco had received his mandatory retirement notice, he'd called in every favor he could think of. But there was no grace this time. He'd stepped on too many people on his way to making colonel, and when he'd been awarded the 437th, that's when some of his peccadilloes had come to light. Falco's boss, a fighter jockey who'd come up the hard way, despised him. And while no one had zeroed in on the cocaine trade, Falco knew it was widely rumored that he was dirty and on-the-take from some unknown source.

A few months ago, when Falco learned his retirement was imminent, he crafted a plan. He'd heard Sonny brag about the value of each shipment— ten to twenty million. He also knew Sonny's organization was top-heavy. Falco had spent some money on biographies of all of the players, and none seemed worthy to approach. The man Falco would meet today had been the best of the bunch, but Falco had chosen to go the other route, hiring Gage Hartline to lead him to the ambush.

And to kill Sonny Calabrese.

By killing Sonny, Falco was beheading the snake. In his estimation, the threats at Alfa Seguridad and Nuestra would go away. Sonny was the dangerous one. But before Falco killed him, the plan had always been to steal a shipment of product. And Falco had known that Hartline wouldn't get a shot at Sonny before he'd even been on a mission. According to what Falco had learned, Sonny waited at least a year before revealing himself to Alfa Seguridad personnel.

But with Sonny gone, Falco wasn't even ruling out the possibility of rebuilding this scheme under his own control. With all his Air Force connections, Sonny would have never gone for it. With Sonny gone, Falco knew he could bribe a new wing commander. It would just take a great deal more money than Sonny would have been willing to pay.

Falco thought back to the connections he had to this upcoming crime. The lawyer, Josephson, had been the one who'd reached out to all the families of the dead. But he'd been paid off and was probably thrilled to be free of the situation. And Falco's pilots could certainly "out" him, but why would they? They were just as dirty as he was. If they ratted, they'd be implicating themselves.

The only wildcard was Hartline. Where the hell was he? If Falco and his new partner could come to an agreement, having Hartline out there causing problems wasn't an option. He had to die, and quickly.

Hartline couldn't learn who I am, could he?

Falco shook his head. No. There's no way.

Regardless, he needed to be erased, post haste.

So, as the late-morning sun baked down on the noisy *Plaza Basílica y Convento de San Pedro*, Falco walked inside the monastery's public hall, crossing the broad stone floor to the main cloister. As he walked, he heard two American tourists anxiously awaiting the monastery's noon tour of the skeleton-filled catacombs. Passing into the cloister, the transformation seemed mystical to Falco, due to the abrupt quiet and tranquility. While the public was forbidden from entering this area, Falco had scoped it out yesterday evening after his arrival. Provided he was respectful, he didn't think anyone would disturb him. He moved through the cloister, sitting on a shaded bench in the green garden. No one said a word to him.

That's where he sat now, his new Walther tucked under his right thigh. He'd purchased the handgun last night—from an underground vendor— along with a few other items. All it had taken was a trip to the bad area of town and the flash of cold hard cash. The gun was locked and loaded and, despite the holy setting, Falco would use it without hesitation. In fact, he had his escape route, along with two alternates, burned into his mind.

A check of his Rolex Submariner. High noon.

Across from him, at the side of the cloister, the heavy wooden door creaked open. A shadowy figure stood in the doorway, scanning the cloister before focusing on Falco. Falco nodded. The shadowy man stayed perfectly still for a moment. Falco eased his hand under his leg, prepared to come out with the pistol.

The door creaked again, pushed open farther as the man stepped into the dim light of the shaded, Romanesque arcade. He wore utility pants with a matching shirt. His richly tanned pate shone, as did the silver pistol emerging glaringly from under his belt. The short, wiry man walked with an elegant confidence and, as he approached Falco, his blue eyes displayed absolutely nothing. His was a bona fide poker face.

Without invitation, Silvan "Sil" Zobrist sat next to Falco.

"Put your hand where I can see it," were Sil's first words, spoken softly with only the slightest hint of Swiss-German accent.

Falco obeyed.

"Where's your phone?" Sil asked.

"Out at my motorcycle."

Sil reached into his breast pocket and retrieved a device that looked like a small iPod. He touched the screen and placed it on his knee. The LED display showed green.

"What's that?"

"Scans for electronics. I'll know if you try to record me or send any type of signal."

"Cute," Falco said. "But I'm on the straight and narrow here."

"Who are you?"

"Like you, I work for Sonny Calabrese."

Sil displayed no emotion.

"And this entire operation, Nuestra and Alfa, is soon to come to a violent end."

"Why do you say that?"

"It will. Believe me."

Sil didn't respond.

"Before it does, I propose that you and I work together."

"How?"

"I propose we work together to steal a shipment of Nuestra cocaine." Falco grew silent, waiting on an answer.

"Why did you contact me?"

"After studying each team member, I felt you were the best one to join me. And I need a partner with your knowledge because I don't know the particulars on how the drugs are handled from ambush to packaging."

"Mister, I don't know what you're talking about."

"Sure you do, Silvan. And based on the recent weights of each shipment and the premium nature of the cocaine itself, I think you and I could *clear* ten to twenty million dollars from a single haul."

"I still don't know what you're talking about."

Falco rolled his eyes before counting facts off on his fingers. "Silvan Zobrist, Swiss by birth and former member of Switzerland's esteemed *Fallschirmaufklärer Kompanie.* You've been a gun-for-hire for decades now, and you're wanted for several murders in Colombia and Ecuador—thankfully for you, the Colombians and Ecuadorians don't know your true identity, but they do have pictures of the killer. You also have a child in Colombia who you don't support. Aside from the authorities who are seeking the murderer, I'm sure the mother of your son, and her four well-armed, Cartel member brothers, would love to know where you are." Falco made his smile fleeting. "Now, can we stop with the games, Sil? I know all about you, Alfa, Nuestra and the theft of cartel cocaine shipments."

Sil glared at Falco. "Theoretically, if everything you just said was true, how do you intend to steal the cocaine?"

"That's for you and me to figure out. And as soon as it's done, you'll kill Sonny."

Sil's voice was sharp. "Kill Sonny Calabrese?"

"Lower your voice," Falco said, looking around. "Yes. After stealing the shipment of cocaine, you will kill him immediately. Surgically."

"You think those around him will just stand by and let that happen?"

"I've thought about that at length. I know all the players, Silvan. I know Calabrese, Mikkelsen, Dinkins, Griffin, Desgreaux and Ortiz."

"You forgot one."

Falco chuckled. "No, I didn't."

"You did."

"Burrell?"

"Yes."

"He's no player, Silvan. He's your fly in the ointment."

"Not anymore. He quit."

Falco closed his eyes and shook his head. "He may have quit the team, but he's here. He's the problem. He's the reason everything is about to come crumbling down."

"Who is he?"

"Before I tell you, I want to know if you're with me."

"I don't know who you are. I don't know what sort of means you have. Hell, you could be working for Sonny trying to set *me* up. It would be just like Sonny to do such a thing."

"I'm not working for Sonny. I have critical information that, when combined with your information, will tell us all we need to know."

"Tell me about Jeffrey Burrell," Sil demanded.

Two older nuns appeared through a creaking door. They crossed the cloister. One frowned at the two men but neither reproached them for trespassing. When the nuns had exited through the door Sil had used, Falco spoke.

"Burrell was my partner."

"Was?"

"The proposal I'm making to you...I made it to him. His name isn't Jeffrey Burrell but he is ex-special ops, a soldier of fortune. He came to Lima, got hired and gained trust. Then you, Silvan, took him on an ambush."

Eyes widening, Sil said, "Were you behind the hit team? The three trucks who tried to steal our shipment? Who tried to kill us?"

Decision time. Tell him or not?

"Well?" Sil demanded.

"Yes, I was," Falco answered. "Burrell didn't know about the hit. I misled him and used him to lead my mercenaries to the ambush. It was a failure, and I learned a lesson from it. And when Burrell realized what had happened, he quit working for me and for Alfa."

"You prick."

Falco shrugged. "That's why I've chosen you, Sil...a true professional. You know how to steal the coke. I know how to get it out of here."

"So, you tried to kill me and failed, but now you want to *cooperate* with me?"

"Don't take it personally."

Sil narrowed his eyes. "You said you work for Sonny, too."

"Yes."

"What do you do?"

"How are the drugs transported after they're repackaged?"

Shrugging, Sil said, "No one knows. The rumor is, the transportation component is the real genius of Sonny Calabrese."

"No. It's the real genius of *me*."

"Explain that."

"It's all done through the unknowing assistance of the United States Air Force," Falco said, pulling in a deep breath afterward. Though he didn't relay who he was, he explained how the drugs were shipped, giving Sil the broad strokes.

When Falco was finished, Sil turned to face the twin towers at the front of the convent. He gnawed the inside of his cheek, as if he were deliberating. "What about Burrell? You said he's going to wreck everything."

"He's pissed, bent on revenge. He's mad at you, at Desgreaux and at me." Falco raised his finger for emphasis. "Burrell has to die before we do anything."

"He's not here," Sil said.

"Oh…he's still here. In fact, I'll have his precise location within twenty-four hours," Falco replied.

"Your soldier of *mis*fortune?"

"He tried to screw me over, and now he's trying to do the same to you."

Sil counted off the elements of the proposal on his hand. "So, to sum up, you propose we rub out Burrell. Then we steal a shipment of coke. Then we kill Sonny?"

"Kill Sonny immediately after stealing the coke. Then we go to ground until all the pieces fall into place. After some time, maybe a year, we consider rebuilding Alfa in a much sleeker fashion and picking up where Sonny left off."

"Fifty-fifty."

Falco nodded. "An even split."

Sil extended his right hand. As they shook hands, Sil touched his left ear with his free hand, making an up and down scratching motion as the deal was sealed. He made sure his motion was clearly visible to the leftmost tower.

*

NINETY-TWO FEET above the cloister, at an easy shooting distance, Desgreaux clicked the safety lever on the L96 sniper rifle. He cursed in a mélange of French and English. Getting up to this ideal firing spot in the monastery's tower had been easy, but getting away after killing a man was going to be the fun part. Watching nuns and tourists scampering around in horror while some asshole with two tidy holes in his head did the death spasm was going to be a hoot.

But not today. *Beck moi tchew!*

Minutes later, the former Green Beret exited through the lower door that was supposed to be locked. In an impious manner, he licentiously winked at two nuns and sauntered away, the long pack on his back bouncing with his gait.

ALTHOUGH SHE despised him as a person, Abi Mikkelsen could have been accused of copying Desgreaux.

It had taken her considerable time to locate an office that met her standards. In full disguise—black wig, spray-tan skin, brown contacts and local attire—she'd searched precisely 38 floors of office buildings, cumulatively. There were three buildings in total that met her requirements. She'd eventually settled on a 60s-era La Victoria office building. The building was located behind Nuestra and the office she'd managed to break into had an excellent view of the rear garage entrance where Sonny arrived and departed.

Situated adjacent to Nuestra, and across the street, was the motel where Gage had scouted the cocaine and where Adriana and Sheriff were currently hidden. Abi hadn't even considered the motel for what she planned to do—it was too low and didn't offer enough privacy.

Now that she'd found the ideal sniping location, she had to figure out a way to get Sonny, her target, out of his armored car. She'd given some thought to this problem. Access to the garage was controlled by a barrier arm that raised if the car was equipped with a transmitter on the proper frequency. Having access to the entire Nuestra security system through Alfa's computers, Abi was able to change the frequency from her mobile device. Since only a few senior people used the small garage, she was able to manually raise the arm as they came and went. And when she wasn't here, she simply switched the frequency back to the correct one.

Abi was taking a gamble. When Sonny's driver approached the arm that wouldn't raise, he would probably get out of the car and walk to security. Abi gambled that Sonny, impatient man he was, would exit the car and walk inside. He wasn't the type to sit in the back of the bulletproof vehicle and wait.

And hopefully his bravado would be his undoing.

The shot was approximately 135 meters in distance—no big deal for Abi or her Howa Type 89 rifle. Fortunately, due to the age and construction of the building she was in, the windows slid up and down. Once the kill shot had been made, she'd simply close the window with her gloved hands, leaving no visible trace of where the shots came from. As she walked, she would change the security frequency back to the original and log out of the system. Abi knew the system's strengths and weaknesses—and while it was robust in its efforts to deter and record intruders, it did not track what its authorized users were up to. There would be no trace of what she'd done.

Due to the lack of surveillance in this office building, and Abi's meticulous precautions, if she could pull off the shot, she felt confident in her ability to escape everything other than a cursory investigation by the authorities. They would know nothing about the internal strife between her and Sonny. Provided Abi left no trail, she'd be fine.

She watched as a silver Ford Focus turned into the driveway from the street. Sil's Alfa Seguridad car. He approached the arm slowly, lighting a cigarette as he waited for the arm to go up. Abi sighted him, the reticle moving over Sil's tanned face. Once his cigarette was lit, he edged the Ford closer to the arm. She touched her finger to the manual button and watched as the arm elevated. Sil idled into the garage and disappeared.

Why is he here?

Abi set the question aside for later examination.

Her biggest question revolved around Sonny's absence. Where was he? It wasn't uncommon for him to have offsite meetings, but she usually knew if he was traveling – and to her knowledge, he wasn't.

She thought about the actual kill shot, assuming her plan with the "faulty" traffic arm worked. Her Howa was fitted with a modified M4 suppressor. It wouldn't silence the supersonic crack of the bullet, but with the echo from the buildings mixed with the considerable traffic noise, it would be difficult for even a prepared observer to determine where the shot had come from.

There were wildcards to this scheme, but Abi had categorized them as acceptable risk. This entire floor was currently unrented. What was the likelihood that a renter would come along in the next few days? And, whenever she did finally make the kill, what if she ran into someone during her hasty exit? Yes, she was in costume, but the police aren't stupid. Sooner or later they'd turn up a witness or two who saw a petite woman exit the building with a guitar case. Or perhaps a security camera would provide visual evidence. With few females on the suspect list, Abi would vault to the top of the Lima Police's most wanted.

But she wouldn't be here to answer any questions.

And, again, Abi was relying on the scandal of what Nuestra really was to remove the heat from the search. Eventually, the powers that be would realize she'd done the world a favor.

Unwrapping a sandwich, she settled in to wait for the balance of the afternoon. Sooner or later, Sonny would show himself at Nuestra. He'd curse the traffic arm, curse his driver and curse his shitty computerized security system. Then, still cursing, he would step from his bulletproof car to walk into the building.

And he'd die.

Chapter Twenty-One

SOMETHING WAS WRONG.

People could accuse Sonny of many things. They could say he was crazy, of course. They might call him a vicious, narcissistic psychopath and, in his estimation, they'd be wrong—but he could see why someone might say it. Other people might just say he was a peculiar asshole. But there was one thing people couldn't say about Sonny...

They couldn't say he didn't have incredible instincts.

And right now, flush with freshly wired-in cash after the Manolo deal, Sonny Calabrese had the distinct feeling that something was amiss.

Sitting in his home office, having just taken a call from *La Bruja*, letting him know that Sil had come to Nuestra looking for him, Sonny was struck with an incredible premonition. He crossed his office and stared out the window at the narrow strip of Pacific in the distance. Taking a Pellegrino from the fridge, he uncapped the sparkling mineral water and took a long pull, allowing the carbonation to sear his throat.

Sonny's first premonition revolved around the mysterious attack that occurred after the ambush. Before the ambush, he'd listened to Abi's concerns. Sonny had heard those concerns many times before and, up until the Manolo ambush, they'd never had any problems. In the end, the attack had been quashed. Now, Sonny's personal intelligence contractors were looking into the past of the dead members of the assault. Initial findings proved all of them to be local guns for hire.

And someone—probably someone Sonny *knew*—hired them. The originator of the hit would be found and dealt with in due time.

That's not why I'm worried.

So, what else?

It wasn't the Manolos. They had no idea that Nuestra was involved in pirating their drugs. In fact, Sonny had impeccable intelligence that the Manolos were currently embroiled in a bloody, three-day killing spree with members of their closest rival, the Garcia Cartel. That, in Sonny's mind, would eventually prove to be a mistake. In his estimation, there wouldn't be a Manolo Cartel much longer, once the Garcias marshaled their considerable forces that reached with long fingers into Bolivia and Ecuador.

258

So, what then? Where's this unease coming from?

Eyes roaming, Sonny viewed the ocean and the strip of beach he could see between the trees. He opened the door, stepping onto the patio and walking into the warm sun. It felt good on his bare skin. He heard a squeaking sound.

Around the corner, parked in the shade, was Sonny's gull-grey Mercedes limousine. One of the young kitchen helpers was polishing the hood of the car. Behind him, sitting in a chair, Pedro, Sonny's butler, watched languidly with a cigarette dangling from his delicate fingers. Parked next to the Mercedes was the company Ford Focus Sonny kept here for the staff.

Pedro started when he saw Sonny on the patio. "Señor! I did not know you were out here. Are you ready to go to work? Leon is nearly finished."

Sonny eyed Pedro, sitting on his ass again. "I'll let you know when I want to go somewhere, Pedro. And I suggest you wash and wax the car and let Leon worry about peeling potatoes."

"Of course, señor."

Smiling at the silent curses being mentally hurled in his direction, Sonny walked back to his office.

Something about the Ford Focus, the company car...

The company *cars*...

Sonny thought through the people with access to Nuestra and Alfa Seguridad cars. Might one of them have done something, some slight misrepresentation of their normal self—a twitch of the cheek, an extra tug on their beard, a slight aversion of their eyes—that set off a subconscious, suspicious receptor in Sonny's highly-attuned brain?

Two company car owners in particular pinged Sonny's radar. The first was Abi Mikkelsen. Her impudence, especially recently, had given him reason to suspect her of disloyalty. And then when Sil claimed she was banging the new man, Burrell...Sonny shook his head, not even willing to think about it.

What about Sil? What were his motivations? Why was he so keen to tell on his boss? And why had he just come to see Sonny at Nuestra? Something about his actions leading up to the private jet flight to Colombia, and on the flight itself, didn't add up. It was clear he wanted Abi Mikkelsen dead. Was it simply because he wanted to move up, or was there more?

Sonny straightened. Could Sil have been behind the hit attempt? Sonny thought through all the angles. Yes, it was possible.

You're not there yet. Don't jump to conclusions. Scrutinize. Be thorough. He took a deep and calming breath.

Everyone was aware—well aware—that during a time of unrest, everything and everyone was open to Sonny's investigations. Nothing was off limits. He walked to his desk, finding his British intel man in his contacts, dialing him. Tony picked up on the first ring.

"Tony, anything new on the dead men who tried to assault my people?" He nodded. "Fine. Keep looking. I actually called about something else. My company vehicles, they're all Fords and all quite new. Can those be tracked?" He listened for a moment. "I'm almost positive they have GPS units, but I don't know the first thing about any software or fleet-tracking we might have purchased. And I can't ask without tipping someone to my curiosity, get me?" He nodded again. "Yeah, I can get you VIN numbers."

Thankful that he was as familiar with the company database as he was, Sonny sat behind his desk and opened several computer folders, finally opening the folder that contained the lease information on the eight company sedans. He right-clicked on each VIN, copying them and sending the list to Tony Killian, the ultra-efficient, ridiculously expensive intel man based in Mayfair, London, England.

At the bottom of his short email, Sonny typed the following: *If the vehicles can be tracked, I want the past week's data on all of them, including addresses of stops, etc. I want this within the hour.*

Sonny clicked send. He leaned back in his chair, placing one hand behind his head and his bare feet up on his desk as he sipped his Pellegrino.

He hoped his instincts were wrong.

THE QUARTET SAT in a circle in the dingy hotel room. Sheriff visited each person, accepting massages of his head and ears before moving to the next. He was in heaven.

Having been fully briefed on the private flight to Lima, Colonel Hunter seemed to be deep in thought. He'd listened to Adriana's testimony, as well as that of Alfredo Nieves. To Alfredo's credit, he'd been nothing short of a gentleman while Gage had been away. In fact, Sheriff seemed to prefer Alfredo over anyone in the room. The smarmy private eye leaned over and readily exchanged tongue kisses with the dog, earning a curled lip and disgusted expression from Hunter.

Slapping his knees to set his stage, Hunter stood and spoke Spanish. "In my estimation, if we're going to do what Gage wants to do, then we've got to own the environment. This is their territory, giving them an automatic edge."

"I don't understand," Adriana replied.

"We need to gain our advantage through surprise, through superior planning and by creating chaos. We'll also need weaponry that's at least as good as what Alfa Seguridad has."

"That'll be a problem," Gage said, shaking his head. "They've got an armory that rivals anything you'd find at Delta."

"I can get you guns," Alfredo offered.

"Thirty-eight specials with tape around the grips?" Hunter rejoined. "No thanks."

Alfredo smiled weakly. "Forties and forty-fives, too."

"If we get desperate, we'll let you know."

"I have an idea," Adriana said, as if something suddenly hit her. She explained in detail.

"Are you sure you want to go down that road?" Gage asked.

Her smile was all the answer anyone needed.

"That may be our answer," Hunter replied. "You," Hunter said, pointing at Alfredo. "You can't go home till all this is done. Got that?"

"As I said when I was first confronted, I don't want to leave. In fact, I want to participate. The American threatened my life."

"He's talking about Falco...Guidry," Gage said.

Hunter tugged on his lip. "We'll see about you participating. For now, stand by."

"With pleasure," Alfredo said, beginning a new round of doggy kisses.

Hunter turned to Gage. "You had four or five ideas on the way down. Any of those crystallize yet?"

Gage eyed each person before nodding his head. "Yeah. When you mentioned owning the environment, that helped bring one idea to the top. I don't have the plan yet, but I think I know where this can all go down. And I think I know how to draw all the rats from their holes and get them out in the open."

He explained.

ADRIANA SAT IN the passenger seat of the rental sedan. Gage drove, with Hunter sitting in the back. Traffic was heavy in the city but had lessened as they'd moved into the run-down residential area. Groups of people gathered on the sidewalks, some spilling into the streets. At a traffic signal, several wayward-looking youths leaned down and malevolently eyed the threesome.

"Are you sure about this?" Gage asked Adriana, keeping his foot on the accelerator in case he needed to run the light.

"Do you have cash?" she replied.

"Yeah."

"Then, yes, I'm sure."

The light changed and Gage continued forward without incident. They'd driven from the motel, entering the San Martin de Porres area just north of the airport. Adriana wanted to introduce her American friends to her cousin, Tomás.

Tomás was a ranking member of a local gang. And, according to her, he specialized in weapons. He was *el armero*—the gang's armorer.

Following her instructions, Gage turned off the barrio street and drove up a small alleyway that was barely wide enough for the car. As the alley narrowed to mere inches on each side of the mirrors, Gage said, "You're certain this is the right road?"

"Keep going. At the top of the hill there's a little covered area. Stop in there and honk the horn three times."

"Hope you got insurance on this car," Hunter muttered. "And I ain't talkin' about the narrow alley."

Gage continued upward as the dingy, trash-littered passage bent to the left. "I hope I'm not going to have to back up when we leave. I'm a good driver, but…"

"Tomás will open the gate so you can go out the other side. Just relax…everything will be fine."

At the top of the steep alleyway, just as she'd said, was a rickety lean-to over the damp road. The roof was constructed of greenish fiberglass, bleeding dull light from a street lamp. Gage pulled into the area and stopped, doing all he could to hide his anxiety over this sketchy rendezvous. He looked in the mirror and shared a look with Hunter, who was probably thinking the same thing.

Helluva place for an ambush.

"I know what you're thinking," Adriana said. "You don't have to worry." She leaned over, pressing the horn three times.

Gage turned as a light came on to their right, illuminating a door. A man exited, shining a powerful flashlight into the car.

"Damn, I don't like this," Hunter grumbled, staring squarely back at the man with the light.

Adriana hopped out, leaving her door open as she spoke native Spanish to the man while she gave him a hug. Gage was able to follow most of their Spanish and the tenor of their conversation gave him a measure of relief—the man was her cousin.

After a minute of speaking, her cousin, Tomás, leaned down into the car, nodding to Hunter before directing heavily-accented English at Gage. "My cousin says you've helped her with a situation. She said you could've been pissed but instead you were cool. Thank you, *mi pata*." He extended a tattoo-covered hand.

"Thanks for helping us," Gage replied, shaking Tomás' hand.

"Just to be straight, I'll help you *if* you have money. I don't own these weapons and I have to account for every bullet. *Entiendes?*" The glint of gold teeth glimmered in the scant light as Tomás smiled.

"*Entiendo.* If you've got what we need, we've got the cash," Gage said.

Tomás straightened, popping the roof of the car twice. "Then don't just sit out here like *vagabundos*...come inside my home." He and Adriana walked in without waiting on Gage and Hunter.

"We're unarmed. What's to stop these criminals from just taking the cash from us?" Hunter growled.

"Her," Gage replied. "And he seems alright. Reminds me of someone I knew in Berga."

"Oh, that's comforting."

"Let's just trust her."

"It ain't her I'm worried about," Hunter replied, stepping from the car.

At the door, Gage took a deep breath and slapped the colonel on the back. In they went, to the unknown.

Chapter Twenty-Two

SONNY STAYED home and even cancelled his evening plans. Though he'd much rather be accompanied by a high-priced escort while dining on steak tartare at the posh new Restaurante Blanco, he'd just gotten the GPS report from London. He was doing his best to make sense of it. His intel man, Tony, had taken more than three hours to compile the information—not the hour Sonny had demanded. Truth be told, Sonny was quite pleased to have gotten the information today. He'd learned years before to work with talented people and to make outrageous demands of them. Oftentimes they obliged him with unexpected results.

As Tony explained in his message, the new Fords were manufactured with fleet tracking software for rental car companies or companies with large fleets. Although Nuestra didn't purchase the option, the tracking still occurred—Nuestra simply wasn't privy to the data. Somehow, Tony had managed to acquire the history for each of the Alfa and Nuestra Ford Focuses.

Using Google maps, Sonny studied the stops each Focus had made. According to Tony, because of how often a car's transmitter pinged the satellite, each stop had to have been for at least five minutes to be recorded. Few stops caught Sonny's eye. Most consisted of residences, Nuestra, Alfa Seguridad, restaurants, health clubs, the beach—places Sonny would expect his employees to go. Setting aside most of the vehicle GPS records, Sonny focused on the cars issued to Abi Mikkelsen and Sil Zobrist.

Abi's stops were nearly the same each day. In fact, if he ever found himself on speaking terms with her again, he would need to tell her to be a bit more unpredictable. Peru is a rather safe country, but kidnappings do occasionally occur. And kidnappers and sophisticated criminals thrive on victims with predictable schedules. Nothing about Abi's GPS history interested Sonny other than the fact that her car was still parked at her house and she wasn't home. But that was another subject.

He flipped to Sil's GPS history and circled six stops that puzzled him. Tony had gone so far as to list the attraction, or attractions, that were near each stop of the automobile.

First on the list of questionable stops was an address near the ocean, south of the city. Sonny wasn't familiar with any of the businesses Tony had listed near this location. Using Google maps, Sonny dialed up the address and viewed the satellite image. As soon as he saw it, he immediately crossed it off the list. In the penthouse of a nearby building was a high-end whorehouse. Though Sonny no longer went there, he'd heard Sil swear by their special "full-body hot oil" massage.

Like the first stop, Sonny was able to reason away the next four stops on Sil's GPS history, although one was a bank that Sonny didn't readily associate with Sil. It was probably nothing. The last one, however, was puzzling.

The stop occurred near the center of the city, next to the Monastery of San Francisco. There were galleries and hotels nearby, but the satellite marked the Focus as having parked in the monastery's lot. Sonny checked the date: Sil had been there just today, at lunchtime. Why would he have gone there? Cold-fish Sil was the last person Sonny would expect to visit a historic monastery.

Were there cameras there that Sonny could somehow access? He shook his head. No, too much time and trouble. Sonny thought back to the imploring speech Sil had made on the Gulfstream, then how he'd squirmed when Sonny had acted dubious.

Sil had always come across as a knave to Sonny.

And now Sil wanted Abi and the new guy, Burrell, dead. His fervor had made Sonny jealous. Sonny had challenged him, and Sil didn't like it. So, why was he at the monastery?

As his hand rubbed his face, Sonny reminded himself that he hadn't shaved this afternoon. He typically shaved twice, sometimes three times a day, despising his facial hair. Each week, Sonny's body hair was removed by two women in his bedroom, using a combination of razors and depilatories. His resulting smooth skin always proved a libido-boost to him and he would either wind up bedding one of the two women or just calling an escort.

Right now, however, all he could think about was Silvan "Sil" Zobrist. Would that little Swiss bastard stoop so low as to use Sonny's lust against him? And, taking it a step further, would he have the gall to try to hijack a shipment of cocaine for his own personal gain?

Sonny thought about Sil's beady blue eyes…

Hell yes, he would.

And everything Sil had said, all his claims, had involved Desgreaux, too. "Me and Desgreaux saw them. Desgreaux and I are sure of it. Desgreaux thinks Burrell is up to something."

Desgreaux…a world-class piece of shit. A good mercenary, yes, but a friend to no one. If Sil *was* in bed with the former Green Beret, he'd better watch his back.

Again, deliberately slowing his brain, Sonny ordered his thoughts. Long ago, he'd learned to remove emotion from tactical planning. Walking into his office bathroom, he turned on the warm water, watching it pour from the waterfall-style faucet. As he prepared to shave his face with his straight razor, Sonny touched the first button on the nearby phone, then tapped the button to put the call over the speakerphone.

"Evening, sir," Sil said, picking up on the second ring. "I came to see you today."

"I heard. Where are you now?"

"Sitting down to eat."

"Come to my home in precisely two hours."

"Would you rather wait till morning?" Sil asked, sounding somewhat anxious.

"Would I have called you if I wanted to wait till morning?" Sonny asked, scraping the razor down his cheek.

A brief pause. "No, sir."

"Two hours."

Sonny touched the button beside the active phone line. He lifted his chin, scraping upward, removing the scant twelve hours of stubble from his face.

Minutes later, when he was finished, Sonny applied an expensive, odorless French lotion to his face and neck. Rubbing his hands together, he eyed himself in the mirror. Sil's tone had contained slight inflections of fear. And why would he be fearful if he weren't guilty?

He wouldn't.

Sonny's instincts were, once again, correct.

Tonight would be interesting.

HUNTER AND GAGE had followed Adriana and her cousin through the residential home. It was small and somewhat cramped with toys strewn everywhere. There was a heavy smell of mint in the home, along with the smokiness of incense. Two toddlers scurried about and, as they waited for Tomás to unbolt an out-of-place steel inner door, one of the toddlers latched onto Hunter's pants leg. Gage couldn't help but be amused. Hunter appeared just about as uncomfortable as Gage had ever seen him.

"What's in the door?" he asked, trying to politely disentangle the kid from his pants.

"My li'l arsenal," Tomás said, lifting the heavy steel bar and opening the door. He flipped on a harsh light and motioned everyone in. After the little boy's mother pulled him away, the foursome entered the small room and the door was shut behind them.

Tomás wasn't kidding when he termed it an arsenal, although it certainly wasn't little. As soon as Hunter was inside the room, he let out a loud whistle and began sliding his hand over a handmade rack containing six MP5 submachine guns. He squatted down and eyed the weapons.

"These are 'N's'," he said, eyeing Gage, referencing the Navy version of the MP5, used primarily by the SEALs. Hunter turned to Tomás.

"Where'd you get these?"

Tomás grinned again, revealing his gold canines in the bright light. "I have many friends," he said, opening his arms in a majestic sweep. He was handsome, muscular and well-defined. His head was shaved, revealing a hairline that pointed in a severe widow's peak. His arms and chest were completely covered in artistic tattoos, most of them depicting religious imagery. Tomás' face and eyes were intense; he reminded Gage of a well-trained pit bull.

Gage eyed the other weapons. There was a row of older-model AK-47s, their wood done in a peculiar blond finish. There was a partial case of American flash-bang grenades. A rack of stout pistols. Gage asked if he could lift one and Tomás nodded without reservation.

The pistols were Sig P227s. When Gage flipped it over, he was more than surprised to see the slide stamped with the words, "Indiana State Police." He screwed up his face and looked at Tomás who, again, smiled that smile of his.

"Get these from a friend, too?" Gage asked.

"Yes. An Americano."

"Looky here," Hunter said.

When Gage turned, he saw Hunter holding a sniper rifle—a distinctive Dragunov like Gage had fired on the range at Fort Bragg. Gage nodded his approval and turned to Tomás.

"Do you have ammo to match everything in here?"

Tomás tapped the stacks of wooden crates behind him.

After a brief conference, Gage and Hunter made their selections of weaponry and ammunition as Tomás stacked the items by the staircase.

"How much?" Hunter asked.

Tomás' nostrils flared as he computed the price. When he eventually replied, Gage glanced at Hunter. Though the old colonel wore his poker face, Gage could tell by his eyes that Hunter was thinking the same thing.

Adriana's cousin had just given them the deal of the week.

The group departed as they came, this time with Hunter trying to walk with two little boys hanging from his legs. Outside, after the trunk of the car was loaded and everyone shook hands, Tomás opened the forward gate.

"I don't know what you're planning on doing but I wish you *buena suerta*," Tomás said.

Gage shook his hand again. "Thanks for your help."

"Watch out for my cousin."

"I didn't want her involved," Gage replied. "But she insisted." Adriana beamed at Tomás.

"Not surprised," Tomás added.

Hunter had just gotten in the car but stepped back out. "Tomás, I just had a thought."

"Please."

"If we wanted your assistance, or that of your...*friends*..."

"Assistance how?"

Arching his brows, Hunter looked at Gage. Gage nodded.

"There is a man who is rumored to have stolen hundreds of millions, if not billions, of product from the cartels," Hunter said. "I would imagine that a group...a *pandilla*, like yours...could be awarded many, many millions for halting this man."

"What are you saying?" Tomás asked, his intensity displayed by his balled fists.

Hunter smiled. "We're going to flush this bastard out and take him and his friends down. And if you want to help us, we'd be pleased."

Gage turned to Adriana. "Do you mind us involving him?"

"He's a grown man," she said with a shrug.

Turning back to Tomás, Gage said, "Would you like to learn more."

Again the smile and glint of gold. It was all the answer Gage needed.

"Keep your phone with you," Gage said. "We'll call you tonight. Be ready. Just you and a few others, cool?"

They shook again.

"Don't breathe a word of this to anyone," Gage added. "Not even the ones you plan to involve."

With that, Gage, Adriana and Hunter drove into the evening traffic.

"I hope you don't mind us involving him," Gage said again. "But we're out of our element and outnumbered. And to pull this off, we're going to need more than one ace in the hole."

"I don't mind," she answered. "And you made a good choice. Tomás is bad…but also good, if that makes sense."

"Makes sense to me," Hunter replied, clapping Gage on the shoulder as he drove. "And it makes complete sense to this one, too."

"Do you still want me to make the call?" Adriana asked.

Gage pulled into a fast food restaurant, parking in the shadows around back. He twisted in his seat. "Before we do this, I'd like to propose my idea again."

Hunter gave a quick shake of his head. "You do that, then you're calling down hell's fury."

"I trust these two enough that they won't turn on us."

"Mistake," Hunter said.

"What are you two talking about?" Adriana asked.

"A couple of the guys I was working with when we got ambushed," Gage said. "I don't think they're truly bad people. Kind of like your cousin."

"And?" she asked.

"And I'd like to warn them off, so we don't end up fighting them, too."

"They might listen to Gage…or they could blow this plan to smithereens and get us killed," Hunter countered.

Gage turned and eyed him. "There's one I trust without reservation. I know where he lives. Let's go see him."

His silver eyebrows hanging halfway over his eyes, Hunter said, "This is your game. If he ain't home, we make the call."

"Deal," Gage replied, quickly backing from the parking space.

"Where does your friend live?" Adriana asked, still puzzled.

"Not too far. In fact, he's right on the beach." Gage headed west as fast as traffic would allow.

GAGE AND HUNTER had taken cover behind the service area of the large beachside condominium complex. The landscape designer had obviously tried to conceal the massive air conditioning system with large plants, providing Gage and Hunter excellent cover while Adriana tried to lure Dinkins downstairs.

"Girl's got balls," Hunter remarked.

"Balls? How about just guts?"

"You been working around women too long. Gettin' all 'P.C' on me." Hunter stared up at the 20-story condominium. "He's a Ranger, huh?"

"Yep. Eleven-bravo and specializes in commo. Compared to the rest of the team, he's alright."

"I hope he doesn't get spooked, snatch our girl and call down the thunder."

"He won't."

They waited quietly before Gage's eyes widened and a look of shock spread over his face. He was facing outward, toward the trail that snaked along the beach between the ocean and rows of condos.

"What?" Hunter asked.

"I don't believe it," Gage whispered.

"Believe what?"

"Stay here. I'll be back but it might take me a minute," Gage replied and burst from the cover.

Hunter moved a stand of jalapa flowers aside, his heart racing as he peered after his soldier who'd grown uncharacteristically alarmed. Gage ran in the grass beside the path. Hunter could see enough of Gage's gait to know he was moving with stealth. Once he exited the lights of the complex, Hunter couldn't see him anymore.

A few minutes later, Adriana arrived with the Ranger named Dinkins. Hunter endured a bit of an awkward introduction with the man, the three of them remaining behind the bushes, having to lean close to speak due to the loud sounds from the massive air conditioning units. Dinkins was wearing shorts, an old t-shirt and flip-flops. As Gage had mentioned, he seemed polite enough but kept his head on a swivel.

"Where's Gage?" Adriana asked.

Hunter shrugged. "He took off running."

Dinkins frowned. "Gage?"

"That's his real name," Hunter explained.

"Whose?"

"Burrell's. Actually it's not but...well, I'll let him explain."

"He took off running?" Dinkins asked.

"Said he'd be right back. He saw someone."

Moments later, Gage returned, holding his splinted wrist tightly to his chest. He was wincing.

And he wasn't alone. With him, both of them partially covered in sand, was a petite woman in running attire. They were both out of breath. After brushing himself off, Gage shook Dinkins' hand. Then he pointed upstairs.

"Your place empty?" he asked Dinkins through gulping breaths.

Dinkins seemed as dumbfounded as the rest of the group but he managed to nod.

"Wait," Hunter interjected. "Who the heck is this?"

"Sorry. This is Chief Abi Mikkelsen. She was my boss and, like me, she'd gone dark. No one knows where she is but she couldn't help herself from taking her daily run. Lucky for us, I hope."

"Lady, you know what we're about to discuss?"

Abi nodded. "After he tackled me, and had to convince two locals that he's not some lunatic, he briefly explained."

"Are you in?" Hunter asked.

"I'd like to know more," she replied, brushing the sand from her body.

Hunter motioned to the building. "How about we all go upstairs, get to know each other a little better and then have a little chat?"

The small elevator admitted a motley crew, two of them still somewhat sandy. Up the elevator went.

Chapter Twenty-Three

HAVING DINED on a salad topped with strips of rare grilled hanger steak, Sonny Calabrese now awaited his visitor in the comfort of his media room. The visitor, of course, was Sil. He arrived right on time. Sonny viewed him on the massive television, watching the company Ford Focus as it climbed the forty-four feet of elevation from the road to the turnout in front of the San Isidro home.

The lone security man, per Sonny's instructions, was to search Sil and disarm him. Sonny watched the search. Then, with the touch of a button, he transitioned the television's feed back to American programming arriving via his roof-mounted satellite. As soon as Sil was given clearance to head up the winding front walkway, the security man radioed and informed Sonny that Sil had been unarmed. While Sonny would have liked to have given credit to Sil for not arming himself, he couldn't. Sil wasn't stupid. He knew he'd be searched. Sonny did, however, give him credit for coming. If Sil hadn't showed up, his absence would confirm that he was a traitor. He still could be, but Sonny's jury was currently out.

Sonny's instinctive unease, however, was as strong as ever.

The front door clicked open and shut. Situated in the middle of the massive, serpentine sofa in his media room, Sonny listened as his Swiss team leader checked each of the rooms in order of probability, starting with the dining room, then the back porch, then the den, then Sonny's office. Finally, Sonny heard Sil's shoes clicking down the long tiled hallway that led to the media room.

"I've only been here a few times," Sil said, standing in the doorway. "I didn't know where to find you." He didn't seem the least bit nervous.

Removing the cigar from his mouth, Sonny said, "And good evening to you, too." He purposefully added a tone of contempt to the greeting, but it didn't seem to unsettle Sil.

"Something up, sir?"

"Stand right there," Sonny said, gesturing to the area directly in front of his 90-inch LED television. On the silenced TV was an NBA game, the light in the darkened room dancing with colorful movement as the Pacers battled the Clippers in Los Angeles.

Sil walked to the spot, frowning. "This is odd, sir, and insulting. It's not hard to see you're upset with me, but I have *no* idea why." He eyed Sonny. "I've done nothing but serve you...and serve you well."

He doesn't act the least bit guilty. But...he's an accomplished tactician. He knows the actions and emotions of an innocent man.

"When did you start banking at the Banco Interamericano?" Sonny asked without preamble, referencing one of the stops from the GPS history.

"Just this past month," Sil replied mildly.

"Why?"

"It suits me better. Excuse me, sir, but isn't my personal banking my own prerogative?"

Ignoring his question, Sonny puffed the Cohiba. He leaned forward, sipping his lemon water before settling in again on the custom, brain-tanned sectional sofa that cost as much as a Porsche. Joining eyes with Sil, Sonny allowed more than a minute to pass.

Sil's icy blue eyes didn't waver.

Maintaining eye contact, Sonny reached into the sofa and produced his well-used M1911 pistol, placing it on the cushion next to him.

After he cocked the hammer.

"Next question," Sonny said, using a melodic voice. "Why were you at the San Francisco Monastery today?"

Sil pulled in a breath through his nose as he crossed his arms. Displaying rare defiance, he said, "I'll say nothing else until you tell me why you're suddenly suspicious of me." He opened his arms. "If you want to shoot me, the man who has served you so well...then have at it."

"I had a gut feeling this morning," Sonny said evenly. "So, following my gut, I pulled the GPS history on your car that I pay for."

Tightening his lips, Sil nodded. "I was meeting someone I didn't trust. That's why we met in such a public place. And as soon as the meeting was over, I came straight to Nuestra to tell you about it. Remember?"

"Maybe you did. But when I wasn't there, you could have called me if it was such a big deal."

"It is a big deal, sir, so I chose to wait until tomorrow when I could tell you in person. Then, when you called, I came here as directed."

Sonny lifted the pistol with his right hand and aimed it at Sil's face.

The Staples Center lights flashed around Sil's silhouette as one of the Clippers made a highlight reel dunk.

"I'm going to shoot you, Sil, and it's going to ruin that television. But, I can buy another television. Hell, I can buy a million televisions. But what I can't seem to buy are loyal people."

Sil swallowed. Finally, a show of emotion.

"Sonny, you're crossing a line that's never been crossed between us. Working for Alfa...for you...has been the pinnacle of my professional life and it's *more* than just the money. It's the organization that we've created together under your leadership." Sil's face visibly softened. "I realize I'm now entreating and showing weakness, so I will say no more about it."

"Who did you meet?"

"A man, Sonny. I met a man who is *our* enemy."

Sonny narrowed his eyes. "No riddles. I hate fucking riddles."

"Sonny...you don't want to know. Believe me. I'm trying to fix it. When you find out what he knows..."

"What are you talking about?"

"It will make things worse for you. It's best you not know."

"Who is he?" Sonny yelled.

Slumping, Sil said, "He calls himself 'Falco.'"

"And?"

"He claims he works for you."

"In what aspect?"

"I don't know, Sonny, but he knows everything. He knows about Nuestra, about Alfa, about the cocaine. He knows we steal from the cartels. He knows which cartels we've hit. He knows who *you* are, who *I am*..."

The next words struck Sonny like a sledgehammer to the chest.

"...and he claims *he* set up the hit on us at the Manolo ambush."

"He knew about that independently? You didn't tip him to it?"

"Hell, no. And it gets worse."

"How?"

"He claims the new guy, Burrell, worked for him...led him to the ambush. He claims Burrell is now a loose cannon and is out there on his own, aiming to take all of us down."

Sonny laughed. He heard himself, realizing it was a strange, flabbergasted sort of laughter, the type a man might use when learning that his spouse has cheated on him with one of his closest friends. To Sonny, the laughter felt reckless and out of control.

"I believe every word this man said, Sonny. He's a threat of the highest order."

Continuing to aim the pistol, Sonny leaned forward and sipped his water. "What did he look like...this Falco?"

"He's an American, maybe fifty…fifty-five. Tight mat of gray hair. Yellowish eyes."

Slowing his train of thought, Sonny asked, "Why did you meet with him?"

"I thought he wanted a payoff. I'd hoped for a chink in his armor, some way we could eliminate him before he did too much damage. So, I agreed to meet him." Sil shook his head. "There's no chink, and he was surrounded by nuns so I couldn't exactly kill him."

As the shock of the revelations faded slightly, Sonny cocked his head. This could all be bullshit, spun from a desperate man who'd gotten caught red-handed. "Why did this Falco pick you?"

"He didn't say."

"Or was it *you* who contacted him weeks ago? Maybe the two of you tried to steal my coke and things went bad."

"Absolutely not."

"Maybe Desgreaux is in it with you, and you two concocted this story about Mikkelsen banging Burrell to throw me off your scent?"

"Not true," Sil said evenly.

"Maybe you're making all this up about Burrell, the convenient new guy, to cover for your sins."

Sil shook his head. "Everything I've said is true."

"Then, tell me, Sil…what does this Falco want?"

"He wants me to help him steal a coke shipment. Then he wants me to kill you and take him on as partner."

"Kill me?"

"Yes, sir."

Sonny screwed up his face. "But what about Burrell? I thought he was a problem."

"Falco claims to know where Burrell is. He says we kill Burrell first." Sil took a step forward. "In case you don't believe me, Falco told me something else that might convince you I'm telling you the unvarnished truth."

"What is it?"

"He claims that we distribute cocaine through the use of U.S. Air Force aircraft. He claims he's the mastermind behind it."

The world spun off its axis.

Collapsing back on the couch, Sonny lowered the pistol and took gasping breaths as Sil continued to speak.

"He claims he has the roster of the dirty Air Force pilots. And he said he has proof of every shipment that has occurred."

Sonny was silent. Sil's revelation changed everything. There is no way he could have known about the Air Force connection. And because he did, it proved to Sonny that at least some of this story was true.

"Do we use the U.S. Air Force?" Sil asked.

Ignoring the question, Sonny said, "Why didn't you just kill him? Why entertain this asshole?"

"I told you, there were nuns everywhere...and he assured me before we met that he's littered the United States and Peru with landmines that will go off if he winds up dead. I believe him."

"Describe this man, Falco, in great detail. You said he has yellowish eyes."

Sil spent several minutes relaying every detail he could recall. By the time he was finished, Sonny knew exactly who he was...

Colonel Troy Guidry, the scumbag wing commander behind the entire Air Force distribution operation. That double-crossing sonofabitch!

In a sudden fit of rage, Sonny twisted to his right and put seven hollow points into the wing of his Turkish-made sofa. Sulfury blue smoke swirled through the room, backlit by the bright television.

When Sonny had calmed down, he and Sil talked for two hours straight.

But Sil hadn't told Sonny the entire truth, and Sil still wanted Abi Mikkelsen gone.

And, despite all he had told Sonny, Sil wasn't so sure he still wouldn't cooperate with Falco.

For now, thankfully, Sonny was on Sil's side.

SIL HAD CONVINCED Sonny to wait until the following day before doing anything about Falco, Burrell or Abi Mikkelsen. Of course, despite Sil telling Sonny *almost* everything, he conveniently left out the part about shaking hands with Falco and making a pact with him. And, thanks to Sil's expert storytelling, Sonny also still believed Abi Mikkelsen was screwing Jeffrey Burrell. Though Sil now knew a bit more about Burrell's dubious past, he dared not clue Sonny in on anything. Why give him more to go on?

But what to do about Falco? And Burrell? And where the hell was Abi Mikkelsen?

The entire situation was incredibly delicate. One little slip-up could bring the world down on Sil, and he knew it. But he also now had incredible intel on the entire operation. Biggest was the Air Force connection—information like that, if Sil played his cards right, could be worth many millions.

Earlier, Sil had come home to his well-appointed condominium and dozed fitfully for a few hours on the couch. Unable to sleep any longer, he arose and made strong coffee in his Turkish press, chain smoking as the sun rose over the whitewashed city.

Dropping his cigarette in his fourth cup of syrupy-black coffee, Sil stood and stretched. It was nearly 6:30 in the morning. He took his iPad outside on the balcony, appreciating the velvety humid air over the dry cold of his air conditioning. He used the encryption program to send a message to Falco, stringing him along.

His head now clear, Sil decided that another meeting with Falco was necessary. Sil rang Desgreaux, waking him. The Cajun's gravelly voice was heaven to Sil's ears—Desgreaux was a man you wanted on your side.

"I've got a plan," Sil said. "Remember the guy I cut the deal with at the Catholic tourist trap?"

"Yeh."

"He's got to go, and soon. Along with your Green Beret friend and the one you call 'the slit.'"

"After dat?"

"After that we decide whether or not we allow our boss to keep breathing."

"I like it."

Sil gave Desgreaux, the former Special Forces weapons man, a very explicit set of instructions.

Chapter Twenty-Four

AT HIGH NOON, Falco sat at a street side café, admiring the ass of his server as she waited on an adjacent table of what appeared to be American tourists. He'd already eaten and was now enjoying the warm, sunny weather as he sipped his sparkling water. Falco hadn't heard a peep from Alfredo Nieves, so he'd spent ten grand on a battery of private detectives. Their mission: find Alfredo Nieves and Jeffrey Burrell. Thus far, Falco hadn't heard a peep about either one.

When his cell phone finally rang, Falco was surprised by the phone number. It was the woman, Adriana, who he'd hired through Alfredo in order to get close to Hartline. Since Alfredo was M.I.A., Falco had been trying to directly reach her for days.

After trying so many times, he was surprised she was calling back.

Falco eyed the phone, performing a hurried risk assessment in his mind. In a matter of seconds, he decided there was little to no threat involved, so he answered the call.

"Yeah?"

"Hi, um…this is Adriana."

"I know who you are."

"You left a message for me to call this number with updates."

At least her English was good. Falco made his tone perturbed. "That was *days* ago. Where the hell have you been?"

"I'm sorry…I couldn't call. I just came back into town this morning, back to the duplex, but it'd been broken into."

"Adriana, you haven't heard from Burrell, have you?"

"Heard from him?"

"Yeah."

"Are you serious?"

"Yes, dear, I am serious," he said, narrowing his eyes at her curious tone.

"We've been together the entire time I was gone."

Sirens blared in Falco's mind. Thundering explosions occurred in the distance followed by brilliant fireworks defeating the noontime sun.

Blackness overcame his vision, streaked by neon lights as his world spun.

Falco swallowed, fighting to control his voice. "Right...sure. And where is Jeff now?"

"He's getting us some lunch. Is everything okay? You sound surprised."

"Fine, dear. Just fine." Dropping a few bills on the table, Falco grabbed his keys and his other phone, struggling to keep from sounding excited. "Does he know that I hired you, Adriana?"

"No! Are you kidding? I really like him and if I tell him that, I don't know how he'd react."

"Very good. I agree. Don't ruin a good thing." Hurrying to his motorcycle, Falco asked, "Where are you now?"

"We've stopped. I'm in the bathroom."

"Stopped? Stopped where?"

"We're in the mountains, at one of those combo gas station/restaurants."

"Why are you in the mountains?"

"We're headed to a place called La Merced."

Falco had straddled his motorcycle and froze. "La Merced, the coffee plantation where he first worked?"

"Yes."

"Why are you going there?"

"Jeff didn't go into detail. He just said something about gathering more evidence, whatever that means."

"How long will you be there?"

"He phoned a man...Abuelito...and made arrangements. We're meeting him and a woman named Abi. Jeff said we're staying the night after the meeting."

Falco again struggled not to worry her with his urgent tone. "Very good, Adriana. You've just earned an additional thousand Peruvian sols. But it's critical I meet Jeff face-to-face."

"You don't want to hurt him, do you?"

"My dear, no. The evidence he's gathering is for *me*. But it's critical we talk."

"Why can't you call him?" she asked.

"It's complicated. He thinks I'm not on his side but, believe me, dear, I am."

"Well, they're having some sort of meeting at midnight."

"Where?"

"At La Merced plantation, behind the huts where Jeff slept. I heard them saying something about avoiding the security cameras. Jeff is meeting the man, Abuelito, the woman Abi, and some other locals. Something about a missing man named Simon."

"This is quite good, Adriana. I will come to see Jeff so he knows I'm on his side. And I will bring you your money and pay you in private. I also have quite a bit of money for Jeff, too," Falco said, using a velvety tone.

And I'll kill all of you.

"Now, Adriana, don't tell Jeff we talked, remember?"

"Of course not. Don't you tell him, either."

"I'll see you this evening. Go now, so he's not suspicious."

"Okay," Adriana answered. "I'm excited about earning the extra money."

"It's been a good arrangement for everyone. See you soon."

Falco stabbed the phone to end the call. He leaned back on the seat of his motorcycle and fist-pumped the sky.

SIL AND DESGREAUX were together, eating burgers at an American-style restaurant as they discussed how best to proceed. Sil's phone rang. He eyed the number. "It's him."

"Mebbee he got good news," Desgreaux mumbled.

Sil answered the phone. "Yeah?" As he listened, his eyes widened. "How the hell do you know that?"

Desgreaux arched his brows. Sil touched the mute button.

"Claims he knows where Burrell will be at midnight."

"B'lieve him?"

Sil un-muted the phone. "How'd you say you learned that?" He listened. "Is she credible?" Listened some more. "Are you absolutely certain? There can be no mistakes if we commit to this." Sil closed his eyes, focusing as he listened. "Okay, hang on a second." He hit the mute button again, his tone optimistic.

"This Falco fellow had hired a girl to get close to Burrell, follow him, that kind of thing. He says the girl had gone missing a few days back but has resurfaced and says Burrell is meeting one of the spic guards, Abuelito, tonight at La Merced, of all places."

Desgreaux curled his lip. "La Merced? Why?"

Sil spoke to Falco again, this time for several minutes. "Hang on." Muted again. Sil looked at Desgreaux.

"Says Burrell is gathering evidence. And along with Abuelito, guess who else he's meeting?"

"Th'slit."

"Yep."

"If dis Burrell dickhead is gatherin' evidence, she tryin' to cut a deal to save her ass."

"La Merced," Sil said, gnawing on his bottom lip. "I can't think of many places better to kill both of them."

"'Zactly. Too good. Could be a trap. I don't trust neither of dem polecats."

"I'd say we could verify they're there with the security 'cameras," Sil suggested, "but Falco said Burrell is arranging the meeting away from the surveillance."

"What about dis guy, Falco?"

"If this meet is really going down, we should kill him beforehand. Then, all we have to do is get rid of Burrell and Mikkelsen. We're scot free after that, masters of our own destiny."

"Where he at?"

Sil touched the mute button. "Where are you?" Checked his watch. "Meet me at nineteen-hundred hours in Tarma. It's the last stop before La Merced. As you pass through town, there's a shopping center with a modern grocery store on the left. I'll meet you on the western edge of the parking lot."

"Perfect," Desgreaux whispered.

Sil listened with closed eyes until his mouth split into a smile. "See you then." He ended the call and slid the phone into his pocket. "We're all set."

"What intel Burrell gone get from Abuelito?"

"Maybe things about Simon?" Sil suggested with a shrug.

"Dat may be why," Desgreaux nodded. "I still think it could be a trap."

"Ideas?"

"How 'bout we trow a lil' green at ol' Abuelito? Po' man like dat, bet he sing like a canary."

"I like it." Sil went through his numbers, smiling when he found the one he wanted. "Here it is."

Before he called Abuelito, Sil eyed his partner. "Assume for a minute that everything Falco has said is true. If Burrell *is* gathering evidence, we're screwed. All it takes is someone like that asshole to tell the authorities about Alfa and Nuestra."

"Or worse, d'cartels."

Sil rubbed his chin. "Burrell's a prick, but he's not stupid. He's probably left poison pills in case he gets killed."

"In udder words, you sayin' we fucked no matter what."

"That's what I'm saying. So, assuming we pull all of this off tonight, what do you propose we do before we disappear?"

"Call Ortiz."

"Agreed," Sil replied.

Desgreaux picked at his teeth with a toothpick. "After we done, we kidnap Sonny an squeeze ever penny we can from his sorry ass."

Sil grinned. "I bet he's got millions in cash. He'd have to."

"Mebbee tens of millions."

"We sweat him. Torture him. Get the cash…"

"And den kill that sumbitch," Desgreaux said with a wicked grin.

"We could give him a choice."

"Hell yeh. Make him squeal like a sucklin' pig at butcherin' time."

"You got a bag packed?" Sil asked.

"Always," Desgreaux replied, leaving a twenty céntimos tip on the table. It was the equivalent of seven cents.

A HALF-HOUR later, an old pickup truck creaked to a stop on the trail off the main road. The driver exited, a cigarette dangling from his lips as he peered uneasily into the thick jungle. He stepped forward, his eyes scanning back and forth. Though there was still sunlight, the dense canopy made the area quite dark. The driver fell backward into the fender of the pickup when a man suddenly stood from the undergrowth. He was camouflaged, carrying an assault rifle and adorned with numerous saplings to break up his outline.

His left wrist was tightly wrapped in a flat black splint.

Abuelito knew him as Jeff Burrell.

"Jeff! You scared the piss out of me."

"Good to see you, *amigo*. Is everything set up?"

"Sí, señor. It's just as you requested."

"Thank you," Gage replied. "Did he call?"

"Sí, Sil called me and offered me a large bonus in exchange for telling him everything."

"Did you stick to the script?"

"Sí, señor. He was very excited when I told him what was going on. He even told me to bring beers and delay you as long as possible."

"Beers, huh? What did he say he was going to do?"

"He told me to get you talking, that they would record our conversation in *la cocina*."

"You know that's not true, don't you Abuelito?"

"Sí, señor. I know this."

"How about the tunnel?"

"It's finished. We dug it in two hours."

"Did you prop it up? This earth is soft."

"Sí, señor. Very solid. There will be no cave-ins."

"Excellent work, Abuelito. I can't thank you enough." Jeff Burrell— Gage—held out a wad of bills for his friend.

"No, Jeff, I cannot take this."

"Then take it for your family, Abuelito. Tonight will be dangerous, and we appreciate your help."

Abuelito tucked the money into his shirt pocket. "Your arm?"

"Hurts like hell. But I'll make it."

"So, I will see you at midnight?"

"You will. Just remember everything I said, Abuelito. No matter what happens, stick to the plan. And make sure you bring that case of beer. Make it conspicuous. It just might save both of us."

Crossing himself, Abuelito stepped back into the truck. He waved and backed away.

GAGE CREPT BACK up the hill, less than three kilometers from where everything would go down tonight. The group was in a perimeter, listening as they ate. Hunter was in the center of the group, reviewing the plan on a makeshift sand table. He stopped and looked up.

"We're on," Gage said. "It's Sil and Desgreaux, for sure. I'm assuming they'll bring Falco and who knows who else."

"They'll bring a platoon," Abi said.

"Agreed," Dinkins added.

"But who else would it be?" Gage asked. He motioned to Dinkins. "You called Griffin and he's way the hell away in Panama. Ortiz is the only one who they might be able to sway."

"As I said earlier," Abi stated, "Ortiz *will* side with them. Count on him being here tonight."

"That all?" Hunter asked.

"No," Abi said, shaking her head. "Sil will hire local guns if he has to. He won't suspect a trap, but he's very careful. He'll want the advantage just in case."

Tomás, Adriana's cousin, stared into a small mirror at the camouflage paint on his face. He smiled, displaying his gold canines as he spoke Spanish, saying, "They can bring a battalion of local guns if they want. That's why you brought us."

Hunter flicked his pointing stick, tapping the mirror. "Put that mirror away, Goldie. Just stick to this plan and you'll get yours."

"Sir?" Gage asked, producing the satellite phone. "Now that we know Sil and Desgreaux are coming, will you let me make the call?"

"This is your game. I'm not in charge."

"But you didn't sound keen on the idea."

Hunter shrugged. "I just think you're inviting trouble if you go that route."

"But it's why I agreed to come here. If I follow through, I've still done as I said I would."

Hunter surveyed the group. "Anyone object?"

Silence.

Hunter looked up at Gage. "Make the call."

SONNY WAS IN his office at Nuestra. The past few days had seemed impossibly long and stressful. Despite all of Sil's reassurances over the veracity of his revelations, Sonny still felt unnerved. He'd either missed something or Sil was flat-out lying to him—because somewhere in all of this, something didn't add up. When he'd arrived, Sonny told *La Bruja* not to disturb him. Since then, he'd been sitting nude, puffing his cigar, running complex scenarios in his mind. At 4:38 P.M., the witch buzzed his phone.

"What is it?" Sonny barked.

"Sorry for disturbing you," she said, not sounding sorry at all. "But there's a caller who went through the main operator. He said he has news for you that could be life or death."

As was his habit, Sonny had been facing the windows as he'd pondered things. He turned his entire body, eyeing the phone. "Did he give a name?"

"No, but he sounds American. I spoke to him and he told me the same thing he told Juana."

"And what was that?"

"Just that he has life or death news and he'll only speak to Sonny Calabrese. Should I take a message?"

"No...I'm going to take the call. You tell Juana not to tell a *soul* that I received this call, got it? Same goes for you."

"Absolutely."

"I'm serious."

"We won't mention it."

"Put him through." Sonny watched as the red light of his line flashed, then it turned green. The caller was on the speakerphone.

Sonny spoke first. "What is the nature of this call?"

"Is this Sonny Calabrese?"

"It is. Who the hell is this?"

"Sonny, you might know me as Jeffrey Burrell, but that's not my real name. My real name is Gage Hartline, and I was recently hired as an operator with Alfa Seguridad."

Perspiration broke out on several areas of Sonny's bare body. He walked to his desk, placing the cigar in the ashtray. Sonny leaned over the phone and supported himself on his knuckles. "I know who you are."

"No, Sonny, you don't. You have no idea, despite the lies you've been told."

"But I do," Sonny countered. "Did you call to brag that you led that piece of shit, Guidry, to my ambush?"

"No, Sonny. I called because I have news for you. Big news."

"What, that you and Abi Mikkelsen are out there angling to kill me?"

"No, Sonny, that's fabricated—a deception aimed at preventing you from knowing the *real* truth about what's been going on."

Unable to help himself, Sonny heard himself ask, "Are you sleeping with her?"

"Abi?" Gage laughed. "Hell no. Did Sil tell you that, too?"

Though it was always harder to tell over the phone, Burrell didn't sound like he was lying. His voice was smooth and confident, the way a person sounds when telling nothing but the unvarnished truth.

"Then what is the real story?" Sonny whispered.

"Listen closely—I will say this once. Because of my background in special ops, and the nature of the missions I've completed after my time in special ops, I was contracted by a man in the United States to come to Lima. As you now know, that man is Colonel Troy Guidry, who called himself Falco."

"I know all this."

"Shut up and listen, Sonny. I bet there's a part of this you don't know."

"Yeah, yeah. Go on."

"My first order of business was getting hired by Alfa Seguridad. Put simply, once I was hired by Alfa, my mission was to gain trust through solid performance. But my mission wasn't to lead anyone to an ambush. My mission was to kill you, Sonny, as quickly as possible."

"So, you're claiming you were duped?"

"I was duped and I unknowingly led those shooters to our ambush. Then I learned what shitbags Sil and Desgreaux are. Ortiz, too, for that matter."

"None of this is news to me," Sonny replied, already bored with this useless exchange. "And when I find you, you're going to hurt like you never—"

Gage cut him off. "The part that is news, Sonny, is the reason I accepted this job."

"To kill me?"

"That was the mission. The reason, Sonny, was the assembly of families of Alfa Seguridad operators. The families claimed their sons were murdered by *you*."

"I thought Guidry hired you."

"He was working for them. It was all a part of his ruse. I didn't know his true identity."

Sonny used his desk handkerchief to wipe his face. Bolstering himself, he straightened, adding bass to his voice as he said, "I don't believe a word you're saying."

"You *do* believe it, Sonny. I met with a nice lady whose son is dead. Her son's name was Jimmy DeLand. Remember him?"

"He went missing and was found in the ocean."

"Yeah, right. 'Went missing.' That happens a lot to your operators."

"We can waste our time talking about—"

"Last thing before I hang up," Gage said, cutting him off again. "The primary reason for my call was to let you know that Sil, Desgreaux and Ortiz are all angling against you. I'm almost certain they will kill Guidry. Then it'll be your turn."

Neither man spoke for a moment. Finally Sonny asked, "What's your motivation in all this?"

"Before I tell you, just remember one thing…I know everything. I know you steal from the cartels. I know you've killed a number of your employees. I know you package cocaine to look like MREs. And I know you distribute all of it…by using Air Force aircraft."

"What do you want?" Sonny asked.

"I want those three bastards who turned on me at that ambush. I want their heads."

"So…kill 'em. I don't care."

"I plan to. In fact, it'll happen at midnight tonight."

"How do you know that?"

Gage explained the La Merced plan.

"Why did you call me?" Sonny asked after he understood the plan.

"Because I'd rather have you as an ally than an enemy."

"What about the families who hired you?"

"I work for money, Sonny. I don't work for causes."

"Can you guarantee my safety if I come tonight?"

"Nope. Hell, we could all die."

"Would you have interest in working for me after all this is done?"

"I'll listen."

"And what about Abi?"

"You'll have to ask her."

Sonny frowned. "Why is she with you, anyway?"

"At the ambush, before we got hit by the gunmen in the trucks…"

"Yeah?"

"There was a young local who appeared with a fishing pole. Sil gave the green light and Desgreaux killed him. He was no threat at all. After that, she checked out on those two assholes."

"Yes," Sonny said. "I did hear about that awful incident."

"They're going to pay."

"So, if I decide to come tonight?"

"You take a helicopter to San Ramón. It's about eight clicks south of La Merced. There's a large field due south of town. No power lines. Tell the pilot to land there. We'll put out an orange X. I will post someone there, till 2100 hours."

"What's to prevent you from killing me?"

"Then don't come. I don't give a shit. But I called you and gave you the truth. And if you *don't* come, I'd suggest you flee, or you're going to wake up tomorrow in a world of shit."

"If I do come?"

"Then maybe you can strike a deal. We'll have a number of the players there. You can be there, or you can run. I'm out…"

"Wait!"

The line was dead.

After sitting in silence for ten minutes, Sonny crushed out the Cohiba and got dressed.

GAGE POCKETED the satellite phone and stared at Colonel Hunter.

"Calabrese is gone," Hunter said. "He'll be halfway around the world by sunup."

"I agree," Gage replied.

Dinkins shrugged. "I don't know enough about him. Ain't never said two words to me."

"No. He'll come here," Abi Mikkelsen countered. "His ego won't allow him to run."

"You sure?" Hunter asked.

"Among other things, he's a narcissist. They're big on self-preservation," she said. "But they're also supremely confident. If we pull this off, he'll simply attempt to use everyone here to his advantage. In fact, Colonel Hunter, I'll wager he offers you a lucrative position."

"I could use some dough," Hunter said, winking at her.

"Alright," Gage said. "Let's wrap this up."

Hunter eyed Abi. "Your airplane ready to go?"

"It'll take me a half-hour to drive there, another half-hour to pre-flight and climb out to altitude."

"Then I suggest you leave here no later than 2100 hours, just to be safe."

She nodded her agreement. Hunter turned to Gage.

"And since you called Sonny, I suggest you better make those phone calls."

Gage smirked as he lifted the satellite phone. Wouldn't these fine Peruvians be surprised to hear from him?

Chapter Twenty-Five

CIVIL TWILIGHT occurred at 6:54 P.M. in Tarma, Peru. The sky had grown a faded purple as Venus shone brightly in the northeast, setting the stage for what would be a beautiful night of star gazing. Not for Sil, though. As far as he was concerned, the best feature of the clear night sky was the absence of a moon. Tonight, the less light the better. Sil watched a helicopter struggle by, headed to the northeast, its green starboard light and white aft light blinking away. The helicopter was flying slowly due to the high altitude.

Probably a rich cartel asshole…hope he smashes into the nearest mountain.

Sil had parked far away from any other cars, facing the cinderblock wall of a business adjacent to the wide expanse of the supermarket parking lot. He had arrived thirty minutes early, giving him an ever so slight upper hand over Falco, who still hadn't arrived. Sil checked his watch. It was time.

The rural supermarket was part of a South American chain. Like its cousins in the United States, this one was massive, with unnecessarily high ceilings and cheery lighting. The damn thing glowed like a forest fire, sitting there behind the wide asphalt parking lot. The store begged patrons to come on in and walk all the way to the back for their inexpensive milk, just so they'd see ten other items they didn't really need. Sil glanced around at what he could see of Tarma. Its elevation was nearly 10,000 feet, giving the surrounding hills a decided wintry appearance. Though there was no snow cover, the temperature up here was chilly. As he brought his eyes back to the rearview mirror, he watched as a motorcycle approached on the main road.

Sil spoke aloud to the car. "Here he comes."

Falco eased the motorcycle into a wide turn, entering the mostly empty parking lot. The headlamp turned to Sil as Falco slowly accelerated across the seven empty rows on his way to the rendezvous on the parking lot's western edge.

The motorcycle stopped two spots away. Falco twisted the key, silencing the BMW's engine. He stared at Sil.

Don't seem impatient.

Sil waited, his left hand casually hanging over the steering wheel.

Falco continued to sit there on the bike, staring. Sil twisted the key for electric power only and rolled down the passenger window with the press of a button.

"Are you going to get in, or do you want me to get out?"

Removing the full-face helmet, Falco cautiously approached the rental car, peering through the rear window. He backed away, standing on the opposite side of his bike as he produced his pistol.

"What?" Sil asked, exasperated.

"What's under the blanket?"

"What do you think?" Sil hissed. "Items for tonight."

"Prove it."

Sil opened his door, storming around the car. Falco crouched down, resting the pistol on the seat of the BMW, aiming it at Sil.

Yanking the back door open, Sil lifted the blanket, revealing several crates and a number of firearms. "Satisfied?" he asked, glancing around. "All your caution is going to get us in hot water with the PNP," he said, referencing the Peruvian National Police.

Falco concealed the pistol and came around the bike. "I've lived this long by being cautious."

"Well, get your cautious ass in the car. Time is short."

The two men sat in the rental car.

"Are you up for this?" Falco asked. He seemed nervous and fidgety.

"Sure I am. But killing is something a man never gets used to. And if he does, I don't want anything to do with him."

"Yeah? How about your teammate Desgreaux? My intel says he's a killing machine."

Sil eyed Falco. "He's a psycho, but he has his place." Checked his watch. "Before we head over there and get set up, I need to know if everything you've given me is the truth."

"I already told you, it is. What's the plan for La Merced?"

"If all goes to plan, we'll use a nice little explosive device. We'll have rifles as backup, just in case. You'll have one, too."

"What about the regular La Merced guards?"

Sil grinned. "Who are you talking to? I'm the number two man at Alfa. I took care of it." He looked forward. "Assuming we get that done, what's your plan going forward?"

"Are you sure Sonny won't know what we did at La Merced?"

"He won't know. Trust me. He thinks Abi and Burrell have lammed it."

Falco was sweating. "Okay. After tonight, you take over and then we take the drugs from your next hit."

"How?"

"We take them when they're being transported to the airport."

"You'll know when that is?"

"I know when the flight will be leaving. If we can't figure it out with that sort of intel, we shouldn't be talking."

Sil sucked on his teeth as he nodded. "Last question...who is Jeffrey Burrell?"

"His legal name is Gage Hartline, but even that's not the name his parents gave him. He actually was S.F. but the government took him off the grid and put him on a black ops team back in the mid-nineties. That went on for more than a decade before something bad went down. The team disbanded and since then he's been a mercenary."

Sil stared. "What else?"

"I chose him after looking at a lot of mercenary types. He's become increasingly violent in the last two years, but he operates with some sort of ethical code. I knew my story about murdered Alfa members would get him hooked." Falco quickly told the story of how he'd used Linda DeLand to persuade Gage.

"Brilliant work, Mister Falco. One last question before we go kill Burrell...er, Hartline and Mikkelsen."

Falco turned to Sil. "Yeah?"

"Who are you? You know who I am and I'm not going one step farther until you tell me who you are."

There was a long pause. "I'm a colonel in the United States Air Force. I'm the man who controls all the distribution. So, we can steal those drugs or...if you've got brass balls...we can take over Sonny's operation and continue to make millions. I was holding my part back till we finished tonight but I just want you to know it's a possibility," Falco said with a shit-eating grin.

Sil eyed the colonel. "I figured it was something like that. Thanks for being straight with me."

"You got it. Now, can we get this over with?"

"Sure. Hopefully it will be quick." Sil placed both hands on top of the steering wheel. He leaned forward, peering upward through the windshield.

"Are you gonna crank the—"

The cabin was jolted by a loud noise. It was a flat, dull sound, like a mallet smacking into a thick rib-eye. Falco jolted briefly before slumping and emitting a modulated sound like an unexpected burp.

Ignoring the spray of warm blood on the right side of his face, Sil reached across Falco's lap, grabbing his right hand to make sure he wasn't holding the pistol. He wasn't.

Falco had been shot in his chest. He was still alive, his bloody mouth opening and closing like a fish. As his chest made sucking sounds, he looked at Sil with wide eyes.

"Guess you weren't cautious enough," Sil said.

Falco's laboring ceased in less than twenty seconds.

Sil twisted the key and rolled up the passenger window. Then, using a moist towelette from a packet he'd brought just in case, he wiped his face and eyes. He hadn't expected Falco to cling to life after an accurate shot to the heart. Now the car stunk of several odors.

Exiting the car, Sil walked around and reclined the electric passenger seat so Falco's corpse wasn't visible. He took a folded blanket from the backseat and covered the body. By that time, Desgreaux had appeared, sauntering over and sitting on the BMW as he smirked at Sil. A guitar case rested on the ground next to him.

"G'shot, I must say," Desgreaux drawled.

"What was it, all of fifteen meters? And you said I wouldn't get sprayed."

"Decided to use ballistic tips at d'last minute. 'Cause some mess but do d'job."

Sil slammed the door. "I get all the blood off my face?"

"All 'cept yo shirt. Ain't no thang."

"These local gun-runners. Where are they?"

"Meetin' us up near Merced."

"Do you know them?" Sil asked.

Desgreaux shrugged. "Met 'em. Dass all."

"Are they any good?"

A shrug. "Doubt it."

"Well, why the hell would you choose them?"

Desgreaux chuckled. "Cracks me up watchin' you get yo lil Swiss panties all in a wad."

"Dammit, I'm serious."

"Dey'll do what we need dem to do, got it? You jus' get me close and

I'll take care of ever'thin'."

"Well, for starters, *you* take the car and deal with this asshole's shit, piss and blood." Sil lifted Desgreaux's faux guitar case and deposited it in the back seat. "Keys are in the ignition."

Desgreaux stepped off the bike.

Pulling Falco's sweaty helmet over his head, Sil cranked the big BMW and rode rather unsteadily away.

One down, two to go, thought Sil. *And then we deal with Sonny.*

The pivotal night was just beginning.

IT WAS DARK and sultry on the La Merced hillside. Whatever western breeze blew from the Pacific had been knocked down by miles of mountains and trees, leaving the coffee plantation sticky with humidity and leftover heat from the hot summer day. The lack of moonlight made the small hillside cabins stand out like beacons in the distance as Sil and Desgreaux watched from the coffee fields 200 meters away. Half an hour left till the meeting.

"You say the kitchen hut is where 'dey meet?"

"That's what she said," Sil whispered into his headset. "She said Burrell...Hartline...will approach from the fields to avoid our surveillance cameras."

"Bout Mikkelsen?"

"I'm thinking they come together."

"I 'gree. Dey gone come in right dere, from d'east," Desgreaux stated, pointing. "On dat access road."

"You're probably right," Sil muttered, eyeing the area through the rifle scope. "These are shit angles. I don't like it."

"Hopefully we ain't gone shoot. My lil firecracker gone do d'trick jus' fine."

Sil rolled over and began preparing his items. "Just make sure you've got your device squared away. When they show, we're getting this done, cleaning up the mess and hauling ass."

"You don't think Sonny'll know about dis?"

Sil turned and eyed his partner in crime. "Not if we hurry. Besides, who's going to tell him? There are no guards here other than the one they're meeting with."

Desgreaux slid two blankets from the tethered bag, handing one to Sil.

"Want me to call Ortiz?"

Sil checked his watch. "Give it ten more minutes. Then call and tell them to approach from the northeast. Have him send the one man with the LMG to the east end of the yard, around the perimeter. If they try to fall back into the yard, he cuts them down. Just like we planned."

The two men continued with their preparations.

ABI MIKKELSEN watched the artificial terrain slide slowly by on her Cessna's GPS. She'd just climbed through 18,000 feet in the specially modified aircraft. While this Cessna—outfitted with a powerful engine, quiet exhaust and stealth prop—was rated with a ceiling of 22,000 feet, Abi could already feel the mushiness of the controls due to the thin atmosphere. She'd have to be extremely careful as she circled La Merced. Her turns would have to be gentle, executed with enough power to prevent a stall in the rarified air.

Pulling in oxygen through the mask, Abi waited until the plantation's center was a kilometer away. She flipped on the imaging system to her right, allowing it to come online as she focused on her speed and heading. Abi glanced over at the mounted screen, about the size of a regular iPad, and immediately noticed two reddish dots on the purple and blue field. She tapped the screen twice, zooming in and marking their position.

"Hunter, this is Mikkelsen," Abi said. Earlier, Hunter had made the decision to use last names as call signs. The radios they were using were hyper-secure. Using call signs, especially among a cobbled-together group, was to invite disaster by confusion.

Hunter's steely voice answered Abi's call. "This is Hunter, go ahead."

"I've got two nice, warm human beings approximately a hundred-fifty to two-hundred meters southeast from the center cabin. Looks like they're prone, over."

"Mikkelsen, you count only two?"

"Roger, I count two."

"Mikkelsen, we will wait the thirty mikes before we start the show. Take a cruise and do another flyby at five mikes before go-time. Copy?"

"Roger, Hunter, I copy. Back at twenty-three-fifty-five."

Abi Mikkelsen set two waypoints and eased back on the throttle just a bit. As she departed the La Merced airspace, she scanned the plantation one more time. Thus far, there were only two warm bodies.

The minutes ticked by.

*

SITUATED WEST-BY-NORTHWEST of where the two people presumed to be Desgreaux and Sil were currently located were Colonel Hunter and his "guest." Earlier, when picking this spot, Hunter had drawn on experience and made an educated guess that the twosome would approach from the east. It had been mildly unsettling to find his position merely fifty meters from the pair, especially since he didn't detect them as they'd approached. But Hunter knew Desgreaux was a highly-trained soldier—one of Hunter's own kind—as was Sil, and underestimating them would be a fatal mistake.

Hunter was situated inside the main bunker they'd constructed earlier, built primarily of sandbags and camouflaged with rich earth and cut foliage. They'd used timbers to create viewing slits that worked perfectly for the AN/PVS-15 night vision goggles that both men wore on their heads.

Just as he had back in the days of his team, Hunter was "quarterbacking" the entire operation. He radioed Abuelito at 2348 hours and told him to drive up the hill and approach the cocina from the west. Hunter answered two brief questions before ending the transmission.

His guest whispered, "Why from the west?"

"It puts the kitchen between Abuelito and those two assholes who are slithering around to the east in the coffee fields."

"They wouldn't shoot him before the meet, would they?"

Hunter shook his head. "I doubt it, but why chance it? Why leave a friendly out in the open?"

"Yeah. I agree." The guest checked his watch. "Ten minutes."

"I know there's ten minutes. I'm good at reading time." Hunter turned, his whisper turning to a hiss. "You wanna do me a favor?"

"What's that?" the guest asked.

"Shut the hell up. Don't talk unless I ask you something."

The guest stared at Hunter.

"I don't like being reminded that I'm sharing a bunker with you," Hunter added.

The guest was Sonny Calabrese. He'd arrived several hours before and had received a limited briefing from Gage and Hunter.

"You don't know me, Colonel Hunter. If you did know me, you'd respect me. While you might turn your nose up at the drug trade, if you truly studied it, you'd learn that fighting it is as useful as shoveling shit against the tide. And what I deal in is no more deadly than cigarettes, booze or even fast sports cars. Car companies, cigarette manufacturers – they get to blame the end-user for dying. But drugs are different…when someone dies, people blame the drug and the people who import it. In the end, it's no different. It's the user who kills himself." The grin that had faded during the little speech reappeared.

"So, Colonel Hunter, as you can see, I'm not all that different from you. I don't add to the flow of illegal drugs. If anything, I slow them. And the money I make comes directly from the cartels. I don't take a dime from the common man. And with all that money, I employ hundreds of people."

Hunter glared at Sonny. "You done?"

"I take it you don't agree with what I just said."

"We've got a job to do tonight, Mister Calabrese. That's all I care about."

"Ever been betrayed?" Sonny asked. "Betrayed by a team member?"

"Can't say I have."

"I guess when large sums of money are involved, betrayal becomes more common," Sonny pondered, peering through the slit. "Regardless, I thank you for coming here to help me."

"I came here to help my friend. Not you."

"Hartline served under you?"

"Yeah."

"Well, by coming here to help him, you're helping me."

"Look at it however you want."

"Here comes Abuelito," Sonny whispered.

The headlights swept over the muddy lot of the La Merced Arabica plantation.

Go-time.

GAGE WAS PARKED below the main entrance of the La Merced Arabica plantation. Adriana sat next to him. He'd run through the plan four times, making her repeat it back to him, along with contingencies, after each time. When the call came through from Hunter, Gage eyed Adriana and her dyed-blonde hair that had been pinned tightly to her head.

"When I reach the cocina, you get your ass inside and go straight into the hole, got it?"

"Yes."

"I'll be right behind you and Abuelito will be in front of you."

"I remember. How will you crawl with only one wrist?"

"I'll manage," Gage replied. "Besides, I took three Advil."

"A person can do anything after three Advil," she replied with a grin.

Gage held out his good fist. "You ready?"

She bumped it. "Let's go."

He eased the pickup onto the main road before turning on the lights. When he reached the plantation, Gage gunned the engine and roared to the cocina, sliding to a stop mere feet away.

The twosome quickly exited the car and walked into the small kitchen. Once inside, Gage shut the door and pulled the two window shades down.

The *meeting* had begun.

SIL AND DESGREAUX had watched everything through their scopes. They'd been somewhat surprised that Hartline and Mikkelsen had driven in through the main entrance. Falco's intel about that had been incorrect. But he had been right about the meeting place. Minutes earlier, Abuelito had arrived and walked into the cocina with a case of beer. Just as he was supposed to.

"You sho' dat was dem?"

"It was them," Sil answered.

"Scope makes things look screwy, but she looked kinda funny."

"It was them. I could see the splint on his wrist. And with that beer, they should be there awhile."

"What if dey come outside to drink?"

"I told Abuelito to keep them inside and he agreed. We just have to trust that he'll follow through." Sil checked his watch. "Five minutes till we move."

"Wan' me to bring Ortiz and his crew forward?"

Sil gnawed on his bottom lip as he pondered this. "No. They're three minutes away. Just tell him to stand by. Tell him we're about to head in."

"You sho you wanna kill dem gun-runners no matter what?"

"After tonight, there will be two witnesses to what happened here," Sil replied, nodding. "Maybe three, depending how Ortiz plays his cards."

Desgreaux grinned. "And after we soak him dry, ol' Sonny be fish food, too."

*

IN THE BUNKER, Colonel Hunter listened as Abi approached La Merced again. She would attempt to circle the plantation and provide constant intel on any movements. Each member of their "team" wore small, pulsing heat tabs on their upper back. The heat tabs gave off no visible light but provided quick identification via thermal scope.

Abi reported the two prone bodies were in the same place. On the northern edge of her scope, she spotted five bodies in a V-pattern, each of them with the pulsing beacon. That would be Dinkins, Tomás, and three members of Tomás' gang. When she banked slightly, she noticed another squad-size element, this group to the northeast. They weren't wearing heat tabs and there were five of them.

Hunter listened to her report before marking the squad-size element's position on his map with a grease pencil.

"I knew they wouldn't come alone," Sonny said.

Hunter eyed him. "Who do you think it is?"

"The twosome will be Sil and Desgreaux. The group to the northeast is Guidry—the one who calls himself Falco—and Ortiz. That's my guess."

"Who's with them?"

"Don't know. Hired guns, probably."

Abi's voice on the radio cut like a knife. "This is Mikkelsen, the two targets to the east are on the move."

"Roger that. Hartline, are you clear of the tunnel?"

"We're out," Gage grunted.

"What's wrong?" Hunter asked, hearing Gage's strange tone of voice.

"I rebroke my wrist when I was crawling. It popped out through the skin. I'm good. Pulled it straight again and cranked the splint down. Commence...I'll be okay."

Hunter paused then shrugged. "This is Hunter...it's showtime, people. Dinkins?"

"Dinkins here."

"Stay on the ready. That squad-size element will be yours."

"Roger that."

Though not one bullet had yet flown, everyone knew that sudden death was one twist of fate away.

SIL AND DESGREAUX had made it halfway to the cocina. They paused, both men scanning the area with their M4s. It was dark and quiet.

Desgreaux pointed. "You see dat cone of light? I'm going just to the right of it. You stop by dat pickup and provide cover. If anyone comes out, smoke 'em."

"Ready."

Desgreaux was off, retreating slightly before making his way down the last slope before the huts. Sil followed. When they'd reached the lowest point, where Desgreaux planned on making his turn, he halted his movement and spoke into the headset.

"Sil, clear?"

"All clear from my vantage point."

"Still clear here," Ortiz added.

"Roger," Sil replied. "Everything's green."

Desgreaux turned and looked at Sil. "Goin'. Stand by."

The Cajun moved northward, weaving in and out of Arabica bushes with remarkable aplomb as Sil followed, taking up his position behind Abuelito's pickup truck.

HUNTER AND SONNY scanned the area with their NVGs.

"You see them?" Sonny whispered.

"Desgreaux ain't gonna cross that light to make his approach. Increases his chances of being spotted," Hunter whispered. "My best guess says they come up in that dark draw over to the south."

And no sooner had he said it than the two figures appeared on the display of the head-mounted NVGs. Desgreaux came first, moving without much caution. He paused once, using a bush for cover, turning as Sil could be seen bringing up the rear with what looked like an M4.

"Contact," Hunter said into his headset. "Hartline?"

"Got 'em," Gage replied.

"Can you see what they're angling to do?" Hunter asked.

"Desgreaux is carrying something," Gage said. "Looks like an explosive device."

"Told you," Dinkins chimed in. "That prick loves to blow things up."

"Roger," Hunter said. "Hartline, you don't want to take them now?"

"They're too spread out. And with their shooters behind us, I'd rather us take them head-on, when they're on their line of retreat."

"Mikkelsen?" Hunter asked. "Any movement?"

"None, other than Sil and Desgreaux," she answered.

"You'll see us coming out from cover in just a second," Gage said. "We're wearing our beacons."

Hunter was next. "Be ready for our two main targets' line of departure. It may be the center lot but I think they'll go the way they came. They'll know it's free of obstacles, it's dark, and it'll funnel them right back out."

"Those backstabbing bastards," Sonny seethed.

"Don't make a sound till they're bagged," Hunter warned.

"I want their heads."

"And you'll have 'em, but you gotta let this play out."

Hunter watched as Desgreaux reached the small kitchen, kneeling in the darkness next to the porch light.

SOMETHING WAS WRONG.

Sil continued to scan the area but something about the situation seemed off. Not unlike Sonny's uneasiness, Sil's came from years and years of commanding special operations teams in deadly situations.

"Can you hear them?" he whispered to Desgreaux.

Desgreaux had just begun to back away when he halted, cocking his head. "Yeah, I hear 'em," Desgreaux said. "Dey speakin' Spanish."

"Alright," Sil answered. "Arm that thing and let's haul ass."

"Done."

As Desgreaux low-crawled back to Sil's position, Sil continued to ponder his uneasiness. Suddenly, the most obvious question he'd come up with earlier suddenly seemed far more important.

Why La Merced?

If Hartline were truly gathering evidence against Sonny Calabrese and Nuestra, what the hell would he get from Abuelito out here at La Merced? Abuelito couldn't give him anything meaningful, even in regard to Simon.

Desgreaux arrived, breaking Sil's train of thought.

"Ortiz, status?" Sil whispered into the headset.

"All clear here," Ortiz replied. "No vehicles and no movement on the scope."

"You ready?" Desgreaux whispered.

"Yeah," Sil replied, following as Desgreaux slowly led them tactically back down the slope. Sil continued to ponder things…

Once the bomb had gone off and they were clear, Sil knew he'd have to make his next moves with alacrity. First he'd call Sonny with the good news that he'd managed to kill Falco. Then, Sil would tell Sonny about a trap he was fearful that Falco had lain. Sil would summon Sonny to Alfa, telling him to hurry, and that's when Desgreaux and Sil would strike.

They'd capture Sonny and torture the hell out of him. They would break Sonny inside of an hour. Blowtorches. Glass rods. Wire-cutters. Then they'd find out about Sonny's available cash and valuables. After that they'd kill him.

But what about other evidence? Would the authorities come after Sil and Desgreaux? There would be a kilometer-long list of people who wanted Sonny dead. Shouldn't matter—Sil had an immaculate false identification, with passport and a full background. He'd be long gone by the time anyone turned the evil eye to him.

And Australia would be a helluva large place to hide.

Sil smacked right into Desgreaux. He'd halted and held up a closed fist as a sign for Sil to do the same. Desgreaux turned, his blackened face making his gleaming eyes seem all the more fierce.

"Dat's gotta be the shittiest tactical movement I *ever* seen," he whispered.

"Lost focus."

"Pay attention. We got 'bout two-hundred mo meters befo' dey buzzard food."

They turned east, headed back to their gear and thermal blankets. Still distracted by his peculiar uneasiness, Sil was unaware of the far more deadly trap that lay just ahead.

GAGE PEERED THROUGH the base of the Arabica bushes, watching the two figures move in his direction. "Are you ready?"

"I've got my hand on the trigger," Adriana responded.

"Hit it when he's about two or three steps away."

"And you'll shoot after Desgreaux goes down?"

"I will. Hope I can hold onto this street cannon with one-and-a-half hands. Look alive...here they come."

He watched as Desgreaux approached stealthily. In twenty seconds, his jungle boots flashed by.

Despite his pain, Gage was grinning.

Chapter Twenty-Six

DESGREAUX WAS doing nothing to clear his way other than watching for obstacles. That's why he never noticed the 3/64" tripwire that had been lightly buried in the coffee plantation's soft soil. Adriana's finger rested on the snare trigger. When Desgreaux was three steps away, she pulled the trigger, watching as the spring snapped the tripwire taut between the trunks of two stout Arabica bushes. With a 270-pound breaking point, the tripwire would easily halt a man in motion.

And it did.

Desgreaux hit the cable, falling hard to the ground, face first. Sil was ten meters behind. He halted when he heard the sound. Just as he began to duck for cover, a shotgun blast emanated from a nearby bush.

Stifling a yell, Gage had managed to hold on to the combat shotgun as it kicked. The shot struck Sil directly in the sternum. It was a non-lethal rubber round, designed for riot control, but still had the potential to kill at a close enough range. But Sil was strong and fit. He survived. However, the round did knock him on his ass, making him certainly wish, at least for a few minutes, that he was indeed dead. Sil's M4 clattered to the dirt as he lay there stunned, mouth opening and closing as he attempted to get a breath.

Inside of two seconds, Gage had pivoted to the right. Desgreaux had held onto his M4 and was already up to his knees and lunging forward, preparing to shoot. Though Gage had pivoted to the right, he wasn't able to get off a shot. He sidestepped to the left just as Desgreaux unleashed a burst from his M4. It missed. Desgreaux, now on his feet, plowed straight into Gage as the two men went down in a heap.

A volley of shots rang out to the northeast.

SECONDS EARLIER, Abi watched the scene from above. She spoke to Ortiz before relaying the intel to the group.

"Ortiz and his squad heard the shots. They're moving in. From your north, they're coming from your two o'clock."

"Range?" Dinkins asked.

"Fifty meters. They're all over you."

"Roger."

Abi's thermal scope suddenly bloomed with light from all the gunfire.

DESGREAUX HAD tackled Gage and remained on top of him. The Cajun pressed the forward grip and laser of his M4 into Gage's throat with tremendous force. Gage had to wedge his right hand under the rifle to keep it from cracking his larynx. His battered left hand was useless, barely clinging to the shotgun.

Desgreaux growled as he bore down on Gage, pressing all of his weight through the carbine and onto Gage's throat. Twisting his head, Gage could see Abuelito behind him, struggling to contain Sil.

Though it didn't matter now, Gage's idea of rubber rounds had been a huge mistake. He'd done it in effort to preserve Sil and Desgreaux for Sonny—the ultimate prize. But after Sonny had displayed his colossal hubris by actually coming here, Gage should have switched to regular buckshot and killed these two assholes.

Didn't matter now. This was *mano a mano*, life or death. Hopefully Abuelito could keep Sil under control. In his struggle, Gage saw Adriana hovering close behind Desgreaux. She seemed paralyzed by fear as she crept closer. One quick swing from Desgreaux's M4 and she was dead.

Though Gage was hardly aware of it, the gunshots in the distance were already dying down, replaced by yells.

As the carbine seemed ready to collapse Gage's larynx, he released the shotgun with his left hand. Bringing the damaged wrist to Desgreaux's side, Gage felt the Cajun's SEAL pup knife. He'd seen it on the ambush.

Even if he could get the knife out, Gage knew the movement might alert Desgreaux.

But he couldn't survive much longer. Even with his strong right arm, the chokehold from Desgreaux was winning out.

This gambit was all that was left. It might be the last decision he'd ever make.

Maybe there was something Gage could do to increase the odds of the gambit working.

Here comes the pain.

In a swift motion, Gage removed his right hand from under the M4, feeling the pressure on his throat ramp up to an agonizing level. Gage's right hand shot up to Desgreaux's NVGs, ripping them off as his thumb dug into the Cajun's left eye.

That caused a reaction.

Desgreaux's sudden movement aided Gage's weakened left hand. He had the SEAL pup knife out in an icepick grip, praying his hand was strong enough to maintain the grip. As Desgreaux pulled back, bringing the M4 with him—presumably for the kill-shot—Gage plunged the knife downward, striking Desgreaux in the backside of his right ribs.

That caused an even bigger reaction.

Though the knife didn't penetrate very far, its tip stuck into the cartilage and caused Desgreaux to spasm. This allowed Gage to scramble away to the left. He grasped the shotgun with his right hand and unleashed a rubber round into Desgreaux's upper body.

The shot knocked the Cajun into the nearby row of Arabica bushes, as if he'd been yanked there by an invisible rope.

"Abuelito," Gage rasped, chancing a look behind him. "You okay?"

"I'm okay now, *amigo*," Abuelito said, his chest heaving. Below him, Sil was bleeding from the forehead, presumably from a strike of the butt of Gage's .45.

"His radio."

"I pulled it off," Abuelito whispered.

Gage leaned over and snatched the headset from Desgreaux's head. The Cajun was trying to sit up. The rubber shotgun round had snapped his humerus—the long bone of the upper arm. His arm dangled as if held by a rope.

"I screwed up," Gage said to Abuelito. "Should've just planned on killing these two assholes."

"Are you two okay?" Adriana asked, emerging from the bushes.

"We're fine," Gage said. "I'm glad you didn't try to intervene. Move back behind us, please."

Gage turned his head to the north. There were no sounds.

"Where do you want Sil?" Abuelito asked.

Gage aimed the SPAS at Sil's face. "Get your hands on your head and slide your ass over there next to your friend."

Desgreaux was now sitting up, leaning awkwardly back against an Arabica bush. He sneered at Gage, muttering unintelligible curses.

When Gage had Sil and Desgreaux where he wanted them, he called in a status report and asked for one in return.

There was no answer. Just a great deal of garbled conversation.

Hunter cut in. "Dinkins, status!"

Finally, Dinkins answered the call. "No more threat," he replied, his voice dejected. "It was Ortiz, alright. He had locals with him, armed to the teeth. They're all dead."

"Your squad?" Hunter asked.

Dinkins let out a long breath, making the radio squelch. "No injuries...but we lost one. That's why all the extra shots. His buddies were finishing these assholes off with an exclamation point."

Gage chanced a look at Adriana. She had a look of horror on her face as she covered her ear pieces with her hands so she could hear more clearly.

She knew.

"Who was it?" Hunter asked.

"Tomás," Dinkins replied. "It was Ortiz who got him. And Ortiz now has about fifty bullet holes in his body."

Though Desgreaux couldn't hear what was being said over the radio, he responded after Adriana burst into tears. He let loose his irritating laugh, a combination between a jeer and a chuckle.

That is, he did it until Gage hammered the butt of the SPAS-12 down onto his nose.

WHEN ABI HAD pronounced the plantation as free and clear, the entire group marshaled a hundred meters below the cocina, using another cinderblock building as cover. Hunter asked Desgreaux and Sil for the specifics on the bomb but neither man would talk. Finally Hunter stepped to Desgreaux and twisted his shattered arm.

Though Desgreaux shrieked like a mountain lion in heat, he still didn't relay any information. But Sil did—he spoke to Sonny.

"The device could be operated by a remote trigger. But Desgreaux put a backup timer on it. Check my watch."

Sonny stepped forward, twisting Sil's wrist. "There's eight minutes left."

Hunter clicked his own watch, as did Dinkins. Behind the group, Gage consoled Adriana who seemed to be holding up better than expected.

Sil began to entreat. "Sonny, I don't know what they've told you, but you've been deceived. We just killed Guidry...Falco...before we came here. And we were going to kill Hartline and Mikkelsen. You know all this. All of this was for you!"

"Do you know how badly I detest a liar?" Sonny asked. "Especially a cowardly liar."

"Can I get a cig?" Desgreaux drawled.

Hunter turned to the Cajun and snorted. "Are you serious?"

"He's serious," Dinkins replied.

"We'll give you a smoke if you'll tell us where Guidry is," Hunter offered.

Desgreaux nodded. "Dead in a car outside'a Tarma, 'bout a half-hour from here. Car's parked a'hind a gas station."

"Get your cigarette...carefully."

While numerous weapons were aimed at his face, the Cajun dug into his shirt pocket with his serviceable hand and deftly retrieved a cigarette, poking it between his lips. He carefully removed his lighter, igniting the cigarette and puffing deeply.

"Ahhh!" he said, sounding as if he were finishing a fine meal.

"Six minutes," Dinkins reminded everyone.

"Let's wrap this up," Hunter said to Gage.

Then, surprisingly, a familiar voice chimed in.

"Sil be lyin' like a sumbitch," Desgreaux said, exhaling smoke like a dragon through his teeth.

"What's that?" Hunter asked.

"He right...we was gone kill Fartline and his slit." Desgreaux grinned wickedly. "Then we was gone come and sweat you, Sonny, 'fore we killed yo ass, too. Was gone take all yo free cash."

"He's lying!" Sil roared.

"No he's not," Sonny said. He turned to Desgreaux. "Though I despise you, I admire your bravery."

Desgreaux smirked up at Sonny as he puffed the cigarette. The smile faded before he said, "Fuck you, Sonny. You ain't shit."

Hunter yanked Sonny back as he tried to deliver a kick to Desgreaux's already badly broken nose.

Gage stepped forward and spoke to Dinkins and the rest of Tomás' gang. "Cover these two." Gage turned to Desgreaux and Sil. "Walk up and sit on the porch of the cocina."

"And die?" Sil cried. "Are you crazy?"

"It's either that, or get shot in the knee and then go sit on the porch. Or, maybe you'd prefer I turn you over to Sonny, here."

"That's what I prefer," Sonny said, still in Hunter's grip.

Desgreaux carefully removed another cigarette, lighting it from the tip of his first. He flicked the first one at Sonny before ambling up the hill to the cocina, his arm dangling like a tube sock with an orange in the bottom. Once there, he sat right next to the explosive device, smoking placidly.

"Four minutes," Dinkins said.

Gage retrieved the shotgun and inserted a buckshot round. He aimed it one-handed at Sil's knee. "No more riot rounds, Sil. I bet I can cut your leg in two with this baby."

The Swissman began to cry.

"Go," Hunter said.

Sil turned and trudged up the hill to the cocina with multiple rifles trained on him. When he was close, Desgreaux used his good arm to pat the porch.

"C'mon up here, sissy boy…let's smoke one till long stick goes boom."

When Sil reached the porch, he crouched instead of sitting.

"He's gonna run," Dinkins whispered.

"Yep," Hunter said, lifting his M4 and training his laser on Sil's chest.

"This isn't right!" Sil yelled.

Desgreaux laughed at his partner in crime. It was a mocking, scornful laugh.

"Keep laughin', dickhead," Hunter warned, eyeing Sil through his scope.

"One minute," Dinkins said.

Desgreaux leaned to his side, resting on his good arm as he smoked. He could have been a weary man relaxing on a lazy afternoon. Next to him, Sil wept openly, shuddering.

Desgreaux could be heard deriding Sil, calling him a pussy in French and English.

Sil suddenly bolted from the porch, running toward the main lot with flailing arms.

Hunter drilled Sil before he made it ten meters. The shot impacted his upper body, probably in the shoulder. Sil fell to the ground, moaning as he squirmed. Desgreaux chuckled.

Time ticked on.

"How long?" Gage asked.

Dinkins touched his Indiglo. "Not long. Seconds."

The last sound from the house was from Desgreaux. He took one last deep pull on his cigarette before flicking it away in a rainbow arch. He checked his watch and could be heard telling Sil that he'd see him in hell.

Then Desgreaux turned his head to the assemblage and yelled "Boom!"

And that's when Desgreaux and Sil ceased to live.

Chapter Twenty-Seven

THE DEBRIS HAD hardly ceased falling before Sonny Calabrese thrust himself to the forefront of the group. The consummate showman, the alpha male, he pumped his fists to the sky as he yelled "yes!" over and over again.

The group was quiet, watching Sonny as he paced, trying to whip them into a frenzy. Nearly everyone in the group was filthy, and all had just had a close encounter with death. Tomás' three fellow gang members were sullen, having just watched their friend die an agonizing death. Adriana clung to Gage's arm, seeming disgusted by the display. Dinkins, Hunter and Gage—all experienced warriors—watched dispassionately.

"Now that's what I call a show!" Sonny shouted, clapping his hands as he smiled at the group. "In fact, I'm pretty sure I saw one of Sil's beady blue eyeballs go whizzing by me."

Gage chuckled. Sonny homed in on it.

"Liked that, did you?"

"I don't particularly enjoy people dying, Sonny, but I can't say I'll miss Sil or Desgreaux."

"Hell no, *we* won't miss them," Sonny exclaimed. "Back-stabbing bastards." He pulled in a deep breath through his nose, opening his arms wide and tilting his head back to the night sky.

Gage spoke up. "Keep in mind, we lost a man tonight, Sonny. A friend to some, and a relative of another."

"I realize that," Sonny said. "I will gladly compensate these fine people for their loss."

"Don't want your money," one of the gang members said through gritted teeth, his English heavily accented.

"You're angry. I get it. That's good. Savor that anger, it'll be useful later." Sonny eyed each person individually. "Allow me to explain…

"For those of you who don't know me, I am Sonny Calabrese, founder and CEO of the Nuestra Corporation. Abi Mikkelsen," he said, pointing upward, "our sexy little eye in the sky, is my associate, as are Mister Dinkins," he said, gesturing, "and Mister…er…Burrell, here." Sonny frowned importantly. "As you might imagine, we've had some regrettable activities

311

transpire recently. While regrettable, they remain completely incidental. My organization can—and will—move forward."

"How's that possible?" Gage asked.

"I know what you're thinking...you're thinking about Guidry, the lynchpin with the Air Force."

"Yes."

"Believe me, I have other allies in the Air Force. Guidry was a glorified pawn. I've also got his deputy commander. Another wing commander. That end of the operation will be just fine once we take care of his passing." Sonny's tone turned reflective as he scratched his chin. "I can read it now...Colonel Troy Guidry was tragically killed in a fall while hiking the high jungles of central Peru."

"Got it all figured out, do you?" Hunter asked.

"I'm fluid, Colonel Hunter. All successful businesspeople are. Plans change. Shit happens. Adapt or die." Sonny pointed at Gage. "And you knew what you were doing by calling me. You might have come down here to kill me for, what, a few hundred grand? But you saw dollar signs and wanted a stake in the big game. I don't blame you."

Sonny's finger turned to Dinkins. "And you, my friend, showed loyalty, and that will be rewarded, believe me. There's a big bonus headed your way."

He eyed Adriana. "I realize the man who died was your relative. I will compensate you as if you had a handsome life insurance policy on him."

Adriana buried her head into Gage's shoulder.

Sonny's three fingers pointed at the gang members. "Do you know how valuable you three can be to a man like me? Savvy locals who know how to get things done? There are innumerable services you can provide me in Lima and all around Peru. I'll bring you three on retainer, a guaranteed ten grand—each—per month. And that's U.S. dollars, boys."

They were silent.

"And you, colonel...that little Swiss prick who's currently scattered all around us was my team leader, a job I'd like you to assume. While I'd rather disclose the terms in private, let's just say if you'll give me five years you can retire on Maui in a mansion and never worry for money again."

"Sounds tempting," Hunter said.

"Bet your ass it's tempting," Sonny laughed. "It's irresistible."

Resting his hands on his slung M4, Hunter shook his head. "No."

"No, you don't want the job?"

"No, it's not irresistible. In fact, it's quite resistible. It's actually detestable."

Sonny's smile faded. "I won't beg you, friend, but I will give you a day to change your mind."

"I'm out, too," Dinkins said.

"And I don't want your filthy money," Adriana added. "Tomás came here to help me, not you."

The gang member who had spoken before spat at Sonny's feet. Then he made a gesture with his hand from his cheek. It didn't look like a friendly gesture.

"Mikkelsen's out, too," Gage said. "She wanted me to tell you."

"Piss on her."

Gage stepped forward. "As for me, I don't want your money nor do I want anything to do with you. While I'm angry at having been deceived by Guidry, I stand behind the real reason I came here."

"You came here to kill me."

"I did."

"Well," Sonny breathed, "if you do that, you're a lying piece of shit. Because you implied you wouldn't kill me when you told me what was happening here tonight."

"I'm not going to kill you."

Sonny took a step backward. "You realize I don't need any of you. I'll leave here tonight and this will be nothing but a speed bump."

"I'll be impressed if you manage to pull that off," Gage said.

"I've made a living outperforming people's expectations of me," Sonny replied.

Gage looked at Hunter and nodded. Hunter lifted his radio and pressed four digits before holding the handset to his mouth.

"Alfredo, this is Hunter. You copy?" He listened. "Good. Lead 'em up."

"What is all this?" Sonny demanded.

"Wait and see," Hunter replied.

Headlights could be seen in the main lot as several vehicles roared up the hill. Sonny turned and began moving away from the group. Gage simply flicked his finger.

Dinkins stepped forward.

Sonny said, "What the hell do you think—"

Dinkins fired his taser, the electrodes striking Sonny in his neck and upper chest, dropping him like a bag of cement. He lay there convulsing as the three vehicles parked at the edge of the main lot.

The first vehicle was a rose-colored Cadillac with a slightly damaged front end. It was driven by Alfredo Nieves, the self-styled private eye who'd just spent days with Adriana in the Lima motel room. Sheriff was with him. As Alfredo tended to the people in the two trail cars, Sheriff bounded to Gage, hopping happily between him, Adriana and Hunter.

The three gang members hoisted Sonny to his feet. One of the gang members trapped Sonny's right arm behind him but didn't torque it. Sonny was still quite out of it.

Alfredo led the two groups to the area behind the lowest building. The first group had arrived in a stretch Hummer limo. There were five people in total, two women and three men. The group followed their leader, a tall man wearing a shiny suit. He wore massive eyeglasses with chunky gold frames and carried a matching cane. Alfredo politely gestured for them to stand off to one side.

The other group had arrived in a white Chevy Suburban with larger than normal off-road tires. This group numbered four—three men following one woman. A petite lady, she was around seventy and wore a tasteful dress with a matching hat. One of the men helped her with her footing when she reached the soft earth. It could have been inferred that her three male escorts preferred high-protein diets to go with all their weightlifting and steroids.

Both groups eyed Sonny Calabrese with palpable malevolence.

Gage stepped forward.

"Sonny, can you hear me?"

Sonny blinked.

Gage lightly slapped Sonny's cheeks. "C'mon, Sonny, snap out of it."

Sonny used his free hand to wipe a string of drool from his lower lip. He cut his eyes to Gage. "I'll get you for this, you bastard."

Gage smiled. "Glad to see your mind is still working after fifty thousand volts. Sonny, I'd like to introduce a few people I'm quite certain you're familiar with." He gestured to the woman. "First, this is Señora Dora Garcia of the esteemed Garcia family. Señora Garcia, this is Sonny Calabrese."

Walking a few steps to the other group, Gage presented his right arm toward the man in the suit and glasses. "And this is Oscar Manolo, of the Manolo family." Gage moved between the two groups. "As I'm sure you're aware, Sonny, these two 'families' have been warring with one another in the belief that they were stealing each other's valuables when, in fact, it was *you*."

"And you, and Dinkins, and Mikkelsen!" Sonny roared, obviously fully recovered from being tased.

"I've already cleared our names, Sonny. And when I presented you the opportunity to come here tonight, I told you I wouldn't kill you, and I won't.

I said you might be able to cut a deal." Gage gestured to both groups. "Well, here's your chance."

"What are you talking about?" Sonny breathed, his chest rising and falling.

"Since you love giving people momentous choices, Sonny, we thought it would be nice to allow you to be on the deciding end, for once." Gage again motioned to the Manolos then the Garcias. "So, Sonny...the choice is yours...who shall you go with?"

Sonny struggled but Tomás' gang member friends easily held him.

"Perhaps they should tell you what they have in mind for you," Gage said. "Maybe, then, you can make a more informed decision." He turned. "Señora Garcia?"

A prim smile flitted across her face. "We've discussed this at length. We will take him to our estate and he will not *depart* anytime soon. We plan to keep him with us, suffering, for a very long time." Her three pitbull escorts grinned and growled all at the same time.

Colonel Hunter whistled and made a quip that had everyone chuckling.

Everyone but Sonny.

"Señor Manolo?" Gage asked.

Sonny's wide eyes darted to the man he'd stolen from.

The Manolo in the Liberace suit smirked. "I shall not be so coy with my answer." He respectfully dipped his head at Señora Garcia. Whatever mirth had existed on his face quickly evaporated as he pointed his cane at Sonny. "I will watch as this *concha* is made to cry like a baby. My sons will use snakes, spiders, rusty blades, dental instruments. He will beg for death. It will be his oasis that is always just a bloody hand out of reach." Señor Manolo wets his lips with his reptilian tongue. "And it will be good."

"How 'bout that?" Hunter replied. He turned to Sonny. "Sucks bein' you."

"Just shoot me," Sonny said, his chin trembling. "I've got millions in cash, Colonel Hunter. I'll tell you where it is. All you have to do is kill me now."

"But, that's not one of your choices," Gage replied. "I've heard you're always fanatical about making your subjects stay within the array of choices."

Gage arched his eyebrows when he noticed another person had joined the audience. She'd slipped in quietly.

Abi Mikkelsen.

"Abi's here, too," Gage said. "Abi...anything you want to say to Sonny before he goes away for a while?" The gang members turned Sonny so he could see her.

She crossed her arms and said, "Sonny, you once told me you were fascinated by the human psyche under duress. You said it often made people choose things they wouldn't normally choose." Abi gestured to the two cartel leaders. "So…fascinate us. Make your choice."

Sonny's eyes darted all around. "And if I don't?"

"We'll make it for you," Gage replied.

After more weeping, Sonny reluctantly made his decision.

True to Sonny's word, most everyone was fascinated.

GAGE AND HUNTER stayed in Lima long enough to wrap things up. Hunter found a friend at the American Embassy, the security officer, and gave him an edited version of the things that had occurred. After Abi informed Gage and Hunter that she, Dinkins and Griffin would stay to face the music, Hunter gave his advice.

"Just tell 'em everything," Hunter said. "Except you might want to tailor your story just a little bit. I'd play dumb about what Nuestra's actual purpose was. I'd just tell 'em I was hired to do high-end security against people who encroached on Alfa's clients. Tell 'em you never fired first and then you started investigating over the last few weeks due to growing suspicion. Make sure you suggest that select Peruvian government officials were in bed with Sonny. Then, after that, I'd just be cooperative. You three ain't who they're looking for."

"I'll head straight over to Alfa and make sure our files are in order," Abi said.

"Mind getting rid of mine?" Gage asked.

Abi winked her reply.

"When this thing blows over," Hunter said, "y'all come on up to Fayetteville. If you're needin' work, I can probably help you."

"Yeah," Gage agreed. "The colonel is like a mini-employment agency. Most of his jobs are hazardous, however."

"Hey, you took this one on your own, smart guy," Hunter replied.

Gage smiled.

Dinkins and Griffin promised to take Hunter up on his offer. Abi, however, said she was planning to go back to Denmark.

"To do what?" Gage asked.

"To rediscover my life," she replied. "I don't know what I'll do, but it won't involve carrying a weapon."

"Aren't you wanted there?" Gage asked.

She shook her head. "There are many stories about me...but no evidence. I'll be fine. I'm done with this life."

Hunter hitched his thumb at Gage and snorted. "Y'know how many times he's said crap like that?"

The group had a good laugh and bade their goodbyes.

As they drove away, Gage made a quick local phone call.

ADRIANA MET them in the executive lobby of the private aviation area at Jorge Chávez International Airport. Hunter quietly excused himself to go find a few trinkets for Alice. Gage led Adriana and Sheriff to a quiet corner as the noontime sun beamed in behind them. Sheriff leaned against her legs while she massaged him behind his ears. Gage again apologized for Tomás' death.

"He knew the risks," she replied.

"Doesn't make it any easier."

"What do I do if the police find out about my involvement in all of this?"

"Be truthful, but don't volunteer too many things. Colonel Hunter received some assurances that Sonny will be the fall guy for all of this."

"Do you think he's still alive?" she asked.

"No telling. If he is, I bet he wishes he wasn't."

"How's your arm?" she asked, wincing at Gage's sling and bandages.

"I'm fine. I'll need surgery in a week or so."

"You need to find a new line of work."

"Believe me, I've tried," Gage said with a halfhearted laugh. "Listen, Adriana, about what happened...I didn't resist you because I don't like you. I'm still just not over my last girlfriend."

She touched her finger to his lips, quieting him. "Don't worry about it. She's probably missing you right now."

"I doubt that."

Adriana gave him a light shove on his good arm. "Go on, now...go find the colonel. Don't worry about me."

Gage waited a moment as Adriana knelt in front of Sheriff, saying her goodbyes. Finally she stood, her eyes sparkling. With a final smile that disappeared like the flame of a match in the wind, she turned and walked away.

Watching her go, Gage wondered what would become of her. Rather than linger, he walked back to the exit that would lead to his employer's private jet. He was ready to go home.

IN A LITTLE more than eight hours, Gage and Hunter arrived at the colonel's farm-style home courtesy of a taxi from Fayetteville Regional Airport. Though it was the last day of February, and dark as pitch, the weather was rather mild for winter. Both men had snoozed on the flight, after Hunter had told Gage to quit his griping about having to go back to Canada to work for the "wacko millionaire." Sheriff, however, had found riding in the posh cabin exhilarating. He'd wandered fore and aft over the entire flight, occasionally rewarded by human food treats from the pilots.

As they'd ridden home in the taxi, Gage had called Linda DeLand—the grieving mother who'd been a pawn in Falco's scheme. While a pawn, her grief was genuine. She'd lost her son, Jimmy, to one of Sonny's bizarre scenarios. Gage didn't go into great detail about what had transpired in Peru. He simply told her that Sonny Calabrese, along with his organization, were no longer a threat.

"Is he dead?" she asked.

"I'm not sure. But, if he is alive," Gage replied, "I'd wager he wishes he were dead."

That was good enough for Linda DeLand.

Hunter and Gage exited the cab, with Gage unclipping the leash and allowing Sheriff to roam.

"I don't want to go back to Canada," Gage groaned, trying to wrap up the conversation about his employer who'd flown them to Peru and back.

"You still have a month off."

"It's not enough."

Hunter clucked his tongue. "Just the simple fact that the man's got a private jet that he lets you use would be enough for me. Hell, I'd work for him till I died."

"You'd have to if you were me," Gage remarked, stretching as best he could with the sling. "Each time I use his jet, it adds six months to my employment."

"Bah. You'll live." Hunter motioned south. "Tomorrow morning, I gotta drive down to Charleston."

"Why didn't you just call that general?"

"I did...told him to meet me in Charleston...told him I've got some serious news about some of his men."

"You could've just told him on the phone."

Hunter shook his head. "If someone told me that my men were running drugs on U.S. birds, I think I'd like to hear it in person. Who knows how many careers are gonna end soon after those words escape my lips."

"Major Wolfe should still have a nice big fish hook-hole in his cheek as the first measure of proof."

"Yeah, I can't wait to tell that part of the story."

Sheriff had run off in the dark and didn't come when Gage whistled. Hunter had a large yard so Gage wasn't too concerned. The two men walked around back, hearing the rear screen door open as the motion lights kicked on. They were greeted by Alice Hunter. She had her hands on her hips, shaking her head as she looked at Gage.

"Look at your arm." Her eyes went skyward. "I'm not even going to ask."

"Don't," Hunter said, climbing the steps and giving her a hug. He produced a small gift from his pocket.

"I'll open it later," Alice said, giving her husband a peck on the lips.

Gage whistled again and called out to Sheriff. "You don't think he got confused and ran off do you?"

"Nah. Just sniffin' around," Hunter said.

"I'll bet he's out at your cottage," Alice said, referring to the storage container.

At that mention, the overhead light above the tiny square porch of the cottage flipped on. The screen door opened and shut, revealing a silhouette. The silhouette was tall and lean and lithe.

And beautiful.

Frolicking around her were Sheriff and another dog, a dog Gage once knew well. His name was Ranger.

Was.

Dropping his bag, Gage hurried across the yard, staring wide-eyed at his Polish beauty. "What are you..." He was too dumbfounded to finish the sentence, his chest heaving with gasping breaths.

"What am I doing here?"

"Yes," he said, smiling on reflex.

"I'm here to say I'm sorry."

Gage bear-hugged her with his good arm. They held their embrace for a full minute.

"Are you back for good?" he managed to ask.

"No," she answered. "You and I both know we can't be together over the long-term."

Crestfallen, but understanding her answer, Gage nodded.

"But we are together now, yes?"

He smiled. "Yes."

"I have nothing to do for two weeks. Do you?"

"No," Gage answered, making his answer loud and clear.

"Then let's enjoy our two weeks."

Gage turned to the flowerbed where the dogs were playing in the scant light. "That's Sheriff, my new buddy. And please tell me I don't have to call Ranger...whatever that name was..."

"Kochanek."

"Yeah."

"Well, that's his name," she said, smiling and adding her full Polish accent. "And, yes, you *will* call him that."

Gage kissed her.

ACROSS THE YARD, Colonel Hunter stood with his arm around his wife, the two of them watching the scene. Hunter shook his head. "Look at that. What a softie he's become."

Alice Hunter elbowed her husband in his stomach, leaving him on the porch.

There was no doubt who commanded the Hunter household.

Acknowledgments

So many readers have written to me asking for more of Gage Hartline. I'm humbled by these requests. I'd never intended Gage's story to continue past THE DIARIES. But I've come to realize that Gage's life will lead him to more adventures. I've sought several friends, and friends of friends, who actually do work similar to some of the activities Gage has been involved with. Sure, I add quite a bit of jelly to the bread to make the story move along. But it's surprising what really goes on out there in the world. And, as the old saying goes, it's amazing what some people will do for money.

This book would have been dedicated in honor of one of my faithful readers, my uncle, Chuck McKeever. Sadly, he passed away just two days before I finished the final draft. Chuck was an amazing man who taught me so many things in life. I could easily fill a book with stories about all he did for me. Suffice it to say, my world is a much less exciting place with him no longer around. I hope I can someday be a Chuck McKeever to others.

What a sweet cover, Nat Shane! Your artistic talents never fail to blow me away.

I'd like to thank three early test readers. Scott Hortis, Phillip Day and Charlie Mink politely slogged their way through this book after the third draft. I heeded their suggestions and the book changed drastically afterward. So, if you didn't like the book...blame them. (Kidding!) Seriously, their recommendations definitely made this book better. Their contributions were invaluable.

Elizabeth Brazeal, my editor, is a caffeine-fueled editing machine. Her keen eye, her knowledge of the written word and her occasional hilarious comments add so much to my mistake-laden work.

My final test readers, Lauren Knight, Lori Bindner and John Humphries helped me polish the book to a readable state.

Finally, Sarah Humphries, my Spanish expert, put the finishing touches on the book's sprinkling of Spanish words and phrases.

Thanks to everyone who helped make this book a reality!

And a big thanks to "Shooter" for the plethora of true-life stories. You're unquestionably insane, but we've known that for quite a while.

I wrote several other books between TO THE LIONS and SOLDIER

OF MISFORTUNE. They are not Gage Hartline novels and they've not yet been released. This time, however, I'm going to acquiesce to the requests of most of my readers and plow straight into the fourth Gage Hartline novel.

I've little clue what the next Gage installment might hold. At this point, all I know is it might involve a request from a wealthy heiress. Someone, probably a relative, is trying to kill her. A great deal of money is at stake. And, I have a feeling the heiress might be quite beautiful. Things may change, so please don't etch any of that in stone.

But Gage will be back. Soon.

Thank you for reading this book.

God bless.

C.

About the Author

Chuck Driskell is a United States Army veteran and part-time writer. He lives in South Carolina with his wife and two children. *Soldier of Misfortune* is Chuck's sixth novel.

Made in the USA
San Bernardino, CA
28 October 2015